Murderers
Prefer Blondes

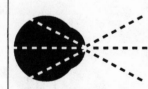

This Large Print Book carries the Seal of Approval of N.A.V.H.

Murderers Prefer Blondes

Amanda Matetsky

Thorndike Press • Waterville, Maine

Published in 2004 by arrangement with The Berkley
Publishing Group, a member of Penguin Group (USA) Inc.

Thorndike Press® Large Print Americana.

The tree indicium is a trademark of Thorndike Press.

The text of this Large Print edition is unabridged.
Other aspects of the book may vary from the original edition.

Set in 16 pt. Plantin by Minnie B. Raven.

Printed in the United States on permanent paper.

Library of Congress Control Number: 2003111457
ISBN 0-7862-6047-5 (lg. print : hc : alk. paper)

For Harry,
who prefers brunettes

As the Founder/CEO of NAVH, the only national health agency solely devoted to those who, although not totally blind, have an eye disease which could lead to serious visual impairment, I am pleased to recognize Thorndike Press★ as one of the leading publishers in the large print field.

Founded in 1954 in San Francisco to prepare large print textbooks for partially seeing children, NAVH became the pioneer and standard setting agency in the preparation of large type.

Today, those publishers who meet our standards carry the prestigious "Seal of Approval" indicating high quality large print. We are delighted that Thorndike Press is one of the publishers whose titles meet these standards. We are also pleased to recognize the significant contribution Thorndike Press is making in this important and growing field.

Lorraine H. Marchi, L.H.D.
Founder/CEO
NAVH

★ Thorndike Press encompasses the following imprints: Thorndike, Wheeler, Walker and Large Pr int Press.

Acknowledgments

Without the love, help, interest, inspiration, and support of the following people, I would have given up long ago, and this first novel of my new Paige Turner mystery series would have no pages to turn: Harry Matetsky, Molly Murrah, Liza, Tim, Tara and Kate Clancy, Ira Matetsky, Matthew Greitzer, Rae and Joel Frank, Sylvia Cohen, Mary Lou and Dick Clancy, Ann Waldron, Nelson DeMille, Dianne Francis, Betsy Thornton, Santa and Tom De Haven, Nikki and Bert Miller, Herta Puleo, Marte Cameron, Cameron Joy, Sandra Thompson and Chris Sherman, Donna and Michael Steinhorn, Karen Plunkett-Powell and Art Scott, Gayle Rawlings and Debbie Marshall, Matt Masterson, Judy Capriglione, Martha Cevasco, Betty Fitzsimmons, Nancy Francese, Jane Gudapati, Carleen Kierce, April Margolin, Margaret Ray, Doris Schweitzer, Carol Smith, Roberta Waugh and her kindly colleague, Saint Joe.

I send extraspecial thank-yous to all my good friends and well-wishers at Literacy Volunteers of America-Nassau County,

Inc., and to my fellow mystery writers and readers at Sisters in Crime-Central Jersey.

Finally, and most importantly, I'd like to thank my co-agents, Annelise Robey and Meg Ruley of the Jane Rotrosen Agency, and my editor at Berkley, Martha Bushko, for their combined enthusiasm, good humor, remarkable skills, sense, and savvy. They made it happen!

Prologue

Okay, here goes. I'm really going to do it now. Starting right this minute, at 9:22 p.m. on Saturday, the fifth of June, 1954, I'm putting these first words down on paper. And I'm going to keep on putting the words down, and stringing them into sentences, for as long as it takes to tell the whole ugly story. Every weekend and every night after work you'll find me sitting in my nightgown at this chrome-edged yellow Formica kitchen table, leaning over this baby blue Royal portable, typing out paragraph after paragraph, and page after page, letting one cigarette after another burn out in the ashtray, until I've produced the complete manuscript of this, my first mystery novel.

Well, it won't be a novel exactly. Most novels are pure fiction, and the story I'm about to tell is true. I know it's true because I was there — right in the middle of things, in some cases *causing* the ghastly events — and I'll be putting everything down exactly the way it happened. All I have to do is change the names and some of the particulars to save myself from lawsuits. This makes it easy for me now, as a writer, since I won't have to devise some ridiculous, far-fetched plot, or invent some oddball cast of characters, just to make the story interesting. But it wasn't so easy for me then, while I was risking my life to *get* the story, and it certainly won't be pleasant to relive the experience.

But I said I was going to do it, and I am. If there's one thing I definitely am *not*, it's a quitter (you'll find that out as this tale progresses). Besides, I've wanted to be a mystery writer since I was a girl of fourteen, reading Ellery Queen and Dashiell Hammett instead of working on my Home Ec projects, and this is the best opportunity I've ever had to fulfill that ambition.

So I'm going to finish this book if it kills me. Which it most likely won't. If I didn't die while I was knee-deep in murder, getting mauled, molested, stalked, and strangled by a homicidal sex maniac, then I probably won't die writing about it.

I know, I know. That's what you call a dead giveaway. Good mystery novelists don't tip their readers off to who will or won't get killed — especially right up front in the prologue. It kind of stifles the suspense. But who on earth do those writers think they're fooling? Anybody who's ever read a twenty-five-cent Mickey Spillane paperback (and nowadays that's just about *everybody*) knows darn well that Mike Hammer isn't going to buy the farm. He's the hero, for God's sake. He's going to go on cracking commie heads, splitting libelous lips, breaking guilty bones, and slaying all the good-looking "skirts" forever, right?

So, I don't see any point in pretending that I might get killed when it's as plain as the nose on your face that I won't. Otherwise, how could I be telling the story? And I don't believe this early revelation will make my novel any the less suspenseful, either. All the provocative, unsettling questions of any successful mystery — the who, what, where, when, why, and how — will still be here in force, buzzing around like bees in your bonnet, keeping you guessing (and squirming).

Trust me. This story will have you sitting on the edge of your seat — or my name isn't Paige Turner.

Awful, isn't it? But the name is true too. I got the latter half of it from my late husband, Bob Turner, who was killed in Korea two and a half years ago. Bob was a wonderful, smart, responsible man, and if General MacArthur hadn't hauled him off to die in that worthless, unwinnable war, I might be living out in Levittown now, driving a pink and white Ford and doing laundry in my brand-new washer and dryer set, instead of fighting the cockroaches for space in my dingy Greenwich Village apartment, working like a dog at *Daring Detective* magazine, and staying up late to grind out a novel that may never earn me one thin dime of income, or even be published at all. I'd also be exquisitely happy and very, very much in love, instead of as lonely and miserable as a Tennessee Williams heroine. But that's another story.

Anyway, as much as I loved my husband, I hate my married name. It sounds like a lousy pun, like a really bad joke — especially in light of my chosen profession. The guys at work (I'm the only female employee) are always making fun of me, saying I'm a real page-turner and so forth, and ever since they found out I was planning to turn my very first *Daring Detective* magazine story into a full-fledged mystery novel, the teasing has — as you can imagine — escalated to a fever pitch.

But it's not the jokes I mind so much, it's the byline problem. Unless I want to become a total laughingstock in the publishing world, I can never use my real name on my work. I can't revert to my maiden name, either (Titmonk is even worse, and I refuse to be the brunt of all of *those* jokes ever again!). So I'm stuck. I'll have to use a pseudonym, and — for an aspiring writer who prides herself on her narrative honesty and hopes to achieve some small level of public recognition and respect — that's a bitter pill to swallow.

My best friend, Abby Moskowitz, the beatnik artist and illustrator who lives next door, thinks I should legally change my last name to Monroe, or Mansfield, or "something blonde and sexy like that," but I could never do such a thing. First of all, I've got brown hair. But most of all, the legal process would make me feel as if I were divorcing my late husband — casting him out in some calculated, coldhearted fashion. I simply couldn't do it. And I would never dishonor Bob's family that way.

So, as far as my personal life is concerned, the name stays. Paige Turner I am, and Paige Turner I will always be (unless I ever get married again, which is highly unlikely since I'm practically over the hill — twenty-eight and still counting — and most men find me too ambitious). Professionally, however, I'll need a pen name.

15

Maybe I'll use Paul Turner, or Pete (male writers get more respect and make much more money), or maybe I'll just use initials. Plain old P. is too boring, but P.J. has a comfortable ring to it. Makes you think of your favorite pajamas. I don't have a middle name, least of all one beginning with J, but so what? If anybody asks, I'll say it stands for Juno (she's the goddess of marriage and the well-being of women, in case you didn't know).

But I'm digressing too much, right? You want me to stop babbling and get on with the story. And I promise I will — first thing in the morning. Right now I'm going to close up my little blue Royal, pour myself a jellyglassful of wine, warm up the old Sylvania, and catch some television before it signs off for the night. *Your Hit Parade* is on. If I'm lucky Gisele MacKenzie will sing a soothing lullaby and send me off to dreamland. A girl could use a sweet dream or two before returning to the scene of a nightmare.

Chapter 1

It was a bright and shiny Monday morning, but I was in a cloudy mood. As the only woman on the staff of *Daring Detective* magazine, I had to get to the East 43rd Street office a half hour ahead of everybody else, unlock the front door, turn on all the lights, open the blinds, regulate the steam, make the coffee, sort the mail, and attend to any other menial tasks that would make life easier and more comfortable for any one or all five of my precious male "superiors."

I had to go through this routine every workday morning, of course, but Mondays were always the worst. After a whole weekend of just being myself — a reasonably attractive, *very* independent twenty-eight-year-old widow with an active and creative mind of my own — it was hard for me to slip back into the role of a sniveling servant.

But I accomplished this transition, as always, with a forced sense of detachment and a hefty dose of determination. I really wanted to keep my job. Not just because it was my only means of support, but also be-

17

cause I believed it would help me achieve my own unusual (for a woman) publishing goals. So by the time my boss, Harvey Crockett, walked in the door that day, the office stage was set and I was poised for duty, with stick-straight stocking seams, a fresh coat of Fire & Ice lipstick, a chipper "good morning," and a big, simpleminded smile.

"Coffee," Crockett growled, giving me his usual one-word greeting. He hung his hat on the coatrack near my desk, combed his fingers through his thick white hair, heaved a noisy sigh, and propelled his huge but very hard-looking belly onward toward the door to his small private office. "Newspapers too," he barked, tossing a baggy, blue-eyed glance over his shoulder.

As Crockett maneuvered his bulk through the maze of desks and drawing tables clogging the large front workroom, I rolled my eyes and made a face at the ceiling. (I'm always doing that. Since verbal expression of annoyance or discontent is considered wildly improper behavior for a working woman, I learned — long ago — to relieve my inner frustrations with a secret stuck-out tongue, or a private cross-eyed contortion. It's safer that way.)

I filled a mug with black coffee, gathered

up the morning papers, and — setting my lips in another imitation grin — entered the boss's office. "Here you go, Mr. Crockett," I said, feeling more like a waitress than an editorial assistant. I set the coffee and papers down on his cluttered desk and took one step back. "Will that be all?"

"No," he said, leaning sideways in his creaky swivel chair and relighting an old cigar stub. "I want a new life. Please get me one right away."

"Would a new cigar suffice?"

"Ha-hmmph." It wasn't a laugh, exactly — more like a cough. "Maybe it would, at that. I could use a good smoke screen."

I smiled, for real this time. "Woman trouble again?" It wasn't often that Crockett revealed anything about his personal life to me, but when he did, it was to complain about his girlfriends. He had two of them. And they knew all about each other. And, for reasons my long-unmarried, extremely self-centered boss had yet to comprehend, the ladies didn't like sharing.

"I took Pauline out for a few beers Saturday night," he told me, "and we ran into Lois on Second Avenue. Lois took one look at me, stuck her nose in the air, and stomped on by, pretending she didn't know who I was. And then Pauline had her garters in a twist for the rest of the evening, asking me what did I see in a tramp like Lois, and why couldn't I settle down with one woman anyway? It got so bad I took Pauline home and went back to the bar by myself. I'd rather drink alone than get soused with a goddamn harpy."

"How kind of you," I said, a bit too sarcastically for my own good.

"Huh?" Crockett shot me a suspicious glance.

"To walk Pauline home, I mean. You could have left her stranded on the street." My impulsive tongue gets me in trouble sometimes, but I'm usually pretty quick with a cover-up.

"Oh," he said, picking up his coffee mug and slurping loudly. "Yeah, well. . . ."

The entry bell on the front door sounded, and I stuck my head out to see who'd arrived. It was Lenny Zimmerman, twenty-two-year-old art assistant. His dark hair was tousled, his bottle-thick glasses were askew, his thin face was bright red, and he was wheezing like an overworked Arthur Murray samba student. For Lenny, this was not an unusual entrance. It was, in fact, the way he *always* looked when he first appeared in the morning. Though he would never admit it, Lenny was deathly afraid of the elevator, and he always took the stairs — all nine flights of them — to and from the office. Ate lunch at his desk every day too.

"Hi, Zimmerman," I said, leaving Crockett's domain and heading for my desk in the front of the main workroom. "Good weekend?"

"Yes, thank you," he gasped, trying not to breathe so hard. Avoiding eye contact and growing even redder in the cheeks, he brushed past me and slunk away to his drawing table in the back. He looked as nervous as a rookie cat burglar. I shrugged and returned to my desk.

As soon as I sat down the front door jingled again, and Mike and Mario walked in. Mike Davidson was the tall, wiry assistant editor and staff writer for the magazine, and Mario Caruso was the short, swarthy art director. Both were married and in their early thirties. Standing next to each other, they looked like young, modern-day versions of Don Quixote and Sancho Panza. But they acted more like Dean Martin and Jerry Lewis.

"Hi, doll," Mike said to me, with an unmistakable tease in his voice. "You're

21

looking mighty fine this morning."

"Thanks," I mumbled, bracing myself for the taunt that was sure to follow.

"Doesn't she look luscious, Mario? I don't know about you, but I'd sure like to turn one of *her* pages."

Laughing so hard you could see his uvula wiggle, Mario slapped Mike on the back, then tossed in his own two cents. "But if both of us try to Turner, then one Paige won't be enough!"

I rolled my eyes at the ceiling again. If I lived to be a hundred, I'd never understand how they could think their repetitive, infantile jokes about my unfortunate name were so doggone funny.

Sniggering and snorting like two drunken frat boys, Mike and Mario stumbled past my desk and staggered down the center aisle of the workroom. When they reached their separate work stations — Mike midway back, at the next desk on the right, and Mario in the rear, across the way from Lenny — the laughter came to a stop. And the cries for coffee started.

"Java alert!" Mario called out, removing his green-and-tan plaid sports jacket and draping it on the back of his chair. He sat down and raked his fingers through his greasy dark hair, grinning impudently.

"I need caffeine!" Mike chimed in, loosening his tie and lighting up a Lucky. He swept one hand over his flaxen flattop, twisted his freckled face into a smile, and gave me a big fat wink — as if the invitation to serve him coffee was both a bountiful and an intimate honor.

I imagined wiping the smiles off their faces with a couple of custard pies (one of the many visual fantasies I use to maintain my emotional equilibrium). Then I stood up from my chair, coaxed my navy blue open-toed high-heeled pumps across the floor, and came to a stop at the table where the electric Coffeemaster, mugs, milk, sugar, and spoons were (thanks to me) always set up. I poured hot coffee into two clean cups (I knew they were clean because *I* washed them out in the ladies' room every night), put sugar in one and milk in the other (just the way the boys liked it), and delivered the steaming potables to their respective guzzlers.

"How about you, Zimmerman?" I asked. Lenny was the only one I ever *offered* to get coffee for, because he was the only one who never demanded it.

"No, thank you," he mumbled, hunching over his drawing table and gazing down at a two-page layout as if it were a sacred passage of the Torah. His nose was so close to the paste-up I thought it might leave a print.

At this point Crockett stuck his head out of his office, growled good morning to the gang, and waved his cup in my direction for a refill — which I quickly provided (with a very sweet mask on my kisser, and a Frankenstein face in my heart). "Did Pomeroy get here yet?" Crockett wanted to know.

"No, sir," I said, wondering why he'd even bother to inquire. Brandon Pomeroy, the lazy and pretentious editorial director of the magazine — and the biggest bane of my pitiful professional existence — never arrived at the office before noon.

I looked at the big round clock on the wall. It was just 9:30. The workday had barely begun, and already I felt as though I'd fought my way through a one-hour girdle sale at Gimbel's. Hoping to lose myself in my work so the time would crawl by faster, I sat down at my desk, lit a cigarette, and started reading and editing Mike Davidson's latest story, "The Corpse in the Coop." It was about a fifty-year-old Fuller Brush Man in Iowa who had raped one of his housewife customers, chopped her to death with a garden hoe, and then chucked her mutilated body in the backyard henhouse.

Like most of the magazine's staff-written clip stories, this one was a prime example of bad spelling, lousy grammar, and poor sentence structure. Worse than that, it was boring. Nobody could massacre a good murder like Mike. *If only Brandon Pomeroy would let* me *write stories for the magazine,* I complained to myself. *I could do a much better job than this!*

But I knew the pompous editorial director would never give me a story assignment. He'd rather drink glue than grant a lowly female a fair shot at a man's salary (I make sixty dollars a week; the guys all make a hundred or more). The only way I could ever hope to become a staff writer would be to research and compose (in total secrecy and completely on my own time) a true crime story so thrilling and well written that it would amaze and delight Harvey Crockett, who might then decide to override Pomeroy's objections and publish my work in the magazine. Knowing this, I was on constant lookout for the perfect subject for the breakthrough opus I was determined to produce.

But thoughts of my own story would have to wait. Right then I had to read and revise "The Corpse in the Coop." I looked down at the messy pages on my desk and shook my head. It would take an hour just to fix the grammar and spelling errors, and no telling how long to embellish the grisly details and spice up the story's intrigue. And if my carefully printed corrections turned out to be too numerous and complicated — making the edited copy too difficult for the typesetter to read — I'd have to retype the whole thing. Just par for the course. At the two-fisted, he-manly headquarters of *Daring Detective* magazine, a woman's work was never done.

"I'm finished with these," Crockett said, dumping the morning papers in a big heap on my desk. "You can clip 'em now. I'm heading over to the Quill for lunch." He grabbed his hat off the rack and trudged toward the door. "If Stafford calls," he said, referring to the head of the circulation company that distributed *Daring Detective*, "tell him to meet me there."

"Yes, sir," I said, watching his wide, flat, gray-flannel-covered rear end disappear through the door. Then I glanced at the pile of crumpled newspapers and silently groaned. One of the many mindless tasks of my daily office routine was to skim through all the major newspapers and cut out all the significant crime stories. I clipped the *New York Times*, the *Herald Tribune*, the *Daily Mirror*, and the *Daily News* every morning, and the *Journal American*, the *World Telegram and Sun*, and the *New York Post* every afternoon. It made for a *lot* of flipping and snipping, and — even though it allowed me to sift through the new murder cases, seeking out killer-diller prospects for my own story — it was not my favorite part of the job. Especially on Mondays, when reports of all the wicked weekend wrongdoings doubled my workload.

But I had to do it, and I had to do it quickly — before Brandon Pomeroy arrived. If the morning crime clips were not sitting — in a labeled and dated manila folder — on his desk when he came in, he'd have one of his angry, alcoholic snit fits. And, believe me, you don't *ever* want to witness one of those.

So, I snatched up the April 26 edition of the *Daily News* and — the very second I finished reading "Brenda Starr Reporter" — began searching the paper's contents for stories of murder, robbery, and rape. There were no such crimes reported on the front page (unless you believe, as I do, that

Senator Joseph R. McCarthy's four-year campaign to destroy the lives of all so-called Communist sympathizers has been a form of murder), but there was a bloody gangland hit story on page two. Somebody had rubbed out one of mob boss Albert Anastasia's closest "associates"; the body was found shot twice in the head and stuffed in the trunk of a car parked in the Bronx.

Knowing Mike would have to write a story about the hit, I cut out the article and set it aside. Then I continued my ghoulish pursuit of newsworthy villains and victims. There were, unfortunately, plenty of juicy felony reports on the following pages, and I was clipping them out as fast as I could find them.

But when I got to page twelve, I froze. And the scissors turned to ice in my hand. There, staring out at me from a small photo printed above the headline BLONDE BEAUTY SLAIN LAST NIGHT, was a murder victim I recognized.

Gasping aloud, I dropped my nose to the newsprint for a closer look at the picture. It was her, all right. No doubt about it. I had a vivid recollection of the one time we'd met. I couldn't remember her name, but her features were unforgettable. Big round puppy eyes, high cheekbones, aristocratic nose, thin lips tilted in the saddest of smiles. Most of all, I remembered her hair. It was pure platinum (if such an unnatural color can ever be called pure), and it was combed into a smooth, sleek, shoulder-skimming pageboy.

Staring down at the newspaper image, I realized I'd not only seen the young woman before, but I'd also seen her photo before. The *same exact* photo. It was a black-and-white headshot, close-cropped on a light gray background — its pretty subject wearing a single string of pearls and a small black hat with a slender black feather curving down over one cheek.

But who was she, how did she die, who killed her, and why?

The story accompanying the photo answered just two of those questions. The victim's name was Barbara — better known as Babs — Comstock. She was a twenty-four-year-old waitress who, according to one gossipy neighbor in her Hell's Kitchen apartment building, had entertained "high hopes" of becoming an actress. But Babs's hopes had been ended, once and for all, by an unknown assailant who had strangled her with a Hopalong Cassidy jump rope (still wound around her neck when the corpse was found), and then deposited her partially naked body in a trash bin near the service entrance of the Woolworth's on 34th Street. No witnesses had come forward, and the police had no suspects. The victim was survived by her parents, John and Elizabeth Comstock, who resided in the family's hometown of Springfield, Missouri.

Neither the victim's name, nor any of the facts reported about her short, unremarkable life, rang a bell with me. I was, in fact, dead certain she'd introduced herself to me under a different name. And she had told me she was a model, not a waitress.

I remembered our meeting clearly. She had come up to the office seven or eight months before, late on a Friday afternoon. All my underworked associates (i.e., all the *male* members of the staff) had left for the weekend, but I was still chained to my desk proofreading galleys. I had just begun checking the last proof when the entrance bell jangled, the office door opened, and a slim, nicely dressed blonde walked in. . . .

"Is Brandon Pomeroy here?" she'd asked, stepping over to my desk and standing politely in front of it — blushing — like a shy Girl Scout trying to sell cookies. She gave me her name and said she had an appointment. She was wearing a form-fitting navy blue suit, a light pink blouse, and a wide-brimmed navy blue hat with a large pink flower on one side. She carried a big black portfolio in one hand and a pink leather handbag in the other. Her blue eyes had a pleading look, and her long shiny hair was bleached so light it was almost white.

"Mr. Pomeroy's gone for the day," I said. "He won't be back until Monday afternoon." I wasn't being very sociable. I was in a breakneck hurry to finish my work and get out of there myself.

"Oh!" she said, crestfallen. Within seconds, her flushed cheeks had turned as pale as talcum powder. "I don't understand," she said. "He said he'd wait for me." Shaken and staggering, she looked as though she might faint.

I jumped to my feet in case I had to catch her. "Are you okay?" I sputtered, lunging around my desk and putting my hand beneath her elbow for support. "Here. I think you'd better sit down. Can I get you a cup of water?"

"I'll be all right," she said, carefully lowering herself into the chair next to my desk. "I just need to catch my breath."

She needed something much stronger than air. A stiff drink, or a jumbo shot of Geritol. "What's the matter?" I asked her. "You seem terribly distressed."

She raised her joyless eyes and gave me a wan smile. "Is it that obvious?"

"You almost collapsed. In my book that's obvious." I returned to my chair on the other side of the desk. "Do you want to talk about it?"

"No!" she cried. "I wouldn't *think* of bothering you with my problems. I'm sure you have plenty of your own."

She was right about that. For instance, finishing my proofreading and getting out of the office for the weekend had become a pressing problem. "Well, then," I said, "if you're sure you're feeling okay, I think I'll —"

"It's just that I need the work so badly," she blurted out, tears welling in her anxious eyes, "and I thought Mr. Pomeroy was going to help me. He said if I came to his office this afternoon and showed him my portfolio, he'd give me a job."

"A job?" I croaked, wondering if *my* job was the one he was planning to give her.

"A photo assignment," she said. "He wanted me to pose for the cover of a magazine."

"Oh," I said, relieved. "You're a model."

"Yes, I am," she said, taking an embroidered handkerchief out of her purse and dabbing her face. "Not a very successful one, though. I guess I'm just not pretty enough."

She wasn't a drop-dead knockout, but she was a lot more attractive than most of the trashy dames who appeared in *Daring Detective*. "Don't be silly. Of course you're pretty enough."

"Thank you," she said, shyly glancing down at her fidgeting hands. "It's kind of you to say that. I may not be really beautiful, but I *do* photograph well, and I'm not afraid of the camera. Would you like to see my portfolio?"

"Okay," I said, with a silent groan. I didn't want to look at her pictures. I wanted to finish my work and go home. But she looked so fragile — so *needy* — I couldn't bring myself to give her the brush-off.

With a grateful smile, she leaned over and unzipped the large black portfolio she had propped against the front of my desk. Then she stood, gathered her wayward strength, heaved the portfolio onto the top of my desk, and pulled it open.

She kept a lot of stuff in there besides

photos. Typed bios and résumés, an appointment calendar, a shopping list, a bunch of bills, a candy bar, a small jar of Pond's cold cream, an extra pair of stockings, and a couple of cowboy comic books (Roy Rogers and Lash LaRue, *not* Hopalong Cassidy). These loose personal items tumbled into view when she opened the front cover of her portfolio. Embarrassed, she quickly turned the first page over to hide the intimate, untidy heap.

"Sorry about the mess," she said. "I was in such a hurry to get here I didn't have time to straighten up."

I laughed. "You talk about your portfolio as if it were your home."

She laughed, too. "It *is*, in a way. My home away from home. The only thing that's missing is a bed." As soon as those words had left her mouth, her good humor faded and her sadness and anxiety returned. "But I've got plenty of photos," she went on, continuing to turn the portfolio pages for me, "and they were all taken by a top professional. At a real studio. I think they're pretty good, don't you?"

"Very nice," I said, looking down at the assortment of glossy photos arranged under the plastic overlays. Some were big, some were small, some were in color, most were black-and-white, some were head-shots, some were full body shots, and all were taken in the same straightforward, sharp-focus style. The lighting and cos-tumes were adequate, but nothing special. If the photographer was a top professional, as she'd said, he must have been having a humdrum day.

"Would you like to leave a few shots for Mr. Pomeroy?" I asked her. "I'll make sure he gets them."

"That won't be necessary," she said. "The photographer already gave him a package of five of my photos. That's why he called me about the cover assignment."

"Oh," I mumbled, not knowing what else to say.

"Maybe Mr. Pomeroy just forgot about our meeting," she said. "Maybe he'll call me back . . . give me another appoint-ment."

"Maybe." *If he's ever sober or interested enough to actually take care of magazine busi-ness.* "I'll tell him you were here."

"Thank you," she said, carefully re-moving her overstuffed portfolio from the top of my desk and zipping it tight. "I guess I'll be going now."

"Are you sure you're feeling okay?" She still looked pale and weak — more like a ghost than a flesh and blood person.

"Oh, yes, I'm fine now," she insisted, picking up her things.

I watched her walk toward the door. She had a lithe figure and good posture, though she was listing under the weight of the large black portfolio. When she reached the door she turned and gave me another sad smile. "Bye-bye," she said, in a voice so frail it vanished instantly in the dormant air.

Taking another close look at the familiar newspaper photo, I realized I'd seen it more than once before. I'd seen it *twice*. First, when I was looking through Babs's portfolio, and then again a few days after that, when I found the same picture in the file room, in a stack of other photos waiting to be sorted and filed (by me, of course). I figured Brandon Pomeroy had put it there — that it had been one of the photos in the package he got from Bab's photographer.

Although I had wondered what had happened to the four other pictures in the package — why they hadn't been included in the stack of photos to be filed — I didn't think too much about it at the time. Brandon Pomeroy had his own way of doing things, and it wasn't up to me to understand. I was just supposed to follow orders. I filed the photo and forgot about it.

I never knew if Pomeroy called Babs back, or gave her another appointment. All I knew was that she hadn't yet been featured on the cover of *Daring Detective*.

Her chances are a whole lot better now, though, I realized with a sinking, cynical heart. *Now that she's been murdered.*

I couldn't stop staring at the photo. Babs's sad round eyes gazed up from the newsprint, locking onto mine. Her melancholy smile seemed to quiver on the page. The long black feather on her little black hat curled around her cheek in the shape of a question mark. I was transfixed. I had a very strong feeling she was asking me for something, and I couldn't shake the sense that I was now connected to her somehow — that Babs and I had suddenly been snapped together, like a couple of pink plastic pop beads.

BLONDE! . . . BEAUTY! . . . SLAIN! . . . LAST NIGHT! . . .

The words flashed in my face like lightning. And rumbled in my brain like thunder. And when the storm was over, and my head had cleared, I knew exactly what it was Babs wanted me to do. She wanted me to write her story.

Okay, okay! So I'm being a bit melodramatic here. I mean, Babs didn't actually *speak* to me, or anything like that. I didn't hear any voices from the great beyond, and whatever lightning and thunder there was came strictly from my overactive imagination. Nevertheless, I *did* feel very, very sorry for the girl, and I was overcome with an intense desire to know who had killed her and why.

And I *did* want to write her story.

Not just for Babs's sake, I confess, but also for my own. I had a very clear conviction that *this* was the story I'd been looking for — the very story that would, if I put forth my best research, reporting and writing skills, earn me the coveted stripes and semi-advanced salary of a full-grown staff writer.

I quickly cut out the article and folded it up in a tight little square. Then, sweeping my eyes around the back of the office to make sure nobody was watching, I stuck the clip in the center pocket of my leather clutch bag, and stuffed the bag into my bottom desk drawer. Sitting forward in my chair, and eagerly searching for more information about Babs's death, I clipped the rest of the *Daily News* as quickly as possible, then madly flipped and snipped my way through the *New York Times* and the *Herald Tribune*.

"Hey, get a load of *her*," Mario called out. "That's what I call a fast-paced Paige Turner!"

"She's a fast one, all right," Mike answered, snickering. "But if she doesn't slow down, she'll reach her climax too quick."

They laughed their heads off for a few seconds, but when I gave *them* the cut by keeping my back turned to their corny horseplay and continuing my clipping crusade, they eventually lost interest and went back to their work.

Halfway through the *Daily Mirror*, I found another article about the Comstock murder. But this one offered far fewer facts than the first. No jump rope, no gossipy neighbor, and no photo at all. I put the clipping into the manila folder with all the other crime snippets of the day, scrawled the date across the face of the file, and deposited it on Pomeroy's desk, where I knew it would languish until the sneering, slow-moving editor finally made his way into the office — probably not until after his three-martini lunch.

I spent my lunch hour in the file room,

plowing through the overstuffed photo file cabinets, searching for the glossy black-and-white headshot of Babs Comstock I knew was there. Trouble was, I couldn't remember where I had put it.

But since I handled all the billing for pictures used in *Daring Detective* and took care of all the filing and refiling of new and used photos, I was on intimate terms with the magazine's cockeyed storage system. So I knew that some pictures were filed by name — either the victim's or the killer's or (in cases where the real pix were unavailable or uninteresting, and crime scenes were re-created) the photographer's — while the huge reserves of nameless stock photos were merely grouped by sex, age, clothing, hair color, location, background, weapon, type of crime, etc.

Although Babs was now a murder victim and would soon have a file all her own, there were — as yet — no folders marked COMSTOCK. And there were no files labeled WOMEN WEARING PEARLS, or LADIES IN LITTLE BLACK HATS. There were, however, about a thousand folders marked BLONDES, and with a sigh the size of a hurricane, I began digging through them — folder by folder, photo by photo, blonde by blonde.

When I was three-quarters of the way through the sixteenth file, I found it: the same thin face, the same peroxide pageboy, the same black feather. I almost shouted "Eureka!" but, fortunately, my voice caught in my throat. I yanked the photo out of the folder and turned it over to check the back. The words STARLIGHT STUDIOS were stamped in black ink on the reverse. There were no red grease-pencil markings, no in-house dates or issue numbers indicating that the print had ever been used. Breathing every bit as hard as Lenny does after his nine-flight hike to the office (and acting just as nervous), I stashed the picture in a manila envelope and tried to hide it from sight in the folds of my full navy skirt. Then I left the file room and scurried back to my desk.

Luckily, Crockett, Mike, and Mario were all still out to lunch. And Pomeroy hadn't come in yet. Lenny was there, of course, slouched low over his drawing table eating a salami sandwich, but I wasn't worried about him. Even if he *did* actually raise his eyes and look in my direction, he'd be so lost in his own self-consciousness he wouldn't notice what *I* was up to.

I quickly stuffed the envelope holding the photo into the drawer with my purse, then took my logbook out of another drawer. I opened it up to the photo billing section, and found the address for Starlight Studios in a flash. After copying it down on a memo pad, I ripped off the sheet with the address, folded it twice, and stuck it deep in the center pocket of my purse, next to the newspaper article. Knowing time was of the essence in every criminal or journalistic investigation, I decided to pay a little visit to Starlight Studios as soon as I got off work.

In an effort to compose myself (and rein in my racing heart), I then reached into the side pocket of my purse, took out my white plastic comb, and ran it slowly through my hair. Patting my thick, shoulder-length waves back into place, I pulled out my new silver compact, clicked it open in my hand, and — smiling slyly at my reflection in the small round mirror — powdered my shiny (okay, *sneaky*) nose.

When Brandon Pomeroy walked into the office two seconds later, I was the picture of innocent perfection.

Chapter 2

"Good afternoon, Mrs. Turner. I trust you've had a productive morning?" Pomeroy's left eyebrow was hoisted to the hilt, and his deep voice was dripping with disdain.

"Yes, sir," I answered. He was only six years older than I was, but he'd made it clear the day he hired me that the "sir" would always be in order. "Mike's new story is ready to go out," I told him. "It's on your desk with the morning newspaper clips."

"What about the cover lines? Have they been proofread?"

"Yes, sir. I gave them to Mario for pasteup."

"And the bluelines?"

"Corrected and sent to the printer."

"Have you finished the backyard mock-up for the next issue?" He screwed his thin lips into a mean little smirk and glared at me through squinted eyelids. He was, I knew, hoping for a negative response — looking for a reason to vent the anger always bubbling beneath the surface of his rigid composure.

"Yes, I finished it on Thursday, sir. Sent it out to the typesetter on Friday." *So there, Mr. Snotty!*

"Any calls?" he growled.

To keep myself from growling back, I imagined a big booger hanging out of his nose and a long piece of toilet paper stuck to the heel of his shoe. "Two, sir. Dirk Pitt from UPI, and freelance writer Jonathan Bliss. The messages are on your desk."

"Is the coffee fresh?"

"Yes, Mr. Pomeroy. I made a new pot twenty minutes ago." It was an outright lie, but I knew he wouldn't find out. Pomeroy never drank coffee after lunch for fear the caffeine would diminish the effects of the gin.

You could smell the booze on him, but you could never detect any other signs that he'd been drinking. His expensive clothes were always clean and pressed — no rumpled or stained shirtfronts; no loose, crooked ties. He walked as tall and straight as a soldier on parade, never swaying or stumbling, and he never, *ever* slurred his words. They came zipping out of his mouth like bullets, heading directly for their intended targets.

Hooking his hat on the rack and smoothing the lapels of his gray suit jacket,

Pomeroy finally abandoned his interrogation of me and stepped over to his own desk, which was across the aisle from mine and Mike's. He sat down and lit up his pipe. He pushed his horn-rimmed glasses higher on his handsome face and, fingering his well-trimmed mustache, looked over his phone messages.

"Get me Dirk Pitt," he said, omitting — as always — the courteous "please." Though he'd come from an upper-crust family and had attended expensive boarding schools and an Ivy League college, Pomeroy rarely showed proof of his "polite" society upbringing (except when he was complaining about poor service, or looking down his nose at everything and everybody — cocktail waitresses and female co-workers in particular). I wasn't surprised he'd never married. He was too selfish to share anything, much less his precious name.

I made the call for him and, while he was talking, grabbed the key to the ladies' room. Raising my hand in the air and dangling the key from my thumb and forefinger (so that Pomeroy would notice it and not give me an argument about where I was going), I stepped out into the hall.

I didn't have to go to the bathroom. I

just needed to walk around a bit, make a few faces, let off some steam. I thought of going down to the lobby coffee shop for a donut — my stomach was beginning to protest the lack of lunch — but I knew that would take too long. Pomeroy would be fuming when I got back. And, hungry though I was, I wasn't in the mood to swallow his preposterous fury. With a petulant toss of my head, I decided the ninth-floor corridor of our large office building was as good a place as any for a cool-down stroll.

There were five other small offices on our floor — two insurance agencies, a private nursing service, a tax accountant, and an employment agency. And at the far end of the wide corridor — down by the elevators and the water fountain — stood the heavy glass doors to a very *large* office, the floor space of which probably equaled that of all the other offices put together. The name Orchid Publications was etched, in ornate purple and gold letters, across the clear-glass-walled entrance, and the walls of the reception area just inside were painted pale lavender. Orchid published an enormous number of second-string women's magazines — romance, movie, and beauty magazines — and employed

46

mostly women on its giggly and frilly staff.

I could have gotten a job at Orchid if I'd wanted to. But I didn't (want to, that is). I'd rather make a thousand pots of coffee, and rewrite a hundred poorly written crime sagas, than compose one weepy I'm-so-pathetic-I-want-to-die confession tale, or conduct one sappy wide-eyed young starlet interview, or write one single caption about the new Persian blue eye shadow every stylish woman simply *must* have in her cosmetics kit this summer. Besides, *Daring Detective* was actually (although semi-secretly) owned by Orchid Publications, so I was *already* an Orchid employee of sorts. So were Harvey Crockett and the others. We were just tucked away in a separate office down the hall (and never invited to the annual Christmas party) because the big shots at Orchid didn't want their company's sparkly feminine image getting tarnished by *Daring Detective*'s gushing blood and gore. They just wanted our gushing profits.

I walked most of the way down the deserted hall and, when I reached the water fountain, turned around to head back. Just then one of the elevator doors snapped open and two young women in small flowered hats stepped out. In their form-fitting pastel suits, white gloves, and stiletto heels, they looked like stragglers from the previous weekend's Easter parade. Chirping and twittering like delirious parakeets, they gave me a joint glance of disinterest, and fluttered off to the sanctuary of Orchid Publications. Then the doors to the other elevator opened, and out hopped Mike and Mario.

Hoping to fend off another terrible joke about my name, I straightened my shoulders and propped one hand on my hip. "Hello, boys," I said. "Have an uplifting trip?" I was trying to act as cool and smart as Brenda Starr, but in my anxious, hotheaded condition, I probably looked (and sounded) more like Woody Woodpecker.

Mario grinned and came closer. Whenever Mario was standing anywhere near me, he *always* came closer. "*You're* more uplifting than the elevator," he said, "if you know what I mean." Wink, wink. Smirk, smirk.

"Then you'd better push the Down button," I said.

Mike laughed, but Mario just leered and moved his chubby body even closer. He raised his dark brown eyes to mine (I'm at least three inches taller than he is) and put his arm around my waist. "Allow me to escort you back to the office, my dear. A beautiful woman like you shouldn't be out in the hall alone." As he began to guide me back down the corridor, his hand slipped (i.e., *slunk*) from my waist to my hip. I knew he was working himself up (or, rather, down) to a full-scale fanny pat, so I extricated myself from his feverish grasp and lurched ahead.

"I think our phone is ringing," I blurted over my shoulder, scampering away like a rabbit. Whenever I'm besieged by Mario Caruso's double entendres and wandering hands, I make up a quick excuse and take immediate flight. It's the simplest of all solutions; he can't badger or fondle me if I'm not there. And I can't tell him to drop dead — a stunt which could easily lead to a public fit of rage (his) and a sudden outbreak of unemployment (mine).

When I got back to my desk — right before Mike and Mario returned to the office — I snatched up the phone and quickly dialed the typesetter. I needed to call for a copy pickup, but I also wanted to make it look as if the phone *had* rung — that my headlong dash away from Mario had been a response to the call of duty, not a calculated escape from his unwelcome advances.

A word to the wise working woman: Do whatever you can to help your male colleagues hold on to their "manly" pride. The face you save may be your own.

Shortly after three p.m. the afternoon papers arrived. The afternoon headlines were much the same as the morning's: testing of the new polio vaccine was scheduled to begin on Tuesday; Ike and Mamie were returning to Washington after their Easter vacation in Georgia; Southwestern Louisiana Institute was ordered by a federal court to admit four Negro students; Juan Perón had won the Argentina election (only three people were killed during the voting); NBC was dropping live coverage of the Army-McCarthy hearings due to poor ratings.

Mob boss Frank Costello was making especially big news that afternoon. His long-awaited trial for income tax evasion had finally gotten under way, and reporters were having a field day. The stories were focused on Costello's illegal financial activities rather than his many heinous acts of murder, but I cut them out just the same. The biographical information and the photos accompanying the articles might prove useful in the future. There were also more articles about the Anastasia mob hit and — even though I knew Mike had already written his story from the morning clips — I snipped them all out. They'd come in handy when I had to do the rewrite.

I cut out the items about the Comstock murder too. Two of the afternoon editions had covered the story, but neither of the brief reports gave even half as much information as the one folded up in my purse. I wanted to rip the new clips to shreds and throw them away (so that Pomeroy wouldn't be reminded of the murder, decide to make it a cover story, and give the assignment to Mike or one of his hotshot freelancers). But I didn't dare. Pomeroy might pick up a newspaper or two on his way home from work and discover my secret deletions. Then hell would have to be paid. Out of my credibility account (which, by virtue of my being female, was already hovering at zero).

I interspersed the Comstock clips between all the others in the folder, hoping that if they weren't grouped together, Pomeroy wouldn't pay them too much mind. If I was lucky — really lucky — the editor's excessive booze consumption would so thoroughly obscure his powers of perception that poor Babs's hideous fate would escape his editorial attention altogether. Then the story would be mine. All mine.

Before putting the clips on Pomeroy's desk, I took a couple of minutes to read Dorothy Kilgallen's column, "The Voice of Broadway," in the *Journal American*. She had recently been covering the scandalous adventures of New York's favorite playboy, Zack Dexter Harrington, and I wanted to see what trouble the mischievous millionaire had gotten into over the weekend.

According to Dorothy, Zack had celebrated Saturday night in style — dining on lobster thermidor and champagne with Ava Gardner at '21' (Frank Sinatra was nowhere in sight), then taking the sultry actress for a whirligig midnight helicopter ride over the city. After depositing the inebriated and airsick Ava back at her hotel, Zack then danced and drank himself silly at the Stork Club, finally heading home to his Park Avenue penthouse at four a.m. with not one, but three anonymous young ladies on his expensively tailored arm.

I smiled and lit up a cigarette. I was interested in Zack Dexter Harrington for three reasons. One, because I found his ridiculous antics amusing; two, because he was ridiculously cute (scores of paparazzi had established that fact); three, because his ridiculously wealthy father — Oliver Rice Harrington — owned and controlled one of the largest publishing empires in the country. Sixty-two newspapers, four major book companies, and over a hundred magazine titles were owned by old man Oliver, including Orchid Publications and — you guessed it — *Daring Detective* magazine.

And my connection to the Harringtons didn't end there. Brandon Pomeroy provided another link in the chain. As the son of one of Oliver Harrington's numerous high-brow cousins, Pomeroy was actually a member of the Harrington family — which was one of the reasons he was always so stuck up, angry, and lazy. Stuck up, because he thought his blue blood ties made him better than everybody else; angry, because when he'd asked his elder second cousin for a position in the publishing industry, he'd been given a lousy job on the staff of *Daring Detective*; lazy, because no matter how little he worked, or how late he came into the office, he knew he wouldn't get fired. I suspected, also, that Pomeroy's pampered pedigree had more than a little to do with his affection for alcohol.

"Taking a cigarette break, Mrs. Turner?"

Seated at his desk behind and across the aisle from mine, Pomeroy fired his sullen words into my back. "I'm glad *you* have time for such unproductive pursuits. But now perhaps you'll be kind enough to take a break from your cigarette break and bring me the afternoon clip file, which I've been waiting for for over ten minutes."

"Yes, sir," I said, rising to my feet and squashing my L&M filter tip in the ashtray. I picked up the clip file and walked it over to Pomeroy's desk. A thank-you was not forthcoming. Mike, Mario, and Lenny were all watching the pathetic little drama, bearing witness to my silent humiliation, looking relieved that Pomeroy's scorn was landing on me instead of them.

"Do you like working here, Mrs. Turner?" Pomeroy asked, in a voice loud enough for all to hear.

"Very much, sir," I answered. *About as much as I like having the flu.*

"Then I suggest you pay more attention to your job. We didn't hire you just to show us how to inhale." As if to prove his own smoking talents, Pomeroy picked up his pipe and puffed it, blowing a plume of fruity fumes in my direction. Then, crooking his mouth in an almost imperceptible smile, he leaned back in his chair and

54

waited for me to reply.

"Yes, sir," I quickly repeated. I knew from experience not to try to defend myself. Back talk of any kind always spurred Pomeroy on. And since the man was sitting there right in front of me, staring at me with his beady brown eyes, I couldn't make any nasty faces. I thought of faking a coughing fit — just to relieve the building pressure — but quickly decided against it. A convulsive physical response would have given the sadistic editor nothing but pleasure.

I finally just heaved a soundless sigh and resorted to my servile little waitress persona. "Will that be all, sir?"

"For now," he said, sitting up straighter in his chair and turning all his attention to the clip file. He had already lost interest in his cruel cat and mouse game. It wasn't any fun playing cat when the mouse was playing dead.

I went back to my desk and looked at the clock on the wall. It was 4:05; only fifty-five minutes to go. After giving Mike's mob story a quick read-through and correcting a few spelling errors, I put it aside for the morning. It would take me longer to fix it than it had taken Mike to write it. I logged in a stack of new invoices, sorted and filed

55

the photos that had just come back from the printer, changed Mike's typewriter ribbon, then made several trips to the ladies' room to clean out the coffeepot and wash all the cups.

By ten after five my desk was clear as an airport runway, and I took off for Starlight Studios.

Chapter 3

Rush hour in Manhattan is, depending on your mood, either a carnival or a zoo. And as I walked downtown from my office at 43rd and Third toward Starlight Studios at 36th and Park, I was definitely in a carny frame of mind. The big warm pretzel I bought from a sidewalk pushcart tasted better than lobster thermidor (no offense to Zack Harrington and Ava Gardner), and being out on the street in the crisp spring air — strutting along with the fast-stepping crowd past all the festive and colorful shop window displays — felt like being on the midway. The cacophony of blaring car horns, cursing cab drivers, and squealing truck breaks sounded like hurdy-gurdy music to me.

I was so excited I could barely breathe. I was working on a story! I was a woman transformed. No longer was I an overburdened, unappreciated, mistreated office drone. I was a courageous and determined seeker of the truth! I was a wildly adventurous woman on a dangerous secret mission! I was a brilliant, shrewd, intuitive, soon-to-be-published writer! (I was also a woman about to dive, headfirst, into her own deathbed, but — thanks to my Brenda Starr bravado and my fixation on becoming the next Agatha Christie — I was too stupid to think about that at the time.)

I hurried west on 36th Street and came to a stop near the corner of Park, at the large brick apartment building housing the private, street-level entrance to Starlight Studios. Tucking my purse and the photo of Babs Comstock under my arm, I took my white cotton gloves out of my jacket pocket and pulled them on. Then I checked my reflection in the closest ground-floor window. My navy wool beret was slightly askew, but I decided the rakish angle made me look more intriguing — more like a *writer* — so I left it that way. Sucking in a chestful of air and exhaust fumes, I limped over to the studio entrance (by this time my high heels were killing me) and pushed the button near the door.

A few seconds passed, and I was buzzed in. A very small, drab hallway led to another door on the right, where the name Starlight Studios was stenciled in large black letters on the battered wood panel. I knocked, but nothing happened. I knocked again, with no response. Finally I gripped the doorknob with my glove and gave it a little twist. To my surprise, the door clicked open, and I stepped into another small, drab hallway. There was an odd smoky smell in the air. The walls were bare, the floor was dusty, and there wasn't a soul in sight.

"Hello?" I called out. "Is anybody here?"

"Yeah!" a male voice bellowed. "In the studio. Come on back."

Somewhat apprehensively, I followed the sound of the voice to the end of the tiny, dark hallway and turned right, toward the light. And suddenly there I stood, all wide-eyed and wobbly, in an enormous, high-ceilinged, white-walled room filled with tripods and cameras and big white umbrellas and spotlights — lots of spotlights — all of which were beamed on a big, busty blonde wearing nothing but a huge Uncle Sam top hat, two star-shaped pasties, and a pair of red, white, and blue–striped panties. She was smiling like there was no tomorrow, and holding several sizzling sparklers in each hand.

"Ouch!" she cried, suddenly pulling her big red smile into a pleated pout. "Can't we stop now, Scotty? These goddamn sparklers are stingin' me! And the smoke's burning my eyes!"

The well-built man bending over the camera stood up straight and raked his fingers through his sandy brown hair. "Just a few more shots, doll. We're almost done. Give me that big, beautiful smile again. And lean over toward the camera a little more. Show the boys everything you've got." Before turning back to his work, he shot me a quick, inquisitive glance.

"Should I wait outside?" I asked, embarrassed. I felt like an intruder — like an accidental witness to some kind of secret sex ceremony.

"No," he said. "Have a seat over there." He gestured toward a dirty gold velvet couch pushed back against the wall. "Be with you in a second." If the half-naked woman had any thoughts as to whether or not I should leave the vicinity, she didn't express them.

I sat down on the couch, put the photo and my purse to one side, and folded my hands in my lap. Lowering my gaze from the model's star-tipped bare breasts to my pristine white cotton gloves, I felt (and certainly looked!) as if I should be sitting in church instead of a cheesecake photographer's studio. I might not dig up any good murder stories in church, I thought with a self-mocking smile, but at least I could

pray for publication. (And, I pondered —
not smiling anymore — for Babs Comstock's brutally departed soul.)

"Hey, can't we do it without the sparklers, Scotty? These ones are all burned
out anyways."

"Oh, all right," the photographer gave in.
"Pitch 'em out of the shot."

As the woman tossed the dead sparklers
to the floor on one side, making sure to
clear the edge of the bright blue paper
backdrop, her breasts bobbed like water
balloons and her Uncle Sam top hat tipped
down over her eyes. "Hey! Who turned out
all the lights!" she squealed, laughing rau-
cously at her own joke. The more she
laughed, the more she bobbed.

Nobody seemed to notice this ribald
spectacle but me. The blonde was utterly
unfazed by her own nakedness, and the
photographer looked as bored as a subway
token teller. Straightening the hat on her
head, the woman struck a few more dopey
poses, and the man snapped a few more
silly shots. Then they were finished.

"Oooh! Oooh! Thank goodness we're
done," the blonde cried. "I've got to go to
the little girl's room!" Hugging her arms
around her fleshy midriff, she made a mad,
pigeon-toed dash for a door on the far side

of the studio and urgently bobbed out of sight.

After spending an inordinate amount of time killing the spotlights, turning on a couple of fans to clear the air of sparkler smoke, changing the backdrop paper from blue to purple, and moving equipment around on the floor, the slow-moving photographer finally sauntered over to me. "Hi, doll," he said, pulling down the sleeves of his black turtleneck. "Sorry to keep you waiting. Shooting a pinup calendar. Did you bring your portfolio?"

"What?" I'd heard his question, but I didn't comprehend it. And I was too busy staring at his shockingly handsome face to try to figure it out.

"You've got one, don't you?" he went on. "I can see you're good looking enough — nice kisser, great legs — but I've got to see how you photograph before I can give you any jobs."

"But, I . . . that's not why —"

"Look, do you have one or not? Because if you don't, you should hire me to shoot one for you. You'll never get any work — not even a shoe ad — without a good portfolio."

I finally stopped gaping at his turquoise

eyes, strong jaw, and cleft chin, and pulled myself together. "I'm not looking for work," I said. "I'm a writer, not a model."

He cocked his head and gave me a curious look.

I stood up from the couch to introduce myself. "My name is Paige Turner," I said. "I work for *Daring Detective* magazine." I muttered the words fast and low, hoping he wouldn't notice the comical combination and start laughing like a hyena.

He didn't even crack a smile. "I've done some assignments for *Daring Detective*," he said.

"Yes, I know. That's why I'm here. I found this photo in our files," I said, retrieving the manila envelope from the couch and taking out the picture of Babs, "and I wonder if you could give me any information about the model."

As I handed him the photo, Miss Fourth of July came bobbing out of the back room. Even with her clothes on — a blue sheath skirt and a fuzzy orange sweater — she jiggled like a minor earthquake. "Bye-bye, Scotty!" she called, heading for the exit. "Gotta go now. I'm workin' the checkroom at Sardi's tonight. Call me later?"

"Sure, doll," he said, never raising his eyes from the picture in his hand. He turned the photo over, took note of his stamp on the back, then turned it topside up again, regarding the image with a look of disinterest on his gorgeous face. "This is Wanda Wingate," he said, handing the picture back to me. "She modeled for me a couple of times. Once on spec, and once for a Juliette Hat Company ad. This pic is from the hat shoot."

Wanda Wingate . . . right! That *was the name she gave me.* "A hat company ad?" I queried. "Then why was this photo in *our* files?"

"I gave it to your editor several months ago, when we met for a drink. He asked for some new headshots. Said he was looking for fresh faces to use in the magazine."

"You gave it to Brandon Pomeroy?"

"Yeah, that's the guy. He's the one that gives me the assignments. Says he likes the way I do corpses."

"Did he want you to shoot Wanda as a corpse?"

"Guess not. I never heard from him one way or the other."

"So Wanda never appeared in a *Daring Detective* layout?"

"You could answer that better than me,"

he said, wrinkling his lightly tanned, perfectly proportioned forehead into a frown. "All I can say is *I* never shot her for *DD*. But maybe some other photographer did. She could have been on the cover for all I know."

I shifted my weight from one sore foot to the other, and forged on. "Wanda Wingate — was that her real name?"

"Probably not. A lot of the girls use professional names. Try to make themselves sound more glamorous. Say, what are you asking all these questions for anyway? What's this all about?"

"Did you read the *Daily News* today, Mr., uh . . . sorry, I don't know your name."

"It's Whitcomb. Scotty Whitcomb. And no, I didn't read any of the papers yet." He was starting to look wary. "What's going on?"

"This very same photo appeared on page twelve of today's *News*, Mr. Whitcomb, but they said the woman's name was Barbara Comstock, and they said that she was dead."

"What?"

"Murdered, they said. Last night."

He cocked his head again. "Wanda? I don't believe it!"

I picked up my purse, took out the clipped article, and handed it to him. While he was reading, I planted myself back down on the couch, crossed one leg over the other, and lit up a cigarette. I needed to get off my feet, but I was also digging in for the duration — determined to sit there as long as Scotty Whitcomb would let me, mentally recording as many details as I could. Details would tell the story.

When he finished reading the article, Scotty handed the clip back to me and sat down on the other end of the couch. He looked a bit upset, but definitely not devastated. "Tough luck," he said. "She was a nice girl."

"Any idea who might have killed her?" I asked, jumping the gun like a witless amateur. After all the detective stories and novels I'd read, I should have known to tread softly — save the tough questions for last.

"Not a clue," he said, offering nothing.

I gave myself a mental kick in the pants, then started over. "Did you know Babs — uh, Wanda — very well?"

"Not really. I did her portfolio, but I only met her three times after that. Once when she came here on a go-see, and twice when she came here to pose."

"You never saw her outside of the studio?"

"Nope."

Ask him something innocuous, I told myself. *Keep him talking.* "Was she a good model?"

"Not very," he said. "Her face was pretty enough, and she had a wow body, but she just didn't have any spark. She was too passive, too lifeless."

I winced at his unfortunate choice of words.

"I got her from the Venus Agency," he went on, "and they're usually pretty good at spotting potential. But they missed the boat with Wanda. I never could sell any of the pictures I took of her, except the shots for the hat company — and that's just because they were on assignment."

"What about her personality?"

"Oh, she was pleasant enough, I guess. A little sad around the edges. Didn't talk much."

"Did she ever discuss her private life?"

"No. And I never asked her about it, either. Didn't want to get involved. I could tell she was attracted to me, but I stayed far away from her, kept things strictly professional. Got more girls than I can handle already."

I didn't doubt the truth of *that* statement. With his looks, Scotty Whitcomb probably had to beat the feverish females off with a folded tripod. "How did you know she was attracted to you?"

"The usual ways," he said. "Batty eyelashes, flirty smiles, blushing cheeks. Whenever I touched her — if I tilted her chin, or straightened her shoulders for a better shot — she trembled with pleasure." A look of disgust flitted across his flawless features. "In my profession, you're exposed to all the worst feminine wiles."

Wiles? I wondered. Babs's flustered responses sounded more like infatuation to me. And did he say *he* was exposed? From what I had seen, his *models* were the ones who fit that description.

Scotty suddenly jumped up from the couch and started pacing the floor in front of me. As he paraded back and forth, from one end of the couch to the other, I couldn't help admiring his broad chest and shoulders, narrow hips, and well-shaped behind. I also couldn't help wondering what had prompted him to take this sudden stroll. Had he become agitated by our discussion? Was he trying to distract me from my inquiry? Or was he just showing off, trying to impress me with his exceptionally fine physique?

And what, I then asked myself, was the *real* reason I was scrutinizing the man's every move so closely? Was I collecting physical data for my story — or was I just another feverish female in need of a good tripod beating?

I considered these questions for a few seconds, but soon stopped trying to answer them. I was in no position to determine Scotty's motives (I'd only just met the man, after all), and I was too worked up by the whole situation — the spotlights, the studio, the *story* — to judge my own feelings objectively. Besides, I wouldn't have recognized my own libido if it stepped up and kicked me in the shin. I hadn't seen the wretched creature for a long, long time. Not since the day I received a certain telegram from the U.S. Army.

After stubbing my cigarette in an overfull ashtray, I gathered my stuff together and stood up from the couch. All of a sudden I was dying to get out of there. "Thank you for your time, Mr. Whitcomb," I said. "I feel I've taken up too much of it already."

"Yeah," he agreed, finally terminating his peacock promenade. "I've got to shoot August and September tonight. The girls'll be here in a few minutes. I'm glad you came by, though," he added. "I might not have known the *News* used one of my pictures if you hadn't told me. Their billing department isn't so great. But now I can send 'em an invoice, so I'll probably get paid pretty quick."

I didn't say anything. But my mind was giving Whitcomb a big fat piece of itself. *You callous bastard, you!* I fumed. *Poor Babs/ Wanda is dead and all you care about is getting paid?*

As I turned and headed for the exit, Scotty followed alongside. "So why did you really come here?" he wanted to know. "You doing a story on the murder for the magazine?"

I had hoped that subject wouldn't come up, but now that it had, I was compelled to reply. "Yes, I *am* writing a story on the murder," I said, "but it's strictly confidential at this point. Please don't mention it to anyone — especially Brandon Pomeroy. If he finds out I said anything to you, I'll be out of a job."

"Sure, doll," he said. "My lips are sealed. But what about the photos for the story? You need somebody to take fake corpse shots?"

My disgust with Scotty Whitcomb was complete. The photographer was willing —

make that eager — to re-create on film the gruesome murder of a woman he had known! "We'll need some photos, I'm sure," I said, imagining a swift bone-crushing connection between his well-formed chin and my white-cotton-covered fist. "But everything's top secret right now, so Mr. Pomeroy won't be assigning a photographer for a while. When he does, though, I'll make certain your name is at the top of the call list."

"Thanks, doll," he said, holding open the door and ushering me into the narrow outlet hall. Not knowing (or caring) if he was behind me or not, I hurtled down the dark, dusty passage, and onward through the next drab hallway, then out through the heavy wood door to the street. When I reached the sidewalk and headed for the corner, I snatched a quick peek over my shoulder. The man stood posed like a model on the doorstep, flashing his perfect teeth in a Starlight Studios smile.

Chapter 4

My carnival spirit was gone with the wind. I was hungry, thirsty, exhausted, and depressed. My high heels weren't mere shoes anymore — they'd become cruel instruments of torture — and my short navy jacket wasn't providing enough warmth in the chilly twilight. Nevertheless, I kept right on walking — marching like a tightly wound tin soldier — toward West 34th Street and the service entrance of Woolworth's five and dime, where Babs's stripped and strangled body had been found.

Something had happened to me at Scotty Whitcomb's studio. I'd begun to really *care* about Babs Comstock — not just as a murder victim or the subject of a story — but as a woman. Having learned that she'd generally been sad and passive, I found myself wondering what (or who) had made her that way. And the discovery that she may have had a crush on Scotty Whitcomb, or at least been attracted to him, had started me wondering about her personal life — whether she'd had a lover, or a boyfriend, or both, or neither. I figured she didn't have a husband, or he would have been listed in the *News* article, along with her parents, as a survivor.

I knew my excursion to Woolworth's might be a waste of time, that the area where Babs had been found would be roped off and already picked clean by the police, but I was drawn to the scene like a moth to a flame (I prefer not to think of myself as a vulture). Yes, I did want to gather some atmospheric details for my story, get a firsthand feeling for the place, but I also wanted to commune with Babs somehow, pay her my in-person, on-the-premises respects, give her my spiritual promise that I would do my very best to find out the truth about her death and present the facts to the public in a responsible, considerate way. I thought if I could approach the actual spot where her poor body had been dumped, I might get close to Babs's ethereal presence — close enough to send (and maybe even receive) an intercelestial message or two.

But good intentions don't guarantee good results. The more I advanced toward Woolworth's service entrance, the more I wished I'd gone straight home. The sidewalk in front of the rear access was roped off, and four police cars were parked in a tight line against the curb. A couple of cops stood guarding the protected area, and several others were pacing the perimeter, swinging their nightsticks and smoking cigarettes, scrupulously scanning the small crowd of onlookers for possible troublemakers. I was surprised by the commotion; I had thought the police would have cleared the scene by now. They must have had a very busy weekend.

A man in a white lab coat was working behind the barricade — probably collecting samples of grit and glass — but I wasn't close enough to see what he was doing. And even though I figured I'd never get up next to the scene, I felt I at least had to try. If I could just get near the caravan of cops, I thought, I could listen in on their conversations, maybe pick up some new details. I hovered at the edge of the crowd for a few minutes, then angled my way in. Wriggling sideways through the clustered bodies, and stepping on a few hapless toes, I finally forced my way up to the front.

That's when I saw him. Detective Sergeant Dan Street. He was standing about fifteen feet away from me, just outside the cordoned-off area of the sidewalk. He was talking to another, shorter man, who was dressed — like he was — in a dark suit, white shirt, hat and tie. They both held paper cups of coffee in their hands. Even in the fading light, I could see Street's jagged profile clearly.

And if I could see him, that meant he would be able — just by turning his head or shifting his eyes — to see me! I gasped and hid behind the broad-shouldered, frizzy-haired woman standing next to me. Then I bent my knees slightly, turned myself around, and — stooping my shoulders and tucking my chin into my chest — duckwalked toward the rear of the crowd as fast as I could. I did *not* want Dan Street to catch me there. If he did, and if he mentioned my presence at the scene to Brandon Pomeroy, my self-designed story assignment — not to mention my secret novel-writing aspirations — could go swooshing right down the editorial drain.

Detective Sergeant Dan Street was, oddly enough, a bona fide member of the *Daring Detective* staff. He had the dubious distinction of being our permanent "police advisor." His picture appeared in every issue of the magazine, right up front near the masthead, along with a wordy, melodramatic write-up about his heroic career with the city's homicide force and his "continuing contribution to the investigative and editorial excellence of this exclusive true crime publication."

It wasn't that Dan actually worked for the magazine, of course. He was just a name, a figurehead, a "front" to make us look official. His only responsibilities were to show up at the office once or twice a year (when some bigwig from Orchid Publications or our distribution company was there for a meeting), and to answer — by phone — Brandon Pomeroy's all-too-infrequent questions about proper police procedure. Dan was, you might say, a paid informant (although NYPD restrictions didn't allow him to actually "inform" *DD* about a murder until the case was closed, which meant his information was, for all magazine-selling intents and purposes, hopelessly out of date).

I had met Detective Street three times: twice when he came to the office for meetings, and once when he came to pick up an overdue retainer check. I wasn't attracted to the man (as I said before, my libido was on the lam) but I did find him pleasant to talk to. And to look at. His jet black eyes crackled with insight and humor, and his rugged features seemed eager to leap into a smile. With his wavy dark hair, dark eyebrows, and strong jawline, he looked like a cross between Tyrone Power and John Garfield. He was thirty-seven years old (I knew this from his *DD* bio), and he had (about three years before I met him) committed a most unusual and scandalous crime: he had divorced his wife.

I learned about the divorce from Dan himself, the day he was sitting in the guest chair near my desk, drinking a cup of coffee and waiting for Orchid's laggard accountant to make out the check for his tardy consultation fee. He had come up to the office to get the check, he told me, so he wouldn't be late with his monthly alimony payment. Although Dan thoroughly disapproved of his frivolous, unfaithful ex-wife, he was determined to make sure she had enough money to take good care of his beloved fourteen-year-old daughter, Katy. That was the only reason he had taken "the clown job at *DD*" in the first place, he said — so he could meet the financial terms of his divorce.

After concluding our conversation about his personal life, Dan and I had gone on to discuss the alarming rise of juvenile delinquency, the new Miles Davis LP, the Giants' latest winning streak, and the great new movie we'd both just seen — *On the Waterfront*, with that exciting young actor

Marlon Brando. It was an altogether agreeable exchange.

But as much as I liked talking to Dan Street then, I didn't want to talk to him *now*. Not while I was busy sticking my nose in his confidential business. Not while I was snooping around an off-limits crime scene like a berserk bloodhound. Not while I was engaged in a secret journalistic crusade that could, if discovered, get me fired.

Finally reaching the fringe of the crowd, I lowered my head still further, and pulled the rim of my beret down over one eye. Then, shielding the rest of my face with the envelope carrying Babs's photo, I scurried out into the busy street and — sticking as close as possible to the string of parked police cars — dashed against traffic, and behind Detective Street's back, up the block to the far corner. Returning to the sidewalk and stopping for a second to catch my breath, I jerked around to survey the scene, to see if my escape had been effective.

And that's when I *really* panicked. Dan Street wasn't standing near the protected area anymore. He was on the move. And he was following me! He was just sixty or so feet away and he was walking — fast! —

in my direction. He wasn't looking at me, though. His head was bowed and his eyes were glued to the pavement, so I couldn't be certain if he had seen me or not. To be on the safe side, I let out a faint squeak and took off like a frantic mouse — around the corner, halfway down the block, and into the first open door I came to.

When my head cleared I was in Woolworth's. The overhead lights were as bright as beacons, and the air was filled with the thick, sweet smell of talcum powder and grilled cheese. From somewhere in the back — the pet section, I presumed — came the titters and tweets of tiny birds. I was standing next to a Lustre Creme shampoo display, which was standing next to a case full of combs, brushes, hairnets, ribbons, and bobby pins. Across the aisle was a large cosmetics counter, the top of which was crowded with colorful exhibits of Tangee lipstick, House of Westmore rouge, and little blue bottles of Evening in Paris perfume. As I glanced around the store to get my bearings, I saw that I was in plain sight of the revolving entrance door — which kept cranking along like a busy subway turnstile, admitting one dazed-looking creature after another.

Fearing that one of those creatures might turn out to be Detective Dan Street, I darted deeper into the store — all the way back to the notions and sewing department — and stationed myself behind a tall wooden counter stocked with bolts of taffeta, cotton, felt, dotted Swiss, and topped with several huge and heavy Simplicity style and pattern books. I figured I would just stand behind the counter and flip through the style books for a while, acting demure and nonchalant, so that if Dan Street did come in and see me there, I could tell him I was shopping for the perfect pattern for the perfect strapless evening dress (thereby impressing him with my seamstress skills *and* my late-night social calendar, both of which were — in reality — sadly underdeveloped).

So I stood there — in my painful pumps on the hardwood floor — for a good ten or fifteen minutes, listening to my stomach growl, and studying dress designs as if I were Coco Chanel herself. But I was an actor without an audience. If Dan had come into the store, he hadn't come over to me. So he probably hadn't been following me after all. And he must not have seen me at the crime scene, either, or then he surely would have been following me, if for no other reason than to say hello. All my gasping and hiding had been for nothing. I felt relieved and ridiculous at the same time.

I was aching to get home and get off my feet, to call a halt to my embarrassing charade, but I couldn't abort the expedition yet. There was one thing I had to do before leaving the store. I closed the pattern book I'd been staring at, picked up my clutch bag and the photo, and headed for the toy section.

The first aisle I came to was full of dolls. There were cloth dolls, rubber dolls, plastic dolls, and porcelain dolls. There were cuddly little baby dolls and floppy Raggedy Ann dolls and pink and frilly Shirley Temple dolls. And there were big, beautiful grown-up dolls — dolls with long legs and long, curly hair and gaudy grown-up clothes. They wore ballet dresses or nursing uniforms or cowgirl outfits or wedding gowns. Most of them were blonde.

But it was the racks and shelves of the next aisle that held the most interest for me — the ones crammed with toys for boys. I walked slowly down the narrow passageway, checking out the bats and balls, catcher's mitts, windup cars, tanks and fire engines, until I came to the western zone — a cluttered exhibit of cowboy hats and cap pistols, fringed shirts and holster sets.

And Hopalong Cassidy jump ropes.

Stopping in my tracks and sucking in my breath, I bent down toward one of the lower shelves and came face-to-face with a large cardboard cutout of Hoppy and his horse, Topper. The kindly white-haired cowboy star was grinning at me, staring deep into my eyes, inviting me to inspect his ample stock of jump ropes, which were coiled — like sleeping snakes — in the attached red, white, and black cardboard display box.

I picked one up and turned it over in my white-gloved hand. It looked so innocent, with its little red wood handles and its tiny, stamped-on line drawings of Hoppy and Topper. The thin cardboard band holding the loosely wound cord together was printed with Hopalong's "autograph." The name was written in rope.

I shuddered and tossed the eighty-nine cent plaything back into the display box. The thought of a child's toy — such a friendly and *harmless* toy — being used as a murder device filled me with horror and disgust. And wonder. I wondered, for instance, who the deadly jump rope had belonged to, and how it came to be on hand at the moment of Babs Comstock's murder. I wondered what kind of killer would even *think* of using a kid's jump rope to strangle somebody. And then I wondered if the murderer had stood on that very spot — right there in Woolworth's — testing the various jump ropes for strength and durability, choosing his weapon with sinister care.

I couldn't answer any of those questions, of course — not *then* anyway — so I started looking around for somebody to help me, a Woolworth's employee who might recall ringing up a recent Hopalong Cassidy jump rope purchase, or remember seeing a woman shopper who resembled the black-and-white glossy I just happened to have in my hand. It was a million-to-one shot, I knew, but what did I have to lose?

There was no saleslady in immediate sight, so I walked to the very end of the toy aisle — out toward the long white Formica lunch counter — to continue my search. And there he sat, swiveled sideways on a chrome and red vinyl counter stool, talking to a waitress in a pink and white uniform, eating a hamburger. With pickles and potato chips. My first impulse was to sneak away before he saw me, but then I thought better of it. I didn't have to hide from Dan Street anymore. I had as much right to be in Woolworth's as he did. I wasn't skulking around a crime scene at that point, I was just catching up on my shopping.

And besides, I was *really* hungry.

"Well, if it isn't Manhattan's most daring detective!" I said, walking over and sitting down on the stool next to Dan's. "I see you've got a new homicide on your plate. What should we call this one? The Case of the Bumped-Off Burger?"

He laughed and wiped the ketchup off his mouth. "How are you doing, Paige? It's good to see you."

"I'm doing fine," I said, "except that I'm starving to death. What's the Blue Plate Special? I hope it's horse."

He let out a deep, hearty chuckle. "You're out of luck. It's turkey and mashed."

"I'll have a frankfurter," I said to the waitress, "with mustard and relish. And a cherry Coke." I really wanted the Blue Plate, but I didn't dare order it. I was afraid I wouldn't have a dime left over for the subway ride home, and the thought of walking all the way down to the Village in my arch-busting, toe-squashing shoes gave rise to dangerous fantasies of suicide.

"How's the magazine business?" Dan asked. "Still knocking 'em dead on the newsstand?"

"It's a bloodbath." I put the photo envelope down on the counter and positioned my purse and gloves on top of it. "The competition can't hold a candle, burning or otherwise. How's the murder business?"

He lifted his hat, combed his fingers through his thick dark hair, and pulled the brim down over his forehead again. "Never a dull moment." His voice sounded a little tired — and a lot sad. "In fact, as much as I'd like to sit and keep you company while you eat, I've got to get back to work now. My dinner break is over."

"Oh," I said, disappointed. I wanted to talk to Dan for a while, share a few thoughts, pick up a few facts. I racked my brain for a way to prolong the conversation. "Are you working nearby?" I asked, widening my eyes into jumbo globes of innocence.

"Very nearby. Right here, as a matter of fact. Around the corner, by the service entrance."

"Really? Somebody got killed at Woolworth's?"

"Not killed here, just dropped off afterward."

"Oh, my!" I exclaimed, acting shocked at first, then looking up at the ceiling with a mask of deep concentration on my face. "Come to think of it, I believe I read about that in the paper this morning. It was a woman, right? A blonde?"

"Right."

"Half nude and strangled."

"Right."

"Do you know who did it?" *God! I'm galloping again! My stupid tongue should be tied to a tree.*

"Not yet," he said, showing no signs of suspicion (either of me or any other questionable characters). "But we'll get the guy eventually. He was sloppy. Left a few pointers."

"Such as maybe he's a Hopalong Cassidy fan?" I blurted.

Dan smiled. "I see you've read the *Daily News*. We managed to suppress that bit in the other papers."

"I know, I read them all." I realized I was acting too bold — revealing too much knowledge and curiosity about the case — but I couldn't help myself. For some unfathomable reason, I wanted to impress Dan Street with my deductive prowess. And as crazy as it was, I also wanted to help him track down the murderer (so that

86

Babs's death would be justly and speedily avenged, and my story would have a dramatic, satisfying solution). Craziest of all was my feeble-minded conviction that I actually *could* help.

"There's a big box of Hopalong Cassidy jump ropes over in the toy section," I proudly disclosed.

He cocked his head to one side, shot me a quick probing glance, then smiled again — broadly. "Yes, we know all about it. But thanks for the tip." His voice had a decidedly paternal tone. "Why all the concern?" he added. "Are you working on a story?"

"No," I lied. "They don't let me write for the magazine." That part was true, at least.

"Well, maybe they should," he said. "Seems like you've got a smart little head on your shoulders."

Though I didn't appreciate his use of the word "little" to describe my head, the rest of Dan's statement left me gushing with pride. My face turned hot, and my insides turned happy. But the cozy feelings didn't last long. Within seconds I was squirming with shame. *Is that all it takes?* I scolded myself. *One offhand compliment from one measly male in a singularly masculine position of power, and you turn into a warm, waggly puppy?* Brenda Starr would never react in such a giddy way, I knew — unless her irresistible mystery man suddenly swooped into the picture. And, man of mystery though he was, Dan Street was *not* irresistible. Or swoopy.

"What other pointers did the murderer leave?" I asked. "Besides the jump rope, I mean." I was trying to recover my self-control, keep Dan talking about the case.

"I can't discuss that with you, Paige. You know that." His eyes gave off a forbidding gleam. "And now I've really got to get back to work."

He stood up from his stool, dropped his crumpled napkin onto his empty plate, and gave a little pat to the little beret on top of my little head. "See you around, kid. Take care of yourself." As he turned and walked away, I swiveled around to watch his progress, forgoing the opportunity to make a face behind his back. Head lowered and hands stuffed deep into his pants pockets, Detective Street proceeded down the aisle, circled the corner, and disappeared behind a tall shelf full of school supplies.

When I swung back to face the counter, my hot dog was sitting on a plate in front of me. I swallowed it — as I had my foolish feminine pride — in one gulp.

Chapter 5

I never interviewed any Woolworth's sales-ladies or unveiled the picture of Babs. I just paid for my hot dog, dashed out of the dime store, boarded the crowded downtown BMT, took a seat next to a dozing Negro woman, and stared at the clanking car's commercial wallpaper all the way down to the Village. Bucky Beaver urged me to use Ipana toothpaste, a couple of curly-haired twins defied me to tell which one had the salon permanent and which one had the Toni, and Esther Williams promised me that Jergens lotion would make my skin soft as silk, even after seven hours of swimming.

Nobody told me how to track down a murderer.

Getting off the train at West 4th Street and climbing the steps to the street, I went south on Sixth, turned right onto Bleecker, and dragged my tired body through the bustling Italian neighborhood I now called home. It was quite dark by then; most of the shops were closed, and most of the local residents were ensconced in their walk-up apartments dining on meatballs and spaghetti. Yet Bleecker Street still hosted a thin parade of people — bearded poets making their way toward MacDougal for the jazz clubs and coffeehouses, college kids prowling for beer and pizza, fashionable fairies strolling the sidewalks in search of forbidden love.

I wound my way through the caravan — bypassing the newsstand, the candy store, the bread shop, the Italian "social club" (i.e., mob hangout), the butcher shop, and the delicatessen — until I finally reached the entry to my building. It was a very narrow, three-story brick structure, with two small storefronts at street level and two tiny duplex apartments upstairs. I lived in the one on the right, over the fish store. With a grateful sigh of relief, I unlocked the front door, ducked into the dim, compact stairwell, and proceeded to mount the steps to my place.

When I was halfway up, the door to the other apartment flew open and Abby Moskowitz, my naughty, nosy next-door neighbor — and best friend in all the world — popped into view. As always, her appearance was electric. She stood tall at the top of the stairs, radiant as a street lamp, vibrating in all her far-out beatnik beauty. She was wearing black ballet slippers, black pedal pushers, and a paint-smeared white smock. Her thick, waist-length black hair was woven into a single braid and draped over her shoulder like a fat python.

"You're late," she said, holding both arms out from her body in a wide welcome. She clutched a drink in each color-streaked hand. "All the ice in your first whiskey sour melted, so I had to make you a fresh one."

"You should've been a nurse," I said, grinning, feeling new life seep into my limbs. I climbed the rest of the steps faster than before, gratefully took the drink out of Abby's left hand, and followed her into her apartment.

Abby's narrow duplex was a mirror image of my own. There was a single room downstairs — a living room, kitchen, and dining area all rolled into one — and two tiny bedrooms and a bath upstairs. A door at the rear of the kitchen led to a rusty metal balcony-cum-fire escape, the steps of which led down to a small courtyard overgrown with weeds and ivy. The upstairs level offered yet another means of escape: a trapdoor in the ceiling that opened out onto the roof. This exit was reachable from a small wrought-iron ladder bolted to the wall outside the bathroom.

In spite of their dwarf-sized dimensions, both apartments were equipped with the commonplace necessities — running water, electricity, radiator heat, a tub and a toilet, a stove and a refrigerator — and both had a measure of old-fashioned charm. The floors were wood, the dainty staircase bannisters were made of wood, and there were windows in every room. Luckily, the rent was somewhat old-fashioned too (just fifty dollars a month), or I'd still be living in one of those horrible-but-affordable women's hotels where you can't play the radio after ten or keep a box of crackers in your own closet.

I'd never have found the apartment if it hadn't been for Abby. She'd told me about it the day we met, ten months earlier, when she came up to the office to show Mario some samples of her work (Abby was a fabulous artist, and beginning to make a name for herself as a magazine illustrator). The gold digger next door had just run off with a Packard dealer, Abby said, and skipped out on the rent, so the owner of the building — a wealthy but warmhearted woman in her eighties — was looking for a new tenant. Preferably a single professional woman. I went to see the apartment and signed the lease that very evening, right after work.

"What a dreamy day I had!" Abby crowed, stirring her whiskey sour with her fingertip. Her deep brown, kohl-lined eyes were gleaming and her wide mouth was stretched in a chalky smile (Abby was one of the first to embrace the weird new white lipstick that was becoming so popular). Suddenly twirling herself around in a full circle, then sailing across the dropcloth-covered floor of her painting studio (the area which, in my duplicate apartment, was still being used as a living room), Abby drew up next to her large wooden easel and pointed at the picture it supported. "If you don't believe me, just blink your peepers at this."

I knew even before looking that it would be a painting of a man. Abby always had a "dreamy" day when she worked with a male model. In this case, the handsome fellow was standing knee-deep in jungle vines, looking startled but very brave, wearing tight khaki shorts and a khaki safari shirt — both of which had (presumably) been clawed to shreds by the ferocious lion shown crouching in the foreground. The shorts and shirt were slashed in all the right places to show off the hero's bulging muscles, and to reveal three deep claw stripes on his broad, hairless chest which glistened — oh, so seductively — with several droplets of bright crimson blood.

"I see you got another cover assignment from *Male Adventure* magazine," I said, pausing to take a sip of my drink.

"Yep," she replied, quickly dismissing my observation with an impatient wave of her paint-smudged hand. "But that's not why I'm so excited, Paige. I'm sitting on the moon tonight! I'm in a torrid trance. Just dig this guy! He's new. His name is Dudley. Today was the first time he ever modeled for me. Isn't he beautiful?"

I walked up to the canvas for a closer look. "Uh, yeah, I guess so. But what's the big fuss about? Most of your models are good looking."

"Not like this. This guy is one hundred percent dreamboat. And one hundred percent man. Nothing queer in *his* cabinet." She brushed a stray wisp of hair off her face, leaving a trace of green pigment on her forehead.

"How can you tell for sure?" I asked. "A lot of models are actors too."

Abby didn't say anything. She just looked me straight in the face, arched one eyebrow to the limit, and shot me a very wicked smile.

I'd seen that smile a dozen times before, and I knew all too well what it meant: Abby had given in (okay, given *out*) once again. Another carnal notch could be carved in the wooden headboard of her rumpled double bed. I let out a disapproving sigh and shook my head.

Though we wholeheartedly agreed on most things — music, art, movies, politics, philosophy, etc. — Abby and I had a slight difference of opinion about sex. I subscribed to the prevailing belief that the act of love should be enjoyed with one's husband; Abby believed it should be relished with any man she wanted. Trouble was, the men she wanted usually turned out to be mere boys — virile young models endowed with less intelligence, humor, and sensitivity than a Polish sausage.

I envied Abby's exuberant abandon, her ability to take pleasure whenever she found it, but I worried about her all the time. She was taking too many risks — with both her health and her entire future. She had gone to the Margaret Sanger Clinic on 16th Street to be fitted with her own contraceptive device, but to my mind she was still playing with fire. The diaphragm was far from foolproof. Abby could still get pregnant. And then what would she do? Have a filthy, illegal, life-threatening abortion, or marry the brainless, boring buck who'd fathered the fetus? Either way, she'd be screwed.

"Stop frowning!" Abby said. "You look like a moralistic old maid. And if you're not careful, that's how you'll wind up — living all by yourself in a rundown apartment with nobody to keep you company at night but Jackie Gleason and the June Taylor Dancers."

"That's how I'm living now!" I said, laughing.

Abby laughed too. Then we each took a seat on the small red couch set in the middle of the room to separate the studio from the kitchen and dining area. Putting my purse, hat, gloves, the photo envelope, and my drink down on the cinderblock and plywood construction that served as a coffee table, I kicked off my shoes, curled my legs up under my skirt, and lit a cigarette.

"I'm glad *somebody* had a dreamy day," I said, inhaling deeply. "Mine was pretty dismal." I sighed and the smoke whooshed out of my mouth in a blue funnel cloud.

"Why?" Abby wanted to know. "Was Little Lord Pomeroy acting up again?"

"Brandon Pomeroy is *always* acting up.

But he wasn't the cause of all my trouble. I created most of that myself." I told Abby about my previous encounter with Babs Comstock, and then I gave her a full run-down of the current day's events, starting with my discovery of the murder report in the paper that morning, and ending with my disturbing expeditions to Starlight Studios and Woolworth's that evening. I showed her the clip from the *Daily News* and the picture of Babs, a.k.a. Wanda, I'd found in our files.

"And you call that a dismal day?" Abby said, incredulous. "I call it thrilling! You're finally starting to live a little. You've been wallowing in widowhood too long, kiddo. It's time to let your hair down and do the jitterbug. Dig it? And it's high time you started working on a story too! I was beginning to think you were all talk and no action."

"Well, I wanted to wait for the *right* story," I said defensively, "and I think this is really it."

"You bet your *shiksa tush* this is it!" Abby clapped her hands in the air and stomped the floor with the sole of one soft black ballet slipper. "It's got everything. Cold-blooded murder and hot-blooded sex! A naked blonde! Hell, it's even got Hopalong Cassidy."

"What makes you think the sex was so hot-blooded? How do you know there was any sex at all?" Like a discriminating detective, I was trying not to jump to quick conclusions.

"Oh, come on, Paige! Where do you keep your brains? In a jar? Whenever there's a naked blonde on the scene, the blood is sure to be hot. Likewise, the sex. You can't go wrong with this one, honey. It's got *Top Story* written all over it." Abby took a big gulp of her drink, leaned back against the couch cushions, and propped her feet up on the makeshift coffee table. "Which reminds me," she added. "Have you picked out a pen name yet?"

"No. I haven't given it that much thought."

"Well, I have," she said, twirling the end of her long thick braid around her finger. "It's really important for your career, you know. Just look at me — I wouldn't get half the work I do if I used my real name." (Abby signed all her paintings "Art Montana."). "It pays to have people — magazine publishers and readers alike — think of me as a creative cowpoke from way out west instead of a pinko Jewish tart from Brooklyn.

"And you need an alias even more than I

do," Abby went on. "You simply can't have a name that makes people laugh. That's certain death for a writer. Paige is cool, but you've got to ditch the Turner. You have to change your last name to something bold and really glamorous. You dig? Something with *chutzpah*. Something brazen and blonde. Grable would be good. Betty made it famous, but you could make it brilliant. Or how about VanDoren, after Mamie — or Gabor, after Zsa Zsa? You couldn't go wrong with either of those."

I found Abby's suggestions ridiculous, but I didn't tell her so. I just put on my most dizzy, vapid, blonde movie star face, and batted my lashes till they stirred up a whirlwind. "I'd rather change my *first* name to Lana," I said.

An hour and a half later — after two more whiskey sours (each), lots of laughs and cigarettes, and several intense discussions about life, love, and the pursuit of murderers — we called it a night. In my still-aching stocking feet, I exited Abby's front door and took four steps across the landing to my own.

Turning my key in the lock and entering my dark apartment, I flipped on a light, put all my stuff down on a kitchen chair, and dropped my shoes to the floor. Then — before loosening my skirt or even removing my uncomfortable garter belt and stockings — I dragged the other kitchen chair over to the coat closet, opened the door, stood up on the chair, took hold of the baby blue case holding my baby blue Royal portable, and pulled it down from the top shelf. Churning with drive and purpose, I withdrew the typewriter from its shell and quickly set it up on the kitchen table.

Abby's pep talk (or was it the cocktails?) had inspired me. New determination (okay, inebriation) was coursing through my veins. My friend was entirely right, I decided. I had been stalling. I had been *talking* about becoming a writer instead of *becoming* one. And the only way to become a writer was to start writing. I would compose the opening paragraphs of the Comstock story that very night, I resolved, just to get the writing process under way. Then I would be fully engaged in the project. I would be committing myself, on paper, to telling the whole story — to finding out the truth about Babs's death. And I would be meeting the challenge of my literary future head-on.

I dashed upstairs to the spare bedroom

— which I planned to turn into an office just as soon as I could afford to buy a desk — and pulled a package of typing paper out of the pile of books and office supplies I had sitting in a box in the corner. I ran back downstairs, grabbed an ashtray, took my cigarettes from my purse, and put everything down on the table next to the Royal. Anxiously filling my lungs with air and tucking my hair behind my ears, I sat down at the typewriter, rolled in a piece of paper, positioned my fingers on the keys, and waited for the muse to strike.

Twenty-five minutes later I was still waiting. There were three cigarette butts in the ashtray, but no words on the page.

Babs's sad smile warped into a mocking sneer.

And then the depression overcame me. My determination and self-confidence turned to water and leaked out all over the floor. Who did I think I was, anyway? Lillian Hellman? Ha! I was acting more like Lucy Ricardo. Whatever possessed me to suppose I could be a real writer? How did my head ever get so big? I might as well face the facts. I was just a hack with a somewhat better than average vocabulary. I was just a secretary who knew how to spell.

And what on earth ever gave me the bright idea I might be clever enough to solve a murder? Had I totally lost my mind? I'd obviously been reading too many Perry Mason novels. And what if, by some incredibly impossible, altogether fantastic fluke of fate, I actually *did* manage to sniff out Babs Comstock's killer? What did I think I was going to do with him? Type him to death? Expose the grammatical errors of his ways?

Fighting the urge to throw myself down on the kitchen floor and curl myself up in a tight little ball of oblivion, I managed to stay hunched over the keyboard for another half hour or so. I forced my fingers to transcribe the words "COMSTOCK CASE" at the top of the paper, and then I drafted a slow and arduous list of all the related information I'd gathered so far — all the random facts, impressions, and details my miserable memory could recall. Then, ripping the list out of the typewriter and leaving it on the kitchen table, I trudged up the stairs, took off my clothes, and laid my pitiful, self-doubting self down to sleep in my pathetic old maid's bed.

Chapter 6

I must have been asking for trouble the next day since I got so much of it. First my alarm clock failed to ring (I'd forgotten to pull out the little thingamabob), and I overslept by a full half hour. Then, as I was stepping in to take a shower, I knocked my shin against the side of the tub so hard it immediately began to swell. By the time I'd gotten out of the shower and started getting dressed — hurriedly hooking on my nylons and straightening the seams — I had a lump the size of a Jax ball on my lower leg. The unsightly wound was right below my hemline, of course.

The green sheath dress I'd chosen to wear was in sad shape too. Like all of the other clothes in my closet that day, it reeked of eau de mackerel — one of the many malodorous hazards of living directly over a fish store. Either Luigi had gotten a big delivery early that morning or his refrigerators were on the blink again. I doused myself with Shalimar perfume, but I knew from experience it wouldn't help. All the stray cats in the neighborhood would probably follow me to the subway.

As I rushed out of my apartment and descended the stairwell chute to street level, I smoothed down my hair and put on my dark green velveteen beret. Luckily, I didn't need a hat pin to keep it on. Even if I'd had one with me — which I didn't — it would have been stupid to try to use it. The way things were going that morning, I'd have inflicted some serious scalp damage.

Scurrying east toward the uptown BMT, I kept flapping the lapels of my green-and-white-checked jacket, trying to air myself out. I didn't lose much of the fish fragrance, but I did lose what was left of my presence of mind. As I dashed down the stairs to the train, I snatched my gloves out of my jacket pocket and — without thinking — put them on. Another groggy slipup (any working woman with half a New York City brain knows you don't wear white gloves on the subway). By the time I reached my first stop, took the shuttle across town, got off at 42nd Street, raced to my office building on 43rd, and took the elevator up to the ninth floor, the palms of my white cotton mitts were black.

So there I was — as worn out, beat down, and hung up (okay, hung *over*) as any hopeless hopeful writer could be — arriving thirty-five minutes late for work, wearing a crooked hat and dirty gloves, sporting a hideous purple tumor on my shin, and smelling like a rancid crab cake. It was going to be a great day.

"What the hell happened to you?" Mike said when I came in. He took note of my appearance, and — judging from the way he wrinkled his freckled nose — my aroma as well, but he didn't make any nasty comments about either. His mind was on more important things.

"There's no coffee in the pot!" he whined. "I tried to pour myself a cup and nothing came out!"

"That's because I didn't make it yet," I said, grinding my teeth and growling to myself like a grizzly. *Why me, Lord?* I hung my jacket on the rack, put my hat and gloves down on my desk, and angrily tossed my self-control into the corner. "Perhaps you noticed that I wasn't here yet?" I fumed, spitting the words in Mike's direction. The sarcasm in my voice was obvious. "It's kind of hard for me to make the coffee when I'm not here. No matter what you may think, I really don't have a percolator grafted to my hip — or keep a spare on the subway."

I had taken Mike by complete surprise. He was so unprepared for any back talk from me, he sat quiet as a monk at his desk, with his eyes popping out of their sockets and his mouth hanging open like a toddler's rear pajama flap.

Mario, on the other hand, wasn't sitting still for any sass. He jumped out of his chair and walked to the front of the workroom, up close to me. Too close to me. "You're acting very cheeky this morning," he said, looking up at me with a smirk on his round, clammy face. "I find that attractive in a woman."

Quick! Somebody bring me a pail of cold water!

"But I don't think Mr. Crockett would agree with me," he threatened, raking his fingers through his slimy, slicked-back hair. "Especially without his morning java." Mario put his gummy hand on my back and gave it a proprietary pat. I wondered if he'd left a grease print on my dress.

I didn't bother trying to amuse myself with any mental comebacks or pie-throwing fantasies. I knew when I was licked. You can't fight City Hall. Or topple the man-made rules. You've got to dance your way around them.

"I'll make the coffee now," I said, side-stepping into my daily waltz (and out of Mario's reach). I grabbed the Coffeemaster off the table and headed for the ladies' room to fill it with water.

"Hey!" Mario called before I made it through the door to the hall. "What's that funny smell?"

"I'm not sure," I said, "but I think it's your hair oil."

The rest of the morning wasn't too bad. Thanks to a good night with Lois (or was it Pauline?), Crockett didn't clobber me for being late. He just chewed on the end of his short fat cigar and cautioned me to "stomp the clock tomorrow." Mike was so shaken by my uncharacteristic outburst earlier in the day that he steered clear of any new confrontations. He didn't make any stupid jokes about my name, and he didn't protest when I changed all the verbs and adjectives in his tepid Anastasia mob hit story. Mario was too busy doing layouts for the new issue to bother with me, and Lenny was as nervous, quiet, and undemanding as always. Brandon Pomeroy hadn't come in yet.

So nobody noticed when I paid an inordinate amount of time and attention to the clipping of the morning newspapers. I scoured every page of every edition looking for more news of the Comstock murder. But there wasn't a word about the case in any of the papers that day. No follow-up articles at all. And not one single recap. Dan Street and Homicide had obviously convinced all the city editors to drop the story completely. But why? Were they just trying to keep the killer in the dark about the details of their ongoing investigation, or were they hiding something important — something they didn't want the public to know?

Whatever the reason, I was glad for the blackout. It would keep Pomeroy and other magazine editors off the Comstock trail, making it far more likely that I might be the only one working on the story. *I could really hit the jackpot with this one,* I realized. *My very first opus might turn out to be an exclusive!* I was thrilled at the prospect, but not so confident about the literary outcome. After my less-than-productive efforts the night before, I felt more capable of walking on water than writing a sensible sentence.

But my storytelling skills could be jump-started later, I figured. Right then I had to develop my crime-busting talents. I had to find out the truth about Babs Comstock's murder, or there would be no story to tell. And I had to work fast, or the trail would be too cold to follow. So when lunchtime finally rolled around, and I had finished all my morning's work, and Brandon Pomeroy still hadn't arrived to throw any roadblocks in my way, I struck out for the Venus Modeling Agency.

The day was clear, breezy, and almost cold. Buttoning my jacket and exiting the crowded lobby of my building, I rushed to the corner and darted across Third Avenue — sprinting through the dense shadows cast by the immense cement, wood, and metal structure of the elevated train. Definite plans were in effect to tear down the Third Avenue el, and service had been suspended at night and on the weekends, but the train was still running on weekdays, up until seven p.m. And there was a stop at 14th Street, just a few blocks away from where I wanted to go.

I mounted the rusty metal steps to the 42nd Street platform and took my place in the motley group of people waiting near the track. The toothless old woman standing next to me was wearing a black kerchief and a raggedy brown coat, carrying a bag of fruit in her arms, and the fidgety boy in front of her had on a heavy orange sweater and a coonskin cap. A skinny Negro stood shivering in his shirtsleeves nearby, and two bobbysoxers clad in fuzzy jackets, felt skirts, and too many crinolines were standing off to the side, sharing a bag of peanuts. Men in gray flannel suits were everywhere.

When the train barreled down and pulled to a stop at the station, I stepped into the nearest car and searched anxiously for a decent seat, which wasn't so easy to find, thanks to all the sleeping Bowery bums: the drunks who rode the el all day for a dime — from the Bowery to 149th Street and back again, and again, and again — trying to stay warm and get some shut-eye. It was safer than sleeping in the park, cheaper than renting a fleabag room, and it allowed them to squander their pan-handled booty on booze.

Eventually I found an empty double and took the place next to the window. A red-haired man in a slouch hat plopped down next to me and began reading the financial section of the *Herald Tribune*. He didn't sniff at the air like a dog, or make any funny faces, or move to another seat, so my fish perfume must have finally worn off. Relaxing into my new nonsmelly status, I took a deep breath and turned to look out the window. Then the train took off again and began racing its way down the track, high above the busy street below, like a roller coaster that had decided to go straight.

I kept gaping out through the dirty train window — and peering *into* the dirty third- and fourth-floor windows of the tenement buildings whisking by — for the entire trip downtown. Apartment after apartment passed my eye, leading me to imagine what it would be like to live in one of them. The elevated track would be your eternally ugly horizon. And the train would clank and thunder past your window every fifteen minutes or so, delivering a bone-rattling shock to your system, and giving every nosy passenger a personal peek inside your bedroom. Fun.

The Venus Modeling Agency was located in the Union Square area, a couple of blocks down from Klein's on Fourth Avenue. It was perched on the second floor of an old brick building, astride a barber shop. The office was small, dingy, and decidedly unglamorous.

"Hello, gorgeous!" bellowed the astonishingly fat woman sitting at the reception desk when I walked in. "Don't you look pretty in your little green beret!" She spread her wide mouth in a smile, and looked me over from head to toe. "You wanna be a model, right? Well, you've come to the right place, girlie. Mr. Gumpert's the best agent in the business. He won't have any trouble finding jobs for you!"

The woman's cheeks were flushed, her chins were wobbling, and her exuberant welcome had left her huffing with exertion. A trickle of sweat seeped down from her frizzy brown hairline, and the bosom of her red and white polka-dot dress was heaving. "Here, take these forms," she said before I could get a word in. She handed me some papers and pointed to a green vinyl couch across the room. "You can sit down over there to fill them out. And while you're doing that, I'll just pop into Mr. Gumpert's office and tell him you're here."

But the woman wasn't *popping* anywhere. Just lifting herself out of her chair and balancing her enormous bulk on her tiny, bedroom-slipper-clad feet took about a century. Then it took another eon for the polka-dot mountain to start moving. If she hadn't been grunting and groaning and gasping for air, I might have told her I wasn't there to apply for modeling jobs —

that I was just looking for some information about one of their models, and was in a desperate hurry to get it before my dwindling lunch hour ran out. As it was, though, I was afraid to upset her or bring a sudden halt to her progress. I thought she might have a stroke. Besides, whoever Mr. Gumpert was, I wanted to talk to him.

After a slow, painful trek to the rear of the waiting room, she opened a door to another room, squeezed her way inside, and closed the door behind her. Promising myself to have a salad for lunch, instead of the cheeseburger and chocolate malted I had planned on, I took a quick look around the drab reception area, and then a long look at the cluster of framed black-and-white glossies hanging on the wall near the couch. A gallery of Venus models, I assumed. There were several blonde bombshells in the bunch, but Babs Comstock wasn't one of them.

For some absurd reason, this really annoyed me. The poor woman was dead — maybe even killed in the line of her modeling duties. Didn't she at least deserve a place in the Venus Agency's innocuous little Hall of Fame? With misguided indignation, I planted myself down on the slick vinyl couch and filled out the forms the receptionist had given me. Using Abby's formula for choosing an effective alias, I gave myself the name of Phoebe Starr (after Brenda) and claimed that I was a twenty-year-old telephone operator by day, who longed to be a lingerie model by night. In answer to the question: Who referred you to the Venus Modeling Agency?, I put down Wanda Wingate.

The polka dot woman squeezed through the back door again and huffed her way back to her desk. "Mr. Gumpert will see you in a minute, honey, soon as he finishes his lunch."

"Thank you," I said, walking over to hand her the completed application forms. "This is such an exciting day for me!" I added, rolling my eyes and punctuating my words with a giddy gasp of elation. "I've been trying to get up the nerve to come here for months, ever since my friend Wanda told me about it. Do you think Mr. Gumpert will like me? Do you think I'm pretty enough?"

"Oh, sure, honey," she said, giving me another once-over. "But what's that purple thing on your leg? It's mighty unsightly. That's not permanent, is it?"

"Oh, no!" I assured her. "Got it just this morning. Banged my shin on the side of the tub."

She giggled like that was the funniest thing she'd ever heard in her life. "Gotta be careful when you're takin' a bath, girlie. Keepin' clean is a tricky business!" Coming from a woman of her size, that was a gross understatement — unless she had six Charles Atlas–trained bathing assistants. And a tub the size of Texas.

"My name's Phoebe Starr," I told her, holding out my dirty glove for her to shake. "What's yours? My friend Wanda told it to me, but I forgot it already."

"Bertha Gumpert," she said, "but everybody calls me Bert."

"It's nice to meet you, Bert. Are you Mr. Gumpert's wife?"

"Heavens no!" she roared. "I wouldn't marry that scrawny runt even if he owned a diamond mine *and* a chocolate factory! It's bad enough being his cousin!" She laughed so hard the room shook.

I laughed with her. The woman's hearty good humor was contagious. "My friend Wanda told me I was going to like you, and she was right! She said you were real friendly and funny."

"Yeah, fat and jolly — that's me," she sputtered. Her cheeks were grinning but her eyes were about to cry. "Gotta keep 'em laughin', girlie. Otherwise, they'll just stare. Or start callin' me names."

Her painful revelation cut through me like a knife. "I'm sorry," I said.

"You and me both, kid!" She started laughing again.

I felt sad for Bert, and I was starting to like her a lot, but I couldn't afford to let her problems outweigh my own. My lunch hour had withered down to a handful of minutes. "Do you remember my friend Wanda?" I asked. "She was a Venus model. Her last name was Wingate."

I thought I detected a sudden stiffness in Bert's demeanor, but I wasn't certain. Before I could get a good look at her downturned face, or search her downcast eyes for signs of recognition, she started huffing and groaning and pulling herself to her feet again. "Can't say as I do, honey," she grunted, laboring to straighten her overburdened spine. "So many girls come in here I can't possibly remember them all by name."

Once erect, Bert picked up my application forms, turned her broad, polka-dot back to me, and began shuffling her worn slippers toward the door to the rear office. "Come follow me, girlie," she said over her shoulder. "Mr. Gumpert must be finished with his sandwich by now."

Chapter 7

Mr. Gumpert looked just like his name. He was small, pale, and stoop-shouldered. His thin brown hair was salted with gray, and his ears were so long the lobes hung past his chin line. As he sat at his desk and studied my application, he tapped a pencil on his large tan blotter and fingered his blue bow tie, gazing down at the forms for a very long time. I sat quietly and uncomfortably — in a straight-backed wooden chair in the very middle of the dreary, windowless room — waiting and praying for him to finish. The smell of ham and cheese still hung in the air.

"Do you have any previous modeling experience, Miss Starr?" Mr. Gumpert asked, finally setting my application aside and looking up at me. His droopy eyes were the color of coffee. With milk.

"Oh, yes, sir. I was in a fashion show once, in high school." I sat up taller and put on a dopey, hopeful-young-model face.

"I meant professional experience." He sounded as bored and weary as a full-time chicken plucker.

"Well, no, I guess not." I lowered my

lashes and tried to blush.

"Do you have a portfolio?"

"No, sir, I don't."

"Well, if you're serious about becoming a model, you'll have to have one made," he said. At this point he perked up considerably, and began looking at me as if I were a cookie on a plate. "I can help you with that — find you a good photographer, get you some nice costumes, and even direct the shoot myself — but it will cost you quite a bit of money."

So that's the game, I said in my head. *Get every bubblebrain who comes in to spring for an expensive portfolio, whether she's good model material or not. Milk her dream till the money flows. Then Venus and Starlight can share the cream.*

"Does that mean you think I'd make a good model?" I simpered, smiling my head off and fluttering my lashes to beat the band.

"Yes, I do," he said. "Big eyes, long neck, full lips, pretty hair. Would you stand up, please, and turn around a few times?"

I rose to my feet and began rotating. "I'm so excited!" I said, in the middle of my second revolution. "I've wanted to be a model ever since the day I saw Rita Hayworth in *Cover Girl*. That was such a wonderful movie! And my friend Wanda said —"

"Stop turning!" he cried as I faced him for the third time. His eyes were fastened on my legs. With a look of horror on his kisser, he suddenly levitated from his chair, leaned over his desk, and pointed at the boo-boo on my shin as if it were a volcano about to blow. "What's that?"

"Oh, nothing! Just a temporary injury. It'll be gone by next week."

"Well, see that it is. You can't pose for a portfolio like that. Both legs have to be revealed completely in case somebody's looking for a stocking model." He straightened his bow tie, smoothed the front of his buttoned-up baby blue cardigan, and sat down again.

I sat down too. "So how much does a portfolio cost? My friend Wanda Wingate had one done, but she didn't tell me how much she paid for it." I searched his face for a reaction to the name, but his features were as placid as pudding.

"A good one will cost you a hundred dollars," he said. "You might be able to get it done cheaper at another agency but, believe me, you'll never get it done better. Your pictures will be taken by a top fashion photographer, and I'll design the sets and poses myself. I know exactly what advertisers and magazine editors are looking for."

"Gee, thanks, Mr. Gumpert. That's really swell of you." I gave him a hesitant smile, then started pouting like Doris Day did, in the recent movie *Young at Heart*, when Frank Sinatra kept acting like a sap and feeling sorry for himself. "But I don't have a hundred dollars," I whimpered, "and it would take me a long, long time to save up that much. Couldn't you maybe get me a couple of jobs *without* a portfolio, so I could make enough to have one made?"

"Sorry, Miss Starr, that's not the way it works."

"Oh," I said, looking down at my grubby gloves, madly searching my brain for a way to bring up Wanda Wingate again without blowing my cover.

I could have saved my energy. Mr. Gumpert did the honor for me. "Your friend borrowed the money to have her portfolio done. Do you know anybody who would make you a loan?"

So he *did* remember Wanda! He even remembered how she'd managed to pay for his so-called services. The question was, what else did he remember about her? Did he recall that she was dead?

"Nobody," I moaned. "All my friends are as broke as I am." I shifted my weight on the hard wooden chair, and focused my attention on Mr. Gumpert's tired eyes. "Speaking of Wanda," I said, "I haven't seen her in quite a while. She must be very busy. Have you been getting her lots of modeling jobs lately?"

His café au lait–colored irises were dormant. "No modeling assignments per se," he said nonchalantly, "but I did get her lined up for some stage and television work. I recommended Wanda — as I do many of my girls — to the Apex Theatrical Agency, and she signed with them a few months ago. So she may have landed a walk-on, or a bit in a commercial, or a radio soap opera role. I could get some work like that for you too — if you had a good portfolio."

I should have smiled and fluttered my lashes again. I should have delayed my next question about Wanda, and camouflaged my concern in a mist of mild indifference. But I didn't have time for anymore play-acting. My lunch hour was officially over — and if I didn't get back to the office before Brandon Pomeroy showed up, my goose would be cooked to a crisp.

"When was the last time you saw

121

Wanda?" I blurted, standing up to take my leave, praying Mr. Gumpert wouldn't notice my overheated curiosity.

If he did, he didn't let on. He remained seated — leaning back in his chair and pulling on one of his elephantine earlobes — as I stood waiting for his reply. "I sent her on a go-see in March," he said, after due consideration, "but she hasn't been back to the office since then."

"Oh. Well, thank you very much for seeing me, Mr. Gumpert. Sorry to rush, but I have to get back to work now. I'll try to scrape up the money to have my portfolio done."

"That's a good girl," he murmured, as I was seeing myself to the door. Then, just as I opened the door and started to walk through it, he tossed me an apparent afterthought: "Hey, I just remembered something," he said. "I *did* see Wanda recently. I ran into her, quite by accident, last week at Bickford's. She was having lunch with another blonde and a cranky little boy in a cowboy hat."

Sometimes the Fates are kind. Sometimes they will take pity on a poor woman in a pathetically confused mental state, and grant her an epiphany of sorts — serve her a big helping of clarity and insight on a silver platter. This wasn't one of those times. As the Third Avenue el hurtled me back toward the office, my third-rate brain hurtled itself into a maelstrom of maddening questions. Who was the other blonde with Babs in Bickford's? Who was the little boy? Did his cowboy hat have a Hopalong Cassidy label? Had it come with an autographed jump rope? How were these people connected to Babs? And why did Mr. Gumpert tell me about them? Had he been merely engaging in innocent gossip, or was he trying to plant leading (or intentionally *mis*leading) information in my mind? Did he even know that Babs, a.k.a. Wanda, was dead?

If only I'd had more time to spend at the Venus Agency, I might have excavated some answers to some of those questions. As it was, though, I didn't even have time to grab a pushcart weenie for lunch. I dashed back to the office with a head full of riddles, a soul full of stress, an ego (okay, id) full of panic, and a stomach full of nothing whatsoever.

Alerted to my arrival by the office entrance bell, Mike, Mario, and Lenny gazed up from their work when I walked in. They all wore the same tense expression on their faces — the kind of shifty, nervous, nonfocused look that says *uh-oh!* Interpreting that look as a sign that I was in for big trouble from our illustrious, no doubt furious editorial director, I took a deep breath and braced myself for a brutal tongue-lashing. Then — not wanting to behave like a coward, or a weakling, or a *girl* — I turned toward Pomeroy's desk to face him head-on.

To my surprise he wasn't there. He was sitting at *my* desk instead.

Seemingly oblivious to the fact that I had entered the office, Pomeroy was crouched low over the wide-open, lower right-hand drawer of my desk (my personal, *private* drawer!), and he was rifling through its contents like a mad dog customs inspector. Some of my things — my hairbrush, my extra pair of stockings, my red silk neckerchief, my black Orlon office sweater — had been removed from the drawer and were heaped on top of the desk, along with the manila envelope holding my secret *Daily News* clipping and the photo of Babs Comstock.

My empty stomach went into convulsions. "What are you doing?" I cried, taking two shaky steps forward. "That's private property!"

Pomeroy snapped his head up, gave me a crooked grin, then straightened his torso against the backrest of my chair. He looked sheepish for a couple of seconds, but soon regained his rigid composure — and his I'm-the-big-bad-boss attitude.

"Do you know what the word *hour* means, Mrs. Turner? It means sixty minutes. It means three thousand and six hundred seconds. That's exactly how long you have for lunch, Mrs. Turner, and if you had chosen to obey the rules of your employment — if you hadn't added sixteen full minutes to your allotted hour — you would have been here when I needed you, and I wouldn't have had to go through your desk myself, looking for the proofs of the Anastasia story."

What baloney! Pomeroy knew darn well the mob story had been written just the day before; that it couldn't possibly have come back from the typesetter so soon. So what the hell was going on here? Was Pomeroy lying to me? Was he trying to conceal his real motive for invading my desk? Or was he just so drunk he didn't know what day it was?

"That story was picked up this morning," I told him. "It won't be back until tomorrow afternoon at the earliest."

He stood up from my desk and stomped back to his own, glaring at me as if I were just a no-good, double-crossing, two-timing dame and he were Albert Anastasia himself. "Call the typesetter and get it back today. I'm pulling it out of the issue."

"But why? That's the biggest story in town right now. Every other magazine will be covering —"

"Save your opinion for someone who cares, Mrs. Turner. Just get on the phone and get that story back. *Now*, damn it!" The grimace on Pomeroy's face bore a striking resemblance to Spencer Tracy's when he was changing from Dr. Jekyll into Mr. Hyde.

"Yes, sir." Without even removing my hat or jacket, I stepped around behind my desk, sat down, and made the call. As soon as the conversation was over, but before I hung up, I snuck the manila envelope from the pile of stuff on my desk, turned my chair toward the wall, and checked inside to see if the Comstock clipping and photo were still there. They were. But what did that tell me? That Pomeroy had failed to uncover my secret stash? Or had he seen the photo and news clip, and decided to leave them there so I wouldn't know he'd found them? Had he actually been searching for the Anastasia story, or something else altogether? More questions I couldn't answer.

Concealing the envelope under a stack of invoices on my desk, I made a big show of hanging up the phone and taking off my hat. Then I swiveled my chair in Pomeroy's direction. "The messenger will bring the story back today, sir," I said, "when he makes the afternoon pickup."

Either the man had suddenly gone deaf, or I had totally lost my voice. There was no reaction at all to my announcement. No growl, no grunt, and certainly no thank-you. Pomeroy just stroked the tips of his mustache, pushed his glasses higher on his face, and buried his nose so deep in the *Journal American* I figured they must have printed a brand new, fully illustrated edition of the Kinsey Report.

Never one to step down from his self-assigned pedestal (no matter how shaky it happened to be), Pomeroy gave me the silent treatment for the rest of the day. So did Mike, Mario, and Lenny, who were being very careful not to do anything that might attract Pomeroy's angry attention to themselves. Unaware of what had happened, and oblivious to the cold-shoulder conspiracy, only Mr. Crockett spoke to me

— to tell me to make him a dentist appointment and get him two tickets for the next Dodgers game.

I was grateful for the standoff. It gave me time to think. The whole time I was placing my personal stuff back in my private drawer, proofreading the current galleys, editing Mike's new story, getting Dodgers tickets, and reviewing the recent invoices for the bookkeeper, I was really thinking about Babs Comstock. And Scotty Whitcomb. And Bert and Mr. Gumpert. And the little boy in the cowboy hat. I was wondering why Brandon Pomeroy was acting so strange, and I was racking my brain to decide what my next investigative move should be. It was like swimming in a whirlpool.

By the time five o'clock rolled around, I was the dizziest, craziest, hungriest woman west of the East River. So as soon as my desk was clear, I grabbed my purse, gloves, hat, and jacket, and made a beeline for the lobby coffee shop, where I ordered — and greedily consumed — the cheeseburger and chocolate malted I'd been dreaming of. Then I stepped into the public phone booth in the lobby, copied down Babs's home address from the directory, and headed — like a suicidal maniac — for the unholy depths of Hell's Kitchen.

Chapter 8

Having a full-blown panic attack is like running for your life around a baseball diamond. You feel safe enough at the outset, but once you leave home plate, the heat is on: you have to reach and pass over three different bases — high anxiety, deep dread, and all-out terror — before you can get back to where you started. *If* you can get back to where you started.

By the time I exited the crosstown shuttle at Times Square, I was already on first base. Zooming underground in a small metal can packed to extremes with oily, sweaty people really does make you feel like a sardine. An anxious, vulnerable, *helpless* sardine. And emerging into the ugly, filthy, noisy neon world of Broadway and 42nd Street doesn't make you feel any better. Especially when it's getting dark and you can't see the shapes in the shadows.

I stood at the famous intersection for a minute or two, shuddering at the signs of human excess and squalor — gawking at the blazing, blinking marquees of the many theaters, hotels, cafeterias, bars, peep shows, novelty stores, penny arcades, strip joints, rifle ranges, and souvenir shops. Then I took a deep breath, hugged my purse in close to my side, and joined the cortege of winners and losers proceeding uptown.

Crossing 44th Street, I caught sight of the Majestic and St. James Theaters, where *Fanny* and *The Pajama Game* were playing, and continuing on to 46th, I passed a Woolworth's dime store, an Arrow shirt store, a Bond's two-trouser suit store, a Loft's candy store, and a Regal shoe store. There was a huge Admiral Television ad on the side of one building, and a gigantic, three-dimensional Pepsi-Cola display on another. And high above it all, on a billboard the size of a drive-in movie screen, gleamed a colossal pack of Camels and the giant head of a handsome naval officer, through whose enormous O-shaped mouth was pumped a continuous succession of machine-made smoke rings.

Buttoning my jacket up tight, and tucking my chin deep into the collar, I hurried away from the eerie crossroads and headed west toward Tenth Avenue and 48th Street, where Babs had lived (and maybe died). I walked as fast as I could and kept my gaze glued to the cement, so as not to make eye contact with any undesirable characters. Having read all about the burgeoning migration of Puerto Ricans from Spanish Harlem to the Hell's Kitchen area, and their heated culture clash with the predominantly Irish community, I knew the region was now plagued by Irish and Puerto Rican gangs — bands of young ruffians who were rumbling in the streets, killing each other, and terrorizing local inhabitants (not to mention non-local intruders, such as myself). I was *not,* therefore, in the mood to make any new acquaintances.

But my mood had no influence over the circumstances, and as I approached Tenth Avenue, I also slid (with a silent scream) into the second base of my panic attack. There — standing in the dim yellow light of a damaged street lamp, stationed like soldiers at the very corner where I needed to turn and head uptown — were three of the creepiest-looking juvenile delinquents I'd ever seen in my life. One was snapping his fingers and kicking at the curb like a deranged tap dancer, another was pacing the sidewalk and letting out loud, howling animal noises, and the third — a huge hulk of teenage surliness — was leaning against the lamppost, chewing on a cigarette and cleaning his fingernails with a switchblade.

Barely breathing, I slowed my steps and searched madly for an Irish bar or a coffee shop to duck into. There were no open storefronts in sight. No other people, either. Just a couple of stray dogs. The squalid tenement buildings to my right were grim and forbidding, and the abandoned warehouse across the street looked like a set for a horror movie. I wanted to turn around and run back the way I'd come, but it was too late. The creeps had seen me.

"Qué pasa, niña?" the dancer croaked, veering away from his cohorts and strutting over to me, snapping his fingers. He brought his thin, pockmarked face so close to mine, and to the foyer light seeping out from one of the tenements, that I could see into the pupils of his eyes. They were spinning like tiny cyclones.

I didn't say a word. I just lowered my head, hunched my shoulders, and continued walking toward Tenth Avenue. Although each step brought me closer to the other two vagrants (and much closer to third base), I felt it was my only option. If I was ever going to find an open bar, or a store, or some other people to protect me,

132

it was going to be on Tenth Avenue. I considered running but I figured my fear would incite them, and they'd start chasing me. And unless each of them was hobbled, as I was, with a tight skirt and high heels, I'd be caught faster than a fattened-up turkey at Thanksgiving. Maybe trussed and roasted too.

"What's your name, chicky?" the dancer said, following alongside, matching me step for step, snapping his fingers in time. Although I knew it would be in my own best interests to answer his question — to try to act brave and just a little bit friendly — I couldn't speak. My tongue was frozen in fear.

"Got a new girrrrrlfriend, Pablo?" The howler stopped pacing in circles and strode over to us. His voice was as high, sharp, and cold as a rooftop icicle. He had a scar on one cheek and was missing several teeth. *"Hola, bambina,"* he said, planting himself right in front of me, forcing me to a standstill. He stared at my face for a couple of seconds, then traced one black-leather-gloved finger slowly around my chin line. *"Muy bonita.* She's a good one."

A good one? I screeched to myself, hitting third with a solid splat. *What does that mean? A good one to rape and torture? A good one to disembowel and dismember?* I was so terrified I stopped thinking of how to escape, and started praying for a quick and painless end to my existence.

"Bring her here," called the knife boy. He was still leaning — indolent and sullen — against the dented metal lamppost, switchblade still clutched in his hand. His black hair gleamed gold in the lamplight, which cast a luminous golden aura around his massive head and shoulders. I was pretty certain the halo was undeserved.

The dancer grabbed hold of my left arm, the howler my right, and — keeping both limbs locked tight in their disabling grip — they pulled me to the corner, into the light. When I saw that the closest two blocks of Tenth Avenue were as deserted as the side street, my heart plummeted to my stomach. And my soul made hasty preparations to take leave of my body.

"Bonita, si?" the dancer asked the knife boy. "Pretty nice chicky." As he spoke, I tried to wrench my arms away, but I was no match for either of my ruthless escorts, who had started laughing and snickering like idiots.

The knife boy didn't say anything. He just looked at me in the same way a rat looks at a piece of cheese. Then he eased open the collar of my jacket, slipped the point of his knife in between the two lapels, and ripped the blade downward in a single, forceful slice. Cleanly severed from their settings, all six of my round, pearlized jacket buttons dropped to the sidewalk and scattered like glittering coins at my feet. Then the knife boy yanked open the front of my jacket, stuck his knife-free hand inside, and squeezed my right bosom. Hard.

If my late husband had been there to see what was happening to me, he would have gone crazy. He would have taken on all three of my attackers at once. He would have kicked their teeth in and broken all their ribs, arms, legs, and fingers. He would have seized the knife boy's switchblade and slashed all three of their juvenile throats.

But Bob wasn't there. Not physically anyway. He must have been with me in spirit, though — giving me courage and spurring me on — because the next thing I knew I was standing up tall as a tree, stamping one foot on the sidewalk, and telling (actually, *ordering!*) the knife boy to keep his filthy hands off me and leave me alone.

"Do you know who I am?" I seethed, looking the beast straight in the eye, screwing my face into a threatening snarl. "I'm a reporter for *Daring Detective* magazine. I've come here to investigate a murder, and to meet up with the cops who are working on the case. And if you don't let me go this very minute, you're going to be in *very* serious trouble." I stopped talking for a second, took a deep breath, and desperately concocted another lie to tell. "The police are waiting for me just a couple of blocks from here," I raged, "and if I don't get there within the next three minutes, they're going to come looking for me. And if they don't find me, you can bet your gutless, flea-bitten balls they're going to find *you!*"

I was flabbergasted by my own valiant (okay, vulgar) performance. And much to my eternal, openmouthed surprise, so was the knife boy. He gave me a miserable sneer and lifted his enormous shoulders in a shrug. Then, looking off to the side — pretending he was bored instead of worried — he clicked his ugly switchblade closed, clasped it in his palm, and told his brutal sidekicks to let me go.

"*No es bonita,*" he said, feigning disgust. "She not beautiful. She not even blonde."

With that, he stepped away from the lamp-post, turned himself around, and — clenched fists stuffed deep into his black leather pockets — began trudging down-town on Tenth. The dancer and the howler dropped hold of my arms and scurried after him like mice. Malevolent, malignant mice.

I stood alone in the light of the street lamp, gasping for air, fighting back tears, and thanking God, and Bob — and any other good spirits who might have been floating around the area — for my sudden deliverance from evil. I had lost all my buttons, but I still had my life. Which was more than I could say for the blonde and beautiful Babs.

One of the first-floor apartments in the tenement building where Babs had lived was lit up like a birthday cake, and music was pouring out into the street — the Four Aces singing "Stranger in Paradise." There were several lively silhouettes on the closed front window shade, and I could hear people laughing and talking inside. As glad as I was to be arriving at such a festive, seemingly safe destination, I couldn't help wondering what the heck was going on. A young woman who had lived in this building had been murdered just four days before, and the neighbors were having a party? Seemed a bit disrespectful to me.

Adjusting my beret, and holding the front of my jacket closed with my hands, I mounted the cracked cement steps to the front door. When I twisted the knob, the door opened easily. Come one, come all. No key or buzzer required. It wasn't until I stepped inside that I saw the note on the wall: DON'T BOTHER TO KNOCK. THE PARTY'S IN 1A.

I held my breath and stood still in the entranceway for a few seconds, taking a quick look around. Ugly green walls, dirty black and white tiled floor, bare wood staircase. The door to 1A was closed and, luckily for me, no party guests were loitering out in the hall. A fast glance at the uneven row of metal mailboxes on my right informed me — in clearly printed block letters — that Babs had lived in 4D.

I kicked off my pumps, picked them up in one hand, and dashed up the stairs in my stocking feet. I didn't want to make any noise during my ascent. (Not that anybody would have heard me; the volume on the record player downstairs could have drowned out the A-bomb.) Huffing from the hasty climb, I came to a stop on four and made a quick survey of the premises. The drab, poorly lit hallway was deserted, and there were four apartments on the floor — two front, two back. D was in the rear, on the right.

Tiptoeing back toward Babs's apartment, I could tell immediately that she hadn't been killed there. There was no Keep Out sign, and no police barricade over the door; it definitely was not a protected crime scene. To be on the safe side, I put my ear to the door and listened for telltale police sounds inside the apartment. It was as quiet as — forgive the expression — a tomb. No cracking of dirty jokes, no blowing of snoopy noses, no clicking and flicking of Zippo lighters, no thunderous coffee slurping. I stepped back from the door, tucked my purse under my arm, and (in lieu of leaving a set of foreign fingerprints at the site) took my gloves out of my pocket and pulled them on. Then — heart banging like a way-out beatnik's bongo drum — I tried to turn the knob.

Nothing happened, of course. Babs's door was, unlike the building's inviting front entrance, locked tight. All my silly fantasies of just waltzing inside, opening a few drawers, and finding all the evidence I needed to catch a killer went poof.

And so did my mental equilibrium. Burning to get inside the apartment, I ripped my gloves off, fished my nail file out of my purse, and jiggled it madly in the keyhole — leaving scratch marks on the face of the lock and almost breaking off the tip of the instrument. Then I rammed the file between the lock and the doorjamb, scraping it up and down, and back and forth, trying my damnedest to pry the bolt out of the socket. I gave no thought to what damage I was doing to the lock, or to what signs of my attempted break-in I might be leaving behind. I just wanted *in.*

After several more minutes of ramming and jiggling, scraping and prying, and puffing and sweating, I renounced the nail file routine and decided to try the old bobby pin trick instead. What a joke! It always worked in the movies, but it was a total dud in real life. All I got for my trouble was a severely bent hair clip and a sprained forefinger. I was just about to pack up my nail file and bobby pin and go home when the door to the apartment directly across the hall flew open.

"Hey, what's goin' on out here? Whaddaya think you're doin'?" A middle-aged woman with bright orange hair, deep red lips, and royal blue eyelids stood boldly in the open doorway, glaring at me as if I were a criminal (which, I guess, at that particular place and point in time, I sort of *was*).

"I . . . uh . . . well, I was just trying to get into this apartment," I stammered. Sometimes honesty is the best policy. Besides, I couldn't think of any other way to explain why I was down on my knees at the door, trying to shove various beauty utensils into the keyhole.

"I oughtta call the cops on you," said the redhead, planting her fluff-trimmed high-heeled mules more firmly on the floor and propping one hand on her hip. She was wearing a sheer but scratchy-looking blue negligee which barely concealed her blowzy, exceptionally well-endowed body. "You got no business bein' here," she added. "The woman who lived in that apartment was murdered, ya know."

"Yes, I know," I said, standing up from the floor and putting my break-in tools back in my purse. In an effort to look more respectable, I slipped my feet back into my shoes. "That's why I'm here," I declared. "Babs was a very good friend of mine."

The woman curved one very thin, very black eyebrow into an inquisitive arch. "Huh! Funny I never saw you around here before. Did you two work together or somethin'?"

"Umm . . . yes, we did," I answered, grateful for the leading question. It was neighborly of her to provide me with such a convenient fabrication. "Babs was a waitress like I am," I told her, "and we worked the same shift at the same restaurant."

"At Schrafft's, right? The one on 58th and Madison?"

"Right." The redhead was so accommodating, I decided it was time to get to know her better. "My name's Phoebe Starr," I said, stretching my hand out for a shake. "What's yours?"

She softened her militant stance and gave me a big red smile. "Margaret Maureen Shaughnessy," she said, vigorously squeezing my fingers (including the sprained one, which was beginning to swell). "That's my honest-to-God real name," she proudly proclaimed, "the one my mother gave me. But hardly anybody ever calls me that anymore."

"Really? Why?"

"Well, I'm kind of famous around here, see? I'm a burlesque dancer and everybody knows me by my stage name. Maybe you heard of me before. My name's Patty Cake."

And I thought Paige Turner was bad.

"Oh, yes, Patty, I *have* heard of you!" I said. "I've seen your picture too." (And I wasn't lying, either. Miss Cake's photo appeared in most of the afternoon papers every Friday, right next to the shots of Honey Bun, Sugar Plum, and Cherry Tart — the other strippers featured at the Footlight Theater on 42nd Street. I'd seen the ads when I was doing the clipping.) "You know Babs had a professional name too," I said, leaping into the fortuitous opening. "Did she ever tell you that?"

"Oh, sure! Wanda Wingate it was. I told her I thought it was too ladylike — that it sounded too much like a stuck-up socialite or somethin' — but she said she liked it that way. It made her feel high class."

"Were you good friends with Babs too?"

"Not best friends or anything like that, but we got to know each other pretty good. We did little things for each other, like pick up a dozen eggs, or sign for a package, or take care of each other's boyfriends when we knew we were gonna be late."

"So you actually met Babs's beaus," I said, trying not to look too interested. "I never saw a one. She *told* me about her dates, of course, during our breaks at work, but they never came by the restaurant to say hello or anything."

"Well, she sure had lots of 'em!" Patty replied, developing a more gossipy tone. "But I didn't get to meet many of 'em either. There was a tough guy named Jimmy who came around for a while, and a nasty little man she called Gunner, but I never laid eyes on the other ones — the good ones, the *rich* ones. Them she always met outside, at the Stork Club, or the theater, or some fancy hotel or somethin'. And they never brought her home afterwards, either. She always got sent back in a car. Sometimes it was a luxury limousine!" Patty's eyes sparkled at the thought.

"Yes, Babs told me about that," I said, counting my lucky stars that Patty was a stripper and, therefore, *trained* to be revealing. "But, you know, it always made me wonder. I mean, how did she get to know all those wealthy men in the first place? I asked her that once, but she didn't want to talk about it, and I didn't want to pry."

"Who cares how she got to know 'em? Maybe she signed up with one a them escort services or somethin'. She never told me. The point is, she was real pretty in a sophisticated kinda way, and she had some classy-lookin' clothes, and she knew how to act around big tycoons to make herself appealin'. And she musta been doin' somethin' right, 'cause they kept comin' back for more. Even the richest ones. You know who she went out with once? Zack Dexter Harrington, that's who! They don't come any richer than that."

Zack? Babs had dated my boy Zack? I was growing giddy from the onrush of information. *Bake me a cake as fast as you can, Patty.* "So she told you about Zack Harrington!" I exclaimed, using my genuine surprise to enhance my phony performance. "I thought I was the only one who knew about him. She said he wanted to keep his personal life secret, and she made me promise to never tell anybody. How did you find out?"

"Oh, she prob'ly never woulda told me about it, if it wasn't for the key."

"What do you mean? What key?"

Patty gave out a raucous laugh and rolled her eyes toward the ceiling. Then she leaned a bit closer, lowered her voice, and went right on talking. "See, one night when Babs went out, she lost the key to her apartment. So she had to wake me up to let her in. And it was five o'clock in the mornin'! Well, when I started complainin' about havin' to get outta bed so early, she

145

told me how sorry she was, and then she told me about bein' out with Zack Harrington. Dinin' and dancin' at the Copa. I guess she thought that would make me so excited I'd forget about losin' my beauty sleep. And she was right! I spent the rest of the mornin' daydreamin' about drinkin' champagne and doin' the mambo with a millionaire."

I giggled and gave Patty an encouraging wink. Then I snatched another question out of the air. "So, since she couldn't get into her apartment, did Babs stay and talk with you for a while? Did she tell you anything more about her relationship with Zack?"

"What makes you think she couldn't get in her apartment? Didn't I just tell you I let her in? She kept a copy of my key, and I had one of hers, just in case we lost 'em or somethin'."

"Oh, really?" I said, heart somersaulting. "Do you still have the key?" If she said no I'd have to kill myself.

"Sure I got it." She brushed a wisp of orange hair out of her eyes and gave me a nervous look. "But don't tell the police, okay? I don't want them to know. They'll just take it away from me, and then I won't be able to get into the apartment to get my jewelry back when the case is over."

It was uncanny. All I had to do was stand there and wait for the woman to give me direction. "You mean Babs borrowed jewelry from you too? That's why I'm here!" I cried. "I was hoping I'd be able to get my great-grandmother's antique brooch back before it disappears forever in a pile of police paperwork, or gets sent to Babs's family in Missouri. That pin means a lot to me, and it has a real diamond in it."

"Gosh! I never thought about that — that they'd be giving all of Babs's stuff to her family. What a dope I am."

"Well, you've got the key, Patty, so why don't we just go in there and get our belongings before they're gone? It's not like we'd be stealing or anything. The jewelry is rightfully ours." I took a deep breath and held it.

She wrinkled her forehead and crinkled her blue eyelids. You could actually see her thoughts flit across her lightly freckled face. When her frown turned into an earnest gawk, I knew I was in. "You're right!" she gasped. "And if we don't get our stuff right now, it could be gone tomorrow! Wait here a sec," she said, turning around and darting into her dim living room. "I'll be right back!"

Chapter 9

The interior of Babs's small, one-bedroom apartment was as rundown as the rest of the building. It was decorated in the all-too-familiar style of all the other living quarters of all the other unmarried, underfunded working women trying to make a go of it in Manhattan: peeling wallpaper (in this case an ugly cabbage rose design); old furniture with worn upholstery (major stains and holes covered by white eyelet doilies); a few faded scatter rugs; thin dime-store curtains.

The police had left the place in moderate disarray. A black wool coat and a gray fox stole (with the head still on) were strewn over the arm of the sofa, their naked wire hangers still lying on the floor of the open living room closet. The doors to all the kitchen cabinets were standing ajar; a stack of melamine dishes, a couple of Kix cereal boxes, and several Campbell's soup cans littered the countertop. In the bedroom, the drawers of the blonde wood bureau had also been left open — stockings, slips, and neckscarfs spilling over the sides.

Against one bedroom wall was a small blonde dressing table, complete with a ruffled skirt and a large round mirror. And sitting on the top of the dressing table was Babs's big white vinyl jewelry box. Patty snatched it up with both hands and sat down on the edge of the bed, resting the box on her knees.

"I hope all my things are here!" she cried, eagerly pulling the lid wide, exposing three pop-up tiers of gaudy baubles and beads. "I loaned Babs my gold charm bracelet, a pair of dangly rhinestone earrings, a silver friendship ring, and my favorite necklace in the whole world — a diamond choker with ruby teardrops. They're not real jewels," she said with a pout, "but they sure do look like it! Nobody can ever tell the difference." Pulling her hair out of her eyes and nosediving toward the open jewelry box, Patty began scrambling through its tangled contents with her fake red fingernails.

"While you're doing that, I'll look around out here," I said, exiting the bedroom and taking a quick turn around the living room, hunting for Babs's big black portfolio. It wasn't there — not even under the couch. Jumping to my feet and brushing the dust off my nose, I made a beeline for the small telephone table near the living room window. I wasn't searching for lost jewelry — I was searching for a lost life. And next to Babs's portfolio, I figured her address book would offer the best leads in that direction.

I yanked open the shallow drawer of the telephone table, stuck in my hand, and felt around for a book-shaped article. To my great disappointment, there were no such objects inside. Just a few loose papers and a couple of pencils. To shed some light on the situation, I snatched my hand out of the drawer and pulled the chain on the small brass table lamp. But even with the extra illumination, I couldn't find what I was looking for. If Babs had kept an address book anywhere near that telephone table, the police had probably confiscated it.

With a sigh of annoyance and frustration, I picked up the loose papers in the drawer and began to sift through them. Nothing of much interest. Just a one-page letter from Babs's mother in Missouri about the box supper at the Springfield Baptist Church, a grocery list, a laundry bill, a shoe repair ticket, and a Woolworth's sales slip. I anxiously checked the sales slip for a charge of eighty-nine cents (the price of a Hopalong Cassidy jump rope), but no such item was listed.

I was turning the papers over in my hand, about to place them back inside the drawer, when I saw something scribbled in pencil on the back of Bab's mother's pen-and-ink letter. I took a closer look and saw that it was a composition of some kind, a poem. It was in the same handwriting as the grocery list, so I felt certain it had been written by Babs herself. There was no title, just six lines of rhyming verse:

> *Scold me if you have to,*
> *Cast me out in the street.*
> *On my finger put no wedding ring*
> *To make my life complete.*
> *Though you'll never be welcome in*
>> *Heaven above,*
> *You'll always be the man I love.*

I was about to read the poem over a second time — try to glean some insight from the silly wording and awkward meter — when Patty suddenly appeared in the bedroom doorway.

"I found everything!" she said with glee. "The choker, the earrings, the bracelet, the ring! See?" Neck, ears, wrist, and finger glittering with all her cheap-but-cherished prizes, Patty struck a traditional stripper pose — hands on hips, large bosoms thrust forward, one leg projected through the front opening of her blue negligee — and shimmied her happy shoulders.

"That's great, Patty!" I said, silently crumpling Bab's poem (and her mother's letter) behind my back, then sneaking it into my jacket pocket. "Did you see my brooch?"

Patty's shoulders sputtered to a stop. "No," she said dejectedly, obviously feeling sorry for me. "I didn't see anything that looks real old, or has a real diamond in it. But you better come look for yourself," she added, brightening a bit. "I mighta missed it."

I stepped back into the bedroom and went through the motions of picking through the jewelry box. "It's not here," I said to Patty, who had plopped herself down on the edge of the bed again and was watching me intently. "Maybe it fell out of the box and rolled under the bed." Dropping down to my hands and knees on the floor, I lifted the bottom of the ruffled bedspread and peered underneath. No sign of Babs's portfolio. Had the police taken that too? Or did Babs have it with her the night she was killed?

"Just a slew of dustballs," I whined, pulling myself up to my feet. "But maybe it's in one of the drawers!" Before Patty could gather her thoughts enough to question my actions, I rifled through all the drawers in both the bureau and the dressing table, looking not just for an address book, but for anything at all that might be considered a clue.

There was nothing. Nothing but a motley stash of cosmetics, bras, underpants, hankies, gloves, garter belts, and sweaters. Nothing but the sad and pitiful remnants of a less-than-stellar life that had been ended all too soon.

Suddenly struck with a deep depression, profound grief for Babs, and a heightened sense of my own mortality, I was about to give up the disturbing scavenger hunt — about to thank Patty Cake for her help and head for home — when something oddly out-of-place caught my eye. On the very bottom of the bottom bureau drawer, barely peeking out from under a jumble of flesh-colored rubber girdles, was a small corner of a black-and-white photograph. A Brownie snapshot. Only the white border and a tiny wedge of the image was visible.

Trying to act as cool as Grace Kelly (but surely behaving more like Gracie Allen), I snatched the photo out of the drawer and held it up to the light. It was a woman and a little boy. They were standing side by side, on a narrow cement path in a children's playground (a set of swings could be seen in the background), holding hands, and looking directly at the camera. The little boy was grinning, but the woman was squinting into the sun, her blonde hair blown back from her face by the wind. Even without the sad smile, or the string of pearls, or the little black hat with the curving black feather, I saw at once that it was Babs.

"Gee, what a cute little boy this is!" I said to Patty, handing her the photo. "Do you know who it is?"

"Yeah, that's Ricky," she said. "I met him and his mother a couple a times, when they came up to visit Babs. The mother's name is Betty. She's an old friend of Babs's. She used to live in Missouri, too, but now she and her husband live in Brooklyn."

"Do you know their last name?" I was practically squealing with anticipation.

"Uh . . . no, not really. They told it to me once, but I forgot it. It mighta been Trott, or Scott, or Potts, or somethin' like that. The husband's first name is Freddy. I remember that 'cause Betty's so damn crazy about the man she couldn't stop talkin' about him. Every time she opened her mouth it was either 'Freddy this,' or 'Freddy that.' It was gettin' on my nerves, if you want to know the truth. She was so proud of herself for bein' a wife and mother it could make you sick. I think it bothered Babs too."

"Is Betty blonde?" I was thinking of Mr. Gumpert's description of the woman with Babs at the automat.

"Yeah, but it's not her real color. You can tell from her eyebrows she used to be a brunette." Patty screwed her face into an exaggerated grimace. "Boy! I wouldn't bleach my hair blonde for nothin'! I bet that's why Babs got herself killed."

Her queer remark grabbed my full attention. "What?! Why do you say that?"

"More blondes get murdered every year than brunettes or redheads," Patty declared. "It's a known fact. I read it in 'Ripley's Believe It or Not!' " Apparently Patty hadn't grasped the full meaning of the final word in the title of Robert L. Ripley's popular (and somewhat less than strictly factual) comic strip.

I smiled to myself and returned my focus to the photo in my hand. "Do you think I could keep this picture?" I said to Patty. "Babs was one of the best friends I ever had, and I'm going to miss her so much. It would be nice to have something to remember her by."

"Sure, why not? The police woulda taken it if they wanted it, and the family must have plenty pictures already. Go ahead and take it if you want to. It's no skin off my back."

"Thanks," I said, quickly slipping the snapshot into my purse.

"Too bad you couldn't find your brooch," Patty said, kindly reminding me of the item I was supposed to be searching for.

"I know," I said with a somber sigh. "But it's obviously not here. Maybe Babs was wearing it the night she was killed."

Patty gasped and put her hand up to her heavily rouged cheek. "Gawd! That would be awful! Then you'd never get it back!" Her devotion to body ornaments was, I thought, a bit excessive. Yet she wasn't wearing a watch. "Say, do you have the time?" she asked me. "I gotta go to work soon."

"It's eight-forty."

"Yikes! I'm supposed to go on at nine. The boss is gonna kill me!" She jumped up off the bed, dashed back into the living room, and crossed to the front door, her backless high heels clacking on the floor.

Suddenly eager to flee the depressing apartment, I followed right behind her. We stepped out into the hall and Patty locked Babs's door behind us. As she let herself back into her own apartment, I thanked her profusely for her help and promised her, once again, I wouldn't tell the police about the key. Then I hastened down the hall and scrambled down the stairs.

The hi-fi on the first floor was still piping popular music throughout the building. Now it was the Chordettes singing their new hit, "Mister Sandman." At the top of their everloving lungs. Seemed like a cruel jest to me. Sandman or no Sandman, nobody in the near vicinity would be getting much sleep that night.

Including myself, I realized with a sinking heart. Because as tired and frazzled as I was — as much as I wanted to fly out the front door, rush straight home, and dive into my lonely single bed — I knew there would be no rest for the weary in the immediate future. I still had a murder to investigate. And a story to write. And a party to attend.

★ ★ ★

I squeezed through the door to 1A and quickly melded into the crowd. Most of the guests were in their twenties and thirties, and still dressed in their work clothes, so I didn't stick out like a sore thumb — even in my beret and buttonless jacket. A few people were sitting on the cheap modern furniture which had been pushed back against the walls of the living room, and several couples were dancing the fox trot in the clearing. Everybody else was standing — packed close together in concentrated groups — holding a cocktail in one hand and a burning cigarette in the other. The air was so smoky you could hardly see, and the loud music made casual conversation impossible.

Still shaken from my encounter with the teenage hoodlums, and from the pitiful desolation of Babs's environment (which was entirely too reminiscent of my own), I decided a drink might calm me down, help me get into the swing of things. If I was going to learn anything about Babs from these lively, laughing party people, I'd have to be a party person too. As I was making my way into the crowded kitchen, where, I assumed, the bar would be set up, I grabbed a handful of peanuts from the candy dish on the counter and stuffed them, all at once, into my mouth.

This was a huge mistake, because the minute I looked up from that candy dish and started chomping on the nuts, I saw him. And then I gulped — a spontaneous nervous reaction which transported dozens of partially chewed peanuts from my mouth down into my throat. And then I choked. Big time. I'm not talking about a regular old gag or cough, where you sputter and gasp your head off for a second or two. I'm talking one of those high-powered, double-barreled, major-league chokes — the kind that explodes like a grenade in your esophagus and blasts shrapnel (in this case half-masticated goobers) all over the room.

"Oh, cripes!" screamed a woman whose pink cashmere sweater was now splattered with snack food and spit. "Somebody hand me a napkin!"

"Jesus! Are you all right?" cried the man closest to me in the kitchen. He began pounding on my back with one hand and wiping wet nut chunks off his face with the other.

"Awrrk!" I answered. I couldn't breathe, much less talk. And I was so embarrassed and distressed I didn't care if I ever drew breath again. Embarrassed, because I'd just made a complete clown of myself in front of a kitchenful of strangers, and distressed, because the man who'd caused me to choke in the first place — the man who was still leaning his shoulder against the refrigerator and staring at me through his hot black eyes — wasn't a stranger at all. He was Detective Sergeant Dan Street, and judging from the deep frown on his otherwise handsome face, he wasn't the least bit glad to see me.

In a total panic, and having absolutely no idea how to explain my presence in Babs's building, I coughed up a few more nuts. Then, in an effort to stop myself from choking (and to give myself some time to think), I frantically reached for the bottle of gin sitting open on the kitchen table. I didn't even *look* for a glass. I just threw back my head, plunged the mouth of that bottle into my own mouth, and started sucking on it like a hungry baby. And I kept right on sucking — and, to my own horror, *swallowing* — until a near third of the gin was gone.

The alcohol burned the skin off my tongue and blazed an excruciating path down my throat. It surged into my stomach like a river of molten lava — an angry, churning torrent of fire — and, for the second time that night, I thought I was going to die. I wasn't choking on the nuts anymore, but I still couldn't breathe. My eyes were bulging out of their sockets, and my ears were roaring like steam engines.

The people around me regarded my performance with a mixture of shock and disgust. You'd have thought they'd never seen a desperate, irrational, out-of-control woman before. But at this point I really didn't care what they thought about me. I didn't care what anybody thought about anything.

"Let's get out of here," Dan said, grabbing hold of my elbow and guiding (okay, *dragging*) me back into the living room. He pushed through the crowd, yanked open the front door, and pulled me out into the hall. Then, turning me around and taking hold of my shoulders, he backed me up to the foyer wall and braced me against it.

"What are you doing here?" he demanded. His fingers were making dents in my upper arms.

I tried to focus my vision enough to get a clear look at Dan's face, to gauge from his expression how teed off he was, but I might as well have been gazing through a telescope filled with water. Everything —

the green walls, the black and white tiled floor, Dan's reddening features — looked smeared and streaky, as if rendered by a toddler with a fistful of finger paint.

I did my best to focus my thoughts, and to control the rubbery movements of my inflamed lips and tongue, but each of those efforts failed as well. "I jush wannidago to a paaarty," I blubbered.

"Don't lie to me, Paige!" Dan raged. "I want to know why you came here, and I want to know *right now*."

His battering words bashed through my defenses, and crumpled the remains of my consciousness. I couldn't see, speak, stand, or even inhale. There was just one thing left for a wildly unstable woman with a bloodstream full of booze, and no air in her lungs, to do. Pass out.

Chapter 10

When I opened my eyes again, I was seated in a fast-moving car. My right shoulder was propped against the locked front passenger door, and my leaden head was rolling back and forth across the backrest, bumping loudly — repeatedly — against the hard doorframe. The window was wide open, allowing a steady stream of cold night air to clobber my face. I felt like a bucket of pig swill.

Somewhere in the murky depths of my skull a few brain waves were stirring. *What's happening? Where am I? Why am I in this automobile? Who's driving, and where are we going?* Looking for simple answers to these fundamental questions, I very slowly and very carefully rolled my head all the way to the left, and focused my gaze on the figure behind the wheel.

As I had feared, Dan Street was in the driver's seat. And from the stern scowl that came over his face when he realized I was conscious, it was clear he planned to stay there. He didn't say hi or even ask me how I was feeling. All he said was, "Sit up straight, Paige, and get hold of yourself. You've got some explaining to do."

I tried to comply, but my motor skills were still rickety. And my cerebrum was still on vacation. "How long have I been unconscious?" I asked, playing for time.

Dan looked at his watch. "Three hours and twelve minutes."

"Oh, my gosh! Where was I all that time?"

"Here in the car with me — keeping me company on my rounds."

"What happened? How did I get here?"

"I'm not answering any more of your questions," he growled, "until you answer all of mine."

"But I can't think or speak very clearly right now," I mumbled, hoping and praying he would pull back and let me be.

I was dancing for rain in the desert. "Tough luck," he said, clenching his teeth between words, "because you're not getting out of this car, or going anywhere, until you tell me what you were doing at Babs Comstock's apartment." Dan's eyes were trained on the road ahead, but his full attention was concentrated on me.

Groaning loudly, and pulling myself to a more upright position, I finally faced the sober facts. It was time for me to tell Dan about my story — and about everything I'd learned during my secret investigation. I would be putting my treasured job in jeopardy, but helping the police catch Babs's killer was infinitely more important than chasing my own eccentric career goals. "Okay, okay!" I said. "I'm ready to confess. Just get me a cup of coffee and I'll come clean."

Dan didn't say anything. He simply continued speeding downtown for several blocks, made a hasty turn onto 8th Street, and then pulled the squad car to a stop at the curb near the next corner, in front of Whelan's all-night drugstore. He got out of the car, slammed the driver's door shut, walked around to the passenger side, and poked his head through the open window. "Milk and sugar?"

"I think I'd better have it black."

"You'd also better be here when I get back."

"I couldn't run away if I wanted to. My legs are still drunk."

A hint of a smile tweaked his lips for a second. But *just* for a second. Before I could take my next breath, the frown flipped over his face again, and he turned to go into the drugstore.

By the time he came back, I was eager to

tell him everything. And as we sat in the squad car in front of Whelan's, drinking our coffee and listening to the crackle and pop of the police radio, I began unfolding my tale.

"I am working on a story about the murder," I admitted. "I lied to you in Woolworth's because I'm not allowed to write for the magazine yet, and if Brandon Pomeroy found out what I was doing, he'd fire me on the spot."

"Just for writing a story?"

"For even presuming that I could. Pomeroy disapproves of assertive females."

Dan turned and gave me a solemn look. "In this case I agree with him."

"What?" I couldn't believe what I was hearing.

"You have to drop the story immediately."

My body turned stiff as a surfboard. "What are you saying? Why should I drop it?" I cried. "I'm doing a good job! I'm going to turn in such a great piece that Harvey Crockett will ignore Pomeroy's objections and make me a regular staff writer! And I want to find out who murdered Babs as much as you do, you know. I've been doing some investigating and I've discovered some stuff that —"

"Hold it right there!" Dan's voice was vibrating with angry tension. "You're way out of line now, Paige. Writing a story is one thing, but interfering in an ongoing homicide investigation is something else altogether. It's stupid, it's dangerous, and it's completely unacceptable!"

"I'm not interfering, I'm just exploring." I was hurt and confused by Dan's attitude, but I still wanted to tell him what I'd learned. "I think I've turned up some important clues," I pushed on. "I found a love poem, and a Brownie snapshot that —"

"Don't say another word." Dan held his large palm up in front of my face like a stop sign. "I don't want to hear about it. If I listen to you, I'll be encouraging you, and that would be the same as cooperating with you. And I could get demoted for that. The department takes a very dim view of detectives who collaborate with meddlers and accept information from unreliable sources."

Well, if that's *the way you want to be about it* . . . I was shocked into silence.

"I'll make this short and sweet," Dan said. "We don't want your input. We want you to butt out. It's for your own safety."

I felt as if I'd been spanked. My face turned hot and I was having trouble breathing. But I didn't want Dan to know the state I was in, so I quickly changed the subject. "Speaking of safety," I said, working to keep my emotions (and tongue) under control, "I had a little trouble up on 46th Street tonight."

Dan perked up and paid attention. "What kind of trouble?"

I showed him my sliced-open jacket, and told him about my run-in with the teenage delinquents. I was hoping he'd feel protective of me and, therefore, soften his hostile attitude. But I also wanted to know what he thought about the incident. "All three of them looked murderous to me," I said, "and the leader, the one with the knife, expressed a definite preference for blondes. Do you think he — or they — could have killed Babs?"

Dan seemed to forget, for the moment, that he had banned all discussion of the Comstock case. "I know the boys you're talking about," he said. (*Boys?* I thought his word choice was tame, to say the least.) "The Ramirez brothers. They're big troublemakers, but they're not the killers. We questioned them at length, and they obviously don't know anything. All three were home having supper when the murder took place. Their mother swears to it."

Aha! I croaked to myself. *So Babs was*

killed around dinnertime! The coroner must have determined the time of death. I was dying to ask for more details, but I didn't say a word (for once).

"Do you know what a lucky dame you are?" Dan went on, in a very firm and forbidding tone. "They didn't kill Babs, but they might have killed you."

"I thought of that," I said, staring into my empty coffee cup.

"So you're going to stop now, right?"

"Stop what?"

"God damn it, Paige! You know what I mean." He made a fist with his face. "You're going to stop pretending you're a hotshot crime reporter. You're going to stop sticking your pretty little nose in this investigation; stop putting your reckless little life in danger. This is a very complex case — more deadly and involved than you can ever imagine — and your secret little search for the story will only screw things up more."

So it wasn't just my head that was little. It was also my nose, my life, and my foremost career goals. "But I feel really attached to Babs now," I exclaimed, trying — but failing — to control my adolescent whine. "And I want to help find her murderer."

Dan stopped frowning and started laughing. Well, actually he was just pretending to laugh. "Ha, ha, ha!" he mocked, curling his lips and crinkling his eyes in artificial mirth. "The lady wants to help! Well, that's very generous of you, Paige, but the only way you can help with this investigation is to bow out completely. Did you hear what I said?" he cried, raising his dark eyebrows and exhaling loudly. "I said back off! We've got a very knotty homicide to unravel, and the last thing we need is to have to worry about you in the process!"

My face grew hotter and my spine stiffened again. "I can take care of myself," I insisted. And I was foolish enough to believe that I could.

"Yeah, right!" Dan scoffed. "That's what Babs thought too."

My ears pricked to attention. What did he mean by that? Did he believe Babs had knowingly involved herself in a life-threatening situation? I tucked this last question away in my mental suitcase, planning to take it out and examine it later.

"Listen, Paige," he said, softening his voice a bit. "I hate to be a bully with you, but you leave me no other choice. If you don't put down your pencil and stop meddling in this case, I'm going to tell

Brandon Pomeroy what you're up to."

I heaved a loud sigh. I was afraid he'd get around to that. "Please don't!" I pleaded. "I'd lose my job for sure!"

"It's better than losing your life."

"Will you at least tell me when Babs's funeral is going to be? I'd like to pay my last respects." *And comb the mourners for murderers.*

"Forget about it. The service will be in Missouri. The Comstocks are having the body shipped back to Springfield as soon as the medical examiner finishes his report. It's your own funeral you've got to worry about now."

"But I should at least give Babs's parents a call and tell them how sorry I am." *And ask them a few probing questions.*

"Absolutely not!" Dan snapped. "They're in a deep state of shock right now. They hadn't seen their daughter in a very long time, and they knew nothing at all about her life here in the city, and the last thing they need is another nosy stranger poking around in their private pain, asking them for answers they don't have."

"I wouldn't poke!" I protested.

Dan slapped his hand against the steering wheel and gave me a dirty look.

"Listen, Paige, I told you to back off, and I mean it. Do not call the Comstocks, or talk to anybody else related to this case, ever again. If you do, I'll find out about it, and I'll go straight to Pomeroy with the news. That's a promise."

"Okay, okay!" I cried, slumping forward in an exaggerated pose of surrender. To continue the fight, I knew, would be futile. "I give up. I'll stop writing the story." (I'd have to start before I could stop.)

"And you'll quit playing detective?"

"You've got my word." (And the secret word was *no*.)

"Good," he said, sticking the key in the ignition and giving it a forceful twist. "Now where do you live? I'll take you home."

In the two years I'd been at *Daring Detective*, I'd never missed a day of work. So when I called in sick the next morning, Harvey Crockett was shocked. And more than a little upset. "But who's gonna make the coffee and clip the papers? I need to have some letters done, and somebody's gotta get me a lunch reservation and an appointment with my barber." The whole time he was talking, he was swiveling uneasily in his chair; I could hear the rusty mechanism squeaking over the phone.

"I'm very sorry, sir," I said, crossing my eyes and sticking my tongue out at the receiver. "I'm in really bad shape today." Truer words were never spoken. My head was splitting, my swollen shin was throbbing, my right bosom was aching, and my sprained forefinger was so sore I knew I wouldn't be able to type.

"What's wrong with you?" Crockett wanted to know.

"Female trouble," I mumbled. Sure, I was lying again, but what else could I say? That I had a terrible hangover and a bruised breast? Besides, I was hoping my answer would embarrass him and make him anxious to get off the phone.

It did. "All right then," he sputtered nervously, "but you'd better get your fanny in here first thing in the morning." Then he promptly hung up — bam! — without a single word of concern. Showing sympathy for others was not one of Harvey Crockett's favorite hobbies.

I plopped the receiver back in the cradle and wobbled back upstairs to bed. I didn't intend to go back to sleep. I just wanted to lie down for a little while; gather my strength; figure out what day it was; see if I could remember my name. But the minute

I hit the mattress, my doorbell started ringing. And ringing. And then somebody started banging on the door. So, cursing under my breath and standing up from the bed, I pulled on my aqua chenille bathrobe and dragged my damaged body down the stairs again.

When I got to the door I was afraid to open it. My tangle with the Ramirez brothers — not to mention the dire danger and death warnings I'd received from Dan Street — had made me a tad nervous. "Who is it?" I asked, in a voice so meek I was ashamed of myself.

"It's me," Abby said. "I was listening for you to leave for work, and when you didn't, I got worried."

Gushing with relief, I let her in.

"Oy vey!" she cried when she saw me. "What happened to you? You look like something the cat spit up!"

"That pretty much describes how I feel," I said, heading into the kitchen area for a glass of water. My mouth as dry as dirt.

"Have you had any breakfast?" Abby wanted to know, cheerfully jumping into her Jewish mother mode.

"Don't mention food!" I begged. "I'm never eating again."

"That could mean only one thing. You had too much to drink."

"Bingo."

Abby let out a knowing laugh, and pushed up the sleeves of her tight red sweater. Then she pulled her long black hair, which had been hanging loose down her spine, into a ponytail, and tied it back with her black silk neckerchief. "Out of my way, kid!" she said, elbowing me aside and lunging toward the refrigerator. "I know the perfect hangover remedy. I got it from that new girlie magazine all the guys are reading, the one called *Playboy*. It'll cure you in fifteen minutes flat."

She took some things out of the refrigerator and the spice cabinet (I don't know what, I was afraid to look) and started mixing a concoction in my water pitcher. I sat down at the kitchen table, squeezed my eyes shut, and covered my face with my hands. I didn't want to see what Abby was doing, and I didn't want to look at my typewriter, which was still sitting open on the table, reminding me of my recent writing failure. I could still hear, though, and when I detected the sounds of an eggshell being cracked and a raw yolk plunking into a pitcher of viscous liquid, I almost barfed.

"Forget it, Abby," I whimpered, hands still over my eyes. "I'd die if I had to drink, or even *look*, at that stuff right now. Pour it down the sink immediately! Can't you just make a pot of coffee?"

"Oh, Paige! You're such a fuddy-duddy. You never want to try anything new!"

"If not wanting to swallow a vat of putrid sludge makes me a fuddy-duddy, then so be it. I'll wear my fuddy-duddy badge with pride."

"Don't you even want to taste it?"

"I'd rather go ten rounds with Rocky Marciano."

With a typhoon-force sigh, Abby gave in. "Okay, baby! It's *your* hangover."

After I heard her pour the sickening stuff down the drain, I slowly opened my eyes. The first thing I saw was my Comstock Case list, the log of observations and impressions I'd typed up on Monday night. It was staring up at me from the kitchen table, demanding that I add all the new data from my latest clue-hunting expeditions.

"Ugh!" I groaned.

"What?" Abby asked, swishing water around in the pitcher, pouring it out, and setting the pitcher upside down in the dish drainer.

"I've got a ton of work to do," I said. "I have to write down every single thing that happened yesterday while the details are still fresh in my memory."

"So what's the problem?"

"I don't have a memory. It went into hiding last night."

Smiling, Abby untied the scarf from her hair and gave her head a vigorous shake. "Don't get your keester in a kink," she said. "My new model isn't coming till noon, so I've got some time to kill. I'll help you find the little devil."

Chapter 11

Two hours, three cups of coffee, and five cigarettes later, I was feeling like myself again — my determined, committed (okay, *committable*) self. I had recalled and related to Abby all the particulars of the day before — my trip to the Venus Modeling Agency, Brandon Pomeroy's suspicious behavior at my desk, my ordeal with the Ramirez brothers, the caper with Patty Cake at Babs's apartment, the filched photo of Babs and Ricky, the nut-choking, gin-guzzling episode with Dan Street — and, in deference to my swollen finger, she had typed up all my notes for me.

To say that my closest friend was excited by my perilous, life- and job-threatening escapades would be an understatement. She was downright exuberant.

"Hot diggety!" she crowed. "You're cooking with gas now, kiddo. You're going to become a famous writer, and you might even catch the murderer yourself!"

"Down, Fido."

"No, Paige, I really mean it. This is wild stuff. You're on to something big."

"Maybe too big."

"Oh, shut up. When it comes to fame and fortune, there's no such thing as too big, you dig?"

"Yeah, but when it comes to staying alive . . ." Dan Street's warnings were worming their way back into my consciousness. What was it he had said? Something about the case being "more deadly and involved" than I could ever imagine. . . .

"So, who do you think killed her?" Abby bubbled. "I bet it was Little Lord Pomeroy."

"What?" I cried. "You're crazy!"

"No, really. Just think about it for a second. Brandon got some pictures of Babs from that photographer, right? Maybe he liked what he saw and called her up for a date. Then maybe he fell madly in love with her, and —"

"Pomeroy never loved anybody."

Abby snorted. "You're probably right about that." She twirled a long strand of hair around her finger and glanced up at the kitchen ceiling. "Then maybe he just lost control of himself and raped her, and then had to kill her to keep her from talking."

"We don't know that she was raped."

"Was she naked when she was found?"

"From the waist down."

"Then she was raped."

"Only the medical examiner knows for sure," I sniffed, refusing to jump to premature — though probable — conclusions.

"Well, if Pomeroy didn't rape or kill her, he's got to be involved in some other way," Abby went on, determined to pin something on my loathsome boss. "Could be he's the private family pimp — always on the lookout for pretty girls for his rich friends and relatives — and maybe he gave Babs's number to somebody else . . ."

The name Zack Dexter Harrington danced through my head.

". . . and maybe that person fell in love with her, and then killed her in a fit of passion, and then called Pomeroy to help him dispose of the body. And now Pomeroy's trying to cover up his involvement, and *that's* why he was going through your desk!" Abby leaned across the table and beamed at me like a spotlight, delighting in her own deductive prowess.

What she was saying had a ring to it, but it didn't feel quite right to me. I stood up from the kitchen table and started pacing the linoleum. "But what was Pomeroy looking for in my desk? And whatever could have made him think that I had be- come involved?" The minute those ques- tions were out of my mouth, I answered them myself. "I guess that photographer, Scotty Whitcomb, could have tipped him off, and told him that I had the photo."

"That's right!" Abby cried. "Now we're getting somewhere!"

"But for some reason I really don't think that's it," I said. The doubt was curling around my skull like a serpent. "I just didn't get the feeling that Pomeroy was suspicious of me. He didn't seem the least bit concerned about me, if you want to know the truth. All he cared about was the damn mob hit story."

"What?"

"The mob hit. Didn't you hear about it? One of Albert Anastasia's boys was bumped off Sunday night. Two bullets to the brain. Mike had done a story on the murder for the magazine, and it was al- ready out at the typesetter, but for some reason Pomeroy was crazy to get it back. He said he was pulling it out of the issue."

"So?"

"So I really do think that's what he was doing at my desk — looking for the Anastasia piece so he could keep it from going to type. He was *dying* to get his hands on that story."

"Hmmmm," Abby brooded. "I wonder why."

"Yeah, I wondered about that too. The hit's the hottest news in town. All of our competitors will be covering the story. Some will even splash it on the cover. I can't imagine why Pomeroy would want to yank it."

"There must be *some* reason."

"Sure, but what?"

"You said the mob guy was killed Sunday night. Wasn't that the same night Babs was killed?"

"Yes, but what does that have to do with anything?"

"I don't know. Probably nothing."

"Right."

"Hey, I've got an idea!" Abby whooped. "Why don't you make a few inquiries at that Italian social club across the street? All the members are two-bit mobsters. Maybe they'll have some inside information."

"I'm sure they do!" I said, laughing. "But why would they give it to me?"

"Because you're a neighbor."

I laughed again. "That's absurd."

"No, really!" Abby insisted. "I'm not kidding. I've met some of those guys and they're not so bad. Most of them live around here, and they care about this neighborhood a lot — like it's sacred ground or something."

"That doesn't mean they care about me."

"Don't kid yourself. They know everything about everybody who lives on the block — including you. They're self-appointed watchdogs, policemen, prosecutors, and judges. Why do you think the area's so safe? No robberies or rapes ever take place around here because all the crooks and rapists in the whole city know the rules. If they ever committed a crime in this neighborhood, they'd pay with their lives, or their *cajones*."

"Oh, I see!" I said, snickering with sarcasm and disbelief. "The gangsters across the way are actually the guardian angels of Bleecker Street. And one of their main objectives in life is to protect my ignorant, non-Italian ass." I stopped snickering and turned serious. "But just tell me this, smarty girl. Which crime family are they connected to, and why in blue blazes would they give me information about a gangland execution?"

Abby was starting to lose patience with me. "Anastasia, Costello, Genovese —

what the hell difference does it make? Each Black Hand knows what the other one's doing. And I'm not saying you should just march in there and ask a bunch of direct questions, for cripe's sake! Then the *dreck* would really hit the fan. But what harm would it do to walk by the club, stick your head in, and say hello? On warm days they always leave the door open. You could strike up a casual conversation with one of the guys — about the weather, or the Yankees, or something — then secretly steer the discussion around to more important things like murder."

I was shocked that she would suggest such a scheme. Didn't she realize how risky a move like that could be? "Oh, come off it, Abby!" I shrieked, throwing my hands up in exasperation. "You make it sound so easy! As easy as getting one of your vain young cover boys to take off all his clothes. For your information, conducting a murder investigation is a little more difficult — not to mention more *dangerous* — than luring a naked narcissist into the sack!"

I had gone too far. Abby's feelings were visibly hurt. "I was just trying to help," she said, lowering her gaze to the tabletop. Her mouth was pinched and her chin was quivering. "But I can see my help is unwanted, so I think I'll be going now." She stood up straight, shook out her hair, and strode to the door.

I wanted to kill myself. "Wait, Abby!" I cried, following her out into the hall. "I'm sorry. I didn't mean to —"

"Excuse my hasty exit," she snapped, pushing open the door to her own apartment and stepping inside. "My new model is due to arrive in five minutes, and I have to get ready to *shtup* him."

When she slammed her door closed it almost hit me in the nose.

I showered and dressed with a heavy heart and a self-reproaching soul. How on earth could I have treated my best friend so badly? Abby had made me coffee, typed all my notes, tried to help me figure out some new angles for my story, and all she'd gotten for her trouble was a pack of insults. I was a swine, a reptile, a rabid bitch. I wasn't worth the paper my list of clues was typed on.

I was, however, eager to get on with my investigation. And, for some strange reason, my flare-up with Abby had actually bolstered my courage — made me less fearful about my own safety. Either I was so disgusted with myself I didn't care what happened to me anymore, or I was so anxious to make it up with Abby I was willing to put myself in peril to win back her approval. Whatever the case, as soon as I finished putting on my white blouse, tapered navy slacks, yellow cardigan, brown penny loafers, and makeup, I threw all caution to the wind, dashed down the stairs to the sidewalk, and then sauntered — as nonchalantly as my nervous legs would allow — across the street and up the block to the social club.

It was a very warm day, and the door to the small unidentified street-level storefront was — just as Abby had said it would be — standing wide open. A short, meaty middle-aged man was leaning against the doorjamb in his shirtsleeves, chewing on his fingernails and staring out at the busy street as if hypnotized. His thin brown hair was slicked back over his massive cranium, and his shirt was unbuttoned all the way down the front, exposing a wide bulge of dirty white undershirt.

I sucked in a chestful of air, sidestepped a few strolling shoppers, and walked right up to him. "Hello!" I said, batting my lashes and pasting on a perky smile. "Beautiful day, isn't it?"

The man took his fingers out of his mouth and turned his large head in my direction. He looked straight at me, but it took him a couple of seconds to break out of his trance. "Huh? What?" He sounded like Ed Norton on dope.

"I said it's a beautiful day."

He squinted at me for a couple more seconds, and then his gluey green eyes suddenly snapped into focus. "Yeah, yeah . . . beautiful," he said, giving me a wink and a very overt once-over. "Almost as beautiful as you."

Yeeuck! I choked back a snotty response and put on my best flirty face. "Why, thank you, kind sir!" I beamed, batting my lashes again. I was trying to imitate Scarlett O'Hara, but in my hung-over, high-strung, hopped-up condition, I probably looked more like Imogene Coca.

He shifted his weight on his short thick legs and winked again. "No problem, toots. I got lots more where that come from."

Lots more what? Eloquent observations? Irresistible come-ons? Oh, goody!

"This is a nice place you've got here," I said, poking my head through the door of the club, sneaking a quick look around. Several grubby card tables — some metal,

187

some wood — hugged the bare beige walls, and a batch of open folding chairs cluttered the bare wood floor. An old refrigerator stood in the far corner of the room, and placed right next to it, on another grubby card table, was a large copper espresso machine. A couple of big, bearish men — with bloated stomachs and arms the size of tree trunks — slouched together at one of the tables in the back, drinking ginger ale and eating meatball heroes.

"I'm Phoebe Starr," I said to the man at the door, coyly glancing down at the sidewalk, hoping my fake name would confuse the beast and shield me from closer scrutiny. "I live over on Barrow Street."

"Oh, yeah?" He was either playing dumb, or just being himself. Hard to tell the difference.

"What's your name?" I asked. If I was ever going to get him to confide in me I figured I'd have to get friendly.

"Name's Tommy," he said. "Like the gun." He crinkled his gooey eyes and snickered loudly. "Get it?" he croaked. "Tommy gun."

"Very funny," I said, smiling till I thought my cheeks would crack and madly searching for something else to say — something that would steer the conversation toward the subject of homicide. "Can I ask you a question, Tommy?" I ventured. This wouldn't have been such a bad opener if I'd had an actual question in mind.

"Shoot," he said. The man had a conspicuous fondness for words related to firearms.

"Well," I began, stumbling, still fishing for a good lead, "do you . . . er . . . do you or any of the other members of your club . . . um . . . what I mean to say is . . ." This wasn't going very well. My tongue was trying to talk straight, but seemed stuck in a permanent stammer. "See, I was just . . . uh . . . wondering if you or any of your buddies . . . er —"

"Quit yer mutterin', girlie! I ain't got all day." The native was getting restless. A very ugly frown was forming on his mallet-shaped forehead.

I stretched my wits to the limit, but still couldn't come up with a smart line of questioning. Streams of sweat were spurting down my sides. Why on earth had I let Abby talk me into this? If I ever got out of this mess in one piece, I'd definitely start seeing a psychiatrist. I took a deep breath and gave myself an imagined slap in the face. Hard. Then I opened my mouth and started to speak, deciding I'd just have to wing it and pray for a safe landing.

"I don't know how to put this, exactly," I said, "but I guess the best thing to do is just tell it how it is. See, I was talking to some friends of mine the other night, and they told me that you guys — I mean you and the other distinguished members of your club — are the neighborhood peace officers, that you keep watch over everybody who lives around here to make sure they don't get robbed, or killed, or otherwise come to any harm."

"Yeah, so?" Tommy's frown was even deeper now.

"So, if that's true — well, I just want you to know I think it's wonderful! I mean, I really, really do!"

"Yeah, so?" he reiterated.

"So, I was just wondering if there are any other clubs like yours in the city," I said, still floundering, still looking for a way to get information without giving any. "I mean, are there other regional fraternities where the members keep watch over the streets, and over all the people who live there, and — well, just generally keep tabs on everything that's going on?"

Tommy didn't reply. He was too busy glowering at me.

"And if there *are* other organizations like yours," I quickly continued, picking up steam, but — unfortunately — no direction, "do you all keep each other informed about what's happening in the various neighborhoods? I mean if something really horrible happened up on 34th Street, say, or in Hell's Kitchen, or up in the Bronx, would you find out all the dirty details way down here?"

"Hey!" Tommy sputtered, taking a step back inside the storefront and narrowing his eyes to razor-thin slits. "What the hell're you drivin' at?"

An alarm went off in the back of my brain, but I was too wound up to heed it. Burning to uncover whatever scraps of information I could about poor Babs's brutal demise, but unable to think of a sly way to do it, I finally just gave up trying to be tricky. I sucked in another blast of oxygen, defied all the flashing danger signs, and marched straight into the heart of the forbidden zone.

"I know your business is none of my business, Tommy," I said, "but this is really very important to me. See, the reason I'm asking all these questions is because a good friend of mine was murdered last Sunday night, and the police don't know who did it, and I thought maybe — just maybe — you or some of your colleagues might know something that could lead the cops to the killer."

There. I'd done it. I'd openly declared the purpose of my mission. It wasn't exactly the truth, but it felt like the truth, and for some delirious reason, I experienced a heady sense of triumph, and then an enormous swoosh of relief.

Which lasted exactly one and a half seconds.

"You got a hell of a lot of nerve, girlie," Tommy said, twitching his jumbo head and inflating his dirty-white-cotton-covered chest to the bursting point. "We don't know nothin' about how yer friend got iced. Don't know who popped him either."

Him? They don't know who popped *him?* My stomach twisted into a knot the size of a station wagon. I hadn't mentioned whether my friend was male or female! Had Tommy leapt to the conclusion that I was inquiring about the mob hit?

"Oh, no!" I cried. "You've got it all wrong! My friend who was killed was a *girl.* Her name was Babs Comstock."

Tommy looked confused but still ready to explode. "Don't know nothin' about that neither," he snapped. "You better come inside and talk to the boys. Tell 'em what you told me." He moved out of the way and motioned for me to enter.

I'd have crawled into a sack of snakes before I'd have gone inside that club. I didn't want a meatball hero, or a cup of muddy espresso, and I certainly didn't want to repeat a pack of senseless lies to three musclebound gangsters whose size forty-six shorts were bursting with vengeful *cajones*. All I wanted to do was run back to my apartment and hide under the bed.

"Sorry, Tommy," I sputtered, "but I can't come in right now! I'm late for a date uptown! I'll see you later." Before he could speak a single syllable, or even raise his eyebrows in wonder, I took off like a racehorse and galloped for the subway.

Chapter 12

My banging heart was making more noise than the screeching northbound express. And my thoughts were so loud I needed mindmuffs. *You've really done it now, Paige. You've laid yourself out in a coffin, and it's just a matter of time till somebody nails the damn thing shut.*

I was sitting tall in my seat on the subway, trying to look composed and courageous, but I was shaking in my white cotton socks. Not only had I just informed a team of local gangsters that I was looking for a killer, but I'd also revealed that I thought they might know who the killer was. If the boys across the street hadn't been watching my every move before, they certainly would be now! Either to protect me or — and this seemed far more likely — to silence me.

Why, oh why, did I have to start talking to Tommy about the murder? Why did I ever start talking to him at all? I didn't get a shred of information from him, and in my harebrained, headlong quest to unearth new clues about the crime, I'd accidentally led Tommy to believe I might be digging for dope about the Mafia killing! *Good work, Paige. You'll be a top mystery author someday. If they bury you with a typewriter.*

I punished myself with such torturous thoughts until I reached my destination. And I chastised myself even more as I plodded — zombielike — out of the subway and up the steps to the street. When I finally emerged into the light at the 59th Street exit, I had almost talked myself into dropping the story.

Almost, but not quite.

I'd already made my way uptown, you see, and the Schrafft's where Babs had worked was just a few blocks away. And how dangerous could it possibly be to sit down and have a snack in a nice, cheerful restaurant, and have a nice, friendly chat with one or two of the waitresses? Seemed like a perfectly prudent pursuit to me. What spot could be safer than Schrafft's? It was a very respectable eating establishment and — to the best of my news-clipping knowledge — had never been the site of a single mob hit.

"Would you like a cocktail?" the pudgy blonde waitress asked. She was wearing the requisite Schrafft's uniform: black dress, white apron, black shoes, white cap. Her plump cheeks looked moist and pink, like two scoops of Schrafft's famous strawberry ice cream.

"No, thank you," I said, suppressing a groan of disgust. I'd rather have taken a bullet than another shot of booze.

"What else can I get for you?"

"A cup of coffee," I said, "and a piece of peach pie."

"Want ice cream with that?"

"Sure."

"Vanilla?"

"Please." It was way past my lunchtime, but I was still more hung over than hungry. The pie a la mode would be just a prop, an excuse for me sit for a while at the highly polished wood and marble lunch counter, grilling the hired help.

Though the lunch hour was officially over, a small group of people lingered in the rear dining room, laughing and talking loudly, ordering martinis and Manhattans. The long counter in the front of the restaurant was empty except for me and the mink-stoled matron sitting at the opposite end, munching cookies and sipping tea.

"Here you go," said the waitress, putting my pie down in front of me. A cup of coffee and a tiny pitcher of cream appeared soon after. "Nice day, isn't it?" she said, sliding the sugar jar closer to my white paper place mat. "You should be picnicking in the park."

"I'd rather be sitting here eating peach pie." I took a big bite just to prove my words. Then I rolled my eyes in pleasure. "Nobody makes it like Schrafft's. A good friend of mine used to work here, and whenever I came by she'd talk me into ordering a piece. I'm addicted to it now."

Her pink cheeks lifted in a smile. "What's your friend's name?" she asked. "Maybe I know her."

I gulped loudly, contorted my face in grief, slumped my shoulders, and let my head hang down between them. "Babs Comstock," I whimpered. "Did you know her? She was the best friend I ever had. She died Sunday night, and I can't believe I'll never see her again."

"Sure I knew Babs," the waitress said, patting my hand in sympathy. "It's really horrible what happened to her. To be murdered like that! The cops were in here questioning us yesterday."

I raised my eyes and gave her a stricken look. "Did they find out anything? God, I hope so. They've just *got* to catch the killer!"

"They will, honey. They will." She patted my hand again. "I'm afraid the police didn't learn too much from us, though. Babs acted kind of stuck up and secretive most of the time, and none of us knew her too good. Except for Doris, that is. Doris and Babs were pretty darn close, so the detectives spent most of their time talking to her. Maybe she gave them some leads."

"Is Doris here today?"

"Sure is. She's workin' the dinin' room."

My pulse quickened. "Do you think I could talk to her for a few minutes? I'd really like to meet somebody else who was friends with Babs. Maybe we can console each other."

"That'll prob'ly be all right, honey. Things are slow right now. And I think Doris is about due for her break. I'll go find out." She patted my hand again and walked toward the back.

I busied myself eating peach pie and vanilla ice cream, both of which were — in spite of my queasy stomach — beginning to taste very good. So good, I gobbled. By the time the waitress came back, with another crisply uniformed waitress in tow, my plate was so clean I thought they might not bother to wash it.

"This is Doris Toomey, honey," the

pudgy blonde said. "She's on her break now, so you two can sit and have a nice talk." She left Doris standing there and worked her way back behind the counter to write up a check for the matron in mink.

Doris looked to be in her late thirties. She was short, skinny, and very mousy. Even in her starched white apron and bright white cap, she looked as drab as a plain brown wrapper. Her plain brown hair was permed into a brittle frizz, and she wore so little makeup her features were almost imperceptible. Only her glasses — which were big and bold and framed in black — made a strong visual impression.

Had this dismal creature actually been a good friend of the blonde and shapely Babs? I wondered. What could the two have possibly had in common? Certainly not their sense of glamour and style! How odd they must have looked standing next to each other in their black and white uniforms — like a set of salt and pepper shakers modeled after Kim Novak and Mr. Peepers.

"Hello, Doris," I said, extending my hand. "My name is Phoebe Starr. I was a good friend of Babs Comstock's." I might have told her my real name and my real reason for being there, but I was afraid she'd tell Dan Street about my visit. "Can we talk for a few minutes? Sit down and I'll buy you a cup of coffee."

She looked as if she might bolt and run away, but after gawking at me for a couple of seconds through her lopsided black-rimmed goggles, she shrugged and settled her wiry body down on the stool right next to mine. "I'll sit, but I don't want any coffee."

"Sure . . . okay . . . whatever you want. I just thought since you and Babs were such good friends, and Babs and I were also good friends, it might be good for the two of us to talk. I mean, maybe we could comfort each other or something. I don't know about you, but I really miss her." A few tears formed in the corners of my eyes.

(I know what you're thinking. You're thinking, "There she goes again, being a great big liar and a phony, acting like she cares about Babs when all she really cares about is her story." But let me tell you, there was nothing fake about those tears. I swear to God. In the two and a half short days I'd been working on the Babs Comstock story, I'd grown so attached to my subject I was beginning to feel like I'd lost a sister.)

Anyway, Doris didn't even notice my

tears because she was blinded by her own. Her scrawny shoulders were shaking and several deep, wrenching sobs escaped her skinny throat. "I . . . I . . . I can't . . . can't believe she's gone." Her words came out in a series of staccato gasps. "She was . . . my only friend . . . the only person who ever . . . really liked me."

I stroked Doris's quavering back and tried to think of something soothing to say. "Yes, I know how much Babs liked you," I cooed. "She spoke about you to me many times. She said you were one of the smartest, kindest, most interesting people she'd ever met." Okay, I *was* being a liar and a phony now. But what harm could a few flimsy falsehoods do? The way I saw it, poor Doris needed all the flattery — false or otherwise — she could get.

"Really?" she croaked, turning her head to gaze up at me. "Did she really say those things about me?"

"Yes, really."

Doris sat up straighter, took her steamy glasses off, placed them on the counter, and wiped her eyes with a napkin. A beautiful smile swam over her face, turning the duckling into a swan (all right, she actually looked more like a goose — but a very delicate, sweet-looking goose). "I'm so glad," she said simply. "It makes me so happy to hear that."

Doris's earnest, straightforward manner was making me feel like a louse. I decided I'd better push on with my inquiry before I went soft and forgot what I was there for. "I still can't believe Babs was murdered," I said bluntly. "Do you have any idea who killed her?"

"No!" Doris cried, replacing her glasses on her nose. "What are you suggesting? How would I know anything about it?" She was getting agitated again.

"I'm not suggesting anything," I quickly assured her. "It's just that I can't help wondering who did it. It's all I can think about. Maybe it was one of her boyfriends. I know she had a lot of them, but she didn't tell me much about them. And I never got to meet any of them in person. Did you?"

"Uh, no," Doris said, becoming interested in the conversation, "but she always told me all about her dates. She told me what she wore, where they went for dinner, what show they went to, if they went out dancing, and so forth. I loved hearing about it! Babs knew I'd never been asked out on a date before, and that I might never have any romantic experiences like hers, so she gave me *all* the details."

"Did she give you her boyfriends' names?"

"Not the last names. There was a Lloyd, and a Frankie, and a Peter, and lots of others, but all I know is the first names. I told the police every one I could remember."

"Did she ever tell you she went out with Zack Dexter Harrington?"

"Oh, yes! She was really excited about that one. But that's the only full name she ever gave me. I told the police about it."

"Did she say anything else about her date with Harrington? Was he nice? Did she have a good time?"

"She had a wonderful time. It was just a few weeks ago. He took her to the Copacabana." Doris's eyes began to gleam, and her thin lips curled into another beautiful smile. "She wore a red chiffon strapless and silver sandals. They had champagne, and filet mignon, and they danced until two. Then they went to his penthouse for a nightcap, and afterward — after they drank another bottle of champagne and listened to three Frank Sinatra albums — he sent her home in a white limousine. She felt like Cinderella."

"Did they have any other dates after that?"

"No, he never called her again."

"Did that upset her?"

"Sure, but it didn't break her heart or anything."

"Why do you say that?"

"Because Babs was a very strong, realistic person. She said her heart had already been broken once, and that was enough. She wasn't going to let it happen ever again."

"Who broke her heart the first time?"

"I don't know. She wouldn't tell me. She didn't want to talk about it."

"She never told me about it, either," I said, feeling it was time for me to add some observation of my own, something to make me seem like Babs's friend in life — not just in death. "Babs was funny that way," I murmured, leaning toward Doris till our shoulders touched. "She'd talk a blue streak about some things, but then if something personal came up — something too painful or emotional — she'd close up like a clam."

"She sure did!" Doris sputtered, nodding vigorously. "I was always really, really careful about that. I never pried too deep in her personal life. I think that's why she liked me."

"Same here," I said. "But there was always one thing I couldn't help wondering about. It really bothered me."

"What's that?"

"Well, Babs had a relationship with a woman named Betty that I never could figure out. I know they were old friends, but Babs really didn't seem to like her very much. She was nuts about Betty's little boy, Ricky, though, and she jumped at every chance she got to see him. I asked Babs about Betty and Ricky lots of times, but she never wanted to talk about them. And she never told me their last name."

"I know who you're talking about!" Doris eagerly volunteered. "Their name is Scott. The husband and wife are both old friends of Babs's from Missouri, but I think they live in Brooklyn now. Babs introduced me to them one day when they surprised her and came in here for lunch."

"She didn't know they were coming?"

"I think she was shocked when they showed up."

"Betty's husband came, too?"

"Yes. He said they were spending a family day in town, taking the boy to a show at the Music Hall."

"Did they seem like nice people to you?"

"Now that you mention it, they weren't very friendly. The woman looked nervous and upset, and the man was cold and standoffish. And you're absolutely right — Babs didn't seem to like them very much. Except for the kid, of course. She really loved that kid. She was always buying him presents and stuff."

I thought of the comic books I'd seen in Babs's portfolio. And of a certain cowboy jump rope. "Did Babs ever talk about her past relationship with the boy's parents?"

"Never. She didn't mention them at all. And I never asked about them, either. Something told me the subject was off-limits. I figured if Babs wanted me to know anything about those people, she would offer the information herself."

"Did you tell the police about the Scotts?"

"There wasn't anything to tell."

I felt Doris didn't have anything more to tell me, either, so — after saying how sad I was about our mutual loss, and how comforting it had been to meet her, and how much I appreciated talking to her — I called for my check. While we were waiting for the other waitress to add up my tab, Doris gave me a shy, admiring look through her big bold glasses and suggested that we stay in touch, that we exchange phone numbers. I hesitated for a split second, then agreed. And you probably won't believe this, but I gave her my real one.

Chapter 13

It wasn't yet five, but the rush hour had gotten off to a snappy start. The sidewalks were pulsing with people — men in three-piece suits and fedoras; women in spring dresses, straw hats, and white gloves. Most of the men carried briefcases, and all of the women wore high heels, which clacked incessantly, like busy typewriter keys, on the pavement. The streets were streaming with cars — yellow taxis, long black Caddies, light green Chevys, baby blue Fords — many of which came fully equipped with cranky drivers, bleating horns, and dingy whitewalls.

The Apex Theatrical Agency was located on Seventh Avenue, between 52nd and 53rd — a long sweaty nine-block trek from Schrafft's. I was glad I was wearing my loafers — especially when I realized, after studying the directory just inside the entrance of the five-story, elevatorless brownstone building, that the agency was up on the top floor. I sucked in my stomach and began the climb, breathing as hard as an overweight tap dancer.

Each floor had a different aroma. The

first smelled like burnt coffee, the second like French fries, the third like cleaning fluid, and the fourth like jasmine perfume (no big surprise — a fragrance distributor was situated on that level). The air up on five, where Apex made its highfalutin home, smelled like used kitty litter.

There were three office doors on the fifth floor. I opened the one with the agency's name stenciled in black and gold on the frosted glass pane, and stepped inside. The smell of kitty litter grew stronger. A scrawny middle-aged woman was sitting at a desk near the door, reading a magazine and singing along with the radio. She gasped when she saw me, stifled her off-key vocalizing, flipped the magazine closed, and slapped it down faceup on the desk. I recognized the cover. It was the April issue of *Careless Love*, one of Orchid Publications's trashy confession titles.

"You scared me!" the woman cried, giving me an accusatory look. "I thought you were Mr. Crawley comin' back!"

"Heaven forbid," I said, smiling. "Is Mr. Crawley your boss?"

"Yeah, and he would fly off his rocker if he saw me readin' a magazine at my desk. He's real fussy that way. A regular Mr. Dithers."

I smiled again. "How long have you worked for him?"

"Over thirteen years," she said with a scowl, "and would you believe he still calls me Miss Faparelli? Ain't that quaint? I think he just likes to remind me I'm not married." She tugged on the collar of her tight purple blouse and patted her dyed black hair, which was pinned up in a scraggly French twist. Several greasy strings of hair had escaped the twist and were dangling, like loose shoelaces, down the sides of her sharp, narrow face.

"Sorry I frightened you," I said.

"I'll get over it," she snorted, leaning sideways to turn up the volume of the white plastic radio sitting near the edge of the desk. Rosemary Clooney was still singing "Hey, There," but all by herself now. "I just love this song, don't you?" Miss Faparelli inquired.

"Sure do," I said, wrinkling my nose involuntarily. I paused and took a fast look around the office, trying to locate the source of the kitty litter odor. There was no cat box in sight, but I eventually spotted two enormous orange felines sleeping on top of the row of file cabinets against the far wall. Case closed.

"So, what're you here for?" Miss

Faparelli wanted to know. "Come to see Mr. Crawley?"

"Yes, but I don't have an appointment."

"That's okay, honey, 'cause he's gone for the day. Went to Coney Island to check out a new magic act."

"Oh," I said, frowning dejectedly.

"What's your name, anyway? Did you want to register with the agency?"

"Umm, yes, I guess so. My name's Brenda BaCall." I decided it was time for a new alias. Phoebe Starr was getting worn around the edges.

Miss Faparelli gave me a sullen, impatient look and shrugged her skinny shoulders. "Listen, Brenda, you can sit down and fill out the forms if you want to. Since you're here already. But that doesn't mean Apex'll take you on. You'll hafta come back for an interview with Mr. Crawley, and bring your portfolio with you."

Ah, the ubiquitous portfolio. Can any Manhattan maiden survive without one? "It's getting kind of late to start filling out forms," I said. "Maybe I'd better come back tomorrow."

"Suit yourself."

"Will Mr. Crawley be in tomorrow?"

"In and out."

"Should I make an appointment?"

"If you want to."

"What time would be good?"

"It's hard to say. You never know what that man will be up to."

She was as helpful as a military roadblock. I decided to back up and drive down a new street. "I really don't know what I'm doing here anyway. . . ." I said, sighing loudly. "I must be crazy! I mean, I'm not a dancer or a singer or an actress or anything."

"Oh?" She gave me another surly look. "You mean you don't wanna be the next Marilyn Monroe?"

I rolled my eyes and snickered. "Not a chance! I don't even want to be the next Harriet Nelson."

"So, what're you doin' comin' *here?*"

"I'm just looking for a job. Any old job."

"This is a theatrical agency, not an employment agency," she sniffed.

"Yes, I know, but . . . see, I met a man in a bar last night who told me all about Apex. And he said you have some important connections — that you have lots of good jobs for unskilled women like me. Women who can't type or take shorthand. He said you could maybe get me something in radio, or television. Something where I could make a lot of money but not have to use my brain too much."

The woman burst out laughing. "Yeah, right!" she crowed. "We got lotsa jobs like that."

"Really?" I said, widening my eyes in innocent expectation.

Miss Faparelli suddenly stopped laughing and turned serious. She put both elbows on the desk, propped her head in her hands, and gave me a peculiar, severe smile. "Sure thing, doll. You don't have to type, or take shorthand, or even file good. You just have to look pretty all the time. Think you could do that?"

"I could try."

"And you have to be nice to the fellas that hire you," she added. "Treat 'em real special."

"That's what the man in the bar told me. He thought I'd be a natural."

"Say, who *is* this guy anyway? What's his name?"

"Let me see, now. It's right on the tip of my tongue. Seems like it's Randy, or Landon, or . . . no, it's Brandon. That's it! Brandon Pomeroy."

"Oh, that bozo. . . ."

"You know him?"

"Yeah, I've seen him around."

"Does he work here?"

"Nah. He's just an acquaintance of Mr. Crawley's. Talks to him on the phone, and comes up to the office every once in a while."

"Is he a talent scout, or something like that?"

"Yeah, something like that." She gave me another peculiar smile, and another shrug of her skinny shoulders. Then she abruptly lowered her eyes and started flipping through her magazine again. One of the cats jumped down from the row of file cabinets behind her, sauntered lazily across the blue linoleum floor, and curled itself up in an orange lump on the brown plaid armchair near the window.

"Look, honey, it's almost closin' time," Miss Faparelli said, licking her index finger and turning another page. "Don'tcha wanna leave now and come back tomorrow? Or maybe the next day?" I was being dismissed.

"I guess that's the best thing to do," I answered. I was ready to go anyway. I tossed my cardigan over one shoulder and took a step toward the door. "Thanks for your help."

"Just doin' my job," she said, looking up from her magazine to make sure I was actually leaving. She watched my progress toward the door and then, just as I was about to go through it, she called out, "Hey, Brenda!"

"Yes?" I said, turning to see what she wanted.

"You better dress more feminine next time you come in." She eyed my slacks and loafers with obvious scorn. "Mr. Crawley likes for a girl to look like a girl."

I zipped back down to the Village as fast as the jam-packed IRT could take me, getting off at Sheridan Square. I hurried up the steps to Seventh Avenue and headed south, toward my apartment. But the closer I got to Bleecker Street, the slower my pace became. And when I reached the corner, I got cold feet and came to a dead stop. Though I was dying to go home, make it up with Abby, fix myself something to eat, watch *My Little Margie*, and go to bed, I was deathly afraid to walk down the block and enter my building. I was scared the syndicate goons across the street would see that I'd come home, and decide to throw me a surprise party. Or a wake.

Making a complete about-face, I retraced my steps to Sheridan Square, took a right turn on West 4th, and then another on Cornelia — which eventually led me to the private gated entrance to the courtyard behind my building. I unlocked the iron gate with the key I kept on my regular keychain, and slipped inside. I never used this entrance (or exit) unless I had to. There was no light in the narrow, dank passage between the buildings, and I was convinced the weedy backyard enclosure had become home to a family of rats.

Gritting my teeth and holding my breath, I dashed down the cracked cement path through the center of the courtyard and climbed the flight of rusty metal steps to the rusty metal landing outside both my and Abby's apartments. A light was on in Abby's kitchen, so I stepped up to her curtainless, glass-paned door and peeked inside.

Not one of my better ideas. My eyeballs were shocked out of their sockets by what they saw. Abby was standing naked as a newborn in the middle of the kitchen floor, with her long black hair hanging loose and her head thrown back, laughing like a lunatic and madly wiggling her bare bottom. This unbridled exhibition caused Abby's arms to jiggle wildly, which in turn caused (in the manner of a Rube Goldberg cartoon) the brisk agitation of the shaker of martinis she held firmly in both hands.

The well-built, well-tanned, towheaded young man sitting at the kitchen table — facing in both Abby's and my direction — was snapping his fingers in the air and grinning his gorgeous head off. His clothes had also been misplaced.

I would have jumped out of sight and ducked through my own kitchen door — leaving Abby and her playmate to their lusty private escapades — but it was too late. The naked young man had seen me.

"Hey!" he called out in surprise, pointing his finger at my gaping visage. "Somebody's out there!"

Abby stopped wiggling and jiggling, and spun around to face the door. When she saw me, her gleeful expression turned into a grimace. "What do *you* want?" she yelled through the closed door, continuing to shake the martinis, unashamed of her absolute nakedness.

I was a bit more disconcerted than she was. My entire body was blushing. "Sorry to bother you," I yelled back. "I just wanted to apologize for what happened this morning."

"But what the hell are you doing back here?" she asked, opening the door and sticking her head out. "Why didn't you come to the front?"

"It's a long story," I said, looking down at my feet. "See, I went to the social club today like you suggested, and I talked to this guy named Tommy, and I said some things I shouldn't have, and . . . oh, never mind! You're busy right now. I'll tell you about it some other time." I began slinking sideways toward my own apartment.

"Oh, no, you don't!" Abby shrieked, sticking her bare arm through the open door and grabbing hold of the sleeve of my cardigan. "Get your ass in here right now. I want to know what happened!"

"Okay," I said. "But you and your boyfriend put some clothes on first."

"God! You're such a prude!"

"Yes, but I'm a lovable one."

I stood by the open door while Abby set the martini shaker down on the kitchen counter, scurried over to the living room coat closet, yanked it open, and began scraping hangers around. She tossed an old trench coat to her boyfriend — who was still sitting at the kitchen table with all his manliness (and mindlessness) exposed — then she pulled out a short red leather car coat and put it on. The jacket barely covered her buttocks.

"Are you happy now?" she asked when she returned to the kitchen doorway.

"No, but I'm less likely to die of embarrassment." *Or envy,* I sadly admitted to myself.

"Then I guess it's safe to let you in." She seized my arm and pulled me inside. Then, after grabbing the martini shaker off the counter and three glasses out of the cupboard, she led me over to the table. "Paige, meet Dudley. Dudley, Paige."

"Hi!" the young man beamed, sitting up a little straighter, looking as simple and sunny as an open-faced cheese sandwich. Abby's trench coat was now tied around his torso like a towel.

"Hi, yourself," I said, pulling a chair out from the table and sitting down with a sigh. "Whose cigarettes are these? Can I have one?"

"Sure thing!" Dudley exclaimed, tapping a Hit Parade out of the pack and happily handing it to me. He flicked open a book of matches and gave me a light. If the fellow was feeling any discomfort due to his partial state of undress, he certainly didn't show it. He looked as snug as a bug in wall-to-wall carpeting.

"Who wants a martini?" Abby chirped. "They're shaken, not stirred." As if we could forget.

"I do!" cried Dudley. His face lit up like

an excited schoolboy's. I half expected him to raise his hand and start waving it at the teacher.

"Pass," I groaned. "Alcohol and I have had a parting of the ways."

Abby poured out the drinks for herself and Dudley, then took a seat at the table. "So you spoke to one of the guys across the street?" she asked, craning her neck in my direction. Her arched black eyebrows were quivering with curiosity. "What did you say? What did he say?"

"I told him I was looking for a killer, and he pretended he didn't know who it was. But that was when he thought I was looking for a mob killer."

"What? What do you mean?"

"I mean I really fucked up, Abby." (I don't often use six-letter words like that, but it was the only term I could think of that fit the way I felt.) I told Abby about everything that had happened with Tommy, detailing my stupid inquiry about the murder and the stupid way I'd indicated my suspicion of mob involvement. I also pointed out that I was now scared to death for my stupid life.

"Why the hell did you give him a fake name?" Abby said. "I *told* you they know who you are! They know your real name, and your real address, and they know you work for *Daring Detective*. The minute you introduced yourself as Phoebe Starr, Tommy knew that you were lying."

She wasn't making me feel any better. "So, what am I supposed to do now? Drop the story? Go hide out in New Jersey? I guess I don't have any choice. My life's not so great, but I'd like to hold on to it as long as possible."

"Oh, don't be such a sissy, Paige!" she sputtered. "I agree that you handled the whole thing badly — that you told Tommy much more than he needed to know — but that doesn't mean you're going to get killed for it. Those Mafia gorillas have better things to do than worry about one silly, flipped-out female who's trying to climb the shaky ladder of success at a cheap detective magazine. You're just a gnat to them. You can fly right in their face and they won't even notice."

"Yeah," Dudley said, as though he knew what we were talking about.

"I hope you're right," I mumbled, but my doubts were more than serious. They were downright grave. "Hey, do you have anything to eat?" I asked, trying to shake off my sense of impending doom. "I'm ravenous."

Eager to accommodate, Dudley skimmed his hand across the top of his dirty-blond brush cut and gazed at me like an ardent puppy. "We got some pizza left over."

Left over from what? I wondered. *A late afternoon breakfast in bed?* "Maybe I'll just have a soda pop."

"Nothing doing," Abby said. "A big investigative reporter like you has to keep up her strength." She got up from the table, sauntered into her adjoining studio, and padded barefoot across the canvas-covered floor. Lifting the pizza box from the paint-smudged table sitting next to her easel, she then waltzed back into the kitchen, put the carton down on the counter, removed the two remaining slices of pizza, and placed them on a plate. She took a bottle of Coca-Cola from the Frigidaire, pried off the cap, then returned to the table and put the pizza and pop down in front of me. "Boom chicky boom," she said, smiling. "Lick the plate clean."

I could tell from Abby's grin she wasn't mad at me anymore. I gave her a grateful nod and dug in. The pizza was cold but I didn't care. Just being back in Abby's good graces provided warmth enough.

"So what did you do after you ran away

from Tommy?" Abby wanted to know. "Did you talk to anybody else? Get any more scoops for your story?" She was literally begging for more information. And I was relishing the attention. For the first time ever, Abby was living vicariously through me. Until now, it had always been the other way around.

I told Abby and Dudley all about my talk with Doris Toomey at Schrafft's and my encounter with Miss Faparelli at Apex Theatrical. Dudley didn't understand a thing I was saying, but he was being attentive anyway. Abby was utterly entranced.

"That's atomic!" she exclaimed. "I'm *kvelling* all over the place! You found out the little boy's last name, and you've established — beyond the shadow of a reasonable doubt — that Little Lord Pomeroy's just a pimp in upper-crust clothing. You're a great detective, Paige! You're gonna solve this thing. I can feel it down deep in my bones."

Her enthusiasm was contagious. "You really think so?" I said, blushing from head to toe again.

"I'm on the square, you dig?" She narrowed her eyes and poured herself another martini. "Forget about *Daring Detective*, Paige. You should be working undercover for the NYPD."

I knew she was exaggerating, but her compliments went straight to my head. "Guess what I'm going to do next," I said, puffing out my cheeks and chest in pride.

"What?"

"I'm going to check out the Scotts and little Ricky in Brooklyn, of course. That goes without saying. But I'm also going to interview Zack Dexter Harrington."

"No kidding!" Abby said. "How come?"

"Because Babs went out with him once, remember? You typed it up in my notes."

"So what? It was just one lousy date."

"Zack Harrington is related to Brandon Pomeroy," I told her. "They're second or third cousins or something."

I watched Abby's face as the full meaning of what I'd just said hit her right between the eyes. "Oh, my God!" she cried, brows arched to the top of her forehead. "Why didn't you tell me that before? That's important!"

"I didn't know how important it was till I spoke to Miss Faparelli. That's when I finally got it into my thick head that Pomeroy might actually be involved. I still can hardly believe it."

"Who's Pomeroy?" Dudley asked, looking more confused by the minute.

"Never mind, daddy-o," Abby soothed.

"Mama will tell you all about it later." She patted his hand to quiet him, then quickly turned back to me. "How the hell're you gonna pin down Zack Harrington? He doesn't talk to anybody. Even Weasel Winchell can't get an interview with him."

"I've got a plan," I said, pausing . . . smiling . . . teasing . . . waiting for Abby to go crazy with curiosity.

I didn't have to wait long. "Well, what the hell is it?" she shrieked, actually grabbing a handful of her wild black hair and pulling it.

"I'm going to corner him on the dance floor at the Copacabana." I had just that minute come up with the idea.

Abby cocked her head and gave me a disapproving look. "Forget about it, babe. You can kiss that *focockta* plan good-bye."

"Why?"

"Because they won't let you in. Unescorted women aren't allowed."

"Oh," I said, dismayed by my naïve oversight, and mad as a hornet that I was born female. I stared down at the table, racking my brain to come up with an alternate plan.

"I can take you there," Dudley said simply.

Abby and I looked at each other and our

eyes popped wide as quarters. "Of course!" we cried in unison.

"Why didn't *I* think of that?" Abby sputtered.

"That's a swell idea, Dudley," I said, grinning with gratitude. "I really appreciate it."

"When do you want to go?" he asked.

"Gee, I don't know," I floundered, trying to gather my thoughts. "It'll take some time to work out the details. First, I've got to figure out a way to find out when Zack will actually *be* at the Copa — and then I have to try to get a reservation for the same night."

"I can take care of both those problems," Dudley said without a blink. "My father is the maitre d'."

Chapter 14

I left Abby's around ten and entered my own apartment — using the front door this time. But I didn't turn on any lights. I wanted it to look, from the outside, as if I still hadn't come home. I stood motionless in my dark kitchen for a few seconds — until my ears became attuned to the quiet and my eyes became adjusted to the gloom. Then I slunk across the floor and headed upstairs. Light from the street lamps and the full moon seeped through my open shades, making it easy for me to find my way to the bedroom.

I took off all my clothes, tossed them in the hamper, and pulled one of Bob's large, government-issued, U.S. Army tee shirts over my head. I sleep in one of Bob's old khaki tee shirts whenever I'm feeling really lonely, whenever I'm truly craving the warmth and solace of a man.

Which is pretty much every night.

But I was especially needy tonight, when visions of Abby and Dudley in a naked embrace next door made me crazy with envy, and thoughts of my own solitude and vulnerability made me wobbly with fear. As for the lovebirds next door, at least I wouldn't have to *listen to* their passionate tweets and whistles; our old building's thick plaster walls were virtually soundproof. But when it came to my own private terrors, I knew nothing could silence them but sleep. I threw myself into bed, curled myself up under the covers, and hugged my knees close to my chest, trying to bluff myself into believing that Bob was there with me, stroking my back, nuzzling my neck, making me feel safe.

That's when I heard it. A slight but sustained grating sound. Which was followed by a sudden snap. Then several faint, almost imperceptible clicks. Which, added all together, sounded exactly like a squeaky doorknob being turned and the front door to my apartment being opened and closed. A bolt of lightning struck my spine. Somebody had broken in! I was certain of it. Somebody was creeping around downstairs!

I sucked in my breath and hugged my knees tighter, praying for divine intervention, begging all the gods and goddesses of all the heavens to tell me what to do next. Should I grab a weapon and rush downstairs to confront the intruder head-on? What weapon should I grab? A pair of nail scissors? The bathroom plunger? Or should I hide in the bedroom closet and hope I'd never be discovered? The intruder probably didn't know I was upstairs, struck dumb in my bed like a deer caught in the headlights, so maybe I should just pull the covers over my head and hold my breath. Maybe if I stayed very, very still and very, very quiet . . .

A loud noise shocked me out of my frozen state. It sounded as if someone had stumbled over a kitchen chair and knocked it down to the floor. I heard some mumbled cursing in a scratchy male voice, and then a string of blatant footfalls as the intruder stomped around the living room and the kitchen, flipping wall switches and turning on table lamps, sending ominous shafts of light shooting up the staircase wall.

I had to make a move, and I knew it. I just didn't know what move to make. Trembling like the coward I was, I got out of bed and tiptoed into the hall, taking care not to step on the creakiest floorboards. Then I just stood there like an idiot, shivering in my timeworn tee shirt, shaking on my shoeless feet, wondering who the hell was in my apartment and why he was knocking over my furniture, and barking out obscenities, and opening and slamming my drawers, and crashing through my cabinets, and generally banging things around like a wild man.

But as much as I wanted to know who the cursing intruder was, I didn't want to meet him face-to-face. He seemed to be in a really bad mood. And for all I knew, he could be armed with a gun. Or a knife. Or a Hopalong Cassidy jump rope. And I, on the other hand, had no means of self-defense at all. I didn't even have on any underpants! To my way of thinking at the time, there was only one sensible course of action for me to take: run for my everloving life.

And the only way to run was up.

I spun on my heels and grabbed onto the handrails of the tiny wrought-iron ladder bolted to the wall outside the bathroom. Placing one bare foot on the first rung of the cold metal ladder, I hoisted myself up and frantically climbed the eight or nine feet to the utility hatch in the ceiling. The rusty latch skreaked when I twisted it, and the heavy trapdoor clanked when I jarred it open, but I didn't think the wild man downstairs had heard me. He was making too much noise of his own.

Mounting another rung of the ladder, I

pushed the hatch all the way open and poked my head through the hole in the ceiling. A blast of cold night air struck my face and I breathed in a snootful of soot. Fighting off a stupendous sneeze, I shoved my arms through the opening and planted my hands down on either side of the overhead passageway. Then I scaled one more step of the ladder and pulled the rest of my half-nude body all the way up to the roof.

The moon shone like a spotlight, making me entirely too visible. I didn't want to attract the attention of any members of the club across the street (or any peeping Tom inhabitants of the apartments across the way), so I quickly dropped down in a crouch to close the trapdoor. Then I crawled on my hands and knees through the grit and soot, across the rough, grimy tarpaper tiles, around a motley assortment of murky protuberances — chimneys, steam outlets, electrical boxes, TV antennas, and the like — until I reached the edge of the roof. A low brick ledge bordered the roof, and I quickly dropped behind it, lying down on my stomach to make sure I couldn't be seen. Then I propped myself up on my elbows, and raised my head just high enough for my bulging eyes to peer over the ledge and down onto the street and sidewalk in front of my building.

Things were pretty quiet down there. A few transients were still passing through the neighborhood — some marching toward the subway, others strolling the sidewalks and gazing into dim shop windows — but all of the local residents were, as far as I could tell, home safe and snug in their beds. Except for me, of course — and three hippos at the Italian social club, who sat smoking cigars and playing cards at a well-lit table near the entrance of their storefront den.

In a total panic, I pushed myself higher on my elbows and raked my eyes from one end of the block to the other, madly searching for someone to help me, for a brave and willing knight in shining armor — specifically Patrick O'Hara, the night policeman who frequently patrolled Bleecker on horseback. But Patrick was nowhere in sight. And neither was his horse, Peggy.

So I made like a statue and waited. I waited for my heart to stop bouncing around in my chest like a basketball. And for some air to return to my convulsing lungs. And for the foulmouthed creep in my apartment to stop turning the place upside down and get the hell out of there.

My scratched and bloody knees were throbbing, my naked rump was freezing, and my elbows — which were insecurely planted in a pile of fresh pigeon poop — were about to give way.

Finally, after what seemed like a decade but was probably just ten minutes, I saw a man emerge from my building. And it definitely wasn't Dudley. The creature was short and stocky, and the top of his large cranium was barely covered with slicked-back strands of straight brown hair. He was wearing a short-sleeved shirt which was unbuttoned down the front, and which flapped behind him in the breeze as he tore out into the middle of the street and then crossed to the other side.

From my perch on the roof, I couldn't see the man's face. But that didn't cause me any serious identification problems. His bulging stomach and dirty white undershirt were recognizable enough. And when the beast made his way straight for the Bleecker Street Mafia Lodge and ducked inside, I knew for sure it was Tommy. Gooey-eyed, nail-biting Tommy. Lady-killer Tommy. Like-the-gun Tommy.

My apartment looked as if it had been raided by a pack of psychotic chimpanzees.

233

Tommy had left all the lights on, so I was able to appreciate the full magnitude of the devastation. The box of books and office supplies in the spare bedroom had been upended — its contents flung all over the room — and every single health and beauty preparation in my medicine cabinet had been swept out onto the bathroom floor. An ugly pink lake had formed beneath the shattered Pepto-Bismol bottle, and my hairbrush and box of bobby pins were buried in an avalanche of Perfect Lady bath powder.

All of the clothes and shoes in my closet had been yanked out and thrown — hangers included — into all four corners of the bedroom, and every drawer in my dresser had been pulled from its slot and emptied onto the bed. The drawers themselves had been tossed, like firewood, into a heap in the middle of the floor. Some of them were splintered and broken. Also broken was the glass in the framed photo I always kept on my bedside table — a wonderful, laughing picture of Bob taken right before he went into the army — and I cried like a baby when I found it smashed under the bed.

The scene downstairs was even worse. My kitchen was in ruins. Everything on the

Formica table had been shoved off onto the floor, all the chairs were overturned, all the dishes were displaced or demolished, and the entire contents of my refrigerator (which, admittedly, hadn't been very appetizing to begin with) were now an oozing mound of sludge on the floor. The mayonnaise and mustard containers weren't broken, but the pickle jar was. And the bottle of milk. Likewise most of the eggs.

The shelves in my living room had been relieved of their books and record albums (all of which were now sprawled in a chaotic jumble near the overturned rubber plant in the corner), and my precious TV set (the nearly burnt-out Sylvania I was still paying six bucks a month for) had been knocked onto its side like a bulldozed tree stump. The floor lamp was lying, appropriately, on the floor, and one end of the couch was sticking out into the middle of the room. (Well, it's not exactly a couch. It's more like an old wooden door, painted black, with nailed-on legs in each corner, a madras-covered mattress on top, and several old orange throw pillows masquerading as back cushions. I made it, in case you haven't already guessed, myself.)

Since all the lights were still on, and the shades still open, I surveyed the wreckage of my life from various kneeling and squatting positions at the outermost edge of each room. I stayed as far away from the windows as possible. I didn't, for obvious reasons, want Tommy — or any of the other hooligans across the street — to know I was home. I toyed with the idea of calling the police, but quickly decided against it. Not only was I deathly afraid of further Mafia retaliation, but I didn't want Dan Street to get wind of what had happened. I was scared of the criminals *and* the cops.

I thought of waking up Abby and Dudley and giving them a tour of the disaster area, enlisting their aid and company for the rest of the night, but I didn't see any point to that either. Abby would feel very guilty about having instigated my meeting with Tommy, and — rather than my getting the sympathy and soothing support I needed so badly at that moment — I might end up having to comfort her instead. I didn't have the energy for that. I didn't have the energy for anything.

All I wanted to do was sneak back upstairs and get back into bed. I didn't care that all the lights were still on. I *wanted* them to be on. The dark held no appeal for me at all. I didn't care that I would have to crawl across a wide patch of linoleum that was flooded with curdled milk, dill pickle juice, and broken glass. What the hell difference would *that* make? I was already wet and smelly — and my knees were already bleeding.

Numb and groggy, I eased myself back onto all fours and began creeping, like a wounded animal, back through the kitchen toward the staircase. I was scooching through the milk and pickles — not thinking, or feeling, or caring about a blessed thing — when I glanced through the legs of the kitchen table and caught sight of my typewriter. It was lying upside down on the floor under the table, next to the overturned table lamp and a pile of ripped and crumpled papers.

My senses suddenly returned full force, and I flew into urgent action. I dove headfirst under the table, pulled myself up on my knees, squatted back on my haunches, and anxiously turned the baby blue portable right side up, checking for damage. If it was broken, I didn't know what I'd do. I certainly couldn't afford to buy a new one.

Luckily, there were no major impairments, just one slightly bent key — the Q — which I managed to straighten with my hands. I figured I'd still be able to use the machine to write my story — which, despite (or maybe because of) all the related mayhem and destruction, I was more determined than ever to produce.

With a heavy sigh of relief, I gingerly pushed the typewriter out from under the table. Then I scooped together the crumpled papers and shoved them out too. After inching my way back to the middle of the room, I stood up just long enough to pick up the typewriter and put it back on the table, out of range of the slowly encroaching river of milk and brine. Then I dropped into a crouch over the pile of wrinkled papers, spread them out on a dry section of the floor, smoothed them out as best I could, and — head spinning like a cyclone — searched through them frantically.

I could have saved myself the trouble. My seven-page list of Comstock clues was gone. So was the snapshot of Babs and Ricky.

With a groan of shock and weariness, I returned to my numb mental state. I blindly crossed through the stream of milk and broken glass, and slowly crawled up the stairs. After guiding my bloody knees into the bedroom, I maneuvered my way around the piles of clothes, shoes, and empty dresser drawers. Then I burrowed my body under the heap of sweaters, socks, and underclothes on the bed, and — turning my face away from the brutal glare of the bare lightbulb in the ceiling — plunged into a deep black sleep.

Chapter 15

Babs woke me up at seven the next morning. She walked right into my dream, sat down on the edge of my bed, and brushed her fingers down my cheek the way my mother used to do. Her blonde pageboy was gleaming, and her upper teeth were sparkling like a strand of pearls. "Hurry up, dear," she said, in a voice so soft and sweet it seemed to be melting in her mouth. "You're going to be late for school."

Poof. My eyes popped open and Babs was gone. In her place was a whopping tangle of slips, cinch belts, and stockings. Under my head was the balled-up sleeve of my red mohair sweater. In the ceiling was a blazing lightbulb, which beamed straight into my brain, forcing me to remember everything that had happened the night before. I whimpered and turned over on my side — thereby unsettling the mountain of underwear on top of me and causing my black lace merry widow to roll down the mountain and flop over my face.

I would have left it there to shade my eyes while I went back to sleep, but Babs's words still echoed in my head: "You're going to be late for school." She was right, I moaned to myself. If I didn't get up out of that bed, and get myself to class (i.e., the office) on time, and get back to work on the Comstock story, I'd never make a good grade on my report, and I'd never graduate from office slave to staff writer.

I pushed myself up on my pigeon-poop-smeared elbows, pulled my blood-and-soot-streaked legs out from under the underwear mountain, and — ignoring the hideous piles of rubble in my bedroom and the tight knot of pain in my head — stood up and limped to the bathroom. Being careful not to walk on the broken Pepto-Bismol bottle, or through the snowdrift of Perfect Lady bath powder, I stepped into the tub and took the hottest shower I could stand.

Twenty-five minutes later, I was reasonably clean, hastily made up, fully dressed in my spectator pumps and lavender shirtwaist (which I'd found on top of one of the piles of clothes in the bedroom), and ready to face the murder — I mean music.

I hurried down the stairs and grabbed a jacket from the clutter of coats on the closet floor. I tried not to look at the smashed eggs and broken dishes. I turned my head away from the overturned TV set and uprooted houseplant. I simply couldn't deal with the destruction now. I'd have to confront it later when I felt stronger, when I wasn't late for work, when I had my sanity back. God knew when that would be.

As I was dashing out the door, I ran smack into Abby and Dudley, who were enjoying a hot good-bye kiss in the hall.

"Oof!" I said, plowing into their clinched torsos and knocking their lips apart. I was glad to see they both had some clothes on.

"Hey!" Dudley yelped. His mouth was chalky from Abby's white lipstick.

"What's the hurry, Murray?" Abby drawled. She looked as slinky and happy as a cream-fed cat.

I wasn't in the mood for chitchat. "Sorry!" I croaked, trying to squeeze my way past them to the stairs. "Can't talk now. I'm late for work."

"Wait a minute!" Abby cried, breaking away from Dudley's embrace and grabbing me by the arm. "We've got news!"

I stopped in my tracks and groaned out loud. My aching head wasn't ready for any new input. "Let me guess," I said. "You two have decided to tie the knot and you want me to be your old maid of honor."

Abby giggled. "No way, Doris Day! This is much cooler than that. You're going dancing at the Copa tomorrow night. Dudley arranged everything with his dad."

"Really?" I said, head snapping in Dudley's direction. "You spoke to your father already?"

"Yep!" He looked proud and goofy — like Li'l Abner after a mud puddle run-in with the amorous Moonbeam McSwine.

"And Harrington's *definitely* going to be there?" I asked him.

"That's what Dudley's daddy-o says," Abby broke in. "He says Zack dines there every Friday night, and always with a different blonde. He likes to go on Friday because that's playboy night, when all the big shots bring their girlfriends. On Saturday they take their wives, and Zack the skirt-chasing bachelor boy gets pretty damned bored with that. Hates having to be polite. At least that's what he told Dudley's old man."

"So tomorrow night it is!" I said, getting excited in spite of myself (and my growing fears for my own physical safety). I looked at Abby and smiled. "Do you have a fancy dress I can wear?"

"Does a flamingo have feathers?"

I laughed and turned to Dudley. "So

243

what time do we meet, and where?"

"About ten o'clock here at my place," Abby answered.

"Pop says we shouldn't get there before eleven," Dudley added. "Gotta wait till the swells are all through eating."

"You mean we won't be having dinner?" I said. I had set my heart on shrimp cocktail, asparagus vinaigrette, a juicy filet mignon, a baked potato piled high with sour cream and chives, and a blazing platter of crêpes suzette. And champagne. Lots of champagne. *No, better stick to ice water.*

"No food unless *you* want to pay for it," Abby said with a dramatic huff. "Dudley's saving all his money for *our* next night on the town. We're dining at Louis's."

I laughed. Louis's was a basement bar off Sheridan Square where you could get the house special — spaghetti and meat-balls with a tomato and lettuce salad — for sixty-five cents.

"Pop's not giving us a table," Dudley explained. "He's just going to sneak us in and put us at the bar. That way it won't cost us anything, except for drinks and tips."

"Good plan," I said, bidding my fanciful feast good-bye. Too bad Dudley's daddy wasn't named Warbucks. "So I'll see you here tomorrow night at ten, right?"

"Check."

"Do you have a good suit?"

"Sure. I got it at Ripley's."

"Then we're all set." I gave him a mock salute and began sidling my way down the stairs. "I've got to run now, kids. I'm really, really late. Thanks so much for everything. Especially you, Dudley. You deserve a gold star for this."

"I'll stick one on his ass," Abby chortled.

By some miracle I managed to get to the office before Mr. Crockett showed up. I cleaned out the Coffeemaster and cups, started a new pot brewing, sorted the mail, and then went through every drawer in my desk, trying to determine if Pomeroy had rifled through my stuff again while I was out. As far as I could tell, everything was in its proper place, including the envelope holding the clipping and picture of Babs, which I'd purposely left to make its presence seem superfluous.

There was a lot of new stuff on top of my desk, though: a batch of newspapers that had to be clipped, a pile of galleys that needed proofreading, a bunch of photos that needed filing, several new stories for me to edit, and a stack of invoices that had to be processed. After looking up Babs's old friends, the Scotts, in the phone directory and writing down their address, I tackled my work with extreme urgency, hoping to finish it all up before five. I wanted to get out to Brooklyn as early as I possibly could — preferably before Freddy Scott got home.

And I might have accomplished this goal if it hadn't been such a screwy day. If Mr. Crockett hadn't come in with a splitting headache and proceeded to bellow at me all morning, demanding coffee, and more coffee, and cold water and aspirins, and a cool compress for his eyes. If Mike and Mario hadn't decided to make up for lost time by needling me with a whole extra day's worth of sneers, jeers, and terrible jokes about my name and gender. If Lenny hadn't picked that day, of all days, to finally open up to me a little bit, to tell me why he was so afraid to ride the elevator (his uncle had been stuck in one for nine hours — with an overweight bookkeeper from his office who went out of her mind with terror and lost all bladder control).

Even though I didn't go out for lunch (Lenny gave me half of his salami sandwich, which I ate while filing the photos), and Little Lord Pomeroy didn't get to the office till two (so drunk and distracted he hardly spoke to me all afternoon), I still had a hard time getting the work done. So when five o'clock finally rolled around, and all my overpaid, underworked colleagues packed up and left for the day, I was still sitting at my desk, madly proofreading galleys.

I was so focused on what I was doing that I didn't react when the office entrance bell rang. It took a few seconds for the sound to register — for me to grasp the fact that someone had opened the door and stepped inside. But when the signal finally did get through, and I finally did look up to see who was there, I almost jumped right out of my skin. It was the world's most photogenic photographer, Scotty Whitcomb — and he was standing right in front of my desk, clenching his fabulous jaw and studying me as if I were the soon-to-be-naked highlight of his next naughty pinup calendar.

"Hi, doll," he said, with the barest trace of a smile. "Remember me?"

"Of course." My pulse was pounding like a tom-tom. What was the man doing here? Why had he come? Did it have something to do with Babs? As far as I knew — in all the time I'd been working at *Daring Detective* Scotty Whitcomb had never come up to the office. Whatever business he'd done with Brandon Pomeroy had been conducted by phone or mail or at Pomeroy's favorite bar. "It's nice to see you again, Mr. Whitcomb," I said. "What can I do for you?"

"You can start by calling me Scotty." He combed his fingers through his sand-colored hair and gave me a wink with one turquoise eye. Was it my imagination, or was the world's most physically attractive (but morally repugnant) cheesecake photographer flirting with me?

"Okay, Scotty," I said, casting my eyes downward, acting slightly bashful, stalling for time. I didn't know how to play this one at all. What was Whitcomb doing here? And how could I glean the most information from his surprise visit? Should I try to back him off, or lead him on? Cool him down, or warm him up? Unable to determine my own best plan of action, I decided to sit back and let *him* carry the ball.

He picked it up and ran with it. "I've got some more headshots for your boss," he said, swaggering back and forth in front of my desk, looking very cool in his crisp white shirt, tan trousers, and brown leather jacket. "I was going to be in the neighborhood, so I figured I'd drop them off and save myself the postage. And besides," he added, abruptly ending his splendid stroll and leaning over the top of my desk, "I've been thinking about you since the day you came to my studio. I was very attracted to you, and I wanted to see you again." He cupped his hand under my chin, and tilted my face up till my eyes met his.

I looked deep into his icy blue-green irises and knew he was lying. Scotty Whitcomb was no more attracted to me than he would've been to Arthur Godfrey in a Hawaiian-print prom dress. But as certain as I was that he was putting on a big act (it takes one to know one), I didn't have a clue what his true motivations were. So I decided to dance along and try to find out.

I batted my lashes and did my best Mae West. "I thought you had more girls than you can handle," I teased, punctuating my words with an arched eyebrow and a sultry smile.

"There's always room for one more."

"Yes, but when the bus is too crowded, I won't get on."

He gave me a cocky smirk and sat down in the chair near my desk. "Does that mean you won't have dinner at the Carnegie Deli with me tonight?"

"Love to, but I'm already booked." I hated to pass up the chance to pump Scotty about Babs over a heaping plate of pastrami and cole slaw — but I was dying to get out to Brooklyn, to see what Freddy, Betty, and Ricky were up to.

"So you've got a hot date," Scotty scoffed. "Is he as handsome as me?"

"She looks like Mort Sahl."

He laughed. It was the kind of laugh where only the voice and mouth are engaged. The spirit is dead or missing. "So call off your plans and come out with me instead."

"Sorry, Scotty. No can do. If I cancel dinner with Aunt Esther again, she'll cut me out of her will."

"Then how about Saturday night?" he stonily persisted.

I didn't say anything. Suddenly, I was as wary of spending the evening with Scotty Whitcomb as I was eager to poke around in his and Babs's shared past.

"We'll go to the San Remo," he said, naming a popular nightspot down in the Village. "It's near where you live, so you can take me back to your place for a nightcap."

I broke out in head-to-toe goose bumps. How did Scotty know where I lived? He must have looked me up in the phone book. Why, oh why, had I given him my real name? I was surprised he even remembered it. And why had he wanted to track me down anyway? Was he really looking for a date? (I didn't believe *that* for a second.) Or was he just hoping I would help him land a *DD* photo assignment? Or maybe he was checking me out for some other reason. Some hidden, homicidal reason.

"So how's everything going, toots?" he went on. "Still working on the Wanda Wingate story?"

Now we're getting somewhere. "Yes, but it's still a deep dark secret. Strictly confidential. You didn't mention it to anyone, did you?"

"Nope."

"I hope you didn't say anything to Mr. Pomeroy!"

"Not a word, doll."

"Good, because if he knew I told you — or *anybody* — the magazine was planning to run this story, he'd can me for sure."

"Do you know who did it yet?"

"Did what?"

"The murder. Do you know who killed Wanda?"

"No, but I've got a few ideas."

"Yeah? Like what?"

"Like I don't want to talk about it." For the dangling carrot trick to work, you've got to keep the root vegetable out of reach.

"Come on, doll. You can tell me. I won't say anything to anybody. I'm just a concerned mourner. I cared about Wanda a lot."

You coulda fooled me, Romeo.

"She was a very close friend."

And your mother was Bridey Murphy.

"Do the cops have any good leads?"

"If they do, they aren't sharing them with me."

Scotty suddenly bounded to his feet and began pacing around in front of my desk again, treating me to another thrilling exhibition of his exceptional physique. Did he stage such a provocative side show for *all* the girls? Had Wanda/Babs been dazzled by his manly mobile charms?

"Say, why are you acting so upset?" I asked him. "You didn't seem so bent out of shape the last time I talked to you."

Scotty stopped dead in his tracks and gave me a sulky rendition of his Starlight Studios smile. "When you first told me about Wanda's death I was in shock," he said. "It took a while for the news, and the pain, to sink in."

"But you said you only met her a few times. That doesn't sound like a very close friendship to me."

"I tried to underplay the relationship. I didn't want you to get the wrong idea."

"And what wrong idea would that be?"

"That Wanda and I were romantically involved. Because we weren't, you know. We were just pals. And I didn't want you to think any different."

"But why did you care what I thought?" *Unless you were afraid my thoughts would lead me to the murderer.*

Scotty leaned over my desk again, bringing his face so close to mine I could see the poorly shaved hairs in the cleft of his gorgeous chin. "Are you hard of hearing or something?" he said, fixing my eyes in his frosty turquoise gaze. "Like I told you before, I was very attracted to you. And I still am, doll." He stood up straight and adjusted his crisp shirt collar. "So we're on for Saturday night, right?"

"I'm looking forward to it."

"I'll pick you up at your place."

"No!" I sounded way too apprehensive, but I *really* didn't want Scotty coming to my apartment. "I've got a lot of things to do Saturday, so I won't be home. I'll meet you at the Remo."

"Suit yourself, doll. Eight o'clock?"

"Fine."

Scotty took several steps back, and then — without leaving a message, or a package of photos, or even a single headshot for Brandon Pomeroy — he turned and strutted smugly toward the door. As he jangled the office doorbell and made his curt, cold-blooded exit, I sat shivering with dread at my desk, wondering if I was behaving like a brave and dedicated crime writer, or just a suicidal fool.

Chapter 16

Bob and I had lived in Brooklyn once. Shortly after he was drafted, and immediately following our secret elopement (our folks back home in Kansas City were opposed to our getting married *before* he went to war), we bought two one-way bus tickets and hightailed it to New York. Our plan was simple: we would pool all our savings, rent a cheap furnished apartment, and devote the month of civilian life Bob had left to making love. Then — when our extended honeymoon was over and Bob had to leave for boot camp — I would stay in New York and look for a job in publishing (which was exactly what I'd always wanted to do anyway). And then eventually — when the war was over and Bob came home — he'd get a good job in Manhattan and we'd find a better place to live.

It was a reasonable plan, and the first part of it was easily and ecstatically accomplished. We found a two-room flat on Ocean Parkway in Brooklyn, stocked the tiny kitchen with a month's supply of canned soup and saltines, hung our clothes up in the small musty closet, tuned the static-prone old Philco radio to the local jazz station, and hopped into bed between our brand-new JCPenney sheets. And in bed we stayed — declaring our undying love, consummating and reconsummating our marriage vows, soaking up each other's heat and scent — until the day Bob was transferred.

It was the fifteenth of March, 1951. Beware the ides. First the army transferred my husband from our warm bed in Brooklyn to a hard, narrow cot at Fort Benning in Georgia. And six weeks later a cramped U.S. troop plane transferred him to the fighting fields of Korea. And seven months after that three bullets to his chest from a Russian-made machine gun transferred him off the earth altogether.

So much for our reasonable plan. There's nothing reasonable about war, and when the world has lost its reason, a plan is as good as a dead battery.

But I'm getting behind myself. I didn't mean to bend your ear with the history of my short but oh-so-sweet marriage to Bob. I just wanted to point out that, having lived in Brooklyn for a while — one month with Bob, eight and a half months on my own — I knew which subway to take out from the city. And I knew which exit would let me off closest to the address of Mr. and Mrs. Fred Scott.

After a fairly swift trip (I caught an express), I climbed out of the dimly lit subway tunnel into the cool darkness aboveground. In the glow of the countless street lamps, I could see that little had changed. The Brooklyn of the present still imitated the Brooklyn of my recent past. Pulling on my gloves, smoothing out my skirt, and choking back my memories, I walked quickly down the busy sidewalk, past the familiar restaurants, delicatessens, launderettes, banks, and clothing shops of Kings Highway, toward the brick apartment buildings and tree-lined curbs of Ocean Avenue.

The building the Scotts lived in was six stories high, and their apartment was on the fifth floor. Fortunately, there was an elevator. I stepped inside, punched the proper button, and rose out of the painful past into the fearful future.

The woman who answered the door to 5C was very pretty. She had a full mouth, even teeth, high cheekbones, and large, wide-set eyes the color of chestnuts. She wore a ruffled white apron over her deep green sateen dress, and her bottle-blonde hair was tied away from her face with a black velvet ribbon. I figured she was in her early twenties.

"Yes?" she said, holding the door just halfway open. She looked nervous and upset, as if expecting a messenger bearing bad news.

"Mrs. Scott?" I asked, smiling so hard I thought my cheeks would crack. "Mrs. Betty Scott?"

"Yes, that's right." Her expression remained anxious and grim. "Who are you? What do you want?" I could hear the TV playing in the background. *The Lone Ranger* was on.

"My name is Phoebe Starr," I said. "I was a very close friend of Babs Comstock's."

Her pretty face recoiled. "What? A friend of Barbara's?" Betty took a big step back from the door. "But why did you come here? What do you want from us?" She seemed on the verge of panic.

"I've been extremely upset about Babs's death," I told her, smiling sadly. "She was gone so suddenly and so violently! And I miss her so much. So I've been looking up some of her other good friends — sitting down with them for a while, sharing memories and talking to them about what happened. It seems to help somehow."

"But how did you find out about us?"

Odd question, I thought. "Well, Babs spoke about you often, of course. And then, when I was talking to Doris Toomey — a waitress over at Schrafft's where Babs used to work — she said you came into the restaurant once and —"

"Hey, Betty!" came a surly male voice from inside the apartment. "What the hell's goin' on out there? Who're you talkin' to?"

Betty wasn't on the verge of panic anymore. She was right in the middle of it. "It's a woman, Freddy," she whimpered. "A friend of Barbara's." She moved further back from the door, swiveled her head to one side, and started wringing her hands in the ruffles of her apron. "What should I do?"

"What does she want?" Freddy bellowed.

"She says she just wants to talk to us."

"Tell her I'm busy."

"I won't take up too much of your time, Mr. Scott," I hurriedly called out, stepping through the door before Betty had a chance to close it in my face. "Can you spare just a couple of minutes, please?" I stuck my head beyond the open door and snaked my neck around it, taking quick stock of the sparsely furnished living room, and seeking out the source of the rude masculine noise.

Freddy was slouched low in a blue Danish-modern club chair, with his knees spread wide in front of him and his head resting against the back of the chair. He was a big, clean-shaven man, with a crooked (broken?) nose, curly brown hair, and a neck the size of a beer barrel. He was wearing gray suit pants and a white shirt. No belt, no tie. His shirt collar was unbuttoned and his cuffs were rolled up over his brawny forearms. He sat facing the TV set, but he wasn't watching the show; his eyes were closed.

The little boy sitting cross-legged on the floor in front of the TV, however, was wide-eyed and enthralled. His elbows were planted on his knees, his head was cupped in both hands, and his neck was stretched out to the limit, craning his small, angelic face so close to the screen it was bathed in a ghostly blue light. In his fringed red cowboy shirt and little felt cowboy hat (white, not black like Hoppy's), he looked like a western windup doll.

"I hate to burst in on you like this, Mr.

Scott," I said, squeezing my way past Betty and marching straight into the living room, "but I really do need to talk to you."

The boy turned and glanced at me for a second, then reverted his rapt attention to the Lone Ranger and Tonto. Freddy opened his eyes and glared up at me, but he continued slouching — insolently — in his chair. He didn't nod, smile, frown, uncurl his fingers, or even draw his far-flung knees together. He just lounged there, languidly, like an enormous lizard in the sun, looking me over from head to toe and breathing heavily through his large crooked nose.

Finally he spoke. "You've got a lot of nerve, sister," he said with an arrogant smirk. "What if I don't want to talk to you?"

I suddenly felt faint. Freddy's manner was so contemptuous — and so menacing — I had the feeling I was standing in the presence of pure evil. Actually losing my senses for a split second, I didn't reply to his question. My tongue was in traction.

"Who the hell are you, anyway?" Freddy demanded, abruptly sitting up straight and sticking out his sturdy, malevolent chin. "What gives you the right to invade my privacy this way?"

Struggling to retrieve my composure, I finally loosened my tongue and started flailing it around. "My name's Phoebe Starr," I sputtered. "Babs Comstock was my best friend in the world. I really didn't mean to invade your privacy, Mr. Scott, but I'm so tormented by Babs's murder I'm going crazy. I can't sleep at night, and I can't stop thinking about the horrible way she died."

"Are your sleeping habits supposed to matter to me?"

"Well, no . . . of course not. But I thought you might care about Babs's death — that it might be upsetting you as much as it is me."

"Think again," he said, allowing his cruel mouth to curl into another ugly smirk. "Babs was no great friend of mine. Or my wife's."

I looked over my shoulder at Betty — to try to judge from her face if what Freddy said was true — but she had shrunk so far back into the shadowy entranceway I couldn't see her features.

"I'm very surprised to hear that," I said, turning back to Freddy, deciding (unwisely, as it turned out) to challenge his authority. I squared my shoulders for a verbal showdown. "Babs told me you all grew up together in Springfield, Missouri — that you were as close as three old friends could be."

"Yeah? Well, Babs was a liar and a tramp. We weren't old friends and we sure as hell weren't close." His mean wide face was growing red around the edges.

I disregarded the signs of his mounting annoyance and forged ahead. "But I know for a fact that she was crazy about your son. She was always talking about how cute and smart he is, and how much she loved him. She bought him a lot of toys, too."

"Didya hear that, Ricky?" Freddy barked to the boy still sitting cross-legged and entranced on the floor. "This nosy dame says Aunt Barbara gave you lotsa toys. Whaddaya have to say about that?"

"Huh?" Ricky replied. He turned his head a notch, but his eyes never left the TV screen.

"How could Babs be Ricky's aunt?" I blurted.

Freddy ignored my question and focused his angry gaze on his son. "Don't 'huh' me!" he exploded, voice boiling over with rage. "Answer me right now, you little runt! Did Aunt Barbara give you a whole bunch of toys, or just a few?"

Ricky's tiny shoulders slumped over in swift surrender, and he stared down at the floor. "Just a few."

"And were they really good toys? Did you like 'em better than the stuff I got for you?"

"No, sir."

"See?" Freddy said, grinning up at me in triumph.

I knelt down at the little boy's side, put my hand on one slumped shoulder, and tried to sneak in one more question. "Did your aunt Barbara ever give you a jump rope, Ricky?"

That's when Freddy bolted. He sprang up from his chair and lunged for the boy like a rabid rattlesnake (if ever a rattler gets rabies). "That's enough TV for tonight," he hissed, poking the kid hard in the back. "Turn it off and go to your room."

Ricky didn't utter a word of protest. All he said was, "Yes, sir." Then he leaned forward, switched off his beloved TV program, rose to his feet, and — holster set swaying lopsidedly on his narrow little hips — walked quietly down the hall to the rear of the apartment (where, I assumed, the bedrooms were located). How old was little Ricky Scott, I wondered. Six? Seven? Hard to tell, since he was acting like he was eighty.

As soon as the boy was gone, Freddy pitched his hulking frame toward me, grabbed me by the arm, and yanked me to my feet. "That's enough for you, too, sister," he said, exerting painful pressure on my elbow and forcibly escorting me back to the front door.

Betty stood by the door like a trained dog. She looked as fretful as a *Beat the Clock* contestant with just three seconds left to balance a stack of paint-filled soup bowls on her head. Face flaming with embarrassment, or fear, she aimed her eyes up at the ceiling and didn't say a word.

Freddy, on the other hand, had one last comment to make. "If you're ever in the neighborhood again," he grunted, giving my elbow an extra-hard twist, "*don't* drop in." Then he shoved me — stunned and speechless — out into the hall and slammed the door.

Chapter 17

By the time I got back to the Village, I'd almost convinced myself Freddy was the killer. He was certainly strong enough to strangle somebody (my aching elbow could testify to that), and as the father of an aspiring young cowboy, he could have had easy access to a Hopalong Cassidy jump rope (whether Babs had bought it or not). I didn't have a clue what Freddy's motive might have been, but any (actually all) of the usual homicidal objectives seemed possible.

He could have been in love — or sexually obsessed — with Babs, and jealous of her other boyfriends (he had, after all, called her a "tramp"). Maybe they'd been having an affair and she'd threatened to leave him. Could be he owed her a bunch of money and didn't want to pay it back. Or maybe Babs wasn't as innocent a victim as I believed she was. Maybe she and Freddy had been working some kind of scam together and he didn't want to split up the booty. Or perhaps she had been blackmailing him over something scandalous or criminal that happened in the past.

See what I mean? The murderous possibilities were endless. And after meeting the man face-to-face, I felt Freddy's murderous capabilities were endless too. I couldn't wait to get home and tell Abby about my new discoveries and suspicions.

Hurrying down Bleecker (and sprinting as fast as I could past the Italian social club), I dashed up the front stairwell of our building, screeched to a stop at the top, and started banging on Abby's door. Not only was I dying to talk to Abby, but I was eager to avoid the hideous upheaval (and the sour milk and pickle juice smell) in my own apartment. And I was in desperate need of a martini, or a whiskey sour, or whatever kind of cocktail Abby might be shaking up that evening.

But to my great disappointment, she didn't answer the door. I knocked and banged a few more times, still nobody came. I put my ear to the jamb, but heard nothing inside. Either Abby wasn't home, or she was upstairs with Dudley (or a brand-new loverboy) and didn't want to be disturbed.

With a heart as heavy as an unabridged dictionary, I turned toward my own apartment and started fishing around in my purse for the key. Not finding it immediately, I heaved a huge, self-pitying sigh, and leaned one shoulder against the door to continue my search.

When the latch clicked open and the door swung wide, I almost fell to the floor inside my dark apartment. I almost had a heart attack, too. Why in God's name was the door unlocked? Had somebody broken in again? Had Freddy known who I really was, and where I lived, and somehow managed to beat me back to my apartment? Was Tommy, or Scotty, or Brandon Pomeroy lurking like a demon in the shadows, flexing his fiendish fingers, itching to strip the clothes off my back and twist my neck into the shape of a corkscrew?

Gasping in distress (okay, *total panic*), I stumbled over to the kitchen table and turned on the lamp. *Hey, wait a minute! What's this lamp doing back on the table? When I left this morning it was on the floor.* With the taste of terror on my tongue, I jerked myself up straight and spun around to look behind me. There was nobody there. Both the living room and the kitchen were completely vacant.

And completely clean, I realized in shock. The couch was snug against the wall, the TV set was upright, the rubber plant was back in its pot, and all my books and record albums were stacked neatly on the shelves. The coats were back on their hangers in the closet. There were no broken glasses or dishes on the kitchen counter, and no cracked milk bottle or shattered pickle jar on the floor. The river of milk and pickle juice had disappeared; the only smell in the air was Bon Ami.

I was about to dash up to my bedroom to see if the same miracle had taken place upstairs, when I saw that my typewriter, which had been repositioned in the very center of the kitchen table, had a slightly crumpled sheet of white paper sticking out of the roller. And the paper had some words typed on it: *You ran off in such a flap this morning, you left your door wide open . . . so Dudley and I saw the shape your place was in. What the holy hell went on here last night? Did you throw a wild party for a bunch of lunatics and forget to invite us? We took the liberty of cleaning up a bit . . . hope you don't mind. Love, Mom.*

I giggled out loud and collapsed in a heap on one of the kitchen chairs. I threw my head back, stuck my legs out, and let my arms dangle down by my sides. Then I sucked in a much-needed chestful of air and started laughing. And I wasn't just chuckling, or chortling, or anything subtle like that. I was practically screaming with giddiness and relief. It was a really weird kind of laughter — the kind that comes from wracked nerves instead of a jostled funny bone — and once I started, I couldn't stop. I laughed so hard I thought my ribs would splinter. I laughed until my shoulders hurt and my eyes rolled back in my head.

I might still be laughing now if the phone hadn't started ringing.

With a sharp intake of breath, I snapped out of my fit and sat up straight in my chair. Who could it be? Should I answer it? Did I want to let anybody know I was home? After two and a half more rings, my curiosity crushed my concern. I darted over to the end table in the living room, sat down on my couch/door/daybed, and picked up the receiver.

"Hello?" I was trying to talk tough like Humphrey Bogart, but I sounded more like a baby chipmunk.

"Paige?"

"Yes. . . ."

"It's Dan. Dan Street."

"Oh, hi!" I said, first gushing with relief, then quickly turning crazy again. Why was he calling me? Had he found out I was still working on the Comstock story?

"Sorry to bother you at home," Dan said, voice dark and rich as chocolate, "but I didn't want to talk to you at the office."

"Oh . . . ? Why not?"

"Didn't want to get you in trouble with your boss."

Uh-oh. He's on to me. Better get my alibis (okay, lies*) in order.*

"And I didn't want anybody there to know we talked."

"Really? Why?" This was starting to get interesting.

Dan cleared his throat and said, "I need a favor, Paige, and you're the only one I can think of to help me."

"Huh?" I was too surprised to speak.

"It has to do with the Comstock case."

"Um-hmmm?"

"You're not still working on the story, are you?"

"Un-unh."

"You stopped when I told you to?"

"Uh-huh." *Will my idiot lips ever utter a real word again?*

"That's good, because things are heating up now and you would've been putting yourself in extreme danger."

"What kind of heat? What kind of danger?" I'm better at questions than answers.

"I can't go into that now. I'll tell you later, after the case is closed — when it's safe."

Oh, brother! First he's ordering me to butt out, then he's asking me to butt in, then he's acting all secretive and serious again. This is getting confusing!

"There is one thing you can do for me, though," Dan said, lowering his voice to a conspiratorial tone. "And it shouldn't put you at any risk at all. If you're careful, you'll be totally secure. I wouldn't ask you," he added, sounding somewhat embarrassed, "but — like I said — you're the only one I can think of who —"

"What do you want me to do?" I blurted. "Question a witness? Shadow a suspect?" If I'd had a tail it would have been wagging.

"I need you to do a little undercover office work."

"Ugh," I groaned. "Typing and shorthand — is that all a woman's good for?"

Dan snickered. "There's no typing or shorthand involved. Just a little filing."

"That's even worse."

"It's important, though, Paige. I'd do it myself, but I don't want to alert anybody that the police are working on this. I need you to do this for me, and I need you to do it first thing tomorrow." His mood had turned dead somber.

"Yes, Sergeant," I said, making a goofy, cross-eyed soldier face and saluting the phone. Good thing he couldn't see me.

I guess my tone gave me away. "Stop fooling around," he growled. "This is serious."

"Sorry," I said quickly, wanting to get on with things myself. "What do you want me to file?"

"The correct word would be *de*-file."

"What?!" That sounded a little perverted to me.

"I want you to take something out of your office file cabinet instead of putting something in."

"Oh."

"But what I'm looking for may not even be there."

"What are you looking for?"

"A picture of Babs Comstock."

I almost fell off the couch. How did he know about *that?*

"I spoke to one of Babs's neighbors," Dan said, "a stripper who lives across the hall. She told me that Babs had been moonlighting as a model. She didn't know what agency Babs was registered with, so I went up to the *Daily News* office to check out the picture that appeared in the paper — the one they ran with their article on the murder — to see if there was any identification on the back of the photo. But there wasn't. No photographer's name, no agency logo. It was clean as a whistle. I asked the editor where he got the picture, and he said one of his reporters had nipped it, frame and all, from Babs's apartment the night she was killed. So there wasn't any billing information either.

"But even without an agency or studio stamp," Dan went on — revealing much more, I'm sure, than he ever intended (including the fact that the police were not in possession of Babs's portfolio) — "I could see the photo was a professional print. It was an eight-by-ten black-and-white glossy — the kind that gets sold to magazines and newspapers, not the matte kind made by portrait photographers. And the background looked kind of cheap, like it was shot at one of the sleazier studios. So, since Babs was a model and all, I'm thinking maybe the photo was shopped around to the romance and pulp magazines — maybe even to *Daring Detective*. Get the picture?"

"I get it." I didn't tell him that I'd already *gotten* it.

"So will you help me out? Will you go

through your files tomorrow and see if you can dig up any photos of Babs?"

"Sure thing, Sherlock."

"You remember what she looks like, don't you? Blonde, long neck, thin lips and nose. The pic used in the paper showed her wearing a black hat and pearls, but there could be other photos too, where she's wearing other things. You think you'll be able to recognize her?"

"I guess so. I still have a copy of the article with the picture."

"Good. This could be crucial to the case, Paige. Any prints you can dig up will be helpful, as long as they've got some info on the back."

"I understand."

"Give me a call if you find anything. You've got my number, right?"

"Right."

"Oh, one more thing," Dan added, almost as an afterthought. "And this is really important. Whatever you do, *don't* let Brandon Pomeroy see you, or find out what you're up to."

"Why?" The plot was thickening.

"Can't tell you that," he said with a sniff. "We're working on an angle that may, or may not, prove out. Just take my word for it," he added, pausing for the proper precautionary effect, "there's a goddamn good reason."

My head felt like an overstuffed suitcase — too small for the tangled heap of information packed inside. I tried to sort it all out, get the facts in order, make some sense out of the whole mess, but my powers of deduction seemed to have shut down for the evening. I needed something to eat. I needed some sleep. Most of all, I needed to talk to Abby. She'd help me organize the clues and come to some crafty conclusions.

But Abby wasn't available, so I settled on feeding myself. I found a dented can of mixed vegetables and an unsmashed box of crackers in the kitchen cabinet, and an unbroken jar of peanut butter in the fridge. Not the most appetizing combination, but I was so hungry, it tasted like manna to me. I had to do without milk, of course, but a bottle of Dr Pepper had somehow survived the demolition, so I didn't go thirsty.

When I finished eating, I knocked on Abby's door again. Still no answer. Deciding to stay up and wait for her to come home (or venture downstairs), I turned on the TV and plopped my exhausted self down on the couch.

The voice came on before the picture warmed up. Sergeant Joe Friday was saying, "It's my job. I'm a cop." Then the familiar *Dragnet* closing theme began to play, and the announcer intoned, "The story you have just seen is true. The names have been changed to protect the . . ." I was asleep before he could say the word "innocent."

Chapter 18

I don't know about you, but whenever I spend the night fully clothed on the couch, I feel cranky in the morning. Especially when I wake up at 4:38 a.m. — with the TV test pattern ablaze in my brain, and all the world's bats abuzz in my belfry.

A hot shower didn't help. A fresh white blouse, a clean black sheath skirt, and a coat of Ruby Flame lipstick didn't make any difference. I couldn't stop brooding, and I couldn't sit still. It was too early to wake up Abby, and it was too late to go back to bed. I finally gave up the ghost — stopped trying to conduct myself in a conventional, ladylike manner. I slapped my green velveteen beret crookedly on my head, pulled my buttonless green-and-white-checked jacket on over my shoulders, and — dashing out into the predawn dusk like a bloodhound with an urgent bladder call — took off for the office.

The entrance doors to the building were unlocked and the lobby lights were on, but the elevators weren't in service yet. I took the stairs two at a time for the first two flights, then slowed to a near crawl (and huffed and puffed my head off) for the rest of the climb up to nine. The hall lights hadn't been turned on yet, but enough morning glow was seeping through the window at the end of the corridor for me to find my office key. Feeling as anxious as a common thief, I slipped it into the lock, gave it a stealthy twist, and let myself inside.

I didn't take off my hat or jacket or begin my morning chores. I just flipped on the lights and swooped over to Brandon Pomeroy's desk. Sitting down in the great one's chair, I tried to open the top right-hand drawer. It was locked. Yet all of the other drawers in the desk were *un*locked. I rifled through them quickly, but — except for a few pencils, pens, memo pads, paper clips, proofs, and production schedules — they were empty. (For the infinitesimal amount of work Pomeroy actually did around the office, he didn't need many tools or materials.)

Knowing that most people who bother to lock one of their desk drawers usually keep the key nearby, I then made an extra careful search of the shallow lap drawer. I pulled it all the way out and stuck my hand to the very back, feeling around in both corners. Nothing but a small package of staples and several stray rubber bands. I felt along the sides of the drawer, and looked under the removable pencil tray, finding only a book of matches and a few loose shreds of pipe tobacco. Finally, as a last resort, I twisted my hand palm up, and brushed my fingers along the underside of the desk top.

That's where I found it — stuck to the top with two strips of Scotch tape. I quickly removed the key from its hiding place and unlocked the drawer.

There were four things inside: an underground pornographic paperback, a half-empty fifth of gin, a stuffed and clasped manila envelope, and a gold-embossed brown leather address book. I opened the address book and madly flipped through it. Aha! Lots of names, addresses, and phone numbers! (What did I expect — dessert recipes?)

Taking a deep breath and straightening my shoulders, I forced myself to calm down. Then I began leafing through the directory one page at a time, starting with A. Virginia Abrahamson, Judy Faye Adams, Lulu Atkins — most of the names were female. Except for one. A business listing for the Apex Theatrical Agency.

And in parentheses under the listing were the names Martin Crawley and Angela Faparelli.

I quickly skipped over to the S section to see if Starlight Studios was listed. It was. And under V, the Venus Modeling Agency. Finally, I sucked in another hefty supply of oxygen, went forward a couple pages, and scanned the W's. And there she was — printed big as you please in capital letters with a blue ink–filled fountain pen: WANDA WINGATE. I felt as if I'd found the Lindbergh baby.

Bolting up from Pomeroy's chair and madly pacing the length of the office, I flipped through the rest of the address book looking for more incriminating evidence. I didn't recognize any of the other listings, but I did see that most of them were female. Aside from Scotty Whitcomb, under Starlight, and Ernie Gumpert, under Venus, the male names were few and far between. There was a Frank and a Jimmy and a Vito — first names only — but that was about it.

Dropping the address book on Pomeroy's desk, I snatched up the manila envelope and quickly, but oh-so-carefully, opened the clasp. I dumped the contents of the envelope out on the desk. It was a stash

of fifty or so black-and-white photos —
mostly eight-by-ten glossies of pretty
young women. Some of the pictures were
close-ups, some were pinups, and some
were nudes. All of the models were blonde.

I frantically searched through the pile
until I found what I was looking for: four
photos of Wanda, I mean Babs — the four
photos Pomeroy had never given me to file.
One was a headshot (no black hat or
pearls, just a white carnation behind one
ear); one was a bra, garter belt, and
stocking shot; and the last two showed
Babs lying down on a bed wearing nothing
but a see-through negligee. The back of
each photo — actually, the back of every
single photo in the entire heap — featured
the Starlight Studios stamp.

I looked up at the clock on the wall. It
was 7:12 — at least an hour and forty-five
minutes to go before the other daring detectives would start to roll in. I made a pot
of coffee, guzzled down a cup, planted myself at my own desk, and quickly typed up
a copy of the names, addresses, and phone
numbers in Pomeroy's directory. When I
finished that, I gathered the Starlight
photos into a neat stack and stuffed them
all back into the manila envelope. All except one — the headshot of Babs I in-

tended to give to Dan Street. (For reasons I couldn't for the life of me explain, I didn't want him to see the three sexier pictures.) I put the envelope and the address book back in the very spot where Pomeroy had placed them — next to the bottle of gin and on top of his dog-eared copy of *Jailbait Nymphomaniacs on the Prowl* — and locked the drawer. Then I retaped the key to the base of his desk top.

After folding up the copied list and stuffing it in my purse, I checked to see if the original photo of Babs and the newspaper clipping about her death were still secure in a manila envelope in my own desk drawer. They were. Good. I had left them there — and I would continue to leave them there — on the chance that Pomeroy might decide to ransack *my* desk again. If he did, I wanted everything in my personal drawer to be sitting exactly where it had been before, looking dormant as could be, giving the appearance of utter inactivity and neglect.

I put the new headshot of Babs in yet another manila envelope, licked the flap, and sealed it. Then I marked it PAID INVOICE (that was the most boring thing I could think of) and put it in my In box. I figured I would leave it there — in plain, unsuspicious sight — until the end of the day, when I would scoop it up and spirit it off to Dan Street. Then Dan would learn about Starlight Studios and start investigating Scotty Whitcomb without ever finding out that I had hit that particular trail before him. Am I smooth, or what?

I was in the process of taking off my hat and jacket when Harvey Crockett walked in. I gave him a dazzling smile and a peppy "Good morning!"

"Coffee," he grunted as usual, and my workday officially began.

"Paging Paige Turner! Paging Paige Turner!" Mario hollered from his desk. When I swiveled around to see what he wanted, he gave me a devilish smirk. "I'm ready to read through the bluelines for the June issue," he said, "and I need you to turn the pages."

"Turn blue," I said, twisting back to my own desk, scowling down at the galleys I was proofreading. It was just 11:35 in the morning, but I had been up for seven hours. I was tired and hungry and in no mood for Mario's stupid jokes. I was also nervous as a nutball — wondering when Brandon Pomeroy would make his insolent entrance, and looking for a good opportunity to call Dan Street.

Luckily, Mike and Mario decided to go out to lunch a bit earlier than usual. As soon as they put on their jackets, tossed me a few zingers, and left the office — and as soon as Lenny became thoroughly engrossed in his salami sandwich — I picked up the phone and dialed Dan.

"I've got a present for you," I said.

"That's my girl," he answered, and the intimate way he said it made me feel warm and proud all over. "What are you doing for lunch?" he asked.

"Eating something, I hope."

"Want to go window-shopping with me?"

I smiled. It was an odd way to say it, but I knew what he meant. He was inviting me to lunch at the automat. "Horn & Hardart?" I asked, just to be sure.

"If that's okay with you," he said.

"It's better than okay. I'm hooked on the macaroni and cheese."

"Then meet me there in fifteen minutes."

"Which one?"

"The one near your office, at 42nd and Third."

"Isn't that a little too close for comfort?" I asked, lowering my voice to a near whisper. "What if Pomeroy's there?"

"He won't be," Dan said.

"How can you be so sure?" I probed, getting excited, wondering if Pomeroy was a definite suspect and if Dan was having him tailed.

"No need to worry your pretty little head about that."

Dan's patronizing statement really ticked me off. I didn't mind him using the word "pretty," but I was sick and tired of him calling my head little. *You wait and see, buster,* I silently vowed. *By the time this case is over my head will be huge!* I could have phrased that thought a lot better, but at least nobody heard it but me.

"What if somebody else from the office is there?" I asked, sniffing haughtily.

"Then we'll say hello and invite 'em to join us — tell 'em we just ran into each other."

"You're the boss," I gave in. "I guess you know what you're doing." I purposely let a tone of doubt seep into my voice.

Dan chuckled. "Yeah, and I know what some other people are doing, too."

"Who? What?" I gasped. I hoped he wasn't referring to me.

"Never mind," he said. "See you at the automat in fifteen minutes. Don't forget to bring my present."

★ ★ ★

I got to the restaurant as soon as I could and laid claim to a table at the far side of the dining room, away from the window. The lunch hour was in full swing and the place was filling up fast. Stenographers, clerks, accountants, beauticians, postmen, taxi drivers, elevator boys, switchboard operators, socialites, high-paid executives — everybody, but everybody, liked to pop nickels and dimes at the automat.

Dan breezed in just a few minutes after I did, spotted me sitting at the table, and walked over and slid into the chair opposite mine. He didn't smile, or say hello, or even remove his hat. He just lifted it off his head for a second, raked his fingers through his thick dark hair, and put it back on again. "So what have you got for me?" he asked, leaning his strong jaw across the table, fastening his deep black eyes intently on my face.

"What's the hurry?" I whined. "The macaroni and cheese is beckoning." I thought I deserved at least one polite offering before getting down to business.

"Facts first, food later," he insisted, pulling himself up straight and giving me a look that said he was the dean of Virtuous University and I was an unruly coed.

"Oh, all right!" I huffed. I peeled off my gloves and slapped them down on the table. This outing wasn't going to be as much fun as I'd hoped it would be. "Here," I grumbled, taking the manila envelope off my lap and handing it to him.

"Thanks."

"Don't mention it."

Dan ripped the envelope open and peeked inside. "Good. You found some photos."

"Just one," I lied, "but it's got a stamp on it."

He slipped the picture out of the envelope, glanced at Babs's smiling image, then checked out the back. "Starlight Studios," he said. "Ever hear of them?"

"Yes, but the name should be singular instead of plural. As far as I can tell, there's just one studio, and one photographer. His name is Scotty Whitcomb."

"Ever meet the guy?"

"Once," I lied again.

"When?"

"Late yesterday, when he came up to the office to see Brandon Pomeroy."

Dan cocked his head and stared at me through narrowed eyelids. "Yesterday? You met him for the first time yesterday?"

"That's right," I said, suddenly feeling

queasy, wondering if Dan knew more about my dealings with Scotty Whitcomb than he was letting on. I toyed with the idea of telling him about my visit to Scotty's studio, but quickly decided against it. If I opened the bag to let one cat out, some of the others might jump out too. I also neglected to tell him I'd made a date with Scotty for Saturday night.

"Did Whitcomb have an appointment with Pomeroy?"

"No . . . no appointment. He just came by the office to drop off some pictures. Pomeroy wasn't even there."

"Was this one of the pictures?" Dan asked, indicating the headshot of Babs.

"No. I found that in the files. No telling how long it's been there."

"Was it ever used in the magazine? Is there any billing information?"

"Never used, never invoiced. If it had appeared in the magazine there'd be crop marks on the front, and other markings on the back — issue date, directions for the printer, et cetera."

"Hmmmm," said Dan, taking another look at both sides of the photo.

"Look, could I have something to eat now?" I said. "I'm so hungry I feel faint." I was telling the truth, but I was also hoping to disrupt the uncomfortable line of questioning.

Dan slid the photo back inside the envelope and set it down on the table. "Sure thing, kid. I'm hungry too." He rose to his feet and looked down at me, finally giving me a smile. A luxurious, wonderful smile. "What can I get for you?"

There was no need for me to get up and peer into the windows myself — I knew exactly what I wanted. "Meat loaf, peas and carrots, two orders of macaroni and cheese, tossed salad with French dressing, a roll with butter, apple pie, and coffee."

His luxurious smile turned cocky. "You sure that'll be enough?"

"I'm a growing girl," I quipped.

"So I've noticed," he said, with a wink. A very *suggestive* wink. Then he turned and headed to the cashier for change.

I felt as if I'd been struck by lightning. Had Dan just made a pass at me? I wasn't sure. He had looked at me in a seductive way, with a gleam of appreciation in his eye, but maybe he'd just been appreciating me for finding the photo. I watched him as he left the change line, grabbed two plastic trays, set them down on the railing running along the wall of chrome and glass food cubicles, and began shoving coins into various shiny silver slots. He looked very masculine, forceful, and . . . well, sexy.

Hey, wait a minute! What's going on here? Why are my ovaries dancing the hula? I took a deep breath, stared down at the floor, and tried not to blush. I couldn't believe it! My long-lost libido was making a sudden comeback. I was — I'm still shocked and embarrassed to admit — getting horny in Horn & Hardart! Abby would be quite proud of me, I knew, but I was thoroughly ashamed of myself.

Feeling damp as a sponge in a steam room, I took off my beret and dabbed at my forehead with a paper napkin. I lifted my hair off the back of my neck and let the cool air circulate underneath. I took several deep inhalations and forced myself to think about filing invoices, instead of reflecting on the way Dan had winked at me, or the way his shoulders widened when he walked, or the way his mouth turned up in one corner when he smiled. By the time Dan came back to the table — balancing two trays piled high with various containers of food and drink — I had myself under control. I was as calm, demure, and self-composed as a nun in church. Well, sort of, anyway.

And Dan was as amorous as a rock. If

the man had actually experienced a physical attraction to me — if he'd ever once thought of me as an appealing, full-grown woman instead of a troublesome, immature tomboy — he'd obviously had second thoughts. There was no trace of flirtation now. His smile was gone, his spine was rigid, and his eyes were darting all over the place, looking everywhere but at me. "Here you go, kid," he said, setting my meal down in front of me, then sinking somewhat sheepishly into his chair.

"Thanks," I mumbled, staring down at the mountain of food on my tray. I didn't feel so hungry anymore.

We had lunch in total silence. Dan didn't say anything when I toyed with my meat loaf instead of eating it, and I didn't mention the fact that he was chewing and swallowing his roast beef sandwich so fast I thought he'd choke. I pretended not to see when he stuffed a whole roll in his mouth at once, and he didn't seem to notice when I listlessly consumed only half of one of my two orders of macaroni and cheese. Neither one of us finished our desserts.

"I hate to eat and run," Dan said, when the silent ordeal was finally over, "but I have to scram." He crumpled his napkin into a ball and tossed it onto his empty plate. Scooting his chair away from the table and rising to his feet, he picked up both our littered lunch trays and deposited them at the cleanup station. Then he returned to the table for the envelope with the photo. "I've got to get back to headquarters now," he said, looking a little self-conscious around the edges. "Have to question a witness this afternoon."

I was dying to know who the witness was, and if he or she was linked to the Comstock case, but I didn't bother to ask. I knew he wouldn't tell me.

"Thanks for lunch," I said, standing up and pulling on my gloves.

"Thanks for the photo," he replied.

Then, without another word — or wink — we walked outside and went our separate ways.

Chapter 19

I couldn't make heads or tails of Dan's conduct at the automat. First he's treating me like a simple messenger and calling me "kid," then he's pumping me for information (without giving me any details in return), then he's flirting with me (maybe) and turning me into a raving nympho, then he's giving me the cold shoulder and behaving like a puritanical mute. If his goal had been to drive me crazy, he had come out a winner.

Shoving these thoughts aside, I hurried back to the office, anxious to be there when Pomeroy showed up. I wanted to watch the man like a hawk, study his demeanor, see if I could determine from his body language and facial expressions if he was a cold-blooded murderer. (Or, more likely, a *hot*-blooded one, since Babs's body was found half naked, and since the supercilious snob seemed to have a secret passion for dirty paperbacks.)

But my sleuthing plans were stymied at the starting gate. Pomeroy never showed his face at the office that day. And he never called in, either, so nobody knew where he was. I imagined that he was over at police headquarters getting grilled by the illustrious Sergeant Street, or down at the Venus Modeling Agency looking over a brand-new batch of portfolios, or up at Apex Theatrical arranging a hot date with a cool blonde for his dear cousin Zack. But I knew I could be wrong on all three counts. There was too darn good a chance he was simply languishing at home, sleeping off a snootful of martinis.

The afternoon went by fast. Mr. Crockett was out of the office at a meeting with our distributor, and Mike and Mario were so busy trying to meet their immediate, heretofore forgotten art and copy deadlines they didn't have time to heckle me with wisecracks or coffee commands. Lenny was, as usual, so thoroughly ensconced in his own timid little world, he didn't bother me at all. So I was free to concentrate on my own work, which included lots of filing, typing, and proofreading.

And more than a little daydreaming. I dreamt I went to the Copa in my Maidenform bra (and one of Abby's snazziest cocktail dresses). Then I swirled out onto the dance floor and swept Zack Dexter Harrington off his feet. Then I became the playful playboy's trusted confidante, and got him to tell me everything, but *everything*, he knew about Wanda Wingate and the wicked way she died (which was the whole truth and nothing but). Then I gave the police the scoop, and Babs's murderer was caught, and I wrote the exclusive story, and Harvey Crockett featured it on the cover, and Mayor Wagner proclaimed me the brightest — and bravest — writer in all of Manhattan.

Pretty good plot, right? Too bad it wouldn't work out that way.

I grabbed a Nedick's hot dog for supper, then hopped the subway for home. I considered using the back entrance to my apartment again, just to avoid being seen by Tommy or any of the other goons across the street, but ultimately decided against it. I was determined to be a daring and fearless heroine, not a nervous little sissy. Head held high and shoulders pulled back, I strutted down Bleecker like almighty Caesar himself (well, Cleopatra, anyway). When I passed the so-called social club, and caught a glimpse of Tommy's dirty undershirt through the window across the way, I got a little sick to my stomach, but I didn't let it show.

It wasn't until I was safe inside the stairwell to my apartment, with the street door closed behind me, that I relaxed my shoulder and stomach muscles. Then I lost my composure altogether. I dashed up the steps and started banging on Abby's door like a fiend who'd smoked too much reefer. "Abby! Abby!" I called. "Are you there? Open the door! Please hurry! Let me in!" I'm so cool sometimes, it kills me.

"Knock it off, Paige!" Abby yelled through the door. "I'm coming, I'm coming!" A couple of seconds later, she yanked the door open and pulled me inside. "What the hell's going on?" she whispered, flipping her long braid off her shoulder and sticking her head out to canvass the dark, empty stairwell. "Is somebody following you?"

"No," I admitted, embarrassed. "I saw Tommy in the window across the Street and got a little crazy.

"I can dig it," she said, smiling, then closing her door and locking it. "I got a good look at him when I went out this afternoon to buy some cheese. He's short, but massive — like a jumbo bulldog. Looks kind of dumb, though."

"Yeah, but he's smart about some stuff. For instance, he sure knows how to break things . . . glasses, dishes, milk bottles, possibly necks."

"Is he the one who wrecked your apartment?"

"The one and only." I took off my jacket, hat, and gloves and tossed them on the couch. Then I flopped down at the kitchen table, lit up a cigarette, and told Abby all about the break-in and my half-nude escape onto the roof. I started to tell her about all the other weird and threatening things that had happened to me since, but she stopped me from going on.

"I'm *plotzing* to hear every little detail," she said, "but now's not the time. Right now you've got to go home, take a shower, put on your sexiest lingerie and dancing shoes, and make yourself up like a glamor girl. And put some makeup on that bruise on your shin! Then you've got to come back over here and we'll find you something smashing to wear. I've got a dress that'll look fabulous on you!" She was more interested in my future Copacabana appearance than she was in my latest crime-busting adventures.

"What's the big rush?" I squawked. "Dudley won't be here for three hours!" I wasn't ready to face the dance music. I wanted to go home and lock myself in for the night. I wanted to get into my U.S. Army tee shirt and aqua chenille bathrobe, have a huge cup of hot chocolate, and watch *Ozzie and Harriet.*

Abby put her hands on her hips, rolled her eyes at the ceiling, and groaned loudly. "Don't fight me, Paige! It takes time to turn a duckling into a swan. I ought to know — I put myself through the painful process every morning."

"So I'll just be a duckling," I said. "Ducklings are cute."

She grabbed her long braid in one hand, looped it around her neck, and pulled it — like a piece of rope — straight up toward the ceiling. Then she stuck out her tongue, popped her eyes wide, and dropped her head to one side, pretending to hang herself dead in the makeshift noose. "Aaargh!" she cried. "You are so exasperating! Will you please do what I tell you to do? Get up off your *tush* and go get ready. After you've done that, and after we've gotten you poured into the perfect dress, we can relax for a while and talk about the case.

"Relax?" I shrieked. "How can I relax when I'm playing hide-and-seek with a vicious killer and the whole goddamn Mafia?" I was getting a little tired of

Abby's sprightly attitude. I jumped up from the kitchen table and stomped over to the couch, snatching up my jacket and the rest of my stuff. I headed for the door, then paused and turned toward my friend. "I'm really scared, Abby," I sniveled, allowing a frank expression of fear to fall over my face. "My knees are actually shaking."

"You'll feel better after you've had a shower," she blithely replied.

As soon as I stepped inside my apartment the phone started ringing. *What now?* I griped to myself. *Must be my doctor calling to tell me I have polio.* I hesitated for a second, then angrily threw my stuff down on the daybed and answered the call.

"Hello, Phoebe?" a quivering female voice inquired. "Is that you?"

"Who?" I said, with a groan of annoyance. I was so out-of-sorts I didn't recognize my own pseudonym. I actually thought somebody had dialed the wrong number.

"Phoebe?" the trembling voice repeated. "I'm trying to reach Phoebe Starr."

Luckily, the memory of the name finally worked its way in through the hole in my head. Instead of dropping the receiver back down in the cradle, I pulled it tight to my ear and sat down. "This is Phoebe Starr," I sputtered. "Who's this?"

"Doris."

"Who?" I didn't have a clue.

"Doris Toomey," she said. "Babs Comstock's friend? Remember me? We met each other at Schrafft's on Wednesday."

"Oh, yes! Doris!" I cried, relieved to have finally grasped her true identity (not to mention my own fake one).

"You gave me your number, you know," she said defensively. "You said I could call you anytime."

"Of course I did," I soothed. "And I'm very glad to hear from you, Doris. How are you doing?"

"Not so good."

"I'm sorry to hear that."

"I miss her so much."

"Me, too," I said, really meaning it. It wasn't strictly the truth, of course — you can't miss somebody you've hardly known — but it was the closest thing to it.

"I can't get any peaceful sleep," Doris moaned, "and I can't stop thinking about what happened. I keep dreaming about her being strangled."

"I've had a few nightmares myself."

"She was the best friend I ever had, you know," Doris said, a series of tiny sobs escaping from her throat. "So beautiful, and so kind. I wish they'd find out who killed her."

"They will," I said with certainty — more from a desire to pacify Doris than from an unshakable faith in the police.

Doris sobbed and sniffled for a few seconds, then seemed to get a grip on herself. "But that's not why I called, you know, just to have a shoulder to cry on. I wanted to tell you that man came to see me. I was so surprised! He came to the restaurant today."

"Who? What man?"

"The one we talked about. Babs's old friend from home. The guy named Freddy, from Brooklyn, with the kid."

Every hair on my body stood on end. "What did he want?" I asked, trying to keep my voice soft, keep the terror out of my tone.

"Well, first he wanted a beer and a club sandwich. Then he wanted to talk about you."

"Me?" My voice had become so small I could barely hear it myself. "Why did he want to talk about me?"

"He said you went to see him at his

302

apartment last night, to commiserate about Babs, and that he didn't treat you very nice. He said he was in really bad shape, and he couldn't stand to think about Babs and the way she died, so he got mad at you and threw you out." Doris paused for a second, then added, "Is that true? Did he really throw you out?"

"Yes," I said, still feeling the rage and humiliation of that dreadful experience.

"He wanted to know where you live, or where you work, so he could contact you to apologize for his behavior."

"Oh, no!" I gasped. "You didn't tell him anything, did you?"

"What could I say? I don't have the slightest idea where you live or where you work."

I heaved a hefty sigh and gave myself a mental pat on the back. Thank God I hadn't furnished Doris with that information.

"I did give him your phone number, though," she added. "I hope you don't mind."

"What?"

"Did he call you yet? He felt really bad about what happened. He said he wanted to talk to you right away, to tell you how sorry he was."

My skin turned into a sheet of ice. "No, he didn't call."

"Good. I wanted to tell you first. I didn't want you to be surprised, and then get upset with me for giving him your number. I wouldn't have done it if he wasn't so sincere, Phoebe. He's really sorry about what happened."

I didn't say anything. My vocal cords were frozen in fear.

"Phoebe? Are you there? You're not mad at me, are you?" Doris had suddenly turned frantic. Her words poured out of the phone like the prayers of a penitent fanatic. "Did I do the right thing?" she pleaded. "Are you okay?"

"Sure, Doris," I said. "Don't worry, I'm fine." No need for both of us to get carted off to the hospital. Doing my best June Allyson, I chirped, "I'll be glad to hear from Freddy. Any old friend of Babs's is a good friend of mine."

"Including me?" she asked, voice vibrating like the wings of a hummingbird.

"Especially you," I declared.

Did you ever notice how one crisis always seems to lead to another? Not in such a way that you get one problem solved, then simply move — in a logical, orderly fashion — on to the next. The troubles always come in batches, like stampeding steers in a cattle drive, trampling each other in the dust. At least that's how things were happening to me.

When I put down the phone and stood up to make my way upstairs for my shower, I saw an odd little wad of paper on the floor. It was white and round, a little bigger than a golf ball. I didn't know what it was, or where it had come from, but judging from its position on the floor — directly underneath the pile of things I'd so violently thrown onto the daybed — I thought it might have fallen out of my jacket pocket. I bent down and picked it up, uncurling the crumpled paper and smoothing out the creases with my fingers.

When I saw what it was, I was mortified. And very, very mad at myself. It was Babs's poem — the one I'd filched from her apartment the night I met Patty Cake (and got plastered at the party downstairs . . . and passed out in Dan Street's arms). The damn thing had been riding around in my jacket pocket for the last three days, and I had forgotten all about it! Some crime writer I was going to be. Just give me a lead and I'll lose it.

Feeling dumb as a tree stump, I moved

over to the light and eagerly reread Babs's handwritten rhyme:

> *Scold me if you have to,*
> *Cast me out in the street.*
> *On my finger put no wedding ring*
> *To make my life complete.*
> *Though you'll never be welcome in*
>   *Heaven above,*
> *You'll always be the man I love.*

I read the words over and over again, looking for hidden meanings, wondering who Babs had written the poem to, or about. It was a man, obviously — a not very nice man — with whom Babs had been madly and obsessively (and stupidly, if you ask me) in love. But who was this man? And why was she so nuts about him? The poem suggested that he was very mean to her. Mean enough to murder her?

I sat down in the kitchen and spread the poem out on the table in front of me. I smoked a couple of cigarettes and stared down at Babs's carefully penciled words for ages (well, ten or fifteen minutes, anyway). I felt certain the verse contained some extremely important message or clue — that Babs was trying to tell me something.

Finally — through the haze of smoke from my cigarette, through the watery lens of my out-of-focus gaze — her communication became clear. It leapt off the creased piece of notepaper like a *Daily News* headline. I squeezed my eyes shut, then opened them again, just to make sure they weren't playing tricks on me. But Babs's message — though somewhat adolescent in structure and design — was distinct and unmistakable. Strung together and read vertically, the capitalized letters at the very beginning of each line of her poem spelled S-C-O-T-T-Y.

Chapter 20

"No, no, no!" Abby cried, tugging on the neckline of the form-fitting black satin dress I had on. "You're supposed to wear it *off* the shoulders, like this!" She pulled on the shiny black material until it slid halfway down my arms on both sides, exposing both shoulders and more than a little cleavage. The dress did look better that way, I thought as I glanced in the mirror, but I felt as if I'd been strapped into a straitjacket.

"How am I supposed to dance in this contraption?" I asked. "I can't lift my arms above my waist! And the skirt is so tight I can only take dinky little baby steps." With an impolite grunt of discomfort, I demonstrated my lack of upper and lower limb mobility.

"That's the whole *idea!*" Abby crowed. "It's supposed to make you look constrained, you dig? Like a bondage queen. Like Bettie Page."

"Who?"

"Nobody you know. She's a model who posed for me once. Nice girl. I met her at a party at Irving Klaw's place."

"Who's Irving Klaw?"

"A girlie photographer," Abby said, getting bored with the conversation. "You wouldn't know him either." She cocked her head to one side and gazed at my reflection. "All you need to know is that you look really, really great in this dress. Zackyboy's pole will pop a hole in his pants when he sees you."

"Then find me another dress!" I yelped. "That's not the effect I'm striving for! I'd rather look interesting, intelligent, intriguing."

"Well, you might as well stay home then. You'll get his attention just as quick that way."

"Oh, come on, Abby! Lots of men are attracted to intelligent women."

"Only if they're blonde, and have huge bongos, and don't use any words with more than four letters." She threw up her hands in exasperation. "Look, do you want to meet Zack Harrington or not? Because if you do, you've got to make a big impression, and you've got to make it *fast*. Looking smart will get you nowhere. You won't even get noticed. But if you look hot and juicy and ready to take on the whole band at once, every *putz* in the place will stand up and sing 'Mammy!' And from what I've heard about Zacky-boy Harrington, he'll be singing the loudest."

I looked down at the floor. I knew Abby was right, but I didn't want to admit it. I didn't think I could carry it off. The thought of barging into the Copa wearing a skintight, off-the-shoulder dress and trying to act like Jayne Mansfield made me cringe. I'd have been much more comfortable donning an apron and impersonating Thelma Ritter.

"It'll never work," I said. "I think I'd better forget the whole thing."

"Over my dead body," Abby threatened, angrily flipping a stray wave of long black hair off her face. "Dudley went to a lot of trouble to set this thing up. The least you can do is hold up your end of the deal."

"But I don't know *how* to act sexy!"

"Of course you do. Every woman does. All you have to do is *feel* sexy."

"But I don't know how to do that, either." I wasn't being quite honest, of course. I had, after all, been married once . . . and then there was my shameful, oh-so-embarrassing heat stroke in the automat that very afternoon. . . .

"Oh, shut up, Paige! You're such a priss! You must feel sexy sometimes, even if it's only in your dreams. All you have to do is recapture that feeling and play it for all it's worth." A sudden flash of inspiration widened her dark, kohl-lined eyes. "Hey, I've got an idea!" she croaked. "Something that'll *really* do the trick!"

"What is it?" I whimpered. I hoped she wasn't planning to stuff any foreign objects into my brassiere.

"Stay right where you are," she ordered. "I'll be right back." She bolted out of the bedroom and headed down the hall, toward the little room she called her "vault of illusions" — the place where she kept all the costumes for her models and props for her paintings. She knocked around in there for a few seconds, then made a breathless return.

"Quick! Put this on," she cried. "I can't wait to see how it looks!" In the bowl of her upturned hands she carried a lapdog-sized mound of soft, shiny, silver-blonde hair.

"Ooooh, what a cute poochie!" I cooed. "What's her name, Fifi?"

"Very funny," Abby sniffed. "But this is nothing to laugh at. This is your surefire, guaranteed, first-class ticket to Zack Dexter Harringtonland. According to Dudley's dad, the gentleman prefers blondes. So pull your hair back and pin it up in a bun," she insisted. "I want to see how this fits." She stood there, holding the wig in her hands, glaring at me like an irate headmistress, until I complied with her demands. Then she shook the wig out and pulled it snug, like a bathing cap, onto my head.

I looked at myself in the mirror and gasped. Abracadabra! I wasn't me anymore. One touch of the magic blonde wand and Paige Turner had disappeared in a puff of smoke. In her place was a siren, a mermaid, a nymph — a freak fantasy creature with long alien waves of platinum silk flowing — like liquid starlight — out of her gleaming skull. "Wow," I said, under my breath.

"That's atomic!" Abby cried, her husky voice filled with awe. "The way you look now, you give new meaning to the word 'bombshell.'"

"Oh, really? Well, what if I explode?" I studied my bold new persona in the mirror, fluffing the silver-blonde locks with my fingers, straightening the black satin cinched at my waist. I could see the liberating advantages of such a disguise — since I didn't *look* like myself, I wouldn't have to *act* like myself — but that still didn't guarantee I'd be able to act sexy. Or even feel sexy. Right now I just felt like an idiot.

"I can't do it, Abby," I sniveled, sitting down in a slump on the edge of her bed. "It's so unseemly. I look brazen and ridiculous. Can't we ditch the wig and find another dress for me to wear? Something more subdued?"

She gave me another disapproving scowl. "Not if you're serious about hooking up with Harrington. Have you forgotten how important this is, Paige? It's crucial! Zacky-boy might know who the murderer is. He might even have bumped Babs off himself."

Abby's words brought me back to the real purpose of my impending Copa excursion. I was trying to hook a savage killer, not a shy intellectual. And I was working to discover the ugly details of a brutal murder. And I was aiming to land a job as staff writer for *Daring Detective*, not *Good Housekeeping*. And if I was ever going to achieve any of these less-than-ladylike goals, I'd have to put my fanny on the line, wiggle it like a tasty worm, and try to reel in the big one.

"Oh, all right!" I groaned, smoothing the tight black satin down over my hips. "I'll wear the damn dress. And the furry hat, too."

"Hey, bobba ree bop!" Abby said, beaming. "Congratulations are definitely in order."

"To whom and for what?"

"To you, sugarpuss, for finally finding your female nerve."

"Forget the congratulations. What I need is a drink."

Abby laughed. "Let's go downstairs, then. I'll make you a *mazeltov* cocktail."

I sat on the small red couch in Abby's studio, nursing a tall Tom Collins, smoking one cigarette after another, fingering the dangly rhinestone earrings she'd made me wear, and giving Abby the lowdown on my latest murky misadventures. My nervous stomach was in a knot, and the hot dog I'd had for dinner was causing its share of distress.

"I don't know if I'm coming or going," I told her. "One minute I'm a fearless, relentless investigator, the next I'm a soggy heap of apprehension and confusion. And what have I accomplished, really? Nothing. Zilch. A big fat zero. All I've managed to achieve is the total smashup of my apartment and the disappearance of my notes. I've even lost the one piece of evidence — the snapshot of Babs and little Ricky — that could hold the most important key to the whole godawful mystery!" My hands were clammy and I was breaking out in a cold sweat under the weighty wig.

"Calm down, sweetie!" Abby's beautiful face was wrinkled with worry for me. "Don't get your *tuchus* in a turmoil. You make it sound a lot worse than it really is. At least you know who wrecked your place. And don't worry about your notes — you can always write them up again. And the picture of Babs and Ricky isn't really lost — it's just in hiding across the street, planted deep in Tommy's shirt pocket or concealed under the espresso machine."

"But why did Tommy trash my apartment and steal that stuff? It would seem that he — or, more likely, his syndicate boss — doesn't want me working on the Comstock story, but what could possibly be the reason for that? Was some Mafia bigwig involved in Babs's murder? Or maybe," I said, recalling an idea I'd had earlier in the day, ". . . maybe Brandon Pomeroy has some connections to the mob. He sure did go crazy about that mob hit story, pulling it out of the issue in a frantic fit. And Anastasia's henchman was killed the same night Babs was. Do you think the two murders really are related?"

"Only God and Albert Anastasia know

the answer to that. And perhaps Brandon Pomeroy. And maybe Zacky-boy Harrington." Abby took a sip of her drink, eyeing me over the rim of her glass. "The question is, are you going to leave it that way? Or are you going to seek out the truth for yourself, and expose it to the rest of the civilized, law-abiding world?"

She was challenging me, and I knew it. If there's anything Abby loves, it's a skirmish. Especially a sex-related skirmish. And this particular skirmish had sex written all over it. Trouble was, *I* was the one who was going to have to fight to the filthy finish line.

"I'll do my best," I said, sighing loudly, doing my best to believe it. "But what if I'm barking up the wrong tree? The more I think about it, the more I think Freddy Scott was the killer. He's really cruel, Abby. I'm not kidding! You should have seen the way he treated his son. It was a horrible thing to watch. The boy's so afraid, he acts like a zombie. And his poor wife, Betty, looks as if she's terrified of losing her own life. God, I wish Doris hadn't given him my phone number!"

"At least he doesn't have your address."

"Right," I said, experiencing only the slightest sense of relief.

"I'd be much more frightened of Scotty Whitcomb if I were you," Abby insisted. "He knows where you live, and where you work — and he knows you're doing a story about the murder. Hell, you've even got a date with him tomorrow night!"

"Thanks for reminding me." If she had knocked me out with a hammer, I would have felt a lot better. I gulped down the rest of my drink and lit up another L&M.

"It's a good thing you found that poem," Abby said, lighting a smoke of her own. "Now you know that Scotty was Babs's lover, and that he lied when he said he wasn't. And since most murdered women are killed by their lovers or husbands, you know that Scotty's a prime — probably *the* prime — suspect."

"What's so good about knowing that? All it does is make me scared to death to go out with him. The poem doesn't prove anything."

"Well, at least you know enough to be really careful on your date. You'll have the sense to stay in a crowded public place, and not go anywhere near his studio or your apartment — right?"

"Right."

"And watch your back at all times."

"Every second."

"And never take your eye off your drink."

"Huh? Why?"

"So he can't slip you a Mickey Finn."

I smiled to myself. It seemed I wasn't the only one in the room who liked detective novels. "You know what I don't understand?" I said, changing the subject before I got too jittery to speak. "How could Babs have fallen so much in love with Scotty Whitcomb? He's very good looking, but he has no soul. Was Babs so shallow that she couldn't see past his handsome face? I'm telling you, Abby, he's so cold, it's downright spooky. I wouldn't be surprised if he killed Babs in the middle of a photo session just because she wouldn't, or couldn't, strike the right pose."

"Well, I can dig that," Abby teased. "It's really tough to work with an unresponsive model."

I laughed, but I felt more like crying. "Maybe Scotty's involved with the Mafia, too," I added, wheels spinning faster and faster. "Maybe *everybody's* involved. What about all those women's names and numbers I found in Pomeroy's desk? Could be Scotty Whitcomb, and Brandon Pomeroy, and Zack Harrington, and the Venus Modeling Agency, and Apex Theatrical, and Albert Anastasia are all hooked up together in some kind of prostitution ring or something."

Abby's eyes grew wide with wonder. "Oooooh!" she said, "I like that idea!"

I was glad *she* liked it. As for me, I was getting sick to my stomach again. It wasn't any fun finally facing the fact that my life was — just as Dan Street had so urgently warned — in serious danger. And, as much as I hated to acknowledge it, all the fabrications and playacting and fake names in the world wouldn't make that danger go away. Besides giving up on the Comstock story (which I definitely did not want to do), or quitting my job and flying off to Alaska, I could think of only one sure way to secure my own safety — dig up the killer before he buried me.

Trouble was, the deeper I looked into the darkness and delved into the dirt, the harder it was to see.

Chapter 21

Dudley arrived at 10:06 p.m., wearing his dark blue Ripley's suit and his goofy Li'l Abner smile.

"You look good enough to eat," Abby told him, giving him a wicked smirk, then a passionate, openmouthed kiss. When she finally tore her lips away, he was in a total daze. "What do you think of our girl?" she asked him, turning him around to face the couch, where I sat in all my blonde, black satin glory.

Dudley looked at me and blinked. "Uh, hello, miss. It's nice to meet you. . . ." He tried to think of something else to say, but couldn't.

"Don't you know who this is?" Abby asked him.

"Uh, no. Should I?" His youthful, well-tanned face was blank.

"Take a good look," she said, grinning proudly and pushing him closer to the couch. "I'll give you three guesses."

Dudley stared down at me for a few seconds, then turned back to Abby. "I give up," he said, getting a little impatient. "Is this some kind of game? 'Cause if it is, I don't have time to play. Where's Paige? She ready to go? We have to leave right now. Pop's expecting us at eleven, and he won't like it if we're late."

"Stop teasing the poor boy, Abby." I pushed myself up from the couch and stood unsteadily in my skyscraper-high heels. "I'm as ready as I'll ever be. We can go now, Dudley — if you're not ashamed to be seen with me."

His blue eyes grew big as baseballs. "Oh, my living ass! Is that you, Paige?"

"Yes, I'm sorry to say it is."

"Well, you sure fooled me! I thought you were one of Abby's models. Or a movie star or something."

"Doesn't she look great?" Abby asked him.

"I'll say!" he exclaimed, shaking his head. "Pop won't believe it when he sees me with a doll like you."

"You're a Petty Girl come to life!" Abby snorted.

"I feel more like a dying clown," I pouted.

Abby groaned and rolled her eyes at the ceiling. "Don't start that again, Paige! If you can't stop sulking and whining, you'd better not go. Where's your *chutzpah?* It's not enough to look torrid, you've got to act torrid, too. You've got to make Zacky-boy's everloving tongue hang out."

I wasn't the least bit interested in the suspension of Mr. Harrington's tongue, but I was desperate to know what it might tell me about the death of one Babs Comstock. "Okay, okay!" I cried, picking up Abby's fur jacket and my evening bag from a kitchen chair. Then — stretching my scarlet lips in a smutty smile, and patting a silver-blonde wave down over one eye — I did an exaggerated Marilyn Monroe walk toward the door. "C'mon, Dudley," I said, with a breathy sigh and an extra twitch of my black satin bottom, "let's get this show on the road."

Very few people take the subway to the Copa. Most patrons get there by limousine, or town car, or at the very least, taxicab. Dudley and I, however, couldn't afford such a swanky arrival. We took the BMT to 57th Street and walked the rest of the way over to the nightclub at 10 East 60th.

After observing our approach on foot (and eyeballing Dudley's cheap blue suit), the doorman glowered at us suspiciously, then pretended not to notice that we were standing there waiting to be admitted. He turned his attention to a rowdy group of well-dressed revelers emerging from a long pale yellow Cadillac and — greeting them with an inordinate number of subservient bows and overly polite pleasantries — motioned them inside. Then finally — after a succession of surly sniffs and a single nod of his hollow head — he let us in too.

Okay, I confess. I was pretty excited about being there. The famous Copacabana! I'd read about it when I was a teenager back home in Kansas City — curled up on the sofa with the latest issue of *Photoplay* — and I was still reading about it now, in every gossip column of every New York City newspaper. All the biggest singing stars performed here — Frank Sinatra, Nat "King" Cole, Perry Como, Peggy Lee — and all the biggest movie stars came here to dine and dance (and be seen by the New York gossip columnists). A lot of other people came here, too — politicians, producers, socialites, oil magnates, industrialists, famous artists and writers — but I hadn't thought I'd ever be one of them.

Dudley helped me off with my jacket and we left it with the hatcheck girl (a beautiful blonde, of course). Then we walked toward the main entrance where Dudley's father was stationed. Dressed in an elegant white-jacket tuxedo, the tall, slim gray-haired man gave his son a quick glance and a smile (and me a wide-eyed once-over), then continued issuing orders to waiters and tending to the reservations of the people who'd come in just ahead of us. When we made it to the front of the line, he shook Dudley's hand, gave me a pat on my bare shoulder, then leaned closer and spoke to us under his breath.

"We're packed tonight," he said, white teeth gleaming in his darkly tanned face (did Dudley and his father share the same sun lamp?). "There's two empty seats at the bar, though. Tony's been trying to hold them for you. But you better get over there quick, before one of the big shots has a fight with his mistress and decides to go sit closer to the booze." He chuckled at his own remark, then turned serious. "And if Monte comes around," he said to Dudley, "try to hide your face. He's only seen you a couple times, so he probably won't remember you, but it's better not to take any chances. If he knew I let you in like this, he'd bust me back to busboy."

"Who's Monte?" I asked Dudley as he whisked me away toward the bar.

"The stooge owner," he said.

I wondered what he meant by that, but my curiosity was quickly eclipsed by the dazzling sights and sounds of my surroundings. Lights were twinkling, ice was tinkling, drums were pounding, girls were dancing, wine was flowing, smoke was streaming, and hot Latin music was shaking the radiant rafters. Looking around at the ritzy Cuban decor, then up and over the heads of the people filling the tables on the lower level, I gaped at the renowned white and gold palm tree–shaped columns and gazed up toward the dimly lit mezzanine (where, I knew from my newspaper clipping and column reading, all the celebrities liked to sit). I wanted to stop walking and just stand there for a second — take in the famous view — but Dudley kept urging me forward, until we reached the two empty seats at the far end of the crowded bar.

"Thanks, Tony," Dudley called to one of the busy bartenders. "I owe you one."

"No problem, pal," Tony shouted back. When he turned to look our way — and got a load of the blonde, black satin me — his eyebrows shot up to the base of his wavy brown hairline. "Whooeee!" he whooped. "What does your gorgeous girlfriend want to drink?"

"Tom Collins," I said to Dudley, sitting down and crossing my legs, batting my lashes at the bartender, trying to get into a Jayne Mansfield mood.

Dudley called out our drink order and sat down next to me. "The wig is working," he said. "All the guys at the bar are staring at you."

I looked up and saw that he was right. Even with the floor show going full blast — even with all eight stunning Copa girls dancing their hearts out in revealing, red-sequined, swimsuit-style costumes — I had become the main attraction. Some of the men sitting at the back tables were gawking at me too. Shows you what a little blonde horsehair can do.

I took a cigarette out of my purse and waited for Dudley to light it for me. "So who is Monte, and why did you call him the 'stooge owner'?" I asked between puffs. "What did you mean by that?"

"Monte Proser owns the club," Dudley said, "but not really. He's the boss in name only. Pop says the real owner is . . ." He leaned over and mumbled into my ear, ". . . Frank Costello."

My naked arms and shoulders broke out in goose flesh. "You mean *the* Frank

Costello?" I whispered.

"Yep. Main man of the mob."

"He's in the middle of a big trial right now," I said, wheels turning. "Tax evasion."

"Yeah, I know. Costello is the biggest —" Dudley cut himself short when the bartender brought over our drinks.

"You gonna introduce me to your girl, Dud?" Tony croaked, setting our glasses down on embossed Copa cocktail napkins.

"Sure, Tony. This is . . . uh . . . this is —"

"Phoebe Starr," I quickly interrupted, then gave out a girlish giggle. "Dudley's cute, but he's not too smart. This is our third date, and he still can't remember my name."

"Well, I sure won't forget it!" Tony said, with a cocky smile. "Better give me your phone number, too, doll — just for safe-keeping."

"Knock it off!" Dudley grumbled, looking annoyed. I couldn't tell if he was acting, or really feeling upset. "Don't you have some work to do?" he said to Tony, who shrugged and went to wait on another customer.

I put out my cigarette and leaned closer to Dudley. "So, you were saying . . ." I murmured.

"Huh?"

"About Frank Costello?" I kept my voice on low volume.

"Oh, yeah," Dudley said, regaining his sense of control. "He's the real owner of the Copa. He owns some of the finest clubs in town. But Pop says he likes this one best, that he comes here almost every night. I'll bet he's here right now, sitting at his regular table up on the mezzanine."

The thought made me shiver with dread — and reminded me of the ghastly chain of events that had brought me, preening and whining, to this opulent den of idols, murderers, and thieves. "What about Zack Harrington?" I asked. "Where does he usually sit?"

"On the mezzanine, of course. Everybody who's anybody sits on the mezzanine.

"Then take me up there. I want to have a look around."

"I can't do that!" Dudley was getting irritated again.

"Why not?"

"Because my dad would kill me, that's why! The mezzanine is for VIPs only. If Pop saw us sneaking around up there, he'd call in Monte's muscleheads and have us thrown out."

"Really?" I asked, draining my drink.

"Yeah, really!" Dudley blustered. "If he

didn't, he'd lose his job! Look, I know you're working on a big story here, Paige, and I know you want to talk to this Harrington guy, but you're just gonna have to wait till he comes downstairs to dance or go to the bathroom or something. Pop did us a big favor letting us in here tonight, and I'm not gonna pay him back by getting him fired." He raked his fingers through his dirty blonde brush cut and gave me a red-faced scowl.

"Sorry, Dudley," I quickly apologized. "Of course I wouldn't do anything to hurt your dad. I just didn't realize . . ."

"Okay, okay!" he said, relieved. He offered me a Hit Parade, then lit it for me. "Want another drink?"

"Sure."

The floor show was coming to a fabulous finish. The drums were rolling, the cymbals were crashing, and the dancing girls were shimmying so fast and so hard I thought their sequins would pop off and soar, like minuscule flying saucers, into the crowd. As the band sounded the final note and fell silent, the ladies in the audience clapped politely and the men broke out in loud cheers and whistles. The breathless Copa girls took several low, bosom-baring bows, then — smiling and waving to the satisfied spectators — wriggled their bright red behinds back to the wings.

When the applause died down and the band started playing "Three Coins in the Fountain," dozens of couples stood up and twirled out onto the dance floor. I sat there for an eternity (okay, three and a half minutes), straining my eyes through the smoke and the glimmer, stretching my nervous neck to the limit, watching for Zack Dexter Harrington to make an appearance.

When he didn't show up, I couldn't take it any longer. I stubbed out my cigarette and stood up on my sky-high stilettos. "I'm going to the powder room," I said to Dudley.

"Do you know where it is?"

"Don't worry, I'll find it," I assured him. Then I stroked my platinum mane, smoothed down my skintight skirt, and wobbled off to look for the stairs to the mezzanine.

Chapter 22

I bravely made my way upstairs, but once I reached my destination, I turned chicken again. What the hell did I think I was doing? What was I trying to prove? Just who did I think I was? (Amelia Earhart came to mind, and we all know what happened to her.) Instead of marching right into the hub of the mezzanine, finding my mark, and making my move, I stood frozen against the back wall, trying to catch my breath and calm my racing heart, hoping no one would notice me.

Fat chance.

"Hey, Goldilocks!" a stocky, balding man at a nearby table called out. "Wanna eat my porridge?"

Ignoring him and his guffawing buddies, and keeping my gaze trained on the plush green and pink flowered carpet, I turned and walked a few yards down the wall, toward the middle of the gallery. But my escape attempt brought only more unwelcome attention. Out of the corner of my eye I saw that other heads were snapping in my direction and many people —

women as well as men — were ogling me. Embarrassed and ashamed of my brazen getup, I wanted to transform my appearance right then and there, go back to being my own understated, mousy-haired self. But it was too late for that. The die had already been cast.

A tall, brown-haired man wearing alligator boots and a tan suede suit got up from his table and walked over to me. "Can I help you, ma'am?" he said in a dry western drawl. "You look like a heifer that got lost from the herd. Why don't you come on over here and sit down with me? My date hightailed it home with a headache."

"Uh, no . . . no, thank you," I said. "My husband's waiting for me downstairs. I just came up here to look for a friend." To add credibility to my words, I raised my eyes from the floor and began scanning them, like searchlights, over the crowd.

"I'll be your friend if you let me, honeypie," he snorted. "I'll be a real goooood friend." I half expected him to whinny.

Do all blondes have to go through this? "Not tonight, cowboy," I said. "My square dance card is full." I turned and hurried away from him, moving further along the back wall.

When I reached a safe distance, and a darker spot in the shadows, I stopped and looked over the crowd again. For real this time. Somehow, during the course of my flight from attention, my courage had made a comeback. And I'd come to an important decision: instead of letting random lady-killers take potshots at me, I would suck in my stomach, stick out my chest, and set my sights on tracking down a *real* killer.

Girding myself for action, I raked my eyes over the throng, seeking out the boyishly handsome, well-known (to me) face of Zack Dexter Harrington. I didn't see him anywhere, but there were a few other faces I recognized. Van Johnson was sitting at a table close to the mezzanine ledge, laughing his head off and nuzzling the neck of a skinny brunette, and the very tired-looking, washed-out redhead sitting with her back to the band, and her head on a portly old man's shoulder, turned out to be the former "Cover Girl" herself, Rita Hayworth. Several local politicians were in attendance (with several tarted-up young women *not* their wives), and Elizabeth Taylor was having a serious tête-á-tête with Montgomery Clift at one of the more distant tables.

At the very last table in the furthest corner of the mezzanine, with his broad back to the outermost wall, sat kingpin Frank Costello. I recognized him — with his slick dark hair, big brown eyes, bulbous nose, fleshy face, thin lips, and very expensive, well-tailored clothes — from his rare newspaper photos, which I always clipped and kept on file at the office. Though I was gripped with repulsion and disgust when I first spotted the man, I couldn't stop staring at him — wondering how such a vicious, brutal criminal could look so gentlemanly, so benign.

But then the stylish don looked up and saw me studying him, and his brutal brown eyes made contact with mine, and I knew in an instant he was no gentleman. Keeping his intense glare fixed on my feverish face, Costello leaned over and said something to the mountainous man sitting next to him. And when that man (who looked like a bone-crushing bodyguard to me) turned and gave me the evil eye, my courage went bye-bye again. All the blood drained out of my brain, my backbone turned to butter, and my extremely cold feet twirled around and took off in the opposite direction.

It was right after that — after I had

dashed back along the rear mezzanine wall and darted back down the steps to the club's lower level — that I bumped into Zack Harrington.

Luck, fate, stupid coincidence — whatever you call it, it was a shattering collision. I was moving very fast, and I guess I wasn't looking where I was going, because the second I turned the corner at the bottom of the stairs, I crashed into the passionate playboy head-on.

"Oof!" I sputtered, toppling backward off my high heels and landing flat on my astonished fanny. My legs were splayed out in front of me — flung as wide as the narrow skirt of my dress would allow — and my dangly rhinestone earrings were rattling like crystal chandeliers during an earthquake. Worst of all, my wig was knocked off-kilter. Quickly grabbing my head with both hands and putting on a hair-tugging show of bewilderment and distress, I managed to straighten it before anybody noticed (or so I hoped).

By some miracle, Mr. Harrington remained standing. I call it a miracle because the man was falling-down drunk. His eyelids were half-closed, his light brown hair was sticking out in all directions, his bow tie was undone, and — though he was still wearing his black tuxedo jacket — his white pleated shirt was open all the way down to his cummerbund. The impact of our smashup had startled him, and rocked him backward a few feet, but he didn't have the foggiest idea what had happened. Swaying like a willow in a windstorm, he just hovered there, sloshing bourbon over the sides of the glass he still carried in his hand, and staring down at me with the goofiest smile I ever saw on any man's face (except for Bert Lahr's).

"Oh! I'm so sorry, sir!" I cried, quickly taking blame for the accident and scrambling to my feet before any of the waiters (or Dudley's father) saw the state I was in. "What a menace I am! I hope I didn't hurt you. Are you okay?"

"I'm fine," he said with a burp. "Jush fine."

"Oh, I'm *so* glad!" I babbled, brushing off my naked shoulders and taking a deep, cleavage-enhancing breath of air. "I simply couldn't live with myself if I caused you any pain!"

"Pain?" he mumbled, still smiling, obviously not feeling any. He was leaning toward my breasts as if they were pillows in need of a head.

"Oh, look! You've spilled your drink!"

"Huh?" He stared down at his wet hand and near empty glass with a look of sheer befuddlement.

"What a shame!" I said, looping my arm through his, trying to hold him upright. "Come with me and we'll get you a new one." I guided Zack, still swaying, back around the corner and through the crowd milling around the bar. Dudley saw us coming and gazed at me in confusion. But after several meaningful jerks of my head, he finally got the message and left the bar, making room for me and my unsteady companion to sit down.

The bartender materialized immediately. "What can I get for you, Mr. Harrington? The usual?"

"Okay," Zack muttered, grinning like a fool.

"And you, doll? Another Tom Collins?"

"Yes, please."

As soon as Tony left to get our drinks, I lit up a cigarette and heaved a huge smoky sigh. Zack Dexter Harrington was mine. But what was I going to do with him? Interrogate him about the murder, or tuck him into the nearest sleeping bag? I wanted him to spill his guts, all right, but not all over the floor.

"The bartender called you Mr. Harrington," I said, leaning closer and speaking into his ear. "Are you *the* Mr. Harrington?"

"No, siree!" he hooted, slapping his hand down on top of the bar and swinging his partially bare, hairless chest toward mine. "Thass my father you're talkin' about, babydoll. Mr. *Oliver* Harrington — ruler of newspapers, leader of men, and master of me!" His words were slurred, but his thinking didn't seem to be.

"Then you must be Zack Harrington," I said, smiling, "ruler of nightclubs, leader of women, and master of ceremonies."

He burst into a brief giggle fit, which ended as soon as Tony put his drink down in front of him. After taking a deep, gluttonous gulp, Zack aimed his half-closed, out-of-focus eyes at me and muttered, "So, who d'ya read? Hedda or Louella? The rumors about me have been greatly — hic! — exaggerated."

"That's not what my friend Wanda says."

"Who?"

"My best friend Wanda," I repeated. "Wanda Wingate." I studied Zack's face for a reaction, but there was no visible response. His handsome, dimpled features remained as soft, relaxed, and indecipherable as several spoonfuls of mashed potatoes.

"Never heard of her," he said.

"How can you say that!" I cried, acting indignant.

"Wha— ?"

"How can you say you never heard of Wanda Wingate when you took her out on a date just a few weeks ago? You brought her here to the Copa, as a matter of fact, for dinner and dancing."

His gray-blue eyes were blank. "Guess I jush don't remember —"

"Don't say that!" I snapped. "She's so crazy about you, it would break her heart if you forgot her."

"Whasser name again? Whass she look like?"

His perplexity seemed genuine, but I couldn't accept it at face value. In the past few days I'd become such a good actor (okay, *liar*) myself, I found it hard to trust anybody else. "Her name is Wanda Wingate," I stressed. "She's blonde and she's beautiful. She's a model!" I added, with an audible exclamation point.

Zack rubbed his face with his hands, then shoved his fingers through his thick beige hair. "I know lotsa models. . . ."

"She wore a strapless red dress the night you brought her here, and you took her back to your apartment for champagne and Sinatra."

"Done that a thousan' times." He belched, giving me another goofy smile. "Lotsa blondes in red dresses. Wanna do it with you, too." He looked at my black dress in dismay. "Le's go to Bergdorf's right now . . . buy you sumpthin' red and silky — hic! — with feathers."

"They're not open yet."

"Owner's a friend a mine. He'll let us in."

I smiled and fluttered my lashes as I knew Abby would want me to do, but I didn't see much point to the flirty charade. Zack was too drunk to respond properly (i.e., become bewitched and tell me all about the murder). It seemed my Copa campaign would turn out to be a colossal waste of time and energy. Still, I wasn't quite ready to call off the expedition.

"I know another friend of yours, too," I said. "Actually, he's your cousin."

"Huh?"

"Brandon Pomeroy. He's your cousin, right? At least that's what he told me."

A look of distaste fell over Zack's face. "Yeah . . . cousin," he grumbled, taking another big gulp of bourbon. "Black sheep, jush like me."

"I thought he was a really nice guy!" I

insisted. "He said I was beautiful — that he was going to hook me up with a good theatrical agent."

Zack let out a knowing snicker. "He'll hook you up all right. . . ." Throwing his head back and sucking down the last drop of his drink, he plunked the empty glass down on the bar and lurched around to face me again. He was trying to keep his torso straight and his heavy eyelids open, but it was a losing effort.

"Did you ever hear of the Apex agency?" I asked him.

"Maybe I did, and maybe I didn't," he mumbled, leaning so far forward I thought he'd fall off his chair.

"An agent named Martin Crawley?"

"I'm gonna crawley all over you. . . ."

Pitching one arm around my neck, and dropping the other down to my lap, Zack took a wobbly nosedive toward my chest. Flinging the full weight of his upper body onto mine, and allowing his head to slide down to my bosom, he snuffled his warm snout against my skin and grunted like a drowsy dog. Then he shuddered . . . sputtered . . . and conked out.

Tony and Dudley got me out from under the wheezing, drunken heap. Tony pulled

Zack's body back into his chair, and laid his lolling head down on the bar. Dudley pulled me out of my chair, and helped me balance on my feet.

"We've got to leave right now," he said, grabbing his cigarettes and my purse off the bar. "Monte Proser saw you sitting here with Harrington and asked my father who you were, and Pop didn't know what to say, so he made up some story about you coming here to look for a job as a Copa girl. He said Harrington saw you standing in the hall and then hustled you off to the bar for a drink. Monte said okay, but that he wanted to meet you later, after Harrington was through with you. So we've gotta get outta here right now, before Monte comes back." He put his free hand on my back and pushed — ushering me along at a very fast pace, through the crowd at the bar and around the corner toward the entranceway.

Dudley's father watched our progress nervously, gesturing for us to hurry. I gave him a big nod of thanks as we rustled by. Then Dudley forged ahead of me and made a beeline for the hatcheck girl. Standing alone in the center of the entrance hall, waiting for Dudley to return with my jacket, I turned to take one last glimpse into the famous, smoky depths of the glamorous Copacabana.

And that's when I saw the man staring at me.

He was standing in the shadow of an enormous potted palm, holding his hat in his hand and leaning lazily against the far wall of the foyer. He was smoking a cigarette, and squinting his eyes, and scrutinizing me as if I were the *Mona Lisa* — or the real Jayne Mansfield.

At first I didn't recognize him. I thought he was just another inebriated, oversexed male on the lookout for a lusty blonde. I thought he was just another Copa Friday-nighter out on the town without his wife. But then I focused on the man's strong broad shoulders, and his large, perfectly formed hands, and his dark wavy hair, and his searing black eyes — and I realized it was Dan Street.

I gasped so hard I almost popped right out of my garter belt. And I came this close to squealing my head off. I wanted to dive behind the hatcheck counter and hide behind the mink and sable coats.

But then I remembered my outrageous disguise, and that I didn't look the least bit like myself, and that Dan might not have the slightest idea who I was. And then I figured if I played my cards right, he might *never* know who I was. So I summoned up all my *chutzpah,* propped one hand on my hip, gave my silver-blonde head a coquettish toss, and winked at Dan the same way he had winked at me in the automat that afternoon (i.e., *very* suggestively).

His smile was so fleeting, I almost didn't catch it.

"Hurry up!" Dudley said, suddenly materializing at my side and slapping Abby's fur jacket over my shoulders. "Let's get outta here." He put his arm around my waist and guided me rather ungraciously toward the exit. Too impatient to wait for the discourteous doorman, Dudley yanked the door open himself and escorted me outside. Then we grabbed hands and bolted for the BMT.

Chapter 23

Abby had waited up for us, and once we'd caught our breath from the mad dash home, we gave her a full report on the Copa fiasco. We were both still feeling panicky, but for very different reasons. Dudley was distressed that we may have gotten his father in trouble, and I was hysterical about everything.

"It couldn't have been a worse disaster!" I blubbered. "Mob boss Frank Costello saw me there, and police sergeant Dan Street saw me there, and Zack Dexter Harrington was so damn drunk I didn't learn a thing about the murder!"

"That's okay, Paige, don't despair. You'll do better next time." Abby meant her words to be soothing, I'm sure, but instead they drove me crazy.

"Next time? Are you out of your ever-loving mind? I'd eat a vat of raw sewage before I'd let there be a next time!" In a childish fit of rage, I ripped Abby's wig off my head and threw it down on her studio floor. It lay on the paint-smeared canvas drop cloth like a dead cat.

"Well, you don't have to get nasty about it," Abby huffed, stooping down to pick up the hairpiece. "I was only trying to help."

"Oh, really?" I screeched, raking my fingers through my damp, matted-down real hair. "Then do me a favor and don't do me any more favors! Your kind of help is dangerous!" The minute the words escaped my mouth I was sorry for them. Abby wasn't to blame for anything. Lady Luck was to blame. More specifically, Lady Bad Luck.

"I'm sorry, Abby!" I cried. "I didn't mean what I said at all. I'm a ranting, raving idiot. I'm just so exhausted, and scared, and tired of running around in circles. And crashing into dead ends. I'm more confused than ever. I'm never going to find out who killed Babs, and I'm never, ever, ever going to get this story written!"

"Yes, you will, sweetie," she said, quickly brushing off my thoughtless assault and swooping over to give me a hug. "Everything's going to work out. You'll see." She pressed her cheek to mine and gave me an encouraging pat on the back.

I felt a little better after that — but not much. "But what am I going to do now?" I said, stepping away from Abby and throwing my hands up in the air. "The police may be on to me! The Mafia may be watching me! Pomeroy probably knows what I'm up to, and Scotty Whitcomb may be planning to strangle me tomorrow night! God! You might as well kill me this minute — spare me the anguish of waiting for the axe to fall."

"I'll tell you what you're going to do now," Abby said, keeping her voice low and under control. "You're going to go home, wash your face, get undressed, get into bed, pull the covers up under your chin, and go to sleep. You dig? And then tomorrow morning — after you've gotten some rest and pulled yourself together — you're going to come back over here for breakfast, and we're going to thrash this whole thing out and figure out what your next move should be."

I wasn't at all sure I wanted Abby to help orchestrate any more moves for me, but I was too mixed up and far too tired — to argue. I suddenly felt as if my bones were made of water. Besides, during the course of my ugly temper tantrum Abby and Dudley had been giving each other some very obvious come-hither looks, so I knew they were eager for me to leave.

"Okay," I said, "I'm going." I picked up my purse and staggered toward the door.

"Thanks for everything, Dudley."

"Sure thing, Paige."

"I'll bring your dress back tomorrow," I said to Abby.

"That's cool," she replied.

"And the earrings," I added, opening the door to let myself out. "Mm-hmm."

Abby probably would have said something more to me right then. She probably would have offered me some phenomenally thoughtful and inspiring parting words of comfort and support — if her mouth had been free. But Dudley already had that covered.

Once inside my own apartment, with the door securely locked behind me, I went straight upstairs to the bathtub, plugged in the rubber drain stopper, and turned the water on full blast. I wanted to soak myself in a hot bath for a century or two. I was so strung out and oversensitive that all my recent injuries — my wounded shin, twisted breast, sprained finger, abraded knees, and now my sorely bruised behind — had started to throb again.

I limped into the bedroom and kicked off my high heels. Then I wrenched myself out of the black satin dress, peeled off my seamed silk stockings, and stripped off my black lace underthings, tossing the whole caboodle on the unmade bed. Naked and trembling, I padded back into the bathroom, turned off the water, and then lowered myself — with a resounding, grateful *ahhhhh* — into the steamy tub.

I'll give you one guess what happened next. Bingo. The phone started ringing.

The unwelcome sound was so laughably predictable, I should never have lost my head the way I did. But it was very late at night, and I was wet and stark naked, and I was already a stark raving mental case. I vaulted out of the tub, darted out into the hall, and dashed — slipping and dripping — down the stairs and through the kitchen to the living room. There were no cunning (or even sensible) thoughts in my head. I never stopped to consider who might be calling me, or how I ought to respond. And it never once occurred to me not to answer the phone. I just snatched the receiver up in my slick wet hand and pressed it to my stupid ear.

"Hello?" I sounded like Jerry Lewis after six cups of black coffee.

"Paige Turner?" The voice was harsh and masculine.

"Yes . . . ?"

There was no response, but I could

hear someone breathing.

"Who is this, please?"

There was another long pause, then a cough.

"Who's there?" I asked again.

A short silence, then a curt reply. "Fred Scott."

I would have wet my pants if I'd been wearing any. "Who?" I asked — not because I didn't know, but because I couldn't think straight and needed to buy a little time.

"Barbara Comstock's old friend."

"Oh," I said, still slow on the uptake. The wheels were trying to turn, but they kept getting stuck. I did have the presence of mind to notice, though, that Freddy had changed his tune — that he was now admitting to a close relationship with Babs. "Old friend?" I repeated. "But I thought you said —"

"Forget what I said last night." He wasn't asking me, he was ordering me. "I was upset. I didn't want to talk about Barbara."

"Why?"

"Because she's dead."

I wasn't sure what he meant by that (other than the fact that Babs was, indeed, dead), but I decided not to push. "It's too horrible," I said. "I still can't believe it."

"Me neither." If there was any pain in his voice, I couldn't hear it.

"So why are you calling me, Mr. Scott? Is there something I can do for you?"

"Yeah." The man was as communicative as a bag of sand. I waited for him to reveal his reason for phoning, but the only sound coming through the wire was the whoosh of his ragged breath.

"What is it?" I prompted. "Do you want to talk about Babs now?"

"Not tonight," he snorted. "It's late."

I looked at the kitchen clock. It was 3:15 a.m. *Jesus! What's he doing calling me up at this hour? Was he hoping to terrify me and catch me off guard? Or did he just wait till he was sure his wife and son were fast asleep?*

"Some other time then?" I asked.

"Yeah."

"When?"

"Don't know. I'll call you."

And then he hung up. Click. No good-bye. No "see ya." No explanation for the late call. No apology for nearly breaking my elbow and kicking me out of his apartment. All Freddy left me with was a clear sense of foreboding and a bad case of the shivers.

I dropped the dead receiver on the hook

and hustled my damp, freezing body back upstairs. The bathwater was still warm, so I got in, reclined against the back of the tub, and sank down until the surface reached my chin. It wasn't until a few minutes later — after I'd soaked away the shivers and mentally reviewed the details of Freddy's startling call for the third time — that I remembered the most startling detail of all: when I had first charged into the living room and answered the phone, Freddy had asked for me by my *real* name.

Sleep was out of the question, so I didn't bother going to bed. I put on an old pink flannel nightgown, a pair of woolen knee-socks, and my aqua chenille bathrobe and went downstairs. After making myself a piece of toast smeared with peanut butter, and a cup of hot tea, I sat down at the kitchen table to eat.

While I was chewing on the toast (and chewing myself out for being a coward, a fool, and a lousy detective), I shot a glance at my portable typewriter, which was still placed — like a preposterous baby blue centerpiece — smack in the middle of the table. And then I really got depressed. Here I was, trying to make a name for myself as a hotshot crime writer, and I hadn't written one word! I hadn't even reconstructed my stolen notes. Or put one single scrap of new information to paper.

I was sitting there feeling very stupid, very scared, and very, very sorry for myself, when something really weird happened. A sudden jolt of electricity shot up my spine, my cranium was filled with light, and I heard a bugle playing reveille. I kid you not. The sharp, staccato notes of the military wake-up call were so loud and clear in my head, I thought the radio had turned itself on. Or that a vigilant soldier was bugling right beneath my window, summoning the sleepy residents of Bleecker Street to formation. Or — and this was the thought that really got to me — that my late husband, Bob, was signaling me from U.S. Army heaven, telling me to snap out of my self-pitying stupor and get my feeble self back on the march again.

So I did. I gulped down the rest of my toast and tea, cleared the table, then turned the typewriter around and pulled it over to face my chair. I sat myself down, rolled in a piece of paper, put my fingers on the keys, and let them fly.

I typed down every little detail of every single aspect of the case I could remember, from the day I'd met Babs at the office, to the moment I cut the Comstock article out of the paper, to the phone call from Freddy I'd just received. I made notes of all the conversations I'd had with all the different people I'd interviewed, and I listed all their physical characteristics and quirks. I described all the places I'd been, and put down all the addresses. I recorded all the particulars of my encounters with Dan Street, taking special care to put down the few tiny bits of information about the case he'd inadvertently let slip. I even scrutinized my own behavior, jotting down all my feelings, actions, and reactions during the five days I'd been following the story.

Five days? Is that all it's been?! I felt as if I'd been tracking Babs's tragic and pitiful saga forever.

When I finished typing the notes, it was 6:30 in the morning — turning light outside. I gathered up the pages (all twenty-three of 'em!) and stuffed them, along with Babs's poem about Scotty Whitcomb and the list of names and numbers I'd copied from Pomeroy's address book, into yet another manila envelope. Then I whisked the envelope into the living room and shoved it deep underneath the madras-covered mattress of my couch/door/daybed.

Seconds later, I was flopped out on top of the mattress, doing a flawless (if you overlook the snoring) imitation of a corpse.

Chapter 24

I didn't wake up until 3:30 that afternoon. I might have slept even longer if Luigi, the owner of the fish store downstairs, and Angelo, the owner of the fruit and vegetable store under Abby's apartment, hadn't decided to disturb the Bleecker Street peace by bawling each other out — at the top of their lungs, in a crazy mix of English and Italian — on the sidewalk right below my living room window. Theirs was an ongoing feud, having something to do with Angelo's beautiful sixteen-year-old niece and Luigi's lazy and lecherous twenty-four-year-old son. It also had something to do with olive oil and scungilli, but I had never been able to figure out *that* connection.

With eyes full of sand and a mouth full of cotton, I pulled myself to a sitting position, then stood up from the couch/door/daybed. So much late afternoon sun was pouring through the living room window, I was half blind. But not so blind I couldn't see the small piece of pink paper that had obviously been shoved under my front door, coming to rest on the floor three feet inside.

Abby often slipped messages under my door, so I figured it was a note from her. Yawning widely, I rubbed my eyes, stretched my back, and shuffled over to pick it up. Then, squinting like a newborn pup, I stared down at the handful of words neatly written, in capital letters, on the blank side of a form-printed telephone message slip, the same kind we used at the office:

STOP NOSING AROUND <u>RIGHT NOW</u>, OR YOU'LL BE STOPPED FOREVER.

It took a few seconds for the words — and their meaning — to crawl into my consciousness. And when they finally did register, I almost *lost* consciousness. Somebody — some dangerous somebody, maybe even the killer himself — had been inside my building, lurking on the landing outside my door, while I was sleeping! Maybe he was out there now! I lunged for the door and yanked it open, popping out into the hall like a clock-sprung cuckoo.

Luckily, the staircase was empty — completely devoid of murderers — or I'd be fertilizer now. I dove for Abby's door and started banging on it, calling out, "Help!

Help! Let me in!" or something equally hysterical. When she didn't answer, I lost what sanity I had left (which, at that point, couldn't have filled a teaspoon), and surrendered to the fear and confusion. I leaned my back against the wall near Abby's door, slid all the way down to my wobbly haunches, and crouched in the corner of the landing like a demented frog. Then I started crying.

I wish I could say I just whimpered and blubbered a bit, but that would be a bold-faced lie (and even though my talents for deception have blossomed since I started working on this story, I said I was going to write the truth — and I am). The fact is I howled my head off. I hugged my arms around my shuddering shoulders and let forth the loudest, deepest sobs I'd ever experienced (except during the days and nights following my receipt of a certain government telegram). I was crying for myself, and for Babs, and for all the other frightened and defenseless females trying to make their way in the brutal world alone.

It was a wonder Luigi and Angelo didn't hear me wailing and come rushing to my aid with a bottle of sedatives, or at least a bottle of Chianti. I cowered on that landing for a full five minutes, weeping and moaning, croaking and sniveling, shivering and shaking, letting the tears gush down my face and the snot run freely out of my nose.

It was disgusting. But tragedy and terror can do that to a person, you know.

Finally, after three or four more minutes of spineless, wet-faced panic and self-pity, I pulled myself together and went back inside my apartment. I double-locked the door behind me, blew my nose, tied my robe tighter around my waist, and started pacing the floor, back and forth — from the far side of the living room to the opposite end of the kitchen — while my cowardice fought my courage for control of my future. Assuming I had one.

In the end my courage (okay, blind determination) won out. I dashed upstairs and took a shower. I put on some makeup and got dressed in the black capris, black sweater, coral neckerchief, and black ballerina flats I planned to wear to the San Remo that night (so I would blend in with the bohemians). Then I scrambled back downstairs, darted over to the daybed, lifted up the edge of the mattress and dug out the manila envelope I had buried there just hours before.

Dropping the mattress and sitting down, I tore open the envelope and fished out the list of names and addresses I had copied from Pomeroy's directory. Then I went through the listings, one by one, starting at the top, until I came to a name with an address nearby. Mitzi Maxwell. She lived just a few blocks away from me, on Perry Street. Burning to find out what Mitzi might know about Babs, or Martin Crawley, or Brandon Pomeroy, or anybody else who might be involved, I grabbed my buttonless jacket out of the closet, plopped my black beret on my head, and strode out into the rapidly fading daylight. Murderers and threatening notes be damned, I had some "nosing around" to do.

Mitzi Maxwell was a medium-tall brunette with a round, plump face, deep dimples, and eyelashes as black as raven feathers. She answered the door of her ground floor apartment wearing a blue-flowered cotton duster over a pink silk slip. The toenails of her bare feet were painted petal pink, and one of her slim ankles was encircled with a thin gold charm bracelet.

"Mitzi?" I asked, looking as innocent and calm as I could (which wasn't easy since I felt as innocent as a skunk and as calm as Milton Berle).

"Uh . . . yes . . . ?" She cocked her head to one side and a long, thick curl of dark brown hair fell over one eye. She was curious but not concerned.

"My name is Phoebe," I said. "I live over on Bleecker and I've seen you around the neighborhood many times. Could I come in and talk to you for a minute?"

Too polite to turn me away, she mumbled, "Well . . . sure . . . I guess so." Then, dimples flashing in a hesitant smile, she opened the door wider and took a step back, allowing me to enter.

It was the smallest studio I'd ever seen in my life. The living area was not much longer than the single bed sitting against the near wall, and the tiny kitchen barely had room for the small round table and two chairs which sat in the middle of the floor, partially blocking the path to the minuscule bathroom. Yet the place was charming. A mix of pictures adorned the cream-colored walls — photos, prints, drawings — and there was a real brick fireplace on the wall opposite the bed. Soft lighting gave the space a pinkish glow, and the air was filled with the warm sweet smell of freshly baked cookies. The radio

361

was playing Vic Damone.

"What's this all about?" Mitzi asked. "Is something wrong? Would you like to sit down?"

"Yes, thank you," I said, answering the last question, but not the first two. I sat down on the kitchen chair nearest the door, slowly crossing my legs and straightening my beret, searching for a good way to start the conversation. Mitzi sat down across from me and lifted her eyebrows in a questioning smile.

"Do you know a woman named Babs Comstock?" I asked her, figuring I'd dive right in and start swimming later.

"Uh, no. . . ." She stopped smiling, but she still looked puzzled.

"How about Wanda Wingate?"

Mitzi paused. She let her gaze go out of focus for a second or two, then snapped it back to attention. Propping her bent elbow on the tiny tabletop, she rested her chin in her hand, and aimed her eyes at mine. Earnestly. "No, I don't know her either. I would remember a name like Wanda Wingate for sure. Look, what's going on here? Are you trying to sell me something? Because if you are, you might as well save yourself the trouble. I'm so broke it's silly."

I gave her a sympathetic smile. "You and

me both. You and me and every other unmarried working woman in this big wide wicked city."

"What makes you think I'm not married?" She was getting her defenses up.

"For two people to live in this dainty place, you'd have to take turns breathing.

Luckily, she laughed. And let down the ramparts. "They say the best things come in small packages, but the people who say that must have brains the size of poppy seeds. Or wallets the size of Wyoming."

It was my turn to laugh. I was beginning to like Miss Mitzi Maxwell — or whoever she was. (From the sound of it, her name was as phony as mine. And Wanda's.)

"Hey!" she said, grinning. "You want a cookie? Ginger snaps. I took 'em out of the oven just a while ago."

Now I liked her even more. "Thanks, I'd love one."

"Milk, too? You gotta have milk with cookies."

"Sure."

While she was on her feet preparing our snack, unable to see my furtive face, I launched my investigation. "So what do you do for a living, Mitzi? Secretarial work?"

"What else is there? I'm too dumb to be

a teacher and too selfish to be a nurse."

"Do you work nearby?"

"No such luck. I gotta shell out twenty cents a day for the subway. I work uptown, for a skinflint tax accountant." She put a glass of milk and a plate of cookies down in front of me.

"Aren't you having any?" I asked.

"I already did." She sat down and flashed her dimples again. "But don't mind me, honey. Dig right in!"

I wanted to keep on chatting — keep the conversation aimed in the right direction — but the ginger snaps got the best of me. And it isn't polite to talk with your mouth full.

Mitzi jumped into the lull. "So why did you come to see me? What did you want to talk to me about?" I could tell from her steady gaze she expected some straight answers.

I swallowed a mouthful of cookie mush, then took a big swig of milk, stalling for time. I didn't know what to say. I wanted to find out if Mitzi was "moonlighting" for Brandon Pomeroy (or Scotty Whitcomb or the Venus Modeling Agency or Apex Theatrical), but how was I supposed to do that? Tell her I was conducting a survey of models and actresses to find out if they were, in actuality, whores?

"I really don't know how to put this," I said, still stalling, wheels twirling in my head. "It's very embarrassing." I gave her a shamefaced smile, then shifted my gaze to my hands, which were clutched in an anxious embrace on top of the table, next to the cookie plate.

"Just spit it out, honey. I've been to the bottom and back. Nothing surprises me." She leaned over the tiny table and patted my wrist.

In the face of so much goodwill, I felt like a total louse. But that didn't stop me from taking a deep breath and spinning a new web of lies. "I went out with some friends to a bar the other night," I told her, "and I met a man in the hall outside the ladies' room. And he bought me a drink. And then he started talking about how pretty I was — pretty enough to be a model or an actress, he said."

"You *are* pretty," Mitzi said, making me feel like the queen of all louses (lice?).

"Then he told me he worked for a big theatrical agent," I went on, "and that he could get me a job in television, being an assistant on a game show, or doing commercials. He said if I bleached my hair blonde I could be another Dagmar."

365

Mitzi didn't say anything.

"So I said, 'Gee, I'd really like that!' I mean, what woman wouldn't want such an exciting, glamorous job? He said I wouldn't have to work very hard, but with a face and body like mine, I could make lots of money. Then he told me to go see Martin Crawley at the Apex Theatrical Agency, and tell him Brandon Pomeroy sent me. He wrote all the information down for me on the inside of a match-book."

Mitzi heaved a heavy sigh, but still didn't say anything.

"So I got all dolled up and went to see Mr. Crawley the very next day," I stumbled on. "I was so excited I could hardly breathe. He called me into his office, and asked me a lot of questions about my professional and personal life, and then he told me I had a lot of potential, but that he couldn't get any television work for me until I had some experience as a model or an actress. He said I'd need a good portfolio, too."

"Don't tell me," Mitzi interrupted. "He said a good portfolio would cost you at least a hundred bucks, right? And you'd need a lot of snazzy new clothes. And somebody to direct your photo shoot, make you look like a star."

"That's right."

"And then he asked you if you had the money."

"Right."

"And you said no."

"Right."

"And he said he could help you get it — *if* you were really committed, and if you were willing to start at the bottom."

"His words exactly."

Mitzi sat up straighter and crossed her arms over her blue-flowered, pink silk chest. "So you told him of course you were committed, and of course you were willing to start at the bottom. And he told you that you could raise the money for your portfolio in the easiest, most pleasurable way imaginable — by going out to dinner with some very rich and powerful men, men who would treat you to the finest food and wine and entertainment, and introduce you to lots of other rich and powerful men."

"Yes," I said, looking down at my hands again. I suddenly felt profoundly sad, as if I were Babs Comstock herself — young, desperate, hopeful, poor, and alive — listening to those very same words for the very first time.

"So, what did you tell him, honey?" Mitzi wanted to know. "Did you sign on the dotted line, or say you weren't that kind of girl?"

"I didn't give him an answer yet."

"So, that's why you're here," she said, slapping the tabletop and fastening me in her genial gaze. "You heard I used to be one of Crawley's girls, and you want to find out what it's like — what 'going out to dinner' really means."

"Yes," I said, "I'm so sorry! I didn't mean to bother you, or embarrass you or anything, but I'm just so confused. Mr. Crawley said everything would be fine, that I wouldn't have to do anything I didn't want to do, but I don't know whether to trust him or not. I mean, is he offering me a real opportunity, or just an opportunity to get really screwed?"

Mitzi threw her head back and laughed. "You may look like a babe in the woods," she said, dimples winking, "but you sure don't talk like one."

"I wasn't born yesterday," I said, smiling. "Just the day before."

"In that case," Mitzi said, chuckling, "I better fill you in. So pay attention, honey. If what you want is a bona fide, honest-to-gosh career in modeling or television, you better forget you ever heard about Apex Theatrical. But if you're just looking for a little extra cash, and a lot of extra boyfriends, then Crawley's your man."

"What's he like? As a boss, I mean."

"Like any other pimp — cold, demanding, heartless, greedy. He's a total queer, though, so you won't have to worry about him wanting to test the merchandise. He'll just want his piece of the profits — which, by the way, usually adds up to about ninety percent."

"God!" I cried.

"God has nothing to do with it," Mitzi muttered.

"What about Brandon Pomeroy? Would I be working for him too?"

"In a roundabout way. But you don't have to worry about him either. He never gets directly involved."

"You mean I wouldn't have to go out with him or anything?"

"You probably won't ever see him again."

"And what about the sex part?" I asked.

"The sex part?" Mitzi looked at me as if I were six years old. "What about it? You *do* know how to do it, don't you?"

"That's not what I meant!" I cried, blushing (for real). "I just wondered if you *have* to do it — if all your dates expect it."

"Some of 'em don't. Sometimes they're shy, or impotent, or simply don't care about getting laid. They just want to be seen with a pretty girl on their arm. But most of 'em do, honey. Make no mistake about it. Most of 'em want it bad, and they expect to get what they pay for. So you'd better be prepared to give it to 'em." Her sweet face turned sour. "And don't kid yourself you'll be making good contacts — improving your chances of becoming a famous model or actress — 'cause that just ain't the way the story goes. You'll be climbing down the ladder, not up."

I thought of poor Babs's quick descent from her home in Missouri, to the fierce and filthy streets of Manhattan, to the broken dreams of love and security, to the humiliation of soul and body, to the final violation of a Hopalong Cassidy jump rope. Her ladder had been short as a step stool.

I peered into Mitzi's black-feathered eyes. "You said you *used* to be one of Crawley's girls. Does that mean you've quit? You don't work for Apex anymore?"

"I quit three months ago," she said, proudly squaring her shoulders and lifting her triumphant chin. "Knew if I didn't get out fast, I might never get out. The parties, the restaurants, the limousines, the money — it's all pretty seductive, you know?"

I nodded.

"But take my word for it, honey," Mitzi insisted, patting my wrist again. "It's a losing game. No woman ever wins it. It's a complete dead end."

Her words were more appropriate than she knew.

Chapter 25

I ate another cookie before I left, but it didn't relieve my hunger. Being stalked, threatened, and terrorized had made me ravenous. I wanted to march right over to the White Horse Tavern on Hudson Street, where all the local writers hang out, for a hamburger and a beer. I wanted to sit at the sacred table — the table where Dylan Thomas had guzzled his final drink — and gorge my psyche as well as my stomach. If, like the recently departed Welsh poet, I was going to die soon, I thought I might as well go out in literary style.

But a woman in a bar all alone? It just isn't done. Not even in the Village. So I went to a coffee shop instead. I had a hamburger and a root beer. And after I finished eating (and checking out the covers of all the detective magazines at the newsstand on the corner) it was time for me to head for the Remo.

I'd like to tell you it was a brisk and purposeful hike, that I strode from Perry to MacDougal with my *chutzpah* intact and my backbone straight as a flagpole. But that would be a big fat fib. I was a nervous wreck. I was walking (okay, trotting) so fast I could hardly breathe, and I kept whipping my head around, looking over my shoulder to see if anybody was following me. I was truly relieved when I reached my destination, even though I knew the killer might be waiting for me inside.

I plunged into the Remo and wriggled my way through the crowd of drably dressed young men and women milling around the entranceway. Many of the males wore beards. It's a Village thing. You rarely see a beard above 14th Street. The females had on dark sweaters, pale lipstick, and so much black eye makeup their lids looked bruised. The smoke was thick as syrup, and whatever air was left was pulsing with the sounds of Thelonious Monk.

Scotty Whitcomb sat facing the door in one of the big wooden booths against the wall. He saw me come in, gave me a little smile (with his mouth, not his eyes), then stood halfway up and motioned me over with a single flick of his hand. Grinning on the outside, groaning on the inside, I scooted across the black and white tiled floor and quickly slipped into the booth opposite him.

"Why don't you come over here and sit next to me?" he said, returning to his seat and sliding closer to the wall, making room for me on his bench.

The last thing I wanted to do was get close to the man. I thought I might freeze to death. "If I sit next to you," I said, forcing myself to be flirtatious, "then I won't be able to see you as well." I knew this reply would satisfy him. In my experience, Scotty Whitcomb liked nothing better than being looked at.

Shrugging and smirking, he slid back to the center of the booth. "Suit yourself," he said, smoothing the front of his black turtleneck and striking an I'm-so-handsome-it's-sinful pose. "What do you want to drink?"

"Scotch and soda," I told him. As you may have noticed, I don't limit myself to a favored highball. Like a dutiful detective, I investigate them all.

While Scotty was summoning the waitress and ordering our drinks, I looked out at the various groups of people clustered around the small tables in the middle of the room. The conversation was flowing as fast as the booze. Most of the lively faces were white, but some of them were brown. Village prince James Baldwin was holding court at one of the tables. That's one thing I like about living in the Village. It's a true melting pot. It's one of the few areas in the city (actually, the whole country) where Negroes and Caucasians can eat, drink, pray, play, love, laugh, and cry together. We even use the same bathrooms.

As soon as the waitress finished taking our order and walked away, Scotty turned to me and said, "So, doll. How's the story going?"

"What story?" I asked, batting my eyelashes and glancing up at the pressed tin ceiling. I hoped my coy response would spur him to spill a few details.

"You know the one I mean." He was annoyed by my charade. "The one about Wanda Wingate."

"Not so good," I said, sighing, telling the truth for once. "I really can't write it until I know who the murderer is."

"And you don't?"

"Of course not! How could I? The police haven't solved the case yet."

Scotty narrowed his eyes and intensified his turquoise gaze. "I thought you were snooping around on your own."

"Are you kidding? I'm no homicide investigator! I wouldn't know a bloodstain from a blob of tomato sauce! All I'm doing is jotting down a few facts, keeping notes for when it's time to write the story."

"But you came to my studio. . . ."

"That was just because of the photo of Wanda I found in our files. It had your stamp on the back, so I thought you could give me some background information on the murder victim."

He narrowed his eyes even more. "What did you do with that photo?" His congenital surliness was starting to show.

"Nothing. I'm keeping it at my desk to use with the story."

"You didn't give it to the police?"

"No. Why would I do that?"

"Because you think I murdered her."

"I certainly do not!" I cried, lying with both hands over my heart. "If I thought you did it, would I have accepted a date with you?"

He softened his glare, but just a bit. "Then why did the police come to see me?"

"I haven't the foggiest idea. Maybe they're just rounding up all the usual lady-killers."

Smirking again, he opened his mouth to speak, but snapped it closed when the waitress appeared with our drinks. She put a Rob Roy down in front of him and a

Scotch and soda in front of me, then hoisted her laden tray and snaked her way toward the next booth.

"Here's to Wanda," Scotty said when she was gone. He held his glass up and shoved it toward me for a toast. "May she rest in peace."

My heart flipped over like a fish. Could anyone who was strangled to death *ever* rest in peace? I clinked his glass and took a sip of my drink, stifling the impulse to splash it in his face. "So the police came to see you?" I asked. "When was that?"

"Yesterday. Late afternoon."

"Homicide detectives?"

"Yeah, two of 'em — a drudge named Boyd and a smart aleck named Street. A couple of the nicest guys you'd ever want to meet," he said sarcastically.

"They questioned you?"

"Street did. He wanted a minute-by-minute account of my life since the day I was born. Boyd didn't say much. He just kept blowing his nose and clearing his stupid throat."

"What did you tell them?" I asked.

"The truth," Scotty said, suddenly sitting back and lighting up a Chesterfield. He leaned his head against the back of the bench and leered at me, exhaling a steady stream of smoke from his perfectly shaped nostrils. "I told 'em where I was last Sunday at seven."

So seven was the time of death. "Where were you?" I probed.

"Home alone, in my studio, setting things up for a photo shoot later that evening. A model named Judy Lovedale. Pinup calendar — Miss June."

Maybe he was, and maybe he wasn't. He certainly didn't have anybody to corroborate his alibi. Except maybe me, I realized in shock, since I had gone to Scotty's studio the day after the murder and he had been photographing Miss July. It wasn't an ironclad defense by any means, but it did follow the right timetable (calendarwise, at any rate). I made a mental note to look for Judy Lovedale on Pomeroy's list when I got home.

"Hey, doll, can we drop this crummy subject?" Scotty grumbled, still leaning against the back of the bench, taking another drag on his cigarette. He blew a couple of smoke rings, then gave me a sultry pout. "I don't want to talk about Wanda anymore. I just want to talk about you. I want to get the hell out of this noisy joint and go someplace nice and private, where I can have you all to myself and tell you how sexy you are."

Ugh. Not again. Why did Scotty keep pretending to be attracted to me? Did he think I'd fall head over heels in love and forget he was a prime murder suspect? Did he expect me to become so infatuated I'd hire him to shoot my portfolio, or help him get lots of *Daring Detective* photo assignments? Did he presume he could seduce me into going back to his place — or mine — where he could strangle me with a jump rope and stop my "nosing around" forever?

I was looking for answers, but not to *those* questions. "Oh, Scotty, that's so sweet," I exclaimed, voice dripping with honey, "but I couldn't possibly go anywhere else tonight. I've been trying to hide it, but I've got the most horrible headache. It hurts so much I can't even bear to sit here any longer." I wrinkled my brow and raised my hand to my forehead. "Please forgive me, but I've got to go home right now, take some aspirin, and go to bed. Thanks for the drink."

I grabbed my purse and slid out of the booth before he knew what hit him. Then I streaked across the floor, pushed through the door to the sidewalk, and started running like a bat out of hell. I figured I'd be halfway home before Scotty regained consciousness and got the check paid.

But I wasn't so lucky. Scotty caught up with me four blocks down on Bleecker, just seconds after I'd crossed Cornelia, smack dab across the street from the Italian social club. He grabbed me by the arm from behind, pulled me to a stop, and yanked me around so hard and so fast I thought he'd dislocated my shoulder.

"Hey, what the hell do you think you're doing?" he screamed into my face, grabbing hold of my other arm as well. "You can't walk out on me like that!" His turquoise eyes were bulging, and his gorgeous mug was scrunched into a hideous wad of rage.

"Let go of me!" I shrieked, trying to wrench my arms out of his painful grip. My purse fell to the ground and popped open, spilling its contents all over the sidewalk. My lipstick rolled into the gutter, and the mirror of my brand-new silver compact splintered into a thousand glittering pieces.

I jerked my head from side to side, madly searching for somebody to help me. But the block was practically deserted, as it often is at night after all the food shops have closed, and the only other people on the street just then — a neighborhood man with his pregnant wife and teenage son — quickly disappeared into their own building. Where were Officer O'Hara and his horse, Peggy, when you really needed them? A couple of frail young fellows came sauntering hand in hand around the corner, but when they saw me struggling with Scotty, they yelped like puppies and ran off in the opposite direction. I cried out to them for help, but they pretended not to hear.

"Shut up!" Scotty hissed, spraying my face with spit. "Shut your stupid mouth!" He shoved me over to the closest building and, slamming my head against the hard facade, pinned my arms against the wall. "If you know what's good for you," he sputtered, grinding my wrists against the jagged bricks, "you'll keep your fucking voice down and behave like a good little girl."

I obeyed the first half of his command. "Oh, really?" I rasped, keeping my fucking voice down to an angry whisper. "Did Wanda behave like a good little girl while you were raping and strangling her?"

I shouldn't have said that.

Scotty lost whatever shred of self-control

he still had. He released one of my wrists, yanked his arm up behind his head, balled his hand into a bludgeon, and started to swing it toward my face. I squeezed my eyes shut and tried to shield myself.

If Scotty's blow had made contact, I'd still be in the hospital now. I'd be drinking my meals through a straw and begging God to reverse the brain damage. As it was, though, his fist never came within a foot of my face. It didn't even get all the way out of the starting gate.

"Aaaargh!" Scotty cried as someone jumped him from behind, spun him around, and pummeled him repeatedly in the head and stomach. At least it *sounded* like that was what was happening. For a few seconds there, I was afraid to open my eyes. And when I finally did open them, Scotty was lying facedown on the sidewalk, with one arm twisted up behind his back, and another man's knee anchored — like an anvil — on his ever-so-handsome ass.

It took me a couple of seconds to realize that the other man was Tommy. Like the gun, Tommy. Apartment wrecker, Tommy. Neighborhood protector, Tommy.

"You okay?" he grunted, turning his massive upper body toward me but keeping his knee firmly planted on Scotty's backside. A beam of light from the corner street lamp illuminated his bulging muscles and dirty white undershirt.

"Y-yes, I think so."

"Nothin' broken?"

"Not that I know of."

"Then run on home now, girlie," he said. "This creep won't bother you no more."

I didn't see any reason to argue with him.

Chapter 26

I bolted up the block toward my building. But when I screeched to a halt at the front entrance and tried to push my way inside, I hurt my shoulder again. The door was, as always, locked tight. And my house keys were — natch! — lying somewhere on the sidewalk down the street, next to my dropped purse and smashed compact, near the shadowy, still-tangled figures of Scotty and Tommy — two men I hoped never to see again in life. Or, more importantly, death.

I pushed the button to Abby's buzzer, but I knew it wouldn't do any good. Her buzzer had been on the fritz for months. Stepping away from the building and peering up at Abby's window, I saw that her lights were on and her drapes were open. I could tell from the moving, human-shaped shadow on her living room wall that she was home — probably standing and painting at her easel — so I stood beneath her tightly closed window and yelled, repeatedly, for her to open the door. She didn't hear me. In desperation, I searched the sidewalk and the gutter for some little stones or pebbles, something to toss against the glass to get her attention.

All I could find was an apple that must have fallen off Angelo's cart when he was closing up for the night. It was the same size as a baseball. Without thinking, I snatched it up in my hand, darted out into the middle of the street, and — doing a swell simulation of Duke Snyder throwing out a runner at home plate — fired it straight through Abby's windowpane.

She heard me then.

Abby shoved open her shattered window, stuck out her head, and shouted down into the street as if she owned it. "Hey! What the hell d'ya think you're doing? I'm callin' the cops! This isn't Pearl Harbor, ya know!"

I would have laughed if I hadn't been so scared. "Abby, Abby! It's me — Paige. Let me in! Let me in!" My voice sounded like a high-pitched foghorn.

"Paige? Is that you? What's happening?"

"Let me in and I'll tell you!"

"Oh!" she cried, finally realizing that I might be in danger. "I'm coming right down!" She slammed her window shut — as if that would cut off the ventilation — then disappeared from view.

I ran over to the door of our building

and stood there, shaking, until she opened it. Then I squeezed past her and shot up the stairs like a rocket.

It was good to be home.

Abby followed me into her apartment, slammed and locked the door behind us, then leapt across the floor to turn off her blasting hi-fi. John Coltrane. (No wonder she hadn't heard me yelling.) "Are you okay?" she gasped. "What's happening?"

"Everything!" I cried, collapsing like a rag doll on her little red couch. I would have given her more details, but I was too busy trying to breathe.

Seeing that I was in no condition to chat, Abby walked over to her front window, and — carefully avoiding the sea of broken glass on the canvas-covered floor — yanked the drapes closed. Then she bent down and picked up the apple, which was sitting on the floor near her easel, as if posing for a fruity still life. After examining the dented missile and wiping it clean with the underside of her paint-streaked smock, she raised it to her mouth and took a bite.

"Want a drink?" she asked, chomping and smiling at the same time.

I was finally able to speak. "Three drinks would be preferable."

She laughed, took another bite of the apple, and headed into the kitchen area. "Screwdrivers okay?"

"Fine." I would have accepted a glass of elephant pee if it had been mixed with alcohol.

Abby brought in our drinks, put them down on the cinderblock coffee table, and sat cross-legged on the floor at my feet. "So how was your day, dear?" she cooed, gazing up at me and madly flapping her lashes. She was parodying the happy little housewife, but I didn't find it so funny.

After gulping down half my drink and lighting one of Abby's cigarettes, I told her about everything that had happened since I last saw her — the phone call from Freddy, the threatening note from God-knew-who, my visit with Mitzi Maxwell, my first mad dash to meet Scotty at the San Remo, and my second mad dash to get away from him.

When I recounted how Scotty had caught up with me across the street from the social club, and how Tommy had saved me from serious head injury, Abby nodded her head excitedly. "See? I told you they protected the neighborhood. A Mafia street is a safe street."

"As long as they don't wreck your

apartment," I snarled.

"So, who do you think left you the love note?" Abby asked. "Tommy, Scotty, Zack, Freddy, or Little Lord Pomeroy?"

"Your guess is as good as mine."

"Well, Tommy sure knows how to open locked doors . . ."

"You can say that again!"

". . . but Scotty's physical behavior is more threatening."

"Than what?" I wailed, crushing my half-smoked cigarette in the ashtray. "Than smashing milk bottles and pickle jars? Than overthrowing TV sets and typewriters?"

"Zacky-boy doesn't seem so menacing," Abby went on, ignoring my cranky outburst, "but you don't know what he's like when he's sober. Could be a homicidal sex fiend in wolf's clothing. And what about Freddy?" she relentlessly proceeded. "If he knows your real name, he knows where you live. You're in the book."

"But how did he get my real name? I never gave it to Doris. All she had was my phone number." I was having trouble breathing again.

"That's a cow of a different color," Abby snorted.

A new thought popped into my brain

and started to take shape. "Maybe Freddy works for the phone company, or has a friend who does. Then he'd have access to their records and could track down a name from a number."

Abby cocked her head and considered my theory. "That would explain a lot."

"Even the note!" I sputtered. "It's written on the back of a telephone message slip!" I was twitching like a bloodhound on the trail of a hot fresh scent.

"Cool it, sister," Abby said, scowling. "Those pink message slips are everywhere — on every secretary's desk in every office in the city. Anybody could have gotten their hands on one of those."

"Right," I said, deflated. "I keep a whole stack of pink pads on my desk. Brandon Pomeroy has some, too."

"Aha! The insufferable Mr. Pomeroy! I was wondering when we'd get around to him." Abby jumped up from the floor and started pacing back and forth in front of the couch, her long black braid swaying with every step. "What's Little Lord Pompous been up to lately?"

"I don't know. He didn't come to work on Friday. He was probably home in bed with a bottle of hooch and a dirty paperback."

"Or scouting for future call girls at the corner bar."

"Or he could have been at police headquarters," I suddenly remembered. "Dan told me he was going to question somebody that afternoon."

"Dan . . . ?" Abby said, stopping short in her tracks and turning to gape at me. She curled her mouth up in a crooked smile and lifted one eyebrow to the peak. "Are you referring to the distinguished Sergeant Dan Street?" she teased. "The tall, dark, and handsome homicide detective you've been avoiding like the plague? The dashing and divorced dreamboat you're not the least bit interested in? The fine, upstanding law enforcement agent you'd never even think of calling by his first name?"

My face turned hot as a griddle. And my forehead broke out in a sweat. In a vain attempt to hide my embarrassment, I picked up my drink and drained it dry. "Could I have another one?" I asked, handing Abby my empty glass and trying not to choke.

"Hey, bobba ree bop!" Abby croaked. Her full lips were stretched in an ear-to-ear grin. "I thought you were starting to flip for Street, but I wasn't so sure. Now it's downright conspicuous — as plain as the nose on your flaming red face."

I didn't say a thing. What was the point of protesting? Abby wouldn't believe me. And besides, I was beginning to wonder if what she had said might be true.

"You can ditch the guilty look, Paige. It's high time you fell for somebody!" Abby declared, heading to the kitchen to refresh our drinks. "You're too young to spend the rest of your life in mourning."

The thought of my late husband brought me up short, and my heart stopped beating for a few painful seconds. I felt like weeping again.

But I didn't. I just poked another cigarette in my mouth and lit it. "Oh, yeah?" I said, taking a quick drag and blowing out a taut stream of smoke. "Well, if things keep going the way they're going, you're going to be the one in mourning — for me."

Abby slammed the refrigerator door and knocked around in the kitchen for few seconds. Then she came back with our drinks and sat next to me on the couch, her pretty face contorted in a grimace of worry. "You're right, Paige. The situation's getting really serious now. Instead of you closing in on the killer, he's closing in on you. I think you'd better stay here tonight."

"Thanks. I don't want to be alone. I

can't get into my apartment, anyway."

"Why?"

"Lost my keys. When Scotty grabbed me, I dropped my purse and everything fell out on the sidewalk."

"Did you lose your nerve, too?"

"Nope," I lied.

"Good. You're gonna need it."

After another hour of heavy clue and motive analysis (i.e., just plain wondering who the murderer could be), Abby and I had a big disagreement over whether or not I should tell Dan about what was happening. She thought I ought to call him up immediately, tell him everything I knew, and enlist his personal — as well as police — protection. But I couldn't bring myself to do it. I simply wasn't ready to admit defeat and give up the ghost.

The ghost of Babs Comstock, I mean. My constant companion and cherished friend. I still felt totally connected to Babs, and responsible for her somehow. If I gave up now, I'd be abandoning her. . . .

And I'd also be abandoning my dream. My dream of tracking down the killer myself, then writing the most explosive, most exclusive murder story ever to hit the national newsstands. My vision of becoming the first female in history to be employed as a staff writer for *Daring Detective* magazine. My hope of winning the admiration and respect of Dan Street and Harvey Crockett, the proper professional courtesy of Mike and Mario, and the overdue honor of a proper paycheck.

"Look, you're not thinking too clearly tonight," Abby said, taking the last swallow of her screwdriver and carrying our empty glasses to the sink. "You should try to get some sleep now. We can talk about all this stuff in the morning."

"Yes," I said gratefully. "Let's talk in the morning." I was eager to end our conversation. My head was spinning and my body was trembling. I wanted to curl myself up in a tight little ball on Abby's tight little couch, and drop off into oblivion. "Do you have a blanket or something? It's kind of drafty in here."

"Very funny," Abby huffed. "Bust a hole in my house, then complain about the breeze."

"Sorry about your window," I mumbled, kicking off my shoes, sinking down into a fetal position on the red sofa seat, and hugging my knees up to my chest. I would have apologized more profusely if my wits had been in working order. It was a wonder I didn't start sucking my thumb.

"I dig," Abby said softly. "Hold on, I'll get you an afghan."

I woke to the sound of pealing bells. And since I'd spent the whole night dreaming that I was being chased by a sex-crazed strangler, my first thought was that the bells were tolling for me — announcing my sudden premature arrival at the proverbial pearly gates. It took me a few groggy minutes to realize that I was in Abby's apartment, not the outskirts of heaven, and that the bells were ringing not for me, but because it was Sunday morning. Time for church.

I sat up on the couch and rubbed my eyes. The drapes were still closed, and the light in the studio was dim, but I could still make out the new painting that was displayed — like a prominent warning sign — on Abby's easel. Probably an illustration for one of the pulps, it was a picture of a beautiful, half-naked blonde, clad only in a torn bra and half slip, sitting on a straight wooden chair with her arms tied behind her back. Standing over the woman and leering down at her lush defenseless flesh was a tough-looking fully dressed man with a very big gun. Not a very comforting image.

Groaning, I got up from the couch, slipped my feet into my ballerina flats, and went into the kitchen for a drink of water. Then I crept upstairs to check on Abby. She was sleeping like a baby — a baby in red lace babydoll pajamas. I tiptoed back down the stairs, took out the broom and dustpan Abby kept in her coat closet, and shuffled over to the window to clean up the broken glass.

When I finished, I pulled open a little peephole in one side of the drapes and peered outside. It was a clear, sunny day. All the shops were closed and the street was quiet. As far as I could tell there were no murderers lurking in the nearby doorways. Pressing my face to the window frame and opening the drapes a little wider, I strained my eyes down the block toward Tommy territory. The door of the social club was closed and the windows were dark, so I figured the mobsters hadn't come in yet. They were probably all over at St. Joseph's taking Communion. Maybe they took Scotty Whitcomb with them.

I was dying to go home, take a shower, change my clothes, add the details of the previous day's events to my Comstock case list — but before I could do any of those things, I realized, I'd have to go outside and look for my keys. I was still dressed from the night before, even had on my shoes, so there was no excuse for delay. I had to strike while the coast was clear (i.e., before I got cold feet and decided to spend the rest of my life on Abby's couch).

Darting over to unlock the front door, I pulled it wide and stuck my head out into the hall. Not a soul in sight. No killers, rapists, or Mafia goons. No playboys, pimps, or photographers. Both the landing and the stairwell were completely empty — except for the odd little mound of stuff sitting on the floor right in front of the door to my apartment. Unable to see very well in the murky hall light, I bent down to take a closer look.

It was my purse! And my lipstick. And my broken silver compact. And my crumpled black beret, which must have been knocked to the ground during my struggle with Scotty, when he slammed my head against the brick wall. My keys were there, too, and I nipped them up in my hand like a thief.

Rather than being crazed and upset that Tommy had broken into my building again, I felt like kissing his big ugly mug — showing my deep, heartfelt appreciation. Maybe I'd send him a thank-you card, or get him a little gift of some kind. A black-jack or some brass knuckles.

Before unlocking my front door, I taped a note to the inside of Abby's door telling her I'd found my keys and would see her later. Then I slipped inside my own apartment.

Too bad I didn't stay there.

Chapter 27

I took a shower and changed my clothes, but I never sat down to work on my story notes. I hopped the subway out to Brooklyn instead, determined to find out more about Freddy and how he was connected to Babs. I had concocted a plan in my head while showering, and I was keeping my fingers crossed it would actually work.

When I emerged from the underground gloom, squinting like a baby mole in the bright sunshine (and constantly checking over my shoulder to see if I was being followed), I headed straight down Kings Highway to the Early Bird Coffee Shop and ducked inside. Sweeping past the line of late-morning breakfasters seated at the green Formica counter running the length of the dingy eatery, I stepped into the wood and glass phone booth in the back corner, sat down on the little flip-out seat, and pulled the heavy door closed.

Throwing all caution to the breeze and shoving a nickel into the slot, I pulled a number out of my purse and dialed it.

"Yeah?" a harsh male voice answered. I

was glad it was Freddy, not Betty. It didn't surprise me he wasn't in church.

"Hello, Fred," I said, doing my best to sound amiable and peppy. "This is Paige Turner. You said you were going to phone me back, but you never did, so I thought I would give you a call instead. I hope that's okay. I mean, I'm not interrupting your breakfast or anything, am I?"

"What do you want?" He sounded angry — as usual.

"Well, two things, really."

"Like what?"

"First of all, I'd like to know how you got my real name." (If I was going to be believable, I felt I had to be honest about *some* of my concerns.) "I only gave you my professional name," I said. "Phoebe Starr. That's the one I always use."

"What difference does it make how I got it?"

"Well, it just surprises me, that's all. Everybody, but everybody calls me Phoebe — all my friends and coworkers, even most of my relatives — and I can't figure out who could have told you —"

"Maybe Barbara said somethin'."

"Impossible. Babs only knew me as Phoebe. I never told her my real name."

"Then I musta got it from that hag waitress at Schrafft's, the one who gave me your phone number."

"Doris doesn't know it either."

"Gee whiz," he said, suddenly changing his tone from menacing to mocking. "Then I don't know where I coulda got it. I guess I just reached up in the sky and pulled it out of a cloud." He was playing with me now, daring me to chase him.

But I couldn't spare the time. "Oh, well, it doesn't matter really," I said, punctuating my words with a soft sigh of surrender. "I was just curious."

"Curiosity killed the cat."

It was an obvious threat, but I pretended not to notice. "The other reason I called is pretty simple," I hurried on, squeezing my eyes closed and praying for divine assistance. I crossed my fingers and popped the all-important question: "Do you still want to talk to me about Babs . . . like you said you did the other night?" I held my breath until he gave his reply.

"Yeah," he grunted. The man was the champ of one-word responses.

"Good. I want to talk to you, too. But I think we should meet instead of talking on the phone, don't you? The phone is so impersonal."

"Yeah."

"Then how about today? At the Schrafft's where Babs used to work. I haven't eaten yet, have you? If you leave now, you could get there by noon."

"Right."

"Does that mean you'll come?"

"Yeah."

I was about to repeat the place and the time when he hung up.

Though I was aching for an egg cream and a donut, I left the Early Bird with an empty stomach — and a mind full of self-doubt. *Oh, brother! I've really tied myself to the railroad track now! Whatever made me think such a half-baked, hare-brained scheme would work? Even Brenda Starr wouldn't attempt anything as daring (okay, dopey) as this.*

Panting my fool head off — and constantly whipping it around to look for furtive (or, as far as I could tell, nonexistent) pursuers — I dashed down Kings Highway to Ocean Avenue, and two blocks over to the red brick building where Freddy and Betty and little Ricky lived. Then, darting behind the tall, thick bank of evergreen shrubs lining the path to the entrance of their apartment house, I sank down in a squat on the soft spring lawn and tried

401

to get hold of myself.

Fat chance. The only thing I got hold of was a loafer full of ants, which is what happens when you plant your foot in an anthill as high as the Chrysler Building. I might have gotten my nose stung, too, if the big hairy bumblebee that circled my face a few times, looking for a good place to land, hadn't finally buzzed off in search of more fragrant flowers.

I hunkered behind that hedge — slapping at ants, swatting off gnats, stifling groans and making faces — for a good ten minutes. My thighs grew numb, my knees started to burn, and my ankles turned itchy from insect bites.

Finally, the front door of the apartment building flew open and someone stomped outside. From my hunched-over squatting position — close to the ground and hugging the hedge — I couldn't see who it was. But I could tell from the heavy footfalls it was a man. A big man. Mumbling and cursing under his breath, he strode down the front path to the sidewalk, turned right, and began walking — in the opposite direction from me, thank God — down the street.

I raised myself up until my eyes cleared the top of the hedge, then I watched him stomp away. He had on a brown sport jacket and a tan fedora. Judging from his considerable height and hefty shoulders, and from the slight edge of curly brown hair visible beneath his hat, I felt pretty sure it was Freddy. And when he suddenly stopped in the middle of the block and turned to step into the street, giving me a good look at his belligerent, broken-nosed profile, I *knew* it was Freddy.

Dizzy with relief, and elated that my crazy plan seemed to be working, I exhaled loudly and partially straightened my cramped legs. Bending over at the waist to stay hidden behind the hedge, I watched as Freddy walked around the green and white Chevrolet parked at the curb, opened the driver's door, and slid in behind the wheel. He fired up the engine, maneuvered the car out of the tight parking space, pulled out into the street, and peeled off like a teenage hot-rodder.

I stood upright and watched his two-tone tail end disappear around the corner. I was about to walk around the hedge and go inside the building when the front door swung open again. Gasping in surprise, I dropped back into a squat behind the bushes, clinched my sore knees in close to my chest, and hoped I was still well hidden. Like any sensible sleuth, I didn't want to be seen at the scene.

High heels tapping a Morse code on the pavement, a woman exited the apartment building and headed down the pathway. She was walking slowly and unevenly, and she wasn't alone. A pair of smaller feet scuffled alongside.

"C'mon, Ricky!" the woman said. "Stop daydreaming and start walking. At the rate you're going, we won't get to the playground before dark!" She sounded snippy and impatient.

Ricky didn't reply. He just sniffled a couple of times and came to an abrupt standstill, directly on the other side of the hedge from me.

"Jesus!" snapped the woman (by this time I knew it was Betty). "What's the matter with you now? You're such a crybaby. Don't you want to go play on the swings?"

He still didn't say anything.

"Oh, I'm getting so tired of this," Betty said, her hostile tone turning into a disagreeable whine. "Why are you always so quiet and unhappy? Don't you like to have fun? Your father said you wanted to go to the playground. C'mon, let's go. . . ."

"Will Aunt Barbara be there?" the little

boy asked. "I like it when she comes."

Betty heaved a defeated sigh. "No, honey, she won't." Suddenly, her voice sounded nicer. Soft, furry, and a little bit sad. "Don't you remember what I told you? Aunt Barbara moved away. She moved all the way out to California — that's all the way across the country — and she won't be able to come visit us anymore."

"Not ever?" His tiny voice quivered like a plucked violin string.

"Not for a long, long time."

Ricky became silent again.

And Betty's impatience made a rapid return. "Oh, stop pouting! I've had enough of your sick puppy act. It's a beautiful sunny day, and I'm not going to spend it standing here moping in the shade. I'm going to the playground. You can come with me and ride the merry-go-round, or you can stay here sulking all by yourself. I don't care." High heels clacking like castanets, she flounced down to the end of the front path, turned onto the sidewalk, and briskly walked away.

Ricky whimpered for a second or two, then dashed after her.

Staying as far behind as I could without losing sight of them, I followed Betty and little Ricky to the playground six blocks away. By the time I snuck into the small park and sank down on the nearest bench, Ricky was sitting on one of the swings, pumping back and forth with listless persistence. He was wearing tan pants and a red plaid shirt. No holster or cowboy hat. The seven or so other children in the playground were laughing, squealing, and playing together, but Ricky was swinging off to the side by himself, dejected and mute.

Betty sat alone on a bench nearby, legs crossed, hands in her lap, face held up to the sun, eyes closed. Her platinum-blonde hair was as sleek and glossy as Abby's wig — or Babs's pageboy. In her shiny red patent leather pumps, gleaming white jacket, and bright blue dress, she looked as American as the flag. The other mothers weren't quite so dressed up, even though it was Sunday.

Too pressed for time to plan a smooth attack, I rose to my feet, walked over to Betty's bench, and sat down next to her. "Hi!" I said. "How's it going?"

Startled, Betty opened her big brown eyes, shielded them from the sun with her hand, and turned them in my direction. When she saw it was me, she almost choked. "Jesus!" she gasped, red lips trembling. "What are you doing here?"

"I was on my way to visit you at your apartment when I saw you and Ricky come around the corner and go into the park. So I followed you here instead."

"What do you want?" Her lips stopped trembling and started scowling, Joan Crawford style.

"I just want to talk to you and your husband about Babs Comstock."

"My husband's not home. He went into the city on business." She looked like Lana Turner now — calm, cool, and painstakingly collected.

Hmmmm. So Freddy didn't tell her the truth about where he was going. "Business?" I asked. "On Sunday? What kind of business is your husband in?"

"My husband's business is no business of yours." Maureen O'Hara at her haughtiest. If Betty had been intimidated by me before, she certainly wasn't now.

"I'm sorry," I said quickly. "I didn't mean to pry." (Which wasn't the truth, of course, but there's nothing new about *that* revelation.)

Betty didn't say anything.

I took a deep breath and continued on. "Actually I'm kind of glad your husband's not here. I've been wanting to talk to you alone."

"But why?" she asked, voice growing shrill.

"I told you. I just want to talk about Babs."

Her spine turned stiff as a fence post. "The poor woman's dead, for Christ's sake. Can't you just let her rest in peace?"

There was that stupid phrase again. "There's nothing peaceful about being strangled," I said.

Betty winced and looked away. She watched as Ricky got off the swing, got on the seesaw, and then tried — repeatedly — to make it go up and down without a partner. I waited for her to say something, but she had closed up like a clam.

"Look, I know this is very unpleasant for you," I ventured, deciding to try honey instead of flypaper. "Babs was a good friend of yours as well as mine, and you must be suffering just as much as I am."

"Not really," she mumbled, still looking away, still idly observing the boy's pathetic attempts at solo teeter-tottering. "Barbara and I weren't that close."

"Didn't you go to high school together in Missouri?"

"Yes," she said, turning to look at me

408

again, squinting in the sun, "but she was a junior and I was just a freshman. She was a popular cheerleader and I was a dreary little nobody. She didn't even know my name."

"So you became friends after you moved to New York?"

"No. We were never friends."

"Then why did you visit her in the city so often? Babs really looked forward to your lunches and get-togethers. She told me all about them."

Betty gave me a creepy smile. "She looked forward to seeing Ricky, not me."

I paused for a second while that bit of news sank in. "Then why did you go to the trouble? What was in it for you?"

"Nothing," she said, gazing down at the grass. "I just felt sorry for her."

I suddenly had the feeling Betty was as good a liar as I was.

"Why?" I exclaimed. "Babs was beautiful, and she had lots of boyfriends, and she was on her way to becoming a successful model. Why did you feel sorry for her?"

"Because she didn't have a husband. And she didn't have any kids. And she was getting old."

"Old?!" I sputtered. "She was only twenty-four!"

"Almost twenty-five," Betty scoffed. "And what man wants to marry a woman that age? Barbara's best child-bearing years were over." As I tensed and said a prayer for my ancient uterus, Betty glanced over toward the seesaw again. But Ricky wasn't there. He was now hanging by his hands from a low bar of the jungle gym, looking limp as laundry on the line.

"Listen," Betty said, turning her hostile eyes back to me, "what's the point of all this? Why are you asking me these idiotic questions? I fail to see how anything I say can help you come to terms with Barbara's death." She looked strong and defiant — not at all the way she had looked the night I showed up, unannounced, at their apartment. She had been pale with panic then. Scared of her own shadow. Or was it Freddy's shadow she'd been afraid of?

"I guess you're right," I said, sighing. "It's your husband I need to talk to."

Bingo. Betty's panic made a speedy comeback. "Oh, please don't bother him anymore," she begged, suddenly wringing her hands in her lap. "He can't help you either. He's very sad about Barbara's death, and he doesn't want to talk about it to anyone. Not even me."

"I didn't get the impression he was sad.

All he seemed to be was mad."

"That's just the way he shows his emotions."

"But he said he wasn't that close to Babs, that they weren't old friends."

Betty looked down at the small white hands still writhing in her lap. "They weren't old friends," she said, pausing to take a deep breath. "They were old sweethearts." She pronounced her words slowly and softly, as if it hurt like hell to say them.

"Oh," I said, not sure what to make of her hushed disclosure. Or of the obvious pain it was causing her. I stayed mum for a few seconds, then finally asked, "Were they sweethearts in high school?"

"Yes," she said, looking as stark and wretched as Vivian Leigh in *A Streetcar Named Desire*. "They were the best-looking, most popular couple in the whole school. He was the star quarterback of the football team, and she was the head cheerleader. They were the king and queen of the world."

"Not for long, obviously."

For some strange reason, my remark put her on the defensive. "They went steady for two years," she said in a huff, "until Barbara quit school and ran away to live in New York."

411

The plot thickens. "Why did she do that?"

"She was just sick and tired of Springfield and wanted to broaden her horizons."

Oh, sure. Babs was so sick of being a beautiful, popular cheerleader, and so tired of having a handsome football hero boyfriend, that she just *had* to quit school and leave her family to seek a brand-new life on the lovely tropical isle of Manhattan. It was a ridiculous, not-to-be-believed story. The question was, who had made it up? Babs, or Freddy, or Betty?

"Was Freddy upset when Babs left?" I asked.

"Just for a little while. He started dating me right after that. And he ended up *marrying* me," she said, tossing her head like a circus pony, "so *I* was the one Scotty really loved."

What did she say? Are my ears deceiving me? Did I just hear what I think I heard? "Who?" I screeched, breathless with wonder. "You were the one *who* really loved?"

"Scotty."

"Scotty who? Who are you talking about?" I was frothing at the mouth now.

"Freddy, of course. Who else would I be talking about? Scotty was his nickname in high school. The guys on the football team

412

started calling him that — from his surname, Scott — and the name just stuck."

"Did Babs call him Scotty too?"

"Sure. Everybody did."

I felt like a total imbecile. Scott, Scotty. Why hadn't I put the two names together before? My powers of detection were downright powerless.

"Are you satisfied now?" Betty said, suddenly shaking off the past and bounding back to the present. She jumped to her feet, stepped away from the bench, and made another ugly Joan Crawford face. "I hope you are," she seethed, "because I've had enough of this useless, boring conversation. I'm sorry Barbara is dead, and I'm sorry for your pain over losing your best friend, but it has nothing to do with me or my husband. So please leave us alone!"

With that, she spun around on her shiny red heels, lunged over to the jungle gym, grabbed little Ricky by the hand and pulled him, surprised and sniffling, across the grass to the playground exit. She was walking so fast he had to run to keep up with her.

Chapter 28

I sat on the park bench in shock, trying to sort out my spinning thoughts and theories. So! Babs had probably written her poem about Freddy Scott — not Scotty Whitcomb! And if that assumption was true, I had been barking up the wrong boyfriend. I tried to calculate the significance of this new revelation, but my brain was upside down. I couldn't calculate the significance of anything . . . anything but my own ineffectiveness.

I was disturbed that I hadn't gotten the chance to talk to Ricky, to ask if he'd ever had a Hopalong Cassidy jump rope. And I was annoyed that Betty hadn't been more compliant, more willing to discuss the true dimensions of her (and Freddy's) relationship with Babs. Most of all, though, I was upset that Freddy, the abusive scoundrel Babs may have been in love with — the mean, violent, easily enraged ex-quarterback who may have wound a rope around her neck and wrung it till her pretty face was blue — was now sitting at a table in Schrafft's, looking at his watch and fuming like a volcano, getting madder by the second at *me*.

Frantic to get to a phone, I fled the playground and ran all the way back to the Early Bird (it being Sunday, everything else was closed). I dove into the booth in the back, looked up a number in the book, and made another call.

After two rings, a woman answered, "Good afternoon, Schrafft's!"

"Hello," I said, trying — unsuccessfully — to keep my voice calm. "Is Doris Toomey working today? May I speak to her, please?"

An eternity passed before she answered me. "Um, yes, Doris is here," the woman finally said, "but I'm afraid you can't speak to her right now. Our employees aren't allowed to take phone calls during their scheduled shifts."

"Oh, please!" I begged. "This is an emergency. Please let me talk to her for just a minute!"

There was a pause, and then a rather loud sigh. "Well, if it really *is* an emergency . . ."

"Oh, it is! It is!" I insisted. "It's a matter of life and death." Truer words were never spoken. Well, not by me, anyway.

"Okay," she said, sighing again. "Hold

on, I'll get her. But you'd better make it quick. It's Sunday lunch and we're packed to the gills." She slammed the phone down on a counter, or a table, or some other flat surface.

Doris picked it up a couple of minutes later. "Hello? Who is this, please?" She sounded astonished and confused — as though she'd never gotten a personal phone call before in her life.

"Doris! Thank God you're there! It's me, Paige — I mean Phoebe! Phoebe Starr!"

"Phoebe? Oh! Is that you? What's the matter? Are you okay? They said it was an emergency."

"I need your help, Doris, but I don't have time to explain. Is Freddy Scott there?"

"What?"

"Babs's old friend, Freddy. The one from Brooklyn with the kid. Is he there? I was supposed to meet him and I'm very late. I need you to give him a message."

"He was here, but he isn't anymore."

"He left already?" I could tell from the screech in my voice — and the sour taste in my mouth — that I was hysterical now.

"Yeah, about five minutes ago. He looked like he was in a big hurry. He sat

alone for a while before he ordered anything, but once his food arrived he just
bolted down his steak and mashed, paid
his bill, and ran out. No good-bye. No
thank-you. No tip."

"Did he talk to you at all?"

"Not a word. But I didn't wait on him.
Marylou Watkins did, and she said he was
acting kind of crazy. Weird and jumpy. She
wasn't surprised when he didn't leave her
any change."

I wasn't surprised either. Freddy didn't
seem like the big-tipper type. "Okay,
Doris," I said, anxious to get off the phone.
"Thanks for the info. You'd better get back
to work now."

"Yeah, my boss is giving me the evil
eye."

"Bye, then. I'll talk to you soon."

"How soon?" she gasped, hanging on to
my words as if they were a lifeline.

"Real soon," I assured her, wondering if
I'd be residing here on earth sweet earth
long enough to keep that hasty promise.

I hung up and dialed another number.

"Homicide," a man's voice answered.

"Detective Sergeant Dan Street, please.
Tell him Paige Turner is calling."

The man let out a scornful snicker.

417

"Paige Turner, eh?" He snapped his gum — loudly — in my ear. "You're out of luck, lady. Street's not here. He went to Harlem to meet a guy named Cliff Hanger." He snickered again.

"No, you don't understand," I cried. "That's my real name, and I really need to talk to Detective Street. Now. It's an emergency!"

"Well, he's still not here," the man muttered. His tone had turned, on a dime, from sarcastic to weary. "Wanna talk to somebody else? Wanna leave a message?"

"No," I said, heart sinking like a corpse in cement shoes. "I'll call back later."

Dropping the receiver back on the hook, I drooped into a slump and let my chin collapse on my chest. I felt defeated and utterly alone. And terrified. Let's not forget terrified. I was so scared, I was ready to make a full confession. I wanted to contact Dan and beg him to meet me at my apartment right away. I wanted to tell him everything I knew about the Comstock case, give him the list of names I'd found in Pomeroy's desk, show him the death threat that had been shoved under my door, and beg him for support and protection (police *or* personal — I wasn't feeling the least bit picky).

But — since I couldn't reach Dan, and since I was keen to get out of Brooklyn before Freddy got back — I summoned all of my energy, straightened my slumping spine, broke out of the phone booth, tore down the aisle of the coffee shop, burst out onto the street, and ran like the devil for the subway. If you had been there to see me, you would have thought I was a mindless, violent criminal trying to escape from the pen, when actually it was the other way around.

Abby was still dressed, or, rather, *un*dressed in her red lace babydolls. She had a bagel in one hand and a paintbrush in the other. "Well, if it isn't Apple Annie!" she said when I appeared, wild and winded, at her door. "Where the hell did you disappear to?"

"It's a long story," I sputtered, tossing my jacket on the table and staggering into her studio (which I had come to think of as my bedroom). "Have you got another bagel?"

"On the counter. There's cream cheese and coffee, too."

I almost kissed her bare feet. "Thank God! I'm so hungry! Just let me get something to eat, then I'll tell you everything."

"Okay," she said, turning back to her easel. She took a bite of her bagel, and applied a few strokes of paint to her canvas while she chewed. It was the same picture I'd seen that morning when I first woke up — the blonde in bondage and the man with the big gun. America's best-selling sex fantasy. I shivered. Replace the revolver with a rope and you'd have a suitable illustration for "The Babs Comstock Story."

I wobbled over to the kitchen counter and scarfed down a bagel. Then I poured myself a cup of coffee and carried it over to the couch.

"I'm through!" I cried, sitting down and taking a quick, scalding gulp. "I can't do this anymore."

Abby put down her paintbrush and propped her hand on her hip. "Can't do what? Wear a wig? Ride the subway? Eat a bagel? Break a window?"

"Any of it!" I said. "I'm finished! I'm really exhausted, and I'm really scared. And if I don't stop playing detective, I'm going to be really dead." I told Abby about how I'd spent my morning — how I'd tricked Freddy into leaving Brooklyn so I could talk to Betty. Then I told her about the two-way nickname.

"Can you believe it?" I wailed. "Freddy

could be the real Scotty — or Scotty could be the real Scotty! I have no way to know which Scotty is Scotty! All I know is that Babs was in love with one Scotty, and one Scotty probably killed her, and now both Scottys want to kill me!" I was in a true tizzy now — just inches from going off the deep end.

"What about Brandon Pomeroy?" Abby interjected.

"Huh?"

"Is there any way you could get hold of his birth records?"

"Wha— ?!" Her left-field question caught me by the hand, pulled me back from the edge. "What are you talking about?"

"Pomeroy's birth certificate. Could you get a look at it?"

"Why would I want to do that?"

"To see if his middle name is Scotty."

That was the slap in the face I needed. I stopped hyperventilating and started laughing. And then I laughed some more. I laughed so hard I almost threw up.

Abby laughed, too, for a few silly seconds. Then she became dead serious. "You're in way over your head now, Paige," she said, pointing her finger at me and wagging it, looking as much like a stern schoolteacher as anyone can wearing red lace babydoll pajamas. "I said it last night, and I'll say it again. You can't wait any longer. You've got to call the police. You've got to call Dan Street *right now!*"

"I already did."

"What?"

"I called him from a phone booth in Brooklyn, but he wasn't there."

"Oh?" She cocked her head and gave me a probing look. "Does that mean you're going to spill your beans?"

"Every last one of them."

"Good girl!" she yelped, springing over to the couch and sitting down next to me. "It's the only thing you can do, Paige. You've got information that could help the police, you dig? Catching the murderer is more important than getting the story."

"Right."

"And if you get killed, you'll never get to write the story anyway."

"Gee, I never thought of that," I said sarcastically.

"So what are you waiting for? You know where the phone is. Go give your future loverboy another buzz."

I balked at her calling Dan my loverboy — future or otherwise — but I didn't say anything. To protest would have sapped my strength, all of which I needed just to stand up and walk into the kitchen to the phone.

I dialed and the same dimwit answered. "Homicide," he croaked, cracking his gum like a cap pistol.

"This is Paige Turner," I mumbled. "Is Detective Street back yet?"

"Nope." He wasn't being polite, but at least he wasn't razzing me about my name.

"Do you know when he'll be back?"

"Nope."

"Can you give me a number where I can reach him?"

"Don't know where he is."

"Then would you take down my name and number and ask him to call me as soon as he returns? It's urgent."

"Okay," he grunted, sounding put out. "I got the name. What's the number?"

I gave him two — both mine and Abby's — just to be on the safe side. Then I hung up.

"What happened?" Abby asked, as I staggered back to the couch.

"Nothing. He wasn't there."

"Is he coming back?"

"I don't know."

"Did you ask to speak to somebody else?"

"No."

"Why not? Maybe they would have sent you a bodyguard."

"I don't want a bodyguard," I said. "I just want Dan." Until the last four words had flown — like arrows — out of my mouth, piercing holes in my frigid facade, I didn't realize how ardently I'd said them. Or how on target they were.

Chapter 29

Embarrassment is a very strong emotion —
sometimes even stronger than fear. And I
was so embarrassed by my unwitting confession of my feelings for Dan that I simply
couldn't stay at Abby's any longer. She kept
smirking, and winking, and giving me so
many self-satisfied, you-can't-fool-me-
you're-madly-in-love-with-him looks, that I
took flight to my own apartment, telling her
I wanted to work on my story notes — get all
the important new facts and clues down on
paper for the police.

I wasn't lying, either. I really *did* want to
do that. Even if it meant being at my place
all alone. Even if it meant flinching at
every tiny noise, and jumping up from the
typewriter every second or two to peek out
the front window, or one of the four glass
panes in my kitchen door, looking for
lurking Scottys.

I finished my notes around five p.m. and
Dan still hadn't called. In an effort to keep
busy (and to keep my sense of impending
doom at bay), I took all my other notes
and bits of evidence out from under the

daybed mattress and spread everything out on the kitchen table, next to the type-writer. I thought if I read through all the details again, and gave Babs's poem, Pomeroy's address list, and the hand-printed death threat another going-over, some heretofore unnoticed sign might spring up off the paper, hit me right between the eyes, and knock some sense into my head. Maybe I already had all the answers, but just hadn't asked the right questions.

First, I looked for Judy Lovedale (Scotty Whitcomb's Miss June) on Pomeroy's address list. She wasn't there. She wasn't in the phone book, either — not under Lovedale at any rate. She was probably listed under her *real* name — Gloggsticker, or Plutz, or something equally unglamorous — but, not having any idea what that real name might be, I couldn't look her up or get her number or call to question her about Babs and Scotty.

Giving up on Miss June, I put Pomeroy's address list aside and picked up the small pink telephone message slip that had been shoved under my door the day before. I held it up to the light and examined both sides. The capitalized and underlined words of the shocking death threat sent another gruesome chill down my spine, but offered no further clues or insights.

Babs's poem, on the other hand, held more promise. Suddenly remembering that she had written it on the back of a letter — a letter from her mother in Missouri — I snatched the poem up and flipped it over to the other side. Although I'd read the letter the night I discovered it in Babs's apartment and found it uninformative, I had little recollection of what it said. Maybe I'd missed something important, something I couldn't have understood at that point in time. With a sharp intake of air, I looked down at Elizabeth Comstock's narrow, rigid pen-and-ink script, and eagerly read her words again.

Just a blob of boring chitchat. The Ferndales had adopted a nasty new dog; the forsythia was blooming beautifully this year; Reverend Wilkes gave a fine sermon last Sunday, and the box supper at the church social that night was very nice. *The whole Askew family was there, and Mitch and Minnie Doone, and even Dorinda and Fred Scott, Sr., who shunned your father and me as usual.* Wait a minute. Back up. Dorinda and Fred Scott, Sr.? Freddy's parents, by any chance? And why would they be shunning the Comstocks?

Several new questions, but no new answers. The remainder of the letter gave an elaborate description of Mom's latest migraine, and was signed, *Best wishes, Mother.* A rather formal farewell, I thought, but what can you expect from a dog-hating, forsythia-loving church lady with a headache?

I put the letter down, stood up from the kitchen table, and started pacing the floor like a loon. I wanted to make a long-distance call to Babs's mother, to offer my condolences and see if she could shed some light on any of my suspicions, but I knew a big phone bill would make me late with the rent. And since I was planning to tell Dan everything anyway, I figured I'd just show him the mother's letter and let him make the call — at the police department's expense.

But where the hell *was* Dan? Why hadn't he called me back? Even if Sunday was his day off and he was spending it with his daughter, Katy, wouldn't he at least check in at headquarters to see if anything critical was happening or if he'd gotten any urgent messages?

Tension rising like the tide, I crept over to the living room window and took yet another furtive peek through the gap between the frame and the lowered shade. The sun had disappeared and the sky was cloaked in dark clouds. It was going to rain. You could feel it and smell it. And sure enough, as I was standing there at the window, staring down through the puckered shade at the darkening street, there was a sudden bright flash of lightning and a bone-cracking clap of thunder. And then the rain came down. Hard.

The people who had been sauntering along the sidewalk beneath my window, laughing and chatting about nothing in particular, were suddenly squealing and whooping and dashing in all directions like idiots, holding jackets and newspapers over their heads, looking for an open doorway or shop to duck into. In a matter of seconds, Bleecker Street had turned into a raging river — and its banks had grown as black as night.

There was another sudden blast of lightning, which caused me to jump away from the window and dart back into the kitchen, and then another earth-shattering crash of thunder — which, I'm sure I don't have to tell you, did nothing to improve my peace of mind.

The grimacing face I saw staring in through the window of my back door didn't calm my nerves, either.

It was a man's face, on a man's head, in a man's gray hat, but that was all I could say for sure. The flash of lightning preceding the second break of thunder gave only a moment's illumination, and when the deep, liquid blackness returned, the face was gone.

My feet were frozen to the floor. I stood in the middle of my kitchen like a statue. Then I crumpled and fell down to the linoleum. After hunkering there for a lifetime — down on my knees and elbows, with my arms wrapped over my head like a schoolkid during an atom bomb drill — some feeling returned to my limbs and I started crawling blindly toward the kitchen door. I was sniveling and slobbering with fear, but I was determined to see who was out there.

Just one good look. That's all I wanted. One identifying glimpse of the face of the man who had murdered Babs Comstock — and who was now searching for an easy, but no doubt odious, way to do away with me.

Somehow, I pulled myself to full height, switched on the outside light, and pressed my nose to one of the glass panes in the door. I could hardly see a thing. Just a lot of darkness and wetness and a rusted metal landing that was now vacant. I combed my eyes down the metal stairway and out into the garden — or, rather, the tangle of weeds and ivy my landlady refers to as the garden — but I still couldn't see anything. The man had either fled the ratty, overgrown courtyard or found a damn good hiding place.

I sank back to my haunches on the floor and crouched there, catatonic, for what felt like an hour but was probably just a few minutes. Every cell in my body was vibrating, but I literally couldn't move. Finally, after the shock had passed, after the paralysis subsided and my brain finally started working again, I began crawling toward the front door. I figured I'd crawl back across the hall to Abby's, have another drink or three, and then crawl up onto her little red couch and stay there until Dan called. Or till the end of time. Whichever came first.

I had almost reached the door when my buzzer rang. And my heart fell out on the floor. Oh, God! Had the killer made his way out of the courtyard and snuck around the block to my front door? Was he now buzzing my apartment, hoping I'd let him in so he could demonstrate his breathtaking rope jumping skills? Vaulting to my feet and creeping back over to the front window, I mashed the left side of my face to the wall, pried another peephole between the shade and the window frame, and shot my eyes down to the rain-splashed sidewalk in front of my building.

Somebody was standing there, but I couldn't see who. All I could see was the watersoaked dome of a big black umbrella.

Desperate to see who was under that umbrella, I lost my wits altogether. I snapped open the shade, stepped over to the middle of the window, and pressed my forehead to the glass. Then I rapped my knuckles against the glass so hard it felt like it would shatter. I wasn't trying to break another window, I was just trying to make a loud noise. Loud enough to be heard over the din of the storm.

I must have succeeded, too, because the big black umbrella glided a few steps back from the building, then tilted up toward my window, revealing the blinking, wet, and oh-so-welcome face of Detective Sergeant Dan Street.

My heart leapt back into my chest, and I bounded over to the door to buzz him in.

"Your phone's out of order," Dan said,

propping his closed umbrella in the corner near the door and taking off his hat. "Must be the weather. I got your message, but I couldn't call you back. Both of the numbers you gave me are out. What's happening? Are you all right?" He was concerned about me, and it showed.

"A man's trying to kill me!" I cried. "He was just here. I saw him looking in through the back door!"

Dan's face broke into a wide smile.

I couldn't believe my eyes. "Why are you smiling?" I screeched. "Utter terror amuses you?"

"Not usually," said Dan, still smiling, "but in this case, yes, I do find it kind of funny."

I was beside myself. "Babs Comstock's murderer was just here, spying on me and looking for a good way to obliterate me, and you think that's *funny?*"

"That was no murderer," Dan said, chuckling. "That was Detective Willy Boyd. He's one of my best men, and he was here to protect you, not kill you."

"Oh." I felt like the Three Stooges, Lou Costello, and Mister Magoo all rolled into one. My face was flaming.

Dan smiled again. "Feel better now?"

"No. Now I feel like killing *myself.*"

He laughed and walked over to the living

room window. After peering down at the street for a few seconds, he reached up and pulled the shade all the way closed. Then he marched through the kitchen to the back door, opened it, and stuck his bare head out into the rain.

"Is he . . . er, Willy still there?" I asked.

"No," Dan said, pulling in his head, closing the door, and wiping his face off with a white handkerchief. "I told him to go sit in the car for a while. He isn't a very good swimmer."

"Well, I'm glad *you're* here," I admitted. "I really need to talk to you. I have a lot to tell you."

"I thought you might."

Dan aimed his jet black eyes at me, and my knees got wobbly. Why was he staring at me like that? Why did he think I'd have a lot to tell him? Was I about to confess to a man who already knew all my sins? Did he realize how scrumptious he looked in his trenchcoat, with his dark wet hair waving over his forehead like seaweed?

"What do you mean?" I coquettishly inquired. When in doubt, act demure (okay, *dumb*).

"I mean it's time for you to tell me what you've learned about the Comstock murder, and why you didn't stop working on the story when I told you to." He took off his coat, tossed it over the back of a kitchen chair, and sat down. The jig was up. He was angry at me, but not furious. Stern face, soft eyes.

"How long have you known?"

"Since Friday night when I saw you at the Copa."

"How did you know that was me?"

He gave me another annoying smile. "I was standing inside the club, near the foot of the stairs to the mezzanine, keeping an eye on a suspect, when a sexy blonde plowed into him and fell flat on her keester on the floor. During the fall, her wig was knocked off-center and I saw that she wasn't a blonde at all. So then I took a closer look at her face and saw that she was you." He wasn't just smiling now. He was grinning his handsome head off.

"So?" I said, a little miffed that he was so tickled, but thrilled that he had called me sexy. "I fail to see how wearing a wig means somebody's working on a story."

"When the somebody in question is you, it's a foregone conclusion. So you might as well just sit yourself down and tell me why you were masquerading as a bombshell, and why you aimed yourself at Zack Harrington."

"Do you want a cup of coffee?"

"Quit stalling."

"I'm not!" I protested, stalling even harder. "Look at you! You're all wet. You've been standing out in the rain and your shoes are soaked. You need something hot to drink. Coffee? Cocoa? Tea?"

He looked down at the runoff beginning to puddle beneath his feet. "Coffee," he said. "But make it snappy. You've got a lot of explaining to do." Stern words, soft voice.

While I was preparing the percolator and putting it on the stove, my thoughts were bumping around in my skull like billiard balls. How much did Dan know? Did he know about my date with Scotty Whitcomb? Did he know Brandon Pomeroy was a part-time pimp? Had he learned anything about Freddy and Betty and little Ricky? Did he know that I was beginning to think he was the most attractive, intriguing, seductive man on two feet?

"How do you like it?" I asked. "Milk? Sugar?"

"Black," he said, loosening his tie and pulling his collar open. This simple gesture made my temples throb.

I gave Dan his coffee, then poured myself a glass of red wine. Just for my nerves, you know. "You want some of this?" I asked, holding the bottle up for his inspection.

His answer surprised me. "Okay," he said. "I'm not on duty now."

"Oh, really?" I purred. All of a sudden I was flirting, doing my damnedest to act like Jayne Mansfield again. "Then why are you here?" I took the bottle and an extra jellyglass to the kitchen table, puffed out my breasts, and sat down.

"Because I want to nail a murderer, and I think you do, too."

He was dead serious, and I felt like a fool. My breasts deflated as fast as my female ego. Then, after a couple of sips of wine, I got excited again. But for a very different reason. Dan was talking to me like an equal! He was here on business. And he hadn't once used the word "little" to describe my head, or my nose, or my unconventional career goals.

Stalling was for sissies. I lit up a cigarette and told him everything I knew.

Chapter 30

Nine cigarettes (six mine, three Dan's) and four glasses of wine (two each) later, my whole story — like my notes and all of my evidence — was out on the table. And Dan was impressed with me. He really was. I could tell by the way he kept shuffling through the pages of my notes and Pomeroy's address list, then shaking his head, and then studying my face out of the corner of his eye when he thought I wasn't looking.

"Instead of scolding you, I should have deputized you," he said, combing his fingers through his damp hair and lighting another Camel. "You dug up a suspect we didn't even know existed."

I was gushing with pride. "Freddy Scott, right?"

"Right. Never heard his name before tonight. I questioned the Comstocks at length, but they never mentioned that Babs had an old boyfriend who was living in the area. I'll check him out first thing tomorrow. What's his address?"

I grabbed a piece of typing paper and wrote the address down for him. "You'd better talk to the Comstocks again," I said. "Ask them point-blank about Babs and Freddy's relationship. Ask them why Babs moved to New York before she finished high school, and why Freddy's parents shunned them at the church social."

"Anything else, boss?" Dan said, in a somewhat teasing, but primarily patronizing tone.

"Yes," I said, ignoring the gibe. "Ask them if Babs was the mother of Freddy Scott's son."

Dan shot me a curious look. "Babs? A mother?"

"That's what I'm thinking," I said. "It would explain why she was so taken with little Ricky, always visiting him and giving him presents."

"Maybe so," Dan said, intrigued but unconvinced. "I'll check it out. Anything else?" His patronizing tone was gone.

"Well, you might need Freddy's license plate number," I added, retrieving the piece of typing paper and writing down the sequence of digits I'd memorized that afternoon. "He drives a two-tone Chevy. Green and white. 'Fifty-three, I think."

"Do you know where he works?"

"No, but I have a hunch he's with the phone company."

"Why do you say that?"

"Because the only true information he had about me was my phone number. And from that he managed to find out my real name. He must have had access to phone company records."

"Clever deduction."

"I'll bet it's *accurate*, too," I boasted, giving my ego another shovelful of fertilizer. "What's more, I'll bet he's the killer. He could have gotten a Hopalong Cassidy jump rope from his son."

"Yes, but if Babs was always buying the boy presents," Dan countered, "she could have had a jump rope with her when she was murdered. Maybe she bought one — at Woolworth's — right before she was murdered. Then anybody could have killed her with it."

"Yes, I know. But I still think Freddy did it. According to *Daring Detective* statistics, tons of murders are committed by old boyfriends."

"That's true," Dan said, "but not conclusive. This case is much more complicated than most. Babs was living a dangerous life, and she was involved with some very dangerous people."

"You mean Mafia people."

"Right."

"Is that why you tried to keep the news of Babs's murder out of the papers?"

"Yes. We didn't want the big boys to know how hard we were working on the case, or how much we'd discovered. And we didn't want them knocking off our informers before we were fully informed."

"Could Babs's death have had anything to do with the hit on Anastasia's sidekick? Both murders occurred on the same night."

Dan gave me an appreciative glance and another sly smile. "You don't miss much, do you? Are all writers so inquisitive and observant?"

"Do all detectives answer questions with more questions?'

Laughing, he crushed his cigarette in the ashtray and stood up from the table. "There's only so much I can tell you, Paige. Not because I don't trust you to keep the information to yourself, but because you might use it to get yourself in even more trouble." He walked over to the kitchen door, pulled it open, and checked out the courtyard again. It was still raining.

"Oh, no, I won't!" I sputtered. "My Dick Tracy days are over. I'm afraid I'll wind up at the morgue myself."

"Smart cookie," Dan said, moving back

through the kitchen and over to the living room window. "Too bad it took you so long to wise up." He stood to one side of the window and peered out around the edge of the shade. Then he repeated the procedure on the other side.

"Okay, okay! So there's only so much you can tell me. But I can't help wondering about Scotty Whitcomb. Do you have any idea what happened to him last night — after Tommy jumped him and I ran away? I mean, Tommy didn't kill him or anything, did he?"

"No, but he's not as pretty as he used to be."

"You've seen him?"

"This morning. Went to his studio to ask him a few more questions. His face looks like chopped steak and he's got two shiners the size of doorknobs. He said he was mugged."

"Poor thing," I said, with a thick slur of sarcasm. Better him than me. "Did you find out anything new? Do you think he's the murderer?"

"He's one of our prime suspects."

"One of? How many do you have?"

"Too many." Stepping away from the window, Dan removed his jacket, dropped it on the edge of the couch/door/daybed, and sat down. The sight of his shoulder holster made me shudder. Propping his elbows on his knees and rubbing his face in his hands, he looked exhausted (but still exhilarating).

I got up from the table and joined him on the couch. "Since you were tailing him at the Copa, I guess Zack Harrington's on your list."

"Yep."

"And Brandon Pomeroy?"

"Yep."

"And Frank Costello?"

Dan snapped his head toward me in surprise. "How did you come up with that name?"

"Well, when Tommy smashed up my apartment and stole my notes, I got a pretty loud message some Mafia honcho was involved. It was obvious that somebody — a connected somebody — wanted me off the Comstock story. At first I thought it was Anastasia, because of the hit, but then I saw Costello at the Copa, and learned that he owns the club, and goes there almost every night. So then I figured he knew Harrington, who's a regular, and maybe cousin Pomeroy, too. And then I wondered if Pomeroy and Whitcomb and Crawley, and maybe even Mr.

Gumpert at the Venus Modeling Agency, were all working for Costello somehow, in some kind of call girl ring or something." I was babbling, but it all made perfect sense to me.

"And maybe Babs was one of their girls," I rattled on. "Could be she got out of hand in some way — got too needy, or started dating somebody she shouldn't have, or threatened to quit or squeal — and Costello decided she was more trouble than she was worth. Maybe he had her bumped off so she couldn't testify against him in court. He's on trial for tax evasion right now, and Babs could have known more about his off-the-books income than it was safe for her to know."

Dan gazed at me admiringly. "You take the cake, kid," he said, in a voice so dark and delicious it made me dizzy. "That's one of the angles we've been working on. Trouble is, the more we find out about Costello's girlie game, the longer our list of suspects grows, and the further we get from finding out the truth. Babs went out with a lot of guys — a lot of rich and sleazy guys — and any one of them could have murdered her. And if Costello wanted her dead, he would have just ordered another hit — which means the killer could be sunbathing in Sicily right now."

"It really *is* complicated, isn't it?" I groaned, realizing there were more pieces to the puzzle than I could possibly count. How could one nice, single, pretty, polite young blonde have had so many male acquaintances with so many possible motives to murder her?

"Tell me more about Brandon Pomeroy," Dan said. "Why do you think he ransacked your desk? Could he have known you were working on the Comstock story?"

"Sure. Scotty Whitcomb could have told him. But I really don't think that's what happened."

"Why?"

"I don't know, it's just a feeling I have."

"A feeling?" Dan scoffed. "You mean a physical sensation or your infallible woman's intuition?"

"Well, both, really," I said, ignoring his disparaging tone. "It's intuition based on sensations. Don't forget I was there, Dan. I saw Pomeroy going through my desk and I heard the anxiety in his voice. His panic was so real I could smell it. And, believe me — if I had been the source of that panic, I would have known it."

"You mean felt it."

"Felt it *and* known it." I wasn't backing down.

"Well, if he wasn't looking for something of yours — something to do with the Comstock story — what *was* he looking for? And why was he so frantic about it?"

"I think the true explanation is the one Pomeroy gave me himself: that he was looking for the proofs of the mob hit story, the one Mike wrote for the magazine. I think he was desperate to make sure it wouldn't get into print."

Dan leaned against the back of the couch — or, rather, the pile of pillows I keep propped against the wall behind the daybed to make it *look* like a couch — and gazed up at the ceiling, giving thought to what I'd just said. A lot of thought. Eventually he sat up straight and concluded, "That makes a certain amount of sense. You're probably right."

Oh, how I loved the sound of *those* words! But I still had some nagging doubts. "What I don't understand," I continued on, "is *why* Pomeroy would be so desperate to pull the mob hit story. There was nothing special — or even very interesting — about the piece. I edited it several times, and it was still just a boring clip job, without a scrap of information that hadn't already been printed in the papers. Why make such a commotion?"

"People under Frank Costello's thumb are prone to making commotions. Otherwise, they might get squashed like ants."

I still wasn't satisfied. "But why would Costello give a whit about that story? His name wasn't mentioned once. The focus was on Albert Anastasia and the man who got murdered."

"And who do you think *ordered* that murder?" Dan said, fastening me in his bottomless black gaze. "I'll give you a hint. It wasn't Red Skelton."

I thought about Dan's comment for a second, but something still worried me. "So what if Costello ordered the hit? That's no reason for him to get so concerned about one stupid little story in one stupid little magazine. *Daring Detective* doesn't have any inside information or proof about anything!"

"It wasn't Costello who was so concerned about the *DD* story," Dan said. "It was Pomeroy. Don't you see? Costello's in the middle of a big trial right now, and he's not in the mood for any extra attention, so he probably sent the word out to all his press people — all the editors and journalists he owns, or those who just owe him favors — to delete or downplay all mob-related articles. And when Pomeroy got the news, he probably went nuts thinking he might not be able to yank Mike's story in time. So he turned your desk upside down looking for the proofs."

"That's nuts, all right."

"It doesn't pay to disappoint Frank Costello. It can, in fact, be quite painful."

"Maybe that's why Tommy wrecked my apartment and stole my story notes — just to get on Costello's good side."

"Maybe."

"And maybe that's why Pomeroy never told Mike to write a story about Babs's murder," I said, getting excited. "Because he knew Costello was involved!"

"Could be," Dan said, heaving a sigh and rubbing his eyes. "But then there's always the possibility he suppressed the story because he killed her himself."

I broke out in goose bumps. I had flirted with the idea of Pomeroy being the murderer, but I hadn't — until that very moment — really believed it might be true. "Did you question Pomeroy at all?" I gasped.

"Of course!" Dan barked. "Several times. We even called him in to headquarters once."

"And what did he say?"

"That at the time of the murder he was at a party at the Plaza. One of Oliver Harrington's big charity shindigs. Zack Harrington was there, too. Pomeroy and Zack corroborated each other's alibi."

"Did you check it out any further? Talk to any of the other guests?"

"God damn it, Paige! How can you insult me with a question like that? I've been investigating homicides a lot longer than you have, you know! You dig up one measly suspect in one pathetic little murder, and you think that makes you smarter than the whole NYPD?" He was really teed off at me.

And rightly so. I was acting way too ballsy for my crime-busting britches. "Sorry," I said, looking down at my lap in shame. (Well, sort of, anyway. It's hard to be ashamed of something you're actually proud of.)

"To answer your ridiculous question," Dan went on, "— yes, we *did* talk to some of the other guests. And both Pomeroy and Harrington were seen at the party. Trouble is, the party lasted from five to ten, and nobody remembers exactly what time they saw them. Either one — or both of them — could have snuck out of the Plaza in middle of the party, met up with Babs somewhere, taken her someplace in a car, raped her, strangled her, dumped her at Woolworth's, and gotten back to the Plaza in time for brandy and coffee."

"So she *was* raped," I murmured.

"Thoroughly," he grunted.

"Then she wasn't a mob hit," I staunchly proclaimed. "Hit men don't rape their female victims. They just rub 'em out and run. It's not passion, it's strictly business."

Dan looked at me as if I'd just sprouted hair on my cheeks and turned green. "Who told you that?" he snapped. "Mother Goose? Contrary to what you *think* you know, some hit men have a real passion for their work."

"Oh," I said, embarrassed by my know-it-all naïveté. I sat quietly for a few seconds, trying to hold my tongue and not make a further fool of myself. But I couldn't keep it up for long. "Correct me if I'm wrong," I said, somewhat self-defensively (and just a tad sarcastically), "but I thought Mafia assassins preferred guns to Hopalong Cassidy jump ropes."

Dan smiled and softened his attitude. "That's usually true, Paige," he said, "but not always. Sometimes they don't want to risk a gunshot being heard. And sometimes

450

they'll just grab whatever's handy — a rock, a piece of pipe, a rope — to use as a weapon. Even hit men need a little variety in their lives."

"Okay, okay! I give up!" I cried. "I was just trying to narrow down the endless list of suspects."

"And your observations are valid," Dan said, still smiling. "Just not indisputable."

He looked so cute I wanted to lick his face.

"So, you think Babs was raped and killed in a car?" I asked.

"Yes, but I don't have any hard evidence."

"You mean it's just a *feeling?*"

Dan laughed, cocked his head to one side, and shrugged his powerful shoulders. "Touché," he said, readjusting his leather holster. "But it's a bit more technical than that. There were some fibers found in Babs's hair that are consistent with several common brands of automobile upholstery. She might have picked those up when her already dead body was being transported to Woolworth's. But there were so many fibers, and they were embedded so close to her scalp, that I think they rubbed off during a prolonged and desperate struggle. The kind of struggle a woman puts up when she's fighting off a rapist or wrestling with a strangler. The M.E. agrees with me."

"What color are the fibers?" I asked.

"A mixture of gray and green."

"Freddy Scott has a car," I said, "and half of it is green."

Chapter 31

You've heard the old expression two's company, three's a crowd? Well, I can testify that it's true. I can also bear witness to the fact that nobody — but nobody — can turn a couple into a crowd faster, or more completely, than my best friend and neighbor, Abby Moskowitz.

Dan and I were sitting just inches away from each other on the couch, having an intimate conversation about automobile upholstery, when Abby rang my bell and started pounding on the door. "Paige! Paige!" she cried at the top of her lungs. "Are you there? Open up!" She sounded frantic.

I got up to let her in, but Dan jumped in front of me and motioned me back, making signs for me to be silent. He took his gun out of his holster, held it up tight to his side, then quietly slipped across the floor and positioned himself to the left of the door.

"What are you doing?" I whispered excitedly. "That's my friend Abby. Put your gun away!"

Dan gave me a look of warning and gestured for me to shut up. He unlocked the door and — still holding the gun up close to his side and keeping his back to the wall — clicked it open about an inch. "Police!" he bellowed, peering sideways through the opening into the hall. "Who's there? Declare yourself!"

"Well, I *do* declare!" Abby said in a wildly exaggerated southern drawl. "It's just little ole me, Abby Moskowitz. Can I come in, please, Mr. Policeman?" Without waiting for an answer, she pushed the door all the way open and flounced inside.

Startled, Dan leapt out into the hall, aimed his gun at arm's length around the landing and down the staircase, then — satisfied that no one else was there — came back inside and relocked the door.

"Paige!" Abby cried, when she saw me standing stiff as a stick in the living room. "Are you okay? I thought you were coming back to my place. I was going *meshugge* with worry! I tried to call you but the phone's not working! What the hell's going on here? Who's the dick with the gun?" Her wide brown eyes were blazing and her long black ponytail was twitching as if it were attached to a real horse. I was amused (okay, *relieved*) to see that she was wearing her painter's smock over her red lace babydolls.

"Dan Street," Dan said, putting his gun back in his holster and nodding in Abby's direction. "Detective Sergeant Dan Street." He looked and sounded so serious I wanted to laugh.

But I didn't. I just chuckled to myself and walked between them, heading to the kitchen for another glass of wine. "Everything's fine," I said to Abby in passing, giving her a pleading, please-don't-embarrass-me look. "Detective Street and I were just discussing the Comstock case."

"Ohhhhhhhhhh?" she cooed, stretching the word out like a long piece of twine and then tweaking it up at the end. Her nostrils flared suggestively. "Well, I'm glad to see the two of you finally got your heads together. Two noggins are better than one, I always say. Wouldn't you agree, Detective Dan?"

"Uh, yeah, well . . ." he stuttered. Was it my imagination, or was he blushing?

"I'm Abby, by the way," she quickly interjected. "Abby, the next-door screwball." She gave him a beaming smile and an outrageous bare-legged curtsy.

Dan threw his head back and laughed. I could tell he found her to be both attractive and enchanting. My jealousy flared up like a brush fire and choked me in the fumes. "Does anybody want some wine?" I screeched, holding the bottle up in the air and brandishing it like a picket sign.

"No, thanks," Abby said, quickly getting the message and kindly putting a lid on her natural seductiveness. "In fact, now that I know you're okay, Paige, I can retreat to my own apartment in peace. May the power of Isis be with you." She clasped her hands together and began backing toward the door, making several little Japanese-style bows in the process.

I could only hope Dan didn't know that Isis was the goddess of fertility.

"Wait!" Dan blurted, stepping in front of the door to halt Abby's progress. "I wish you wouldn't go yet."

"Why shouldn't she?" I howled from the kitchen, sounding — even to myself — like a threatened alley cat.

"Because I've got to leave," Dan said, turning his ardent black gaze toward me, "and I don't want you to be alone."

"Oh," I said, somewhat mollified. "It's nice of you to be concerned. But I was going to spend the night at Abby's anyway."

"Good. Then you can go over there right

now." He turned his eyes toward Abby again. "That okay with you?"

"Sure thing, Sarge. As long as she brings the bottle of wine. And don't you worry about us at all. If the killer shows up, I know exactly where to kick him."

"It won't come to that," Dan said, smiling. "I'm leaving Willy here for the rest of the night. He'll stay on watch outside and make sure both of you are safe."

"Willy?" Abby said, getting excited. Mention the name of a man — any man — and she starts panting like an overheated poodle.

"Detective Willy Boyd," Dan explained. "My left-handed right-hand man. He's smart, he's strong, he packs a mean pistol, and his aim is dead center."

"Oooooh," Abby whimpered, turning all limp and lusty. What a sop she is sometimes! "But it's pouring rain outside," she wailed. "Willy could catch pneumonia and die! Shouldn't he and his pistol stay indoors with us? I'd feel ever so much safer that way." Ever so much *sexier* was what she meant, of course.

"Detective Boyd's job is to stop an intruder *before* he intrudes, not after," Dan said. "After could be too late. Besides," he added, giving Abby one of his famous winks, "like all good dicks, he's got a good trench coat."

"Listen!" I said, jumping in to break the tension (*my* tension). "I'll gladly stay at Abby's tonight. And we'll keep the shades down and the curtains drawn and the doors locked tight. And Willy Boyd will guard the gates and keep us safe from harm. But what about tomorrow? What should I do tomorrow? Should I go to work and keep tabs on Brandon Pomeroy, or should I stay home and hide in the closet?" Like any self-respecting paranoiac, I was thinking ahead.

Dan walked over to me, put his hands on my shoulders, and gave me a strong, steady look of assurance. "Don't do anything out of the ordinary," he said. "Go to work and act perfectly normal. But keep your eyes wide open. I'll plant a plainclothes watchdog in the lobby, and another one on your floor, to make sure you're okay. If you're reasonably cautious and careful, nothing bad will happen to you. I promise. He was so solicitous, and so certain of his purpose, that I was putty in his capable hands.

"Aye-aye, Captain," I said, feeling as supple and unflappable as Eve Arden in *Our Miss Brooks*. If he had told me to swim the English Channel with both arms tied behind my back, I would have taken a deep breath, cracked a couple of wry jokes, and then plunged into the water headfirst.

Dan took my story notes and bits of evidence with him when he left, saying he'd have someone at headquarters make copies for me. Then Abby and I locked ourselves up in her apartment and wedged high-backed wooden chairs under the knobs of both the living room and kitchen doors.

We huddled together on her little red couch for a while, eating graham crackers and drinking the rest of the wine and trying to act as if we weren't scared of anything or anybody, until Abby went upstairs to bed, saying she had to deliver her new painting to *Spicy Mystery* magazine first thing in the morning. I turned off the lights, slipped out of my loafers, curled up on the couch in my clothes, and — much to my great surprise — slept like a lobotomized baby for the rest of the night.

I woke up to the smell of coffee and the sound of Abby's high heels clicking across the kitchen linoleum. She was wearing normal apparel for once — a black sheath skirt and a blue blouse with big black buttons. Her painting was wrapped in brown paper, tied with cord, and propped against the wall by the front door, ready for transport.

"Morning, sunshine," she said when I sat up and rubbed my eyes. "I gotta run. The art director told me if I didn't deliver my masterpiece into his hairy little hands by eight a.m., I shouldn't deliver it at all. Something to do with lost press time. It's still raining like a bitch out there. There's coffee and a leftover bagel."

"Thanks," I said, still in a sleepy fog.

Abby yanked the chair out from under the front doorknob and shoved it back toward the kitchen table. Wiggling into her raincoat, she picked up her painting and umbrella, opened the door, and popped out into the hall. "Catch ya later, alligator," she said, giving me a brave little wave and a smile before disappearing down the stairs.

Waking all the way up in a hurry, I vaulted off the couch, darted over to the open door, and strained my eyes down the dark stairwell. "Wait!" I cried.

But I was too late. Abby was gone. I was alone. And alone was definitely *not* where I wanted to be. Forgoing the coffee and bagel, I zipped into my own apartment, dashed up the stairs, took a lightning-fast shower, and got dressed for work.

It wasn't until I had dashed back down the stairs to the kitchen that I saw the thin silver strip of daylight streaking across the linoleum floor. And it wasn't until I had spun around on my heels to locate the source of the silver strip of light that I saw the narrow opening in the kitchen door. And it wasn't until I saw what was sticking through the very bottom of the narrow opening in the kitchen door that I realized something horrible had happened. Something worse than horrible.

It was a finger. A single crooked, motionless, gray-looking finger. It lay curved like a comma on the floor, beckoning me forward, bidding me to open the door wide and gaze upon the rest of its body — its large, masculine, rain-splashed, trench coat–covered body. Its sprawled, strangled, brown-haired, blue-faced body. Its undeniably dead body.

I fell to my knees on the wet metal landing next to the corpse, rain pouring down my face like tears, screams shrieking from my soul without making a sound. It was Detective Willy Boyd. I knew it was. His gray hat had tumbled just two feet away from his head, and his cold gray gun was lying on the landing, just inches away from his lifeless left hand.

He looked as if he'd been dead for a while — a couple of hours at least. Raindrops were pelting his upturned face — bouncing off his bulging eyeballs, filling his shocked, gaping mouth to the brim. And twisted tight around Willy's neck — so tight it cut deep into the flesh of his pitifully swollen purple throat — was a three-foot long section of wire. Actually, a sheathed bundle of wires.

Looked like telephone cable to me.

Chapter 32

I went back inside and — though I felt pretty sure the killer wasn't still there — took a frantic tour around my apartment, peering in closets and under the bed. I guessed that the murderer *had* been inside — looking for me, no doubt — but, thank God, he was long gone now.

I positioned the kitchen door the way I'd first found it, propped lightly against the gruesome finger, and — legs shaking so hard I thought they might fold — slowly walked into the living room toward the phone. I was doing my best to stay calm — trying to be as brave and sturdy as my late husband had always been in a crisis (which wasn't the least bit easy, since I was soaked right through to the skin and every wretched cell in my body was screaming bloody murder).

I picked up the receiver and waited, in a daze, for the dial tone. It never came, of course. My phone still wasn't working.

And neither was my brain, I guess, since I never considered running downstairs to the fish store, or down the street to the deli, to call the police. I had a vague notion that I should report the murder at once, and then wait for the police to get there to tend to the corpse and begin conducting their investigation, but I was too crazed to put that notion into action. All I could think to do was slam down the useless phone, grab my jacket and purse, and take off for the safety of my populated and (hopefully) staked-out office.

I forgot to take my umbrella, so by the time I got to the subway my jacket was as wet as the rest of my clothes. I stood shivering on the northbound platform — nowhere near the edge, but right in the middle of the heavy rush-hour crowd — waiting for the uptown train. I wasn't taking any chances. For all I knew the murderer could have been sneaking up behind me, looking for the opportunity to push me down onto the merciless metal tracks.

When the train screeched into the station, I squeezed my way inside, grabbed onto an overhead strap with both hands, and hung there like a side of beef for the entire trip. I was chilled to the bone and in a deep state of shock. A zombie in a drenched dress and jacket, wearing squishy high heels. When I finally reached my stop and let go of the strap, I could barely move my bloodless arms. They felt as if they'd been wrenched out of their sockets.

Emerging out of the subway into the dim gray daylight, I saw that it had finally stopped raining. So instead of waiting for a crosstown bus, I walked (okay, *ran*) the rest of the way. By the time I reached Third Avenue, I was so feverish and overheated my clothes had dried on my back. Only my hair was still damp, and it clung to the sides of my face like clay.

Don't do anything out of the ordinary, Dan had said. *Go to work and act perfectly normal.* But how was I going to act normal when I was now some lowly, steamy, crouched-over swamp creature who had — just twenty-five minutes ago — stared smack into the face of a dead man?

I raked my fingers through my hair, straightened my bowed spine, and forced one foot to step in front of the other until I made my way across Third Avenue and up the block to the entrance of my building. I was almost on time — just fifteen minutes later than usual. If I moved really fast, I figured, I could open up the office, call the police and tell them what happened, and still make the coffee before Harvey Crockett sauntered in.

I entered the lobby of my building on full alert — head swiveling in all directions. I scanned the crowd inside, looking for Dan's promised bodyguard — but if he was there, he was indistinguishable from the rest of the raincoated, rainhatted herd. Nearing hysteria, I peered back through the glass walls to the street, looking for murderers, or Mafia hit men, or anybody else who might be stalking me. My heart was thumping so hard I thought my chest would explode.

And when I saw Brandon Pomeroy walk up the crowded sidewalk and step into the revolving glass door leading to the lobby, it really *did* explode.

Not literally, of course. Just figuratively. But that figurative explosion was enough to blast me into the stratosphere. What was *he* doing here?! Why was he so early?! Not once in all the two years I'd been working for *Daring Detective* had Pomeroy ever, ever, ever gotten to work before noon.

What could have prompted this shocking change in my demon boss's behavior? Did he have an ulterior scheme? Was he hoping to catch me in the office alone? Could it be that he had killed somebody earlier this morning and was now feeling so powerful and excited he wanted to do it again?

★ ★ ★

Panicked over Pomeroy's sudden appearance — and terrified of being trapped in an elevator with him — I lunged across the lobby and propelled myself through the door to the staircase. Then I started running up the stairs as if my life depended on it (which, at that point in time, I was pretty damn sure it did).

I wasn't thinking very clearly but I did sort of have a plan. I figured when I got up to the ninth floor, I'd open the door just a crack and look for the plainclothes detective Dan said would be stationed there. If I found him, great: I would solicit his protection, tell him about Willy Boyd, and we would report the murder together. But if Dan's watchdog wasn't there? I would blast out of the staircase, streak across the hall, bound into Orchid Publications, hide behind the receptionist's desk, and call the police myself. (Okay, okay! So it was a pretty lousy plan. But what do you expect from a woman whose entire central nervous system had gone haywire?)

I was out of breath by the time I reached the fourth floor. My high heels were crippling my progress, and the mad dash across town from the subway had left me with zero energy. Midway between the fourth and fifth floors, I staggered to a standstill on the gritty cement steps, grabbed hold of the metal handrail, and — humped as low as Hugo's hunchback in that creepy, cobwebby bell tower — began groaning and gasping for air.

I was making so much noise it's a wonder I heard the footsteps behind me. Hard, fast, heavy footsteps that came to a halt just seconds after my own. I whipped my head around to see who it was, but the stairs behind me were deserted. I knew somebody was there, though — probably right around the corner of the fourth-floor landing because I could hear breathing. Harsh, raspy, monsterlike breathing.

Oh, my God! I shrieked to myself. *Somebody really is stalking me!*

I shouldn't have been so surprised, I know. Every murder mystery I'd ever read had featured a horrid, hair-raising scene like this. But this wasn't fiction; this was real life. *My* life. And I was astonished. Truly scared to the bone. A gallon of adrenaline flooded my bloodstream and I started scrambling up the stairs again. Up toward the fifth-floor door. If I could just make it out of the stairwell and into the hall, I told myself, I might be safe.

I managed to hold on to this thought for

a full three seconds. Then I heard the heavy footsteps coming after me again, and felt a massive, meaty hand grab hold of my right ankle. My foot was yanked out from under me and I fell, like a duffel bag full of rocks, face forward onto the jagged cement steps. My shins, knees, thighs, and ribs cracked against the sharp edges of the steps, and my chin came down hard on the fifth-floor landing.

If my tongue had been between my teeth when I fell, I'd be speaking in sign language now. But, fortunately for me (if anything about this atrocious ordeal could be called fortunate), my teeth were clenched and my tongue was spared — which was more than I could say for every other organ and bone in my body. I felt completely smashed and broken, as if I'd fallen off a cliff onto a huge pile of bricks. I couldn't move, breathe, or see anything but stars.

I was still conscious, though, so I was fully aware when the big meaty hand let go of my ankle and grabbed hold of my shoulder, yanking hard and twisting me over onto my back on the uneven stairs. My spine seemed to snap in a thousand places and the back of my head conked loudly on the landing. And then my eyes

— which had been squeezed shut against the fear and the pain — popped wide open and I stared straight into the feral face of my attacker.

"You stupid filthy bitch!" Freddy Scott spat, spraying my face with saliva. He was leaning so close I could see the tiny capillaries in his crooked nose. "You don't know when to stop, do you?" Clamping one hand tight around my neck, he kept my head anchored to the landing and cut my air supply in half. I tried to scream, but only a squeak came out. I tried to claw his face and kick him away, but he threw his hard, heavy body down on top of mine, pinning my arms and legs to the cement with his ex–football player's weight.

As he writhed on top of me, grunting like a pig and grinding his hips into mine, I realized — to my absolute horror and disgust — that he was becoming sexually aroused. Another jolt of adrenaline shot through my veins and I struggled with every ounce of strength I had left to wriggle out from under him.

It was impossible. And my spasmodic exertions just made him more excited.

"You like it like this, don't you, bitch?" he snorted, clenching my neck even tighter, staring down at me with a grotesque smirk on his face. "Guess I'll have to fuck you before I kill you."

If I had been able to speak, I would have told him to go fuck *himself* — but I was fighting for air, not self-expression.

At that point Satan (or Freddy or Scotty or whatever ugly name you want to call him) reached down with his free hand and yanked the skirt of my dress up to my waist. Then he shoved his hand up under my slip and tried to pull down my panties.

The optimal word here is *tried*. Because the more Freddy tugged and pulled and jerked and twisted — the harder he strove to separate me from my underwear — the more completely he failed. The lower half of my female anatomy remained firmly and hermetically sealed. It was the first time in my life I'd ever been glad to be wearing my ultratight, heavy-duty, thick rubber Playtex panty girdle.

If I had been able to laugh, I would have roared in Freddy's face — but I was too busy gagging to gloat. The ceiling above me was spinning. My lungs were withering in my chest. My consciousness was waving bye-bye. . . .

Furious and frustrated, Freddy gave up trying to rape me and focused all his efforts on killing me. He locked both hands

471

around my neck and — grinning like a psychotic gargoyle — squeezed my throat completely closed. Then he pressed down hard on my larynx with both thumbs. There was no oxygen left on the planet. My world turned black and my soul began to seep, like a thin sweet fog, into the airless atmosphere.

I was, to put it plainly, a goner.

Almost.

But not quite, of course.

You knew that already, right? I mean, I *told* you I wasn't going to die, remember? What I didn't tell you, though, was how I was going to survive, which is a pretty amazing and exciting tale unto itself. Since I was choking to death at the time, I'm a little fuzzy on some of the details, but here — to the best of my understanding and recollection — is what happened:

At the very moment I was leaving my physical body and floating over to the other side, somebody dragged Freddy off of me and pulled his hands away from my neck. Presto! My windpipe was clear, and what would have been my last gasp became a deep, resurrecting breath of life instead. Oxygen flowed into my lungs like a river, and — coughing, wheezing, and gurgling to beat the band — I took in great huge gulps of the wonderful stuff.

As soon as my vision cleared and my brain regained some function, I pulled myself up to a sitting position on the landing and looked down toward the loud snorting and growling noises where two men were fighting on the steps. Freddy was much bigger than his opponent, whose face I couldn't see since he was flat on his back on the stairs and Freddy was standing over him, gripping him by the collar and punching him repeatedly in the nose. All I could see was the top of the man's head, which was covered with dark brown hair and being thwacked from side to side with each crushing blow of Freddy's formidable fist.

I tried to rise up and rush to my rescuer's aid, but my knees buckled and I crashed right back down to the landing. I tried it again and the same thing happened. I wondered if my legs were broken. Wanting desperately to help the man who had just helped me, I took off one of my navy leather pumps and hurled it — pointy, metal-tipped high heel first — toward Freddy's fiendish forehead.

Bull's-eye.

The heel of my shoe didn't puncture the skin and poke a hole in Freddy's skull the way I'd hoped it would, but it *did* bop him soundly on the head and get his attention. And as Freddy reared back to see where the torpedo had come from, he stopped — for just a split second — pummeling the face of the man who had saved my life. And that split second gave my gallant hero just the time he needed to pull his knees up to his chin, aim his feet at Freddy's chest, and then kick both legs out straight at once — a canny maneuver which lifted Freddy's bulky frame to a full upright position, then sent him careening backwards down the stairs.

Screaming and shouting obscenities, Freddy tumbled like a giant wooden puppet down the long hard flight of steps. You could actually hear the nauseating sound of bones breaking against cement. He hit the fourth-floor landing with a loud, crunchy thud, and then everything was quiet. Dead quiet.

I pulled myself up by the metal handrail and looked down at Freddy's motionless, splayed-out body. He was lying on his back. His startled eyes gaped up at me, seeing nothing. His large head was cocked at such an impossible angle, I knew immediately his neck was broken.

474

The dragon had been slain.

My knight in shining armor was seated a few steps down from me, upper body curled over his thighs, face buried in his hands. His thin shoulders were shaking and he had started to cry. I quickly lowered my rear end to the landing and began scooting down to his level, one step at a time. There was a pair of smashed eyeglasses on one of the steps, and I narrowly avoided sitting on the splintered lenses.

When I reached my hero's side and saw the pool of blood at his feet, I almost stopped breathing again. "Are you okay?" I cried, throwing my arm around his back and holding on tight. I was wild with worry. "Please be okay!" I begged. "You saved my life! I couldn't bear it if you were hurt." I didn't know who in the world he was, but I loved him with all my heart.

He heaved a great sigh and his shoulders stopped shaking. His final sob got caught in his throat. "I think I'm okay," he croaked, turning his poor battered face in my direction.

I didn't recognize him at first. Not without his glasses. And not with the blood dripping out of his nose, over his lips, and down onto his chin. But as I gazed into his anxious eyes, and felt the strong vibrations of his nervous energy — and caught a whiff of the salami sandwich that lay crushed on the step below — I finally grasped my hero's unlikely identity.

"Lenny!" I whooped, heart leaping in giddy surprise. "Is that you?"

"Yeah," he said, wiping his bloody nose and mouth on the sleeve of his olive green slicker. "At least I think it's me. Hard to tell without my glasses."

"Oh, Lenny," I cried, snaking both arms around his chest and giving him a breathless hug of gratitude. "He was strangling me! I was almost gone. You saved my life! How can I ever thank you?"

"Who *was* that guy, anyway? And where is he now?" Lenny shot his nervous, nearly blind eyes down the staircase. "Did he run away?"

"Uh, no."

"Then what happened to him? Where did he go?"

"He didn't go anywhere."

"Huh? What do you mean?"

"He's not gone. He's still here."

"What the hell are you —"

"He's dead, Lenny. He fell down the stairs and broke his neck. His body's lying on the landing beneath us."

Lenny's blood-streaked face crumpled

into a wad of horror. "You mean I *killed* him?" He looked as if he might start crying again.

"No, you just kicked him. The *fall* killed him, and it's lucky for both of us that it did." I hugged Lenny again — so tight I almost strangled *him*.

But I could feel his tortured muscles relax in my embrace. "So who the hell is he?" Lenny wanted to know. "Why was he attacking you?"

I didn't have the strength — or the presence of mind — to explain. "I'll tell you later," I said, not mentioning the names of Babs Comstock or Freddy Scott or Scotty Whitcomb or Brandon Pomeroy or Martin Crawley or Zack Harrington or Albert Anastasia or Frank Costello or Willy Boyd or even Dan Street. I looked down at the body of the dead murderer, then cast my eyes up to the heavens (where I imagined the avenged ghost of Babs Comstock to be lounging comfortably on a cloud), then gazed over at the unwitting young art assistant who had brought the whole sorrowful saga to its crazy but correct conclusion.

"It's a long story," I said, smiling, thanking my lucky stars that I'd finally be able to write it. And that Lenny was afraid of elevators.

Epilogue

Neither of my legs were broken. In fact, the only thing broken during the entire staircase brawl was Lenny's rather large nose. (I'm not counting the bones in Freddy's neck, because who cares what happened to him?) Anyway, Lenny's nose got fixed, and all my various wounds were tended to, and we both bounced back to fighting shape in no time.

I looked a little the worse for wear (lots of new black-and-blue marks joined forces with the older, yellowing bruises on my breast, knees, and shin), but I could still walk and talk — a condition which pleased me immensely, but seemed to annoy some of my male coworkers no end.

Brandon Pomeroy, for one. He was furious at me for helping to uncover his nasty little pimp operation before he managed to destroy the incriminating evidence in his desk drawer (which, by the way, was the true purpose of his early arrival at the office that fateful day). He was also really mad that I had discussed his dirty secret with Dan Street, who then informed our communal commander, Oliver Rice Harrington, who in turn told Little Lord Pomeroy that if he didn't clean up his act and start applying himself — full time! — to his *Daring Detective* job, he'd not only be fired, he'd be disinherited altogether.

Pomeroy could have gone to jail, of course, and probably would have, if Big Boss Harrington hadn't greased a few powerful palms (Dan Street's *not* included), and if Pomeroy hadn't agreed to give evidence against Martin Crawley — the real head of the busted Apex Theatrical Agency call girl ring — who's now behind bars awaiting trial on procurement charges. (Actually, Frank Costello was the *real* real head of the Apex enterprise, but it'll be a frosty day in hell before Pomeroy or Crawley, or anybody else for that matter, agrees to give evidence against him!)

Anyway, Pomeroy is still the editorial director of *Daring Detective* magazine, and I'm still the receptionist/secretary/bookkeeper/news clipper/proofreader/story editor/file clerk/coffee maker. I've also been given the title of staff writer — thanks to the fast-selling exclusive inside story I wrote about the Babs Comstock murder, which Harvey Crockett decided to feature on the cover. But all that new title means is that I now get to write an occasional full-length article or story in addition to all my other office duties. And my salary has climbed to seventy dollars a week.

I had hoped for seventy-five, but I'm not complaining. A ten-dollar-a-week raise is more than most working women receive in a lifetime. Besides, if I ever finish this novel I'm working on (the one you may be reading right now), and if it ever actually gets published, then I'll be a bona fide *author*, and well on my way to achieving great fame and fortune. That's what Abby says, anyway.

But I'm getting too far ahead of myself, (okay, far too *full* of myself), and if I don't stop daydreaming and keep on typing, I may not finish this novel at all. I mean, I've got a lot of loose ends to tie up here! And I know Babs wouldn't want me to leave anything out.

Especially the part explaining the motive — the reason (if you can possibly call it that!) that poor, dear Babs was killed. You know all of the other major details — the who, the what, the where, the when, and the how. But — unless you've already put the pieces of the pitiful little puzzle together (as I finally, but oh-so-belatedly managed to do) — you don't know the why. And in many murder mysteries — factual or fictitious — that's the most tragic and intriguing detail of all.

So I'm going to save that part for last. (Sorry, but a mystery writer's got to keep up the suspense somehow!)

In the meantime, I'll fill you in on some of the other interesting particulars, things I didn't learn about until later — after Freddy tried to kill me but got himself killed instead; after Lenny and I helped each other up the stairs to the fifth floor, then up the remaining four floors (in the elevator no less!) to the office; after the undercover cop who was planted on the ninth floor notified Homicide and called for an ambulance, and the paramedics took care of me and Lenny, and Dan Street came rushing in like a crazed canine, with his tail between his legs and his other plainclothes playmate in tow. (*That* not-so-vigilant fellow had, by the way, been purchasing a donut in the lobby coffee shop when I entered the building and ducked into the stairwell.)

Dan was so upset about what had happened to me — and so mad at himself for not keeping me safe — that he could hardly speak. But after staring at me intently for a full five seconds, and then pulling me into his arms and hugging me so tight I lost my breath again, he gave me a sheepish pout and a curt apology. And after he recovered from *that* humiliation and regained his normal cocky swagger, he proudly advised me he now had all the proof he needed that Freddy Scott had murdered Babs Comstock. (I had all the proof *I* needed, too, but I didn't say anything snotty. I just rolled my eyes at the ceiling and gave him my standard simpleton smile.)

Freddy's car had been found, Dan said, parked in the street just two blocks away from the office. And not only did the fibers from the car's green and gray upholstery seem to match the fibers found in Babs's hair, but Babs's big, black, overstuffed portfolio had been discovered under a dirty maroon stadium blanket in the trunk. Crammed into the bulging portfolio were a pair of high heels, a red sheath skirt, a pair of torn panties, a mangled garter belt, two shredded silk stockings, and a small, crumpled brown paper bag, which had — judging from the Woolworth's sales slip and the ripped trademarked packaging inside — once contained a Hopalong Cassidy jump rope.

And that's not all, folks. There was a big

box of tools in Freddy's trunk, too. Telephone repair tools. And one of those implements was a cable cutter — the very same one, we later found out, that Freddy had used to sever the wires outside my apartment, simultaneously cutting off Abby's and my phone service and detaching the three-foot length of cable with which he strangled Willy Boyd. Though Freddy had been promoted from telephone installer/repairman to a company desk job two years earlier, he'd never surrendered the tools of his manual trade, or forgotten how to use them.

Freddy Scott, it seems, never forgot or willingly surrendered anything.

As for the *other* Scotty — Whitcomb's gorgeous face has healed, but his gargantuan ego hasn't. He came up to the office the other day to deliver some fake corpse shots to Brandon Pomeroy, and he was too ashamed to even look at me, much less talk to me. This suited me just fine, thank you very much, since I wish I'd never laid eyes on *him* at all. No matter how handsome he happens to be. He's a lying womanizer and a cold-blooded creep, and if Tommy hadn't beaten him to the punch that night (the night of our so-called date), *I'd* be the one who had spent four weeks in solitary, hiding out in the dark with two profoundly black eyes and a batch of bloody bandages on my face.

I was shocked when it turned out Whitcomb had nothing — zilch! — to do with the Apex call girl ring. I had figured him for one of the principal players. But he didn't even know the sex-for-hire scheme existed. Can you believe that? When he'd sent all those sample headshots and cheesecake photos to Pomeroy, he'd actually thought the girls were being considered as future magazine models — not potential prostitutes.

That's not to say Scotty was totally blameless in the seduction and corruption of Babs Comstock. He was involved in the sleazy portfolio scam with Mr. Gumpert and the Venus Modeling Agency, and he did talk Babs into posing for some almost-but-not-quite-nude photos, and he did see to it that those photos reached the malignant, manipulative hands of Brandon Pomeroy. And if there were any true justice in this dog-eat-dog (okay, dog-*shtup*-dog) world, there would be a mandatory jail sentence for guilt by association.

But there isn't. And all the Scotty Whitcombs, Mr. Gumperts, Martin Crawleys, Brandon Pomeroys, and Frank Costellos of this world will go on making easy money from young women's starry dreams, and pandering in the profits of their photogenic bodies — while all the Wanda Wingates, Patty Cakes, and Mitzi Maxwells will keep on trying to make a living by selling their dreams and their bodies short. That's just the way it is. And that's the way it always will be — as long as human nature keeps calling the shots, and humans keep responding to the call of nature.

Hey, do I sound like Edward R. Murrow, or what? Maybe I could get a job writing for him! That would really twist the noses of some people I know. People like Mike and Mario who, by the way, were so shocked and dismayed by the sudden elevation of my salary and office standing they actually stopped hounding me for coffee and heckling me about my name. (For a while, anyway. Once they heard I was working to turn my Babs Comstock story into a full-length novel, their masculine insecurities got the best of them, and they started tormenting me more than ever.)

Speaking of my farcical name, I still haven't decided on a nom de plume for my novel. Abby is now pushing for Paige Blondell — not so much because of the actress Joan, but because the name sounds so, well, blonde. Doris thinks I should use Phoebe Starr, just because she's used to it.

You remember Doris Toomey, don't you? The mousy Schrafft's waitress who was Babs's best friend? Well, she's a good friend of mine and Abby's now, and she's not so mousy anymore. Abby dyed Doris's hair red, taught her how to use makeup, and talked her into buying some tight sweaters and a new pair of glasses shaped like cat eyes. Good-bye, Mr. Peepers — hello, Susan Hayward! Since her radiant, tight-sweatered transformation, Doris has been out on three dates, with two different guys. I think Babs would be really happy for her.

But I'm babbling too much again, right? And you're not in the mood. You want me to stop futzing around and tell you why Freddy Scott killed Babs Comstock. And I'm going to do that — I really am! — just as soon as I throw on some clothes and run down to the candy store for a fresh pack of cigarettes. Can't write without my weeds!

Hold your horses, I'll be right back.

Okay. I'm ready now. Sorry for the delay, but you know how it is. This has been a long hard journey for me, and I'm going to need a crutch (i.e., lots of L&M filter tips) to walk the final mile. I had to gather all the depressing facts myself — from Betty Scott and Babs's mother, Elizabeth Comstock — because the police didn't give a skinny rat's tail why Babs was killed. They knew Freddy was the murderer, and they knew Freddy was dead. And that was all they needed to know. Their case was closed.

But mine wasn't. A good mystery writer has to provide a credible, clear-cut motive. So, ignoring Dan's rather hot-blooded suggestion that I quit snooping and leave well enough alone, I made another unannounced appearance in Brooklyn, hoping to have a nice long chat with Freddy's grieving widow. And this time my wishes were granted. Betty wasn't exactly glad to see me, but she wasn't exactly grieving, either. And with her abusive husband out of the picture, and her own survival no longer at stake, she was more than willing to reveal her side of the story.

Babs's mother, on the other hand, wasn't so forthcoming — for reasons that became apparent during our tense, drawn-out, long-distance phone call (it cost me a bundle, but with my new raise I could almost afford it). Her own role in the drama had been somewhat less than commendable so she was less than eager to discuss it. But after I made a slew of soothing comments, and promised on a stack of Baptist Bibles not to sully the "fine, up-standing" Comstock name, she divulged a few key details.

Blending Elizabeth's and Betty's stories together — and editing out their more self-serving observations — I came up with what I believe is a fairly accurate account of the events and emotions leading up to Babs's murder. It may not tell the whole truth, and nothing but the truth but the only ones who really know the truth are Babs and Freddy, and they're not talking. So, you'll just have to take it from me. The following pieced-together, partially conjectured explanation is the only one you're likely to get:

Yes, Babs *was* little Ricky's real mother. She'd gotten pregnant when she was sixteen, in the middle of her junior year in high school. Freddy was the baby's father and the only boy Babs had ever made love with — if getting mauled in the backseat of an old Studebaker after every winning football game can be called making love. For Babs, it *was* love, of course — sincere and submissive sweet-sixteen love — and she wanted nothing more than to marry her star quarterback boyfriend and to give him a beautiful child.

But Freddy wasn't so crazy about that idea. And neither were his parents. They believed their son when he told them he'd never laid a finger on Babs Comstock, and they forbade him to ever date "that lying tramp" again.

After Freddy refused to marry her, Babs faced equally strong opposition from her own parents. They treated her like a moral leper, making it clear she would not be allowed to have her "bastard" baby in their house. Or even in their town. It would, they insisted, bring disgrace to the whole family. So, as soon as Babs began to "show," she was sent to a "home" in upstate New York, where she was supposed to wait out the rest of her pregnancy, give birth, and then give the baby up for adoption.

When the little boy was born, however, Babs found she loved him too much to let him go. Instead of signing the designated adoption papers, kissing her son's fuzzy little head good-bye, and going back to Springfield as instructed, she wrapped the infant up in her blue wool bathrobe, tucked him into a canvas laundry bag, snuck him out of the "home" in the middle of the night, and grabbed a Greyhound for New York City.

Nobody, but nobody, had any idea where Babs and the baby had gone. Six months went by, and still no word. Mother and child were safely out of reach — their whereabouts completely unknown.

But then Babs herself changed the script. She wrote (and mailed) a long, heartfelt letter to Freddy (big mistake). She told him how much she still loved him and she told him how wonderful his little son was. Then she confessed how hard it was for her to take good care of the boy by herself (yet another massive error in judgment).

She and the baby had a room in a respectable East Side boardinghouse, she wrote, and their sixty-nine-year-old landlady was a cheap and willing babysitter, but no matter how many hours she worked as a waitress, and no matter how much she scrimped on food and clothes, she still had trouble paying the bills. And she was so terribly lonely. She missed her darling Scotty so much. Didn't he still love and miss her, too? Wouldn't it be wonderful if he could come to New York and they could get married? Then little Ricky would have a father — his real father — and they could all live happily ever after.

It was a sweet and suitable proposal — except for one teeny-weeny problem: Freddy was already married.

After Babs had been sent away, Freddy hadn't wasted any time. He had appraised all the available girls at Springfield High and picked out a cute new sweetie for himself — Betty Tarbutton, sexiest frosh in the fold. First he flirted with her in the lunchroom, then he felt her up in the hall outside the gym, then he drove her home from school and told her she could be his steady girl if she bleached her hair "bare-nekkid blonde" — the way he liked it. And then soon after that — right after Betty went platinum and Freddy scored the winning goal in the biggest game of the season — he pinned her down on the back seat of his "Studeo," strapped his huge hand over her whimpering mouth, stripped off her white cotton underpants, and made another touchdown.

Betty got pregnant, of course. And this time Freddy's parents weren't so easily deceived. Finally facing the fact that their son was a lying cad, they turned a deaf ear to his protests and forced him — kicking and squealing — to do the "right thing." So — eight days after his high school graduation, but three years before hers — Freddy told another pack of lies at the altar and made Betty an "honest woman." (Does that familiar phrase disgust you as much as it does me?)

Five months later Betty had a miscarriage. Her doctor said she might never be able to have children — something to do with the Rh factor.

Four months after that Babs's letter to Freddy arrived.

Three months after *that* Freddy and Betty moved to Brooklyn.

Babs was brokenhearted to learn that Freddy already had a wife, but she allowed him to see his son occasionally, and after a short adjustment period, the lives of all concerned settled into an acceptable, if uncomfortable, routine. Freddy went to work for the phone company, Betty took a job in a ladies' hat shop on Kings Highway, Babs continued slaving around the clock at Schrafft's, and baby Ricky spent all his days nestled in the arthritic arms of an absentminded gray-haired stranger.

But that was just the kickoff. And it wasn't long before Freddy intercepted the ball. He went to Babs's room one night after work and gave her the dreadful news: he was taking little Ricky to Brooklyn to live with *him*. The boy *belonged* to him, Freddy insisted, and he was going to take him home that very night. He had it all arranged. Betty would quit her job and become a full-time mother, and Babs would get to visit the kid on weekends. And if Babs was really, really good — if she behaved herself and worked hard enough to become a decent provider — then her child would be returned to her someday. And she could be his mother again. Or so Freddy promised.

Babs cried and screamed and begged and pleaded and swore she'd find a way to make enough money to take better care of the boy, but Freddy wasn't having any. The boy was *his,* and he wanted him *now*. It didn't matter what Babs wanted. It had *never* mattered what Babs wanted. It didn't matter what Betty wanted, either.

The fact that Babs was unable to fight off Freddy's "fatherly" advances says more about the *man*-powered world we live in than it does about the strength of Babs's character. Babs was a high school dropout, an unwed mother, a "fallen" woman, and a social outcast. She had no power at all. And the mere fact that she was female meant, in all likelihood, that she would never be able to provide adequate support for her son on her own.

She tried, though. Oh, how she tried! After Freddy stole little Ricky away to Brooklyn, Babs moved into a cheap apartment in Hell's Kitchen. She took every extra job she could find, and saved every penny she could get her hands on (except those she used to buy gifts for her son and to pay for her modeling portfolio), hoping to build a big enough bank account to earn little Ricky's return. She waited on thousands of tables, took in sewing and ironing, cleaned other people's apartments, and worked the Kresge gift-wrap at Christmas time — all the while searching high and (mostly) low for modeling jobs.

Six years later she was still living in Hell's Kitchen, and her bank account was still hovering at the near poverty level.

That's when Babs — then known as Wanda — became one of Martin Crawley's girls. And that's when the money (not a lot, but at least some) started coming in. And that's when Babs went begging to Freddy and told him she was doing pretty well now, so could she please, please, please have her son back?

I'll give you one guess what his answer was.

Bingo.

It wasn't because Freddy had grown to love little Ricky and couldn't bear to part with him. It was that he wouldn't give up control. And because he wanted a son to carry on his precious name. Instead of keeping his promise, Freddy admitted, he'd decided to keep the boy — and change his last name to Scott.

At this point, Babs lost her head. Disregarding her own safety and total lack of leverage, she made the fatal mistake of threatening Freddy — telling him that if he didn't give Ricky back to her, she'd take the matter to court. It was a sadly empty threat. If Babs had gone to court, her new call girl career would have been discovered; she would have been branded an unfit mother, and she would have lost custody of her son forever. But Freddy didn't know this. He was afraid she might win. And he wasn't about to let that happen. Plus he was really, really mad.

So, we all know what happened next. Around seven o'clock in the evening on Sunday, the twenty-fifth of April, 1954, Babs Comstock was eliminated. We don't know the exact particulars: when or where Babs and Freddy met that disastrous day, how Freddy lured or forced Babs into the backseat of his car, how long she struggled against his brutal assault, or why he dumped her poor raped and lifeless body at Woolworth's. We just know that an abominable murder took place, and that a lonesome little cowboy was deprived — for the second and final time in his short unhappy life — of the mother who loved him.

I hate to tell you where little Ricky is now. Would you believe they sent him to Missouri to live with Babs's parents? That's like putting a gerbil in a cage with two condors. But, according to Dan, there was nowhere else for the boy to go. Betty didn't want him (Betty had *never* wanted him), and the child welfare authorities decided it wouldn't be at all proper for Ricky to live with his father's — the *murderer's* — parents.

The state offered to place Ricky in a foster home, but for some undoubtedly hypocritical reason, the Comstocks turned them down flat. (It's my guess that once everybody in their community knew that Babs had been murdered, and that she'd had a son, the Comstocks felt compelled to take the little boy in. If they hadn't, all the good souls of the Blessed Jesus Baptist congregation would have thought them unchristian, and that would've been even worse than being labeled the parents of a filthy slut.)

Anyway, I loathe the fact that Ricky is now living with people who wish he'd never been born. But there's nothing I can do about that. All I could, (and did) do, was write him a letter telling him how beautiful his mother was and how much she adored him. I know he got my letter because at the end of my phone conversation with Elizabeth Comstock, I made her swear on all that's holy that she'd give it to him. (In this case, the pen — or rather, the threat of what I might do with it — *was* every bit as persuasive as the sword.)

Since little Ricky doesn't know me, or who I am — and since he probably doesn't even know how to read very well yet — my letter may not mean much to him now. Or ever. But I'll bet he's glad to have the photo I sent him: the Brownie snapshot I found in Babs's apartment — the one where he's holding hands with his mother in the playground.

I got the picture back from Tommy several weeks ago, when I simply marched across the street to the social club and asked for it. Pretty gutsy, right? I was shocked by my own defiance! And while I was there I asked Tommy why he busted up my apartment. I didn't get much of an answer ("boss's orders" was all he said), but I did get an apology, which smoothed my ruffled tail feathers and made me feel a little better about living on Bleecker between Sixth and Seventh — where the Village meets Little Italy; where artists, writers, beatniks, and queers share the sidewalks with merchants and mobsters. The *paesanos* can be cruel sometimes, but at least they're courteous. As protective as they are destructive. I can live with that.

Abby says I'm a changed woman now — that working on the Comstock story has made me bolder and braver than I ever was before. She says I'm more of a *shamus* and not so much of a *shnook*. I'm not so sure about that. Yes, I *did* track down a murderer, and my actions *did* lead to the murderer being caught (okay, *killed*), and I *have* become the first-ever female staff writer of a national detective magazine. But that doesn't mean I'm any stronger or more self-assured than I was before. I still feel like a glob of mush inside.

Especially whenever I see Dan Street — which has been pretty often lately, I'm happy to say. We've had dinner together a few times, and we went to hear Miles Davis at the Village Vanguard, and he took me to a picture show the other night — Alfred Hitchcock's *Dial M for Murder*, starring Ray Milland and Grace Kelly (yet another movie where the husband tries to kill his wife — his *blonde* wife). Abby keeps asking me if I've *shtupped* Dan yet, but I just smile, wink, and tell her to mind her own business.

She isn't fooled, though, and I'm sure you're not, either. I've become daring enough to defy *some* of our society's sex-restrictive conventions, but not *that* one. Not yet, at any rate. (If Dan and I ever go back to Horn & Hardart there's no telling what could happen. . . .)

Hey, guess what! I think I've actually finished writing this novel! There's really nothing left for me to relate. No more characters to introduce, or scenes to describe, or clues to reveal, or action to convey, or motives to explain, or suspense to prolong. In short, no more pages to turn.

So, if it's all the same to you, I'm going to sign off now. I'm going to close up my baby blue Royal, send a few silent blessings up to my dear friend Babs, grab my cigarettes, and scoot on over to Abby's to celebrate. She's created a brand-new cocktail for the occasion — a frothy pink concoction she calls the Living End — and I'm dying to have one (okay, *three*).

About the Author

Amanda Matetsky has been an editor of many magazines in the entertainment field and a volunteer tutor and fund-raiser for Literacy Volunteers of America. Her first novel, *The Perfect Body*, won the NJRW Golden Leaf Award for Best First Book. Amanda lives in Middletown, New Jersey, with her husband, Harry, and their two cats, Homer and Phoebe, in a house full of old movie posters, original comic strip art, and books — lots of books.

The employees of Thorndike Press hope you have enjoyed this Large Print book. All our Thorndike and Wheeler Large Print titles are designed for easy reading, and all our books are made to last. Other Thorndike Press Large Print books are available at your library, through selected bookstores, or directly from us.

For information about titles, please call:

(800) 223-1244

or visit our Web site at:

www.gale.com/thorndike
www.gale.com/wheeler

To share your comments, please write:

Publisher
Thorndike Press
295 Kennedy Memorial Drive
Waterville, ME   04901